Praise for *When the Night Bells Ring*

"*When the Night Bells Ring* is the most terrifying vampire tale in half a century. Jo Kaplan could make a bucket feel haunted, and the horrors she populates old mines and frontier towns with arm the dark with nightmares for days after a reader visits them. Truly, it's a brilliant novel of survival, greed, and corruption that lingers in the mind like a wound that won't heal." —**Jef Rouner, author of *Stranger Words***

"Kaplan's compelling page turner—Daaayam! If you want a thrill ride full of twists and turns, you don't need a roller coaster; read this book! A story within a story; a horrific thriller within a haunting suspense. I see this as a movie that everyone will talk about." —**Catherine Jordan, reviewer for HorrorTree**

"Set in an unforgiving, sun-bleached desert landscape, *When The Night Bells Ring* is a terrifying, yet hauntingly beautiful novel with a cast of resourceful, fierce women determined to survive their circumstances . . . Engrossing, atmospheric, and shot through with claustrophobic horror, this is the kind of story you can get lost in." —**Paulette Kennedy, author of *Parting The Veil***

"I soon found myself consuming page after page of compelling narrative of likeable characters and horrific circumstance." —**Ginger Nuts of Horror**

"Jo Kaplan has fashioned an experience like none other, where forgotten curses and future terrors collide. Highly recommended for horror fans whose TBRs consist of VanderMeer-worthy climate disaster novels and the creepiest of creature features, reading *When the Night Bells Ring* is like slinking through a mine shaft with only a single, dying flashlight to rely on . . . while behind you, the sound of footsteps—and the tinkling of bells— grows ever-louder." —**Christa Carmen, author of *Something Borrowed, Something Blood-Soaked***

WHEN THE NIGHT BELLS RING

WHEN THE NIGHT BELLS RING

JO KAPLAN

CamCat
Books

CamCat Publishing, LLC
Fort Collins, Colorado 80524
camcatpublishing.com

© 2022 by Jo Kaplan

Hardcover ISBN 9780744306118
Paperback ISBN 9780744306101
Large-Print Paperback ISBN 9780744306156
eBook ISBN 9780744306316
Audiobook ISBN 9780744306231

Library of Congress Control Number: 2022933557

Book and cover design by Maryann Appel
Artwork by eakgaraj

5 3 1 2 4

FOR JAKE

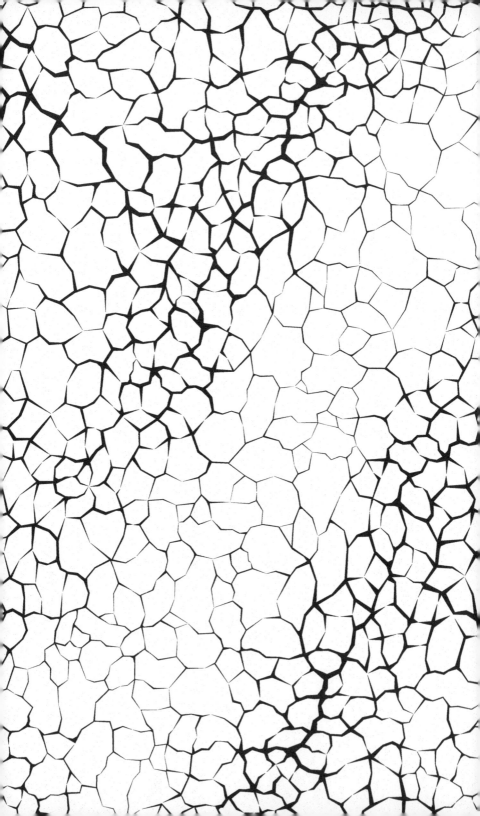

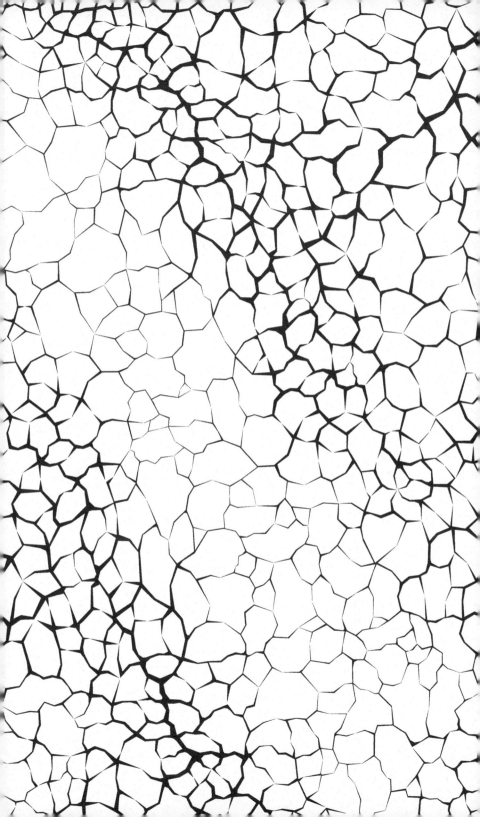

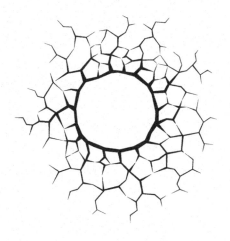

THE DUST DEVILS

TWO LONG TRACKS MADE snakes in the red dirt, their scales formed by tire tread. From high-enough up, you could almost see them wriggling through the heat-shimmered air. The only sign of their creation in this vast empty desert was a plume of dust whose twin voices grumbled their low warning. *Keep away*, they might say to the birds, if there were any birds in the sky.

But the birds were gone from here now, like most anything alive.

Inside the cloud, or just at its forefront, two motorcycles cut the horizon. A white, relentless sun pummeled the figures who rode them—figures of denim and dust.

One raised an arm, signaled to the other, and they slowed to a stop.

Tugging a red sun-faded bandana from her mouth, Mads called out, "Too hot." Her voice was like the motorcycle's: coarse, choked with grime.

Her partner spoke through her own bandana, which had been a dark blue, once, before it turned the vague almost-gray of the sky. "Can't stop here. No shade."

"Sun's been up for hours, though. We can't keep going." She propped up the bike, slid off, dropped to one knee. "We can dig to cooler ground."

Waynoka yanked the bandana from her face. Her lips, chapped and flaking off like old paint, were pulled into a frown. While Mads found a spade in her pack and punched its blade into the dry dirt, Waynoka brushed grime from the wheel spokes and checked their gauges. "Running low," she said. "Should have taken those bicycles instead. Won't be any gas to siphon out here."

Mads barked a laugh as she pulled off her jacket. "Wouldn't have made it this far. Bicycles mean pedaling. Pedaling means sweat. Sweating means losing water."

"Like you're not sweating anyway."

After half an hour of digging, they lay in the long hole surrounded by mounds of dirt, propped their bags under their heads and opened a solar blanket just big enough to cover them both. The cool dirt at their backs was like a balm on scorched skin. They slept a few restless hours, then rose as twilight fell, from red to blue, and shared a stick of leathery old jerky. Mads tried to shake the dirt from her curly mane, but it was futile.

The dust was unshakable here in the dry, dead desert. Maybe there had been patches of green here, once, but they were long gone now.

They waited until the sun gave up the ghost so they could sit a while and watch the stars come out before they continued on their way. Their voices carried across the desert, but there was no one around to hear them.

"My Very Excellent Mother Just Served Us Nine Pizzas."

"Yeah, but Pizza ain't a planet."

"Well, that's how I learned it."

Mads crumpled up the jerky wrapper and tossed it aside, where it crinkled as it slowly expanded. "How many people you think nine pizzas would serve?"

"A lot."

"Sounds like your very excellent mother just served you high cholesterol."

"You don't even know my mother," said Waynoka. "And she would never." They lay in silence while the wrapper finished its crinkling and went still, before a passing wind took it away like a plastic bird. "Is it a planet though, or not?"

"It was, and then it wasn't. Not big enough or something. It's all semantics anyway."

"Guess it doesn't matter now."

"No. Guess not."

Mads stood up and fixed a pair of grimy pool goggles over her eyes, pulling her bandana up over her mouth and nose. Waynoka nodded.

The dust devils took off again.

░░

AND THEN, IN THAT endless nowhere, out of the nothing, there was . . . something.

"You see that?" Waynoka pointed at an angle from their trajectory. Rocky hills hunched black against the night, rising jagged into mountains, like giants creeping. But she wasn't pointing at the hills. She was pointing at the smaller shapes that stood at the base of the hills.

Mads wiped at her goggles. "What is it?"

"Not sure."

They changed course. The shapes drew closer, looming out of the dark. The dust devils slowed enough that they had to keep balance with their feet, toeing the ground away.

They passed a sparse series of clapboard houses that whistled as the wind worked its way through gaps in wood, warped and crooked with age. One shack still had a door attached, and the wind swung it open and shut with an arduous groan. Further on, the buildings clustered closer together. They came upon a dozen crumbling structures along a stretch of dirt that might once have been a small town's Main Street. Waynoka imagined what the buildings had been in their heyday—maybe a quaint general store, a bank with iron vaults, gambling halls, and saloons. Now they were rotted shells, the bones of long-dead buildings. Some looked burned out, scorched down to their blackened foundations; others stood on the force of stubbornness alone.

"It's a town," said Waynoka. "Why don't we stop here?"

Mads frowned at the sky. "Dawn's a long way off, still. We could cover a lot more ground if we kept going."

"Even if we do make it all the way to New York—I don't think one extra day will make a difference."

"Don't be dense. Every day we stay in the desert is another day closer to dying of thirst. At least if we get farther east, we'll find something to drink."

"You don't think there could be any water *here*, do you?"

Mads frowned. She looked around at the ruins lining either side of Main Street. "Doubt it. This place looks dry as a bone."

"At least we can rest here. There's shelter—safer than staying out in the open. Under the sun."

"Always playing it safe," said Mads, shaking her head. "If we'd played it safe back in LA and gone with that group to the encampment, we'd have had all our shit taken in that police raid like the rest of them. We'd never have left."

"I'm not playing it safe. I'm playing it *smart*."

Mads sighed. "All right, fine. We'll stay here for a day. See if we can find any water. And then we're gone. New York will only take so many refugees before they start turning people away like they say they're doing in Chicago."

"Then we'll pick somewhere else," said Waynoka. "I hear Canada's nice."

Pulling a flashlight from her pack and winding it up, Mads followed its beam into the nearest building. Shadows crept around the edges of the light as it asked the ceiling how many spiders lived in its corners. The floor was dirt. The walls had buckled under the weight of the roof where jagged holes punched through to the sky. She came out again and shook her head.

It wasn't the first ghost town they'd come across. Some, you couldn't even tell how long they'd been standing. Could have been abandoned for centuries; could have emptied out only last year, when the climate had really started to blister the desert and make it uninhabitable. When the temperature rose, and the water dried up, and it was too late for an apathetic populace to give up any of the luxuries that had brought them all to this point of no return.

Newly abandoned towns wore battle scars from hours in the sun and drifts of sandy dirt, but you could still see the memory of life in their shattered TV sets left in the living rooms, dusty treadmills, and the square holes in the walls where A/C units had been looted.

Not here, though.

"This place is old," said Mads. "Been empty long before the decline started. I'm talking eighteen hundreds, maybe."

Waynoka tipped her bottle carefully against her lips for a small sip of warm water that was mostly backwash. She didn't like the look that crept across Mads's face.

"You know what this is?"

Waynoka raised an eyebrow. "Bunch of decrepit old buildings."

"Boomtown," said Mads. "West was full of them. People coming to mine gold, get rich."

"Great. Let's mine some gold. That'll solve all our problems." Waynoka put away her bottle, pulled her jacket collar over her neck, and crossed her arms. The temperature still dropped at night, even out here, cooling the sweat they had built up in the heat of day.

"Know what that means?" Mads looked excited now. She didn't wait for Waynoka to take a guess. "Means you were right. There probably *is* water here."

"Did you just admit I was right about something?"

"No, listen. Lot of these old mines are flooded."

"You want to drink stagnant mine water."

"Better than piss," said Mads.

A tumbleweed rolled toward them, pausing intermittently in its wandering, until it was close enough for Waynoka to put her foot on it and flatten it. "Don't mines usually have toxic runoff?

"Oh please, at this point, toxic runoff is the most common by-product of civilization. Your body is probably, like, seventy-five percent toxic runoff."

"Huh. I guess you really *are* what you eat."

"More like, you are where you live."

Waynoka looked around at the wasteland and could not deny it.

"Look, we'll check to make sure it's not toxic. Plus, we'll boil it."

Waynoka sighed. "You *sure* there'll be water down there?" She finished stepping on the tumbleweed and looked up again at her partner, at the gleam in Mads's eyes, the moonlight on her teeth. "Because if you're wrong, we *will* be drinking piss again."

The wind tried to take the misshapen tumbleweed, pushed it feebly, and it tilted though it didn't give an inch. It wasn't round enough to roll anymore. The wind gave up and wandered away to howl through the cracks in the buildings, haunting the old dead town. Behind Mads, the moon's crooked rictus mirrored her own eager grin, the few stars that pierced through the dusty air mimicking her shining eyes.

"Trust me."

STARS AND PLANETS AND the moon and anything that glowed gave the buildings form and presence, at least enough to know they were there. They walked down the dirt road, trying to find a building that still had an intact roof; most yawned open to the elements. A walkway made of wooden planks ran along the fronts of the buildings, sheltered in places by an overhanging roof held up by splintered posts. A few faded old signs spoke of a time and place that felt utterly foreign to Waynoka: one sign, hanging crooked, boasted a blacksmith; another read, FEED & SEED.

Mads shined her flashlight on one half of a pair of swinging doors, the other long gone. The circle of light crept up the crooked entryway to find letters worn to near illegibility.

"Saloon," she read. "Think they got any whiskey?"

"Sure," said Waynoka. "And dancing girls. Gunfights. Ghosts of cowboys."

Mads pushed the remaining door; it swung inward, and a rotten board at its middle fell away in a cloud of dust. Pulling her bandana over her mouth, she stepped through, let the flashlight rove around the old saloon, revealing it in fractured bits. Against the far wall stood what was left of the bar. The light found a broken bottle, grimed over, dry of whatever substance it had once contained; pink bubble letters painted on the bar, newer graffiti that cheerfully announced "Hell"; a barrel, half-rotted away, bloated out of proportion.

The decay was palpable, apocalyptic; the air smelled like the death of civilization. How many people had once sat in this saloon, drinking the bitter elixir that would take them away, if only for brief respite, from a life of fruitless toil?

They sat against the graffitied words and laid out their bags. Listened to the wind creeping in. Outside dawn was paling the sky, but it was still dark in here, a cool shadow of the past.

Waynoka pulled the rubber band from her hair, shook it out, retied it away from her face. Stray dark wisps clung to her angled jaw. She blew them from her chapped lips. "What are we waiting for?"

"Hmm?"

"Let's go find the mine. It'll be easier in daylight."

Mads didn't answer for a moment. She eyed her partner. "Chill out, eager beaver. Ever heard of heat stroke?"

"Ever heard of dehydration?" Waynoka snapped. She stood up quickly, stumbled, leaned against the sagging bar.

"Easy," Mads said without getting up to help her. "Sit down, kid. We need to rest up. It'll hit one-twenty out there in a few hours."

Waynoka found her balance, let go of the bar, sucked frustrated breaths through her nostrils. She crossed her arms, stood over Mads. "Don't call me 'kid.' You're not that much older than me."

"I'm old enough." Mads cleared her throat, her voice like gravel—the voice of a woman in her sixties, not forties.

"Well, you don't need to treat me like a child," Waynoka continued. "I'm obviously capable of taking care of myself. Or did you forget which one of us snagged all that camping equipment before the REI was picked clean?"

Mads snorted. "Oh, please. If I hadn't come along, you'd still be sitting around at some evacuation center, waiting for the world to go back to normal."

Dust spiraled dizzily in the air as the sun started to peek through cracks in the walls, throwing bright lines on the floor like alien code. Waynoka exhaled slowly and sat down. She pulled a paperback from her rucksack, the cover worn to shreds, pages soft and feathered at the bent edges, and angled the book against the bands of light to read. Not that she needed the light. She had read the book a dozen times, practically knew it by heart. But it was the only one that had survived the fire. Eventually she gave up, the light too poor to make out the small type. She closed the book and put it away.

"You know," said Mads, chewing her words as if they were food, as if they could produce saliva for the desert of her mouth, "I feel like I would fit right in here, back in the old days. Sitting here, drinking themselves insensible. What else was there to do? They were like us. Bored as hell by the damned monotony of survival. Ever think of that? Ever think we have more in common with them than some people who are still alive?"

Waynoka slid down, lay with her head on her bag, shut her eyes. "Don't talk so much."

But Mads remained sitting, her arms draped on her knees, staring into the cracks of darkness she could just make out in the rough wood. "At least they had something to drink," she said. Waynoka turned over, turned her back to Mads. "If there was whiskey here, I'd drink it all. I'd drink till I didn't care anymore. Then I'd drink some more. I'd drink till I was dead."

"Why don't you make like the dead now," Waynoka's muffled voice drifted up from where her face was pressed against the canvas of her bag, "and shut up."

⬚

THE SALOON DOOR RATTLED. Waynoka shot up, pulled her knife and flashlight, watched the door swing slowly inward. Darkness crawled in behind it; the sun had already set. They'd slept a while.

She put the knife handle in her mouth so she could crank the flashlight, then aimed its light at the swinging door, waiting for it to tilt inward enough so she could see behind it. The ghost of a cowboy pushing his way into the abandoned saloon for a drink long dried up. An outlaw looking for an enemy, in death, to kill again. Someone like them, a climate refugee traversing the desert for the promise of the East, the promise of rain.

But there was nothing there. It was only the wind knocking.

She reached over to the lump beside her, shook its shoulder. Wild hair shifted as the body tilted limply onto its back. Mads's face was like clay in the circle of the flashlight's glow.

Waynoka leaned in, listening for breath. The face was corpse-still even as the circle of light started to tremble.

She reached out, tentatively, and put her hand on her partner's cheek.

Mads's eyes popped open, then immediately squeezed shut again.

"You trying to blind me?"

Waynoka moved the light away. "You sleep like the dead."

Mads stretched languidly, cat-like. "Narcoleptic tendencies. Sorry to scare you, darling."

"Come on. Lazy ass." Waynoka stood up, tucking the knife away.

But Mads only sat up, pulled a plastic package out of her bag, and peeled it open. She offered Waynoka a handful of unsalted peanuts. Though she chewed them to a fine powder, they went down gritty, like swallowing dirt.

It took her longer than Mads to finish chewing; by the time she'd choked down the nuts, Mads was on her feet with her pack hitched up on her back.

"You're bringing everything? Thought we could make this home base while we look."

"Never know."

Waynoka opted to lighten her own load on the assumption they'd be back before daylight. She took out her paperback book, the small pan they used when they had occasion to cook something over a fire (though she kept the pot for boiling water), the solar blanket, a spare pair of jeans rattier than the ones she wore, a roll of duct tape, and her bow saw. She pulled out a bundle of nylon string, then reconsidered and kept it in. There was no telling when you'd need it. The bag seemed deflated now, like a sorry balloon, but the straps didn't cut into her shoulders as much without the extra weight.

Locked and loaded, they crept out of the dilapidated saloon, let the door swing behind them, haunted by their absence. The night was still. A haze of dust haloed the moon.

It was strange to walk through a dead town. A dead town nobody even knew was still here—far from any real roads, and farther still from anywhere livable, after the decline. And still, after hundreds of years, the marks people had made on the earth remained. They'd last longer than their inhabitants, but eventually, one by one, the buildings would crumble, and there would be nothing left.

Waynoka didn't like to say it, but when she had too much time to think, she figured that was the way it ought to be. Hadn't humans done enough damage? Sometimes she felt like a ghost drifting through what remained of her life, following Mads because Mads was the only thing living, alive, like a blazing light.

Compared to the vibrant, grimy, sweaty *aliveness* of Mads, Waynoka felt like a walking corpse. As if she'd died in the fire, then latched onto the first interesting person who came along.

Her spirit haunting Mads.

They passed the fossilized remnant of a dead tree, its limbs like burnt matchsticks.

Waynoka's foot crunched down on a hard protrusion from the earth, and she shined the flashlight at it. Something round, like a polished stone. With her toe she prodded it free from the dried glue of the dirt. Another light kick and it rolled over so that a pair of dark eye sockets stared up at her. She cried out, nearly tripped in her haste to step away from it.

Mads swiveled around. "What?"

Recovering from the shock, Waynoka aimed her flashlight to get another look. "It's a skull."

"Animal skulls are probably all over the place around here," said Mads. "I wouldn't be surprised if—"

"No." Waynoka bent down. The fleshless grin, the holes where eyes had been, stared stark in the white circle of light. "It's human."

As she moved the light slowly over the ground, she noticed several other suspicious shapes scattered in the dirt. Bones.

"Guess they didn't quite make it to the cemetery." Waynoka looked up as Mads pointed with her own flashlight to a shape in the distance.

A narrow wooden church loomed over a little graveyard with a handful of crude stones standing crooked in the dirt. Leaving the bones behind, they made their way toward the church, whose steeple reared up into the black sky. They shined their flashlights over eroded etchings on the stones in the graveyard, finding names and dates from the 1800s. Nearby a cross stood, crooked, made of old, dried-out wood.

"Why did they include cause of death? Seems cruel, like their lives didn't matter—only the end. Look, this one died of ague." Waynoka moved her flashlight slowly over the etchings, black dirt caked in the crevices. "What the hell even is that?"

"I don't know. Some kind of sickness."

"Well, I wouldn't want that on my headstone."

"What would you want?"

Waynoka kept wandering. "I don't know. I don't think about it."

"I know what mine would say." Mads reached to wipe dust away from the headstone before her. "Madelyn 'Mads' De La Cruz: Made it East, lived a long fucking life."

Waynoka didn't say anything.

Mads stood up quickly, her light trained on the stone she'd been wiping clean. There was something uncertain in her face. Waynoka turned, raised an eyebrow. "What?"

"Nothing." Mads moved her light away, aimed it far from the cemetery, where it dissipated into nothing, swallowed by the vast dark of the desert.

"What is it?"

"There's a mine here for sure. Good news."

Following her as she stepped away, Waynoka trained her own light on the headstone. It froze there on the bleak engraving. "Died in mine collapse," she read.

The words fell like a boulder.

"They probably cleared out the debris," said Mads as she looked intently at the rocky hills around them, holding up her flashlight as if its beam would go farther from sheer force of will.

"Too dangerous."

The light whirled, glared in Waynoka's face, leaving Mads a black blotch. Waynoka put up her hand, watched the light make rays around her fingers. When it was finally lowered, she blinked against a starry miasma, catching only a glimpse of Mads's face as she turned away.

"Then stay here," said Mads, her voice scathing. "Find yourself a nice headstone and lie down in front of it."

Without looking at her or waiting for a reply, Mads marched away. As her form receded into the dark, a thrill of panic rose up Waynoka's throat and she hurried after, her own light swinging wildly. For a moment she thought she'd lost her—then the light caught on a mane of curly hair, and she breathed quickly through her nose as she caught up.

"It's not the only way," Waynoka said when she'd worked up enough saliva to open her mouth. Still not turning or slowing, Mads marched on, toward the rocky hills that looked like the hunched backs of demons. "Hey." Waynoka grabbed her by the shoulder.

"*What?*"

Her flashlight beam drifted left, searching for something, anything— and in the edge of its light, Waynoka saw a figure standing there, inching away from the glow, keeping to darkness. Watching them.

She froze, afraid to move the flashlight where it would land on the figure that stood just outside of its beam.

"You see that?"

By the look on her face—the way the muscles froze and her gleaming eyes locked in the far distance—Mads did.

"I've been feeling like we're not alone this whole time," Waynoka confessed, her voice a bare whisper, the sound of a tumbleweed. She thought of the saloon door swinging back and forth.

"Of course we are. Look around you. Not exactly where I'd want to spend my retirement."

"There's someone over there."

The hollow of Mads's throat jumped as she swallowed. The figure was too far away to have heard the whisper, but the night was still and carried pin drops in its silence. The figure didn't move. Was it following them?

"Who else could be here?" Mads whispered back. "*Here?*"

The idea of a person in this forsaken place rattled Waynoka. Like a person standing on their own grave.

"What do we do?"

They waited. Waynoka would have preferred to stumble across an animal. Hell, even a ghost would seem more at home here.

"Fuck it." Mads shifted her flashlight beam right onto the figure before it could move away.

They both sucked in a sharp breath.

Standing in the dim, dispersed glow was a tall thin cactus, its withered limbs almost in the shape of human arms.

Mads shoved Waynoka, not very gently. "You trying to spook me?"

"I saw it move."

The light drifted over and around the uncanny cactus—brown, desiccated. Though Waynoka wanted to stay away from it, her partner drew closer, pulling out her knife.

"What are you doing?"

"We can chew the meat."

"Sure, if you want to puke your guts out."

Mads lowered her knife and turned, raised her eyebrows.

"Most cacti are toxic. Only a few types are edible."

"Is this one of them?"

The cactus twisted on itself, bulging in strange places like a malnourished child. Divots near the top gazed out darkly like the hollows of eroded eyes. "I don't know."

Gleaming eyes, a mottled green and brown, made wide, round discs in Mads's ashy face, her freckles like scattered dirt. She ran her tongue over cracked and feathered lips, raised her knife again to the cactus, its tip grazing the fine needles, a desperation in the grip of her hand—but then she lowered it again, and with it released the air from her body in one long exhale of defeat.

She turned her light to the uneven landscape ahead, the sullen rocks that clustered at the base of cruel mountains. This place had a strange, unsettling atmosphere, but maybe that was the nature of ghost towns. They'd bustled with life, once, but now knew nothing of humanity. They were leftover relics reclaimed by the wounded earth. Civilization slowly fossilizing as it faded to antiquity. And someday all of earth's cities would be hollow tombs decaying slowly over the eons to their final entropic states, unless some other creature intelligent enough to wonder who had built them came upon the earth to possess it and to wonder who or what had ruined it in the first place.

They walked away from the town, toward the mountains. Mads found what looked like an old trail or road, and they kept to it, thinking it might lead them somewhere. The farther they got from the town, the more

Waynoka regretted leaving so many of her things in that saloon, but there was no way she would double back now. Instead she turned every so often to track the vanishing buildings with her flashlight.

"Would've been a quicker trek on the bikes," Waynoka pointed out.

Mads shook her head. "Waste of gas. A walk won't kill you."

They climbed up the sloping path, stumbling over the uneven terrain. "Are you sure we're going in the right direction?"

"If there's a mine, it's got to be around here," said Mads.

The land grew hilly with scrub-choked rock. Waynoka had to walk carefully to avoid tripping. Ahead of them, the moonlight revealed more broken buildings—a tall structure stitched with support beams that looked like a good breeze would send it toppling. "Is that what I think it is?" said Waynoka.

As they passed the building, directing their flashlights to the mountain-side ahead, the entrance to the mine appeared: a rusted rail led into a black mouth in the rock framed by crooked wood supports.

"*Brazo Poderoso, asísteme,*" Mads murmured.

Waynoka stepped closer to the opening, which swallowed her light like a black hole. "I would be surprised if God was listening."

"Doesn't hurt to check."

The mouth of darkness led to a long stone tunnel that echoed their footfalls with vaguely sinister chuckles. Otherwise, it was quiet—the kind of closed-in quiet where you could hear your own heartbeat. At least outside, the open desert had the occasional call of the wind. There was movement out there. In here there was only stillness.

Waynoka reached out to the wall and felt cold, rough stone. The walls were craggy, like the choppy surface of a stormy sea, petrified in place. Rocky edges gleamed in the light. Support beams above splintered where they stood, looking too feeble to hold up the tons of rock crushing down on them.

The deeper they went, the thicker and staler the air. They felt farther and farther away from fresh air, and ever more enclosed. The narrow tunnel did nothing to assuage this feeling. The ground was uneven around the rusted tracks, rising and falling. At one point, the tracks vanished and a drift of broken rock forced them close to the low ceiling, compelled them to crawl on hands and knees.

Died in mine collapse, thought Waynoka.

"Hey," said Mads, pausing to shine her light straight up, through the narrow crevice that opened high above them, the two walls of rock stitched together by wooden beams. It went up and up. "This is probably where they found a vein of ore. Look how much of the mountain they took out."

"How much farther you think the mine goes?"

As it turned out, much farther.

They wound their way through turns in the tunnel, at every moment wondering if it wouldn't be better to go back but unwilling to voice this to the other. The rock shifted from dark granite to light—almost pearlescent—and back again.

"If there's water in here, it's probably farther down," said Mads. "It would pool on the lowest level. Right?"

"Great," said Waynoka. She did not relish the idea of descending deeper, and part of her hoped they would find no means of getting to a lower level anyway. Was it cowardly to hope for failure so they could leave this place?

Sometimes she felt like all she was capable of was questioning, worrying, hesitating. She wished she could be more like Mads. Confident. Proactive. Fearless. She hated that sometimes, she *did* feel like a kid next to Mads, even though she liked to think of them as partners, equals in their quest to survive a world turned upside down.

Down the passage, their footfalls echoed and crunched on bits of rock ground near to powder. After a little while, Mads abruptly halted and threw out her arm to stop Waynoka from stepping past her.

"What?"

Without a word, Mads lowered her flashlight so Waynoka could see the square of perfect blackness before their feet.

A mineshaft.

They crept closer to the hole in the ground, the crunch of their shoes filling the silence around them. Mads crouched at the edge, where a piece of rock dislodged and crumbled away, pattering the walls on its way down. Waynoka held her breath for a beat until the wayward pieces clattered somewhere at the bottom. She couldn't tell how far down it was.

"Where do you think it goes?" Waynoka asked, her voice leaving ghostly whispers in the darkness.

"Another level." Mads aimed her flashlight straight down, where its beam faded into the muted depths. An old wooden ladder clung to the side of the shaft plunging away beneath them. Waynoka thought of the warped and splitting timber that tenuously held up the buildings back in the town. How long did wood stay preserved underground? "We can go down and check it out."

"That doesn't seem very safe."

Mads raised her light and rolled her eyes. "No, it doesn't." She stood and clipped her flashlight onto her belt. "We going, or what?"

Waynoka looked again at the dark hole and the ladder. Thinking of the few sips left at the bottom of her canteen, she murmured, "Or drink piss again." She nodded.

A few of the rungs had rotted out, so they had to carefully feel their way down with their feet before dropping their weight, contorting themselves so they could stretch a leg down to the next rung if one was missing. Lacking miner's helmets, they had to move by feel alone. Waynoka breathed slowly through her nose to combat the panic that the blind dark drove into her like a rusty nail. She knew if she reached out, she would feel the walls within arm's length, the only way out to crawl back up the ladder or continue into the abyss.

Down it was.

As soon as their feet hit bottom, they wound up their flashlights. Waynoka released a slow sigh of relief and looked back up the shaft, but she couldn't quite make out the top anymore.

"See? That wasn't so bad," said Mads.

Waynoka turned away from the ladder. Ahead lay another narrow passage of jagged rock and darkness. She wondered how much farther they'd have to go.

※

SEVERAL MORE SHAFTS DOWNWARD, and the surface seemed impossibly far away. The sky—cruel as it could be, blazing with monstrous sun—was like a distant dream.

Neither Mads nor Waynoka could tell how long they had been down there. Time had no meaning underground.

They were just shining their flashlights ahead, tasting the air for moisture, when they heard it: far in the distance, the tinkling of a bell.

"Where did that come from?" Waynoka slashed her light behind her. "I knew it. It's . . . whoever was following us. I *told* you."

Mads didn't move. They listened to the dying echo of the jingling as it bounced from wall to wall of the underground labyrinth. Finally, she shook her head. "That didn't come from above."

"What?"

She pointed her flashlight down the next shaft, into the darkness below. The light didn't reach the bottom. "It came from down there."

Waynoka shivered. In that moment she regretted having started down that first shaft instead of turning back immediately. Dread crept into the corners of her brain.

"Let's go back up."

She looked at her partner's appalled face and tried to explain.

"Look how deep we are already, and we still haven't found water. Let's at least go back up, get our bearings, make a plan of attack." Her breath caught in her throat. She hated herself for even suggesting it.

"You want to give up now?" said Mads, her voice coarse and dry. Her eyes gleamed, and perhaps if she'd had any extra moisture to spare, they might have been watering. Her flashlight lit up the desperation of her face, dusted now with the black dirt that hung in the air of the mine. "There's nothing for us up there. Nothing for miles around."

Waynoka let the words settle heavily into her bones. Go back up to the surface, expend the energy climbing up all that way, and surely die of thirst before they could even think of coming back down.

"How long have we been down here?" she whispered, keeping her voice soft so that it wouldn't echo on the walls. She tried to control her shivering. "I'll go crazy down here."

Mads reached out and grabbed her wrist, and though the grip was hard on her narrow bones, the touch of her warm skin felt solid and reassuring. "Don't worry. You won't go crazy down here." She cracked a grin. "You're crazy already."

Waynoka wanted to push Mads, or hug her. She couldn't decide which. The tinkling had long since faded, but she listened for it anyway in the space between breaths.

They sat to regain their energy. Mads pulled out a stale power bar. She broke it in half and gave the slightly larger piece to Waynoka, which made Waynoka feel bad, but it wasn't as if she could decline it. She ate it ravenously, even though it tasted like cardboard. When she leaned her head back against the wall, it felt cool and damp.

She sat up, turned around. Put her hand flat on the wall.

Mads quirked an eyebrow, then leaned forward and licked the rock. "Well?"

"A little wet," she said. "Tastes . . . salty? Metallic, kind of."

Waynoka tentatively touched the rock with the tip of her tongue, then dragged it along to lap up any moisture she could.

They grinned at each other.

"We must be getting close." Mads stood up, recharged, like when you rub two dying batteries in your palms to work up the remaining juice. She shined her flashlight down the shaft again. "I bet you anything, we go down one more level, we'll find water."

If it really was that close, they couldn't turn back now.

Waynoka thought about the long climb back up and out of the mine, and the possibility of water just below them. She clipped her flashlight to her jeans and tightened the straps of her pack. "All right," she said. "Let's go."

They started down the ladder.

Mads went first, testing out the rungs with each step down and calling out when she came upon a bad one so her partner would know to tread carefully. Each of the previous ladders had been surprisingly intact, had held their weight, so Waynoka could not help but start to think maybe it was supposed to be this way—they were *meant* to find water down there. She could feel it in her bones now. And when they found it, she would drink until her bladder remembered what it felt like to be full.

She wanted it so desperately. Nothing else mattered, when it came right down to it—nothing but the taste of cool water in her parched throat.

The sound of a rending crack jolted her from these thoughts.

Mads yelped with surprise, and a whoosh of air ruffled Waynoka's hair.

Without thinking, Waynoka hurried down another two rungs, thinking only of water, of rivers and lakes and ponds. It all happened too quickly for her to register. She heard the thump below just as her foot met open air and open air and open air—no rungs at all—and then the rung she gripped in her hands, which held her body's weight, broke, and she plummeted into the dark.

▨

THE GROUND, WHEN IT slammed into her, seemed to jar her bones loose. Seemed to squeeze the air from her lungs, leaving her panicked and breathless, until they remembered how to inhale.

Coughing in the dusty air, Waynoka could only lie there, winded and aching. Her pack had cushioned her fall, but a throbbing pain drove spikes through her skull, and when she touched her scalp, she felt something warm and sticky on the back of her head.

"Mads?" she grunted, rolling onto her side so she could reach into the pack for her flashlight. It took great effort to wind it up, the sluggish trickle of time too slow for her manic mind.

She found Mads clutching her leg. Blood had soaked through her torn jeans, which revealed the abnormally lumpy shape of the knee, scraped raw, shattered. A shard of something protruding from it. At first Waynoka thought a piece of broken rock had lodged itself in Mads's knee. *Let it be a rock*, she thought as she shined the light on it.

It wasn't a rock.

Dreading what she would find above, Waynoka raised the flashlight to the shaft they'd just come down.

The ladder was broken.

A pile of rubble sat at its base, and it was missing all its rungs up until the point they'd fallen from. She could barely see the intact rungs high above, far too high to reach.

"Oh God," she said. "Oh God, oh God."

※

WAYNOKA HADN'T FELT SO afraid since the Great Valley Fire two years ago—evacuated from her tiny studio apartment in the dead of night, the hills raging red and casting a yellow jaundice over the sky, the air choked with ash, flames leaping across the highway, helicopters dropping their insufficient retardant overhead. Chaos. Everything burned, from Sunland to Studio City, and then across Tarzana, up into Simi Valley. Nothing was safe, not even the money-lined fortresses of Bel Air. There, and in other places that had continued watering their lawns during the most severe drought on record, as if everything was normal, the willfully oblivious had finally had to concede that ignoring the problem of climate change wouldn't make it go away. No one could continue just going about their lives as usual.

She remembered hunkering down in a grade-school gymnasium with a hundred other evacuees all crammed together on the rubbery floor, feeling strangely calm after the terror of running through the burning neighborhood, feeling calm, even, that her apartment was likely on fire. There wasn't anything in it she loved—not the lumpy IKEA futon or the photos of her parents smiling with disappointment from their frames, not the bed she'd shared in a handful of failed romances, nor the bamboo plant she barely managed to keep alive. Maybe the thrift-store bookcase whose shelves bent inward with the weight of half a decade of dog-eared paperbacks. Certainly not her laptop, which liked to blue-screen on her when she was halfway through writing an article that would earn her just enough for a few tacos and a box of Franzia.

Already she wasn't missing any of that, and something about this realization felt dangerously bleak, until she considered maybe it was a chance to start fresh, the way she had when she'd first moved out to LA to make a life here. Maybe it was a blessing in disguise.

Then a voice to her right said, "Not exactly my first choice for a Friday night on the town." She turned, startled by the friendly familiarity in the voice, even though she didn't know this person. A woman sat next to her, knees to her chest. An impressive mass of russet curls haloed her freckle-spotted face, which was otherwise a golden shade that suggested mixed ancestry. She wore a leather jacket, even though it was warm in the gym, as if to defy her surroundings. When she parted her lips, a plume of white smoke leaked out, and she gave a little cough, then wryly turned her mottled green and brown eyes to Waynoka.

When Waynoka didn't say anything, the woman held out her long silver vape. Waynoka declined.

The woman shrugged and hit it again.

"Should you be doing that? There's kids around." Waynoka looked to see if anyone else had noticed. "And we're in a school."

The woman laughed out more smoke. "You gonna tell on me?"

Waynoka shrugged. "It's not illegal."

"*Gracias a Dios*, prohibition is over. Now we can smoke up in the apocalypse."

Unable to help herself, Waynoka snorted.

"So what are you going to do while the world burns?"

Waynoka looked at the woman, unsure what she was asking. She supposed she was going to sit here in this gym with everyone else until the fire was contained. But what was beyond that? The idea of going back to normal seemed absurd. The only certainty was that things were going to continue to get worse. Wasn't that what the scientists had been saying for decades? Every single one of those annual worldwide summits produced a report about the dangerous increase in temperature, and year after year, the politicians said we have to do something while still doing nothing. Waynoka's old therapist had told her that half of her patients had climate anxiety. Everyone was worried, especially the people who didn't have the power to do anything about it. Was it too late, now? Was this the end of the world?

Her phone was dead in her pocket, and all the outlets in the gym had long since been commandeered by teenagers whose dead eyes reflected scrolling screens. She wondered if there were any water fountains nearby.

When a long minute passed and Waynoka still hadn't said anything, the woman proffered her vape pen again. This time, Waynoka took it. As she inhaled, the woman held out her hand and said, "By the way, I'm Mads."

※

AS SOON AS SHE'D taken Mads's hand, that was it. She knew she would follow this woman to the ends of the earth. Her presence was magnetic. Just being around her seemed to recharge Waynoka's spirit.

And when it took weeks to contain the fire, when the swath of destruction had permanently changed the landscape of Los Angeles, when thousands of people had been displaced from their homes with nowhere to go, she'd hopped onto the back of Mads's motorcycle and they'd driven around the labyrinthine streets of the LA basin, stealing when they needed to, sleeping on the beach, sheltering in abandoned parking structures. Until it became clear things weren't getting better, at least not in LA. The government finally said, "Our bad," and gave up. Transportation had all but ground to a halt. Airlines had finally been forced to shut down, compelled by the fact that their pollution had irreversibly fucked the environment. Gas stations were shuttered, but it was too little, too late, and no one had bothered to build up the infrastructure needed for widespread clean energy. Millions died of heat and thirst, and the lucky few who could afford the sky-rocketing cost of living shrugged their shoulders and said good riddance to the poor and homeless. Most of the West, outside a few urban centers and the coast, had become a wasteland—an inhospitable desert, climate-ravaged with blistering heat. No one lived there anymore, and it effectively blocked off the West Coast from the supposedly fertile East, which itself was drowning in hurricanes.

So they had to find their own way through.

※

"WILL YOU STOP THAT," Mads said through gritted teeth. Waynoka hadn't realized she'd still been chanting her panicked litany. She snapped her lips together. Prayed for calm.

Mads groaned and pushed herself to her feet, her bad knee remaining bent as she steadied herself on her other foot, her hands braced on the wall. She cried out and sat back down.

Waynoka kept the flashlight aimed upward, giving Mads a good look at the broken ladder.

"Not like I'd be able to climb it anyway," said Mads. She looked at her knee. "Tell me that's not bone. Is that bone?"

"Don't look at it," Waynoka told her.

"Right, the old 'pretend it's not there and it disappears.' If only I were a toddler. Damn my object permanence."

Waynoka choked out something that was neither a laugh nor a sob, rather a sound she associated with hysteria. She felt muddled, oddly separate from her own emotions, as if someone else were feeling them. Her head seemed to waver far above her body, like a balloon, only tentatively connected to the rest of her. Was this what panic felt like?

"We're trapped," she said. Her head gave a massive, stomach-churning throb. She wondered if she had a concussion. "We're never getting out of here."

"There'll be another way out." Mads gritted her teeth and tried again to stand. Failed. And then the numbing quality of shock must have worn off, or the attempt to stand had set off a new burst of pain. She screamed, a sound like her throat tearing. It echoed around them, up the vacant shaft.

The screaming didn't last long. She tired herself out quickly. They sat in silence, amid the pile of debris left by the broken ladder. After a while Mads said, her voice hazy, as if she were stoned, "It doesn't feel so bad anymore. I think I can walk."

This time, with help, she managed to get to her feet, leaning against the wall and breathing heavily through her nose. Beads of sweat lingered on her brow. Her leg buckled beneath her, but Waynoka held her upright, Mads's breath coming out in a high keen like a wounded dog might make.

When she was sure Mads wouldn't collapse, Waynoka picked up Mads's pack and switched it with hers. "Here. Mine's lighter." Mads grudgingly took the bag and awkwardly swung it onto her back while trying to keep her balance.

"You sure you can walk?"

"I'll manage."

Waynoka shined her flashlight down the passageway ahead, trying not to wonder how they would ever find their way out of here, trying not to imagine what would happen when they found a way out that Mads wouldn't be able to scale, trying not to think of her partner's shattered knee as a death sentence, the way it might have been hundreds of years ago and hundreds of miles from civilization.

Deeper and deeper.

In the deep underground, footsteps give way to ghosts. Panic gives way to fog. Darkness to darkness. A dull throb aches through the hollows of fear, muted but insistent, and the body shambles forward even while it screams that forward is the wrong way to go.

Ahead, beneath wooden struts that had split down the middle, the tunnel was blocked by a mound of rock.

"The collapse," Mads wheezed, leaning against the wall to relieve pressure on her trembling leg.

Waynoka looked up at the low ceiling and wondered how long it would hold up the eternity of heavy stone above their heads. She thought of an ant squashed beneath the sole of her shoe. "We should have stayed," she said. "We should never have left."

"Stayed and what? Joined the homeless camp in Venice?" Mads pushed herself off the wall. "Hang on." She inched toward the collapse of rock, shining her flashlight at the dark spot where the boulders met the wall.

"Don't," said Waynoka, thinking about fissures in the ancient mine, the merest breath on that horrible rock pile sending the rest of the ceiling down on them, but Mads started to crawl over the rubble, moving clumsily to avoid her injured knee coming into contact with the jagged edges. Waynoka felt her breath catch in her throat, which made her want to cough, but she feared a cough would send the tunnel imploding.

"There's an opening here," Mads called out, leaning forward with her flashlight. "Might be big enough."

"Are you crazy?"

"You got a better idea?"

Waynoka bit down on her lip so hard she tasted the coppery tang of blood. She welcomed the way it brought saliva springing to the surface of her tongue. Maybe she could just drink her own blood. Who needed water?

"The air is probably bad, if it's been shut up all this time," she said as Mads continued shimmying over the rocks. "It could poison us before we even know anything's wrong. It could suffocate us."

The tinkling of a bell splintered her litany of warnings. It jangled, high and metallic, its echoes obscuring the source's direction, at least from Waynoka's standpoint. But Mads froze in her climbing, waiting for the jingling to die away, before she whispered, "It's coming from in there." She looked at Waynoka. "See? There must be some kind of airflow. Maybe a way out."

Waynoka took a moment to lean back, her face slicked with sweat, dizziness in its pinched edges. A warning throb spiked through the back of her head, reminding her there was a wound that she couldn't see. "You really want to go through that little hole?"

"Haven't you ever seen a horror movie?" Mads said. "You have to go deeper to get out."

Waynoka didn't dare say what she was thinking. Or you go deeper to die.

She followed Mads over the precarious jumble, treading with care even though it felt solid. Only once did a small rock slip free and tumble away, ricocheting with an overblown clatter in the confined space that nearly made her heart rip through her chest. When she was sure no other rocks were about to fall away, she continued forward. Mads reached the opening, took off her pack, and shoved it in ahead of her.

It was only when her partner had started slithering through that Waynoka really saw it.

The dark hole was barely big enough to squeeze into on her belly, like a worm. Mads held her flashlight in front, her other arm wedged in at her side to help her inch forward. Low grunts emerged from the back of her throat, the tunnel's edges ripping into her bloody knee, dragging away slivers of flesh from the sticky, shredded denim. The grunts became gasps, short screams, but she kept going.

Just as her feet were disappearing into the dark, she stopped. Her voice was muffled. "The pack is stuck."

Waynoka took off her own pack and remembered the switch. She was carrying the full one. No way would it fit through. That is, if Mads even got the deflated pack through in the first place. That is, if there was anything to get through to at all beyond the mine's ever-narrowing throat, if it didn't hit a dead end or spit them out in a tomb.

"Never mind," came her partner's voice, floating back through the confines of the passage. "Got it."

She continued worming forward until she was far enough in that Waynoka couldn't stall any longer. Leaving Mads's pack on the cave-in's detritus and guiding her way with the flashlight that whitewashed the tight, rough walls crowding in around her shoulders, she followed.

The narrow walls bore long scratches, and Waynoka couldn't help but think of someone trapped in here, trying desperately to claw their way out, until their fingernails popped off against the rock.

"Shit." Mads again.

"What?"

"Flashlight went out, and I can't . . ." She grunted. "Can't wind it. Not enough space to—my other arm is back."

Waynoka stared at her partner's feet and tried to tell how far in she had gotten. Her foot told her she was full-body deep. There was no shimmying back.

"Just keep going."

And if the tunnel only narrowed further? And if she got irrevocably stuck in the increasingly narrow space? And if they were only shimmying down the throat of the mine into its belly with no exit—

Mads pushed ahead, and then she gave a sound of surprise. Her feet disappeared, and Waynoka heard the sound of her flashlight winding. The taste of freedom on her lips, she pushed forward at a reckless pace, scraping up her elbows, and finally the passage spat her out into the chamber in which Mads sat, shining her flashlight around, the deflated pack beside her.

Where they'd emerged appeared to be . . . a storage room?

Old equipment had collected around the edges of the chamber. A broken wheel, relic of some cart once used to haul ore. A corroded wheelbarrow. A half-rotted wooden crate.

But there was something fundamentally strange about this room. It looked lived in: a moldering pile of rotten rags—strips of cloth, possibly small bundles of hay, tufts of wool—sat against one wall. The sooty remains of a long-stale fire lay in the center of a small circle of stones, as if someone had built a fire pit, though with very little airflow in here, the burnt ash smell pervaded everything. The air was dry, stagnant.

"What the hell is this place?"

Mads dragged herself to the pile of rags. "I think this is someone's bed."

Trying not to gag at the thought, Waynoka looked at the crate and saw a dried-up bottle of ink and a leather-bound book sitting on top, as if the crate had been fashioned into a makeshift table. She tried to imagine the kind of person who would stay in this suffocating cave, sleep on that pile of old rags, sit in front of this crate, and . . . do what? She stepped closer to get a look at the book, its cover cracked and wrinkled with age. Maybe some kind of ledger for the mine? But what sort of person would keep a ledger down here in the dark? She reached out and brushed a finger over the layer of grime on its cover, and her heart jolted at the sound of the bell again, except this time piercingly close.

At the far side of the room among a cluster of shadows, Mads stood at the opening to another tunnel, this one taller than the last, tall enough to go through if you just stooped down, and she had a mystified grin on her face. Dangling from the top of the tunnel's entrance was a rusted little bell. She flicked it again and sent its strident peal through the room.

The ringing shivered over Waynoka's flesh.

She worried Mads was going to start crawling down this next tunnel; she wasn't sure she could step past that little bell. Relief washed over her when Mads stepped out of the low entrance and collapsed on the makeshift bed. But the relief didn't last long. Still aiming her light at the bell, as if waiting for it to ring again, she noticed a peculiar coloring on the rock wall above it, and shifted the light upward, to shine full on the stone.

"What the fuck is that?"

Mads looked. They both stared for a long moment.

It was a cave painting. It reminded Waynoka of the petroglyphs she'd seen in the Black Hills back in South Dakota where she'd grown up—rock art made by the ancestors. It was a striking reddish hue, most likely ochre.

The drawing was a simple one: a person-shaped stick figure surrounded by lines that radiated out from it, the way a child might draw the rays of a cartoon sun.

Waynoka turned to Mads and asked, "How old do you think that is?"

"Do I look like an archaeologist?" said Mads.

Waynoka went closer, touched the red, felt the powdery substance on her fingers. "I honestly have no idea how people date these things. Could be prehistoric. Could be a hundred years old."

Mads tilted her head, still staring at the red figure. "Kind of creepy, don't you think?"

Waynoka did not want to agree. It was a piece of history, quite possibly a remarkable find, maybe an ancient work of art from some long-ago people who had inhabited this area.

It was an indication that human beings had survived this long, and would keep surviving—at least, as long as they didn't destroy everything around them first. As long as they could find a way to let the earth survive too.

But there was something vaguely ominous about it. Maybe it was the piercing red spots that had been left for eyes.

She wished she had something to block off that opening beneath the painting. Knowing it was there, but not knowing what lay beyond it—that's what made her uncomfortable.

"I'm just going to take a peek," she told Mads, and shined the flashlight into the opening. Not because she wanted to, but because she couldn't just ignore it.

Another tunnel, leading off into the dark.

She ducked under the bell and took a few steps farther, to see how far she could see.

At the far edge of the light, where it started to fade, was a shadow.

Waynoka gasped and dropped the flashlight. She heard it clattering over the stone, and another sound in the distance, a chuckling—she dropped to her knees to grab the light—her knee came down on something soft that made her give a little shriek, and she rolled away, snatching up the flashlight and turning it wildly until she saw what she'd knelt on.

A dead bat.

She lifted the light again and strained her eyes to see into the distance of the tunnel, but there wasn't anything there, at least that she could make out. The light threw strange shadows against the craggy rock, and she realized that's all she had seen, just a shadow cast by the rock at an angle that made it look like a figure standing there. Just like with the cactus, back at the town.

"What was that?" Mads called from behind her.

Waynoka quickly retreated through the opening with the bell. "Nothing. I stepped on a dead bat."

"Great. If we find water, we can make bat soup."

Waynoka made a puking sound and smiled when Mads laughed.

It was easy to break down the old wooden crate, which splintered readily against the shovel Waynoka had found leaning against the wall. With the flint she was glad she'd kept in her pack, she got a fire going, and even though it filled the room with the choke of smoke, having only those two passageways for outlet, the warm light imbued the place with small joy. They put away their flashlights. Mads stayed on the pile of rags, and Waynoka let her; she didn't want to touch the foul bed. The ground was uncomfortable beneath her, but it would have to do. She remembered the book that she had set aside so she could break down the crate, and she retrieved it, settling down beside the fire as she creaked open its dusty cover.

"What is it?" Mads said.

Inside, two words had been inked onto the first page of brittle paper, which Waynoka read by the light of the snapping fire, which sent jagged shadows around the chamber.

"It says it's a diary. Lavinia's diary."

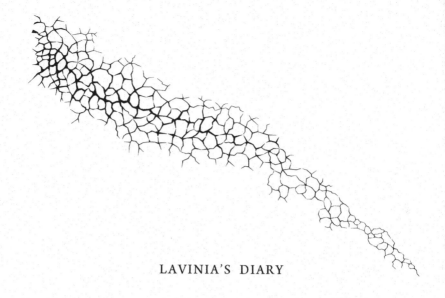

LAVINIA'S DIARY

July 26, 1869
    Passed 3 graves. Made 12 miles.

July 28, 1869
    Passed 1 grave. Made 15 miles.

July 29, 1869
    Passed 6 graves. Made 17 miles.

August 1, 1869
    Passed 8 graves today.

    I begin to weary of counting them. I started doing so in my last diary and thought I might continue in this one, but it is a bit dispiriting. Shall I attempt to leave the grimmer matters out of you?

    Then what should I ever talk of?

August 3, 1869

Today we found a little child's skull, picked clean by vultures and inscribed with a rhyme. Oscar wanted to keep it, but I bade him leave it where it was. It gave me an all-overish feeling, or maybe it was the sight of Oscar cradling it the way Sophie cradles her dolls: youth clinging to a perfect memento mori. Leave it to the boy to enjoy such a macabre poem! The sun hardly dares to kiss his tender flesh, perhaps tasting something of death on him. The rhyme goes:

> *The wagon wheel did break,*
> *They prayed to all the saints.*
> *Woe! Came the snake,*
> *Now they're naught but haints!*

August 8, 1869

What a barren waste we find ourselves in, ever more the Great American Desert! How the land shimmers with heat like a sea of flame! A strange and arid territory whose dominion is silence, broken only by the weary yoke of oxen and the belabored wagon wheel. And yet, the fierce clarity of the sky holds a kind of majesty. There is an attractive dreadfulness about the place that I cannot explain.

It is as wild a country as I have ever seen.

Last night we heard a band of coyotes offering melancholy calls to the dark. I almost felt sorry for them, just as starved and thirsty as we are. It was a fine night, though. The moon was fat and lustrous.

August 15, 1869

It is excessive hot today. Made only 8 miles. We stopped early, for the oxen and cattle were worn from the heat and starving on what little hay we can afford them.

At dusk, John Henry caught two jackrabbits, which made a fine feast for us. I made a jackrabbit stew. I thought it turned out quite well, but

Sophronia did not seem to enjoy it, as she passed hers over to Oscar to finish. I asked her if she would prefer a nice fish chowder instead.

August 20, 1869

We are passing into a more mountainous landscape that instills in me terrible, wonderful feelings. I am aware, somehow, that we are a part of this little moment in the course of history.

We, like the pilgrims before us, travel into the strange unknown, the dark beyond the setting sun. Every moment we pull farther from civilization into the primitive wilderness.

As we draw closer to them, the monstrous heights of the mountains fill me with astonishment and wonder. I feel close to the sky and yet these precipitous peaks are closer still. Vast granite escarpments, ornamented with prickly pears and sagebrush, pierce the Heavens, a picture of unearthly grandeur. And even with the blooming cacti, there remains a haunting desolation to the wilderness.

In all our lonesome toil, I am happy for a brief period of awe.

August 22, 1869

I suspect Sophronia is not well. It will not do to fall ill in this foreign land. We are but strange travelers here.

One of our cattle seems on the verge of collapse. We have passed many dead cattle on the way, which gives me an ill feeling.

Passed 2 graves today.

Made 16 miles.

August 24, 1869

Sophie is most certainly ill. She will not take food.

We have parted ways with the company to go on to our own destination. The other outfits continue farther west. By our guidebook, it will not be long now, to Virgil.

We are completely alone.

August 25, 1869

Sophronia's fever has worsened. There has been no rain to fill our buckets and we have passed no streams. We have lost two of our three cattle, one which fell from thirst, and the other which lay down soon after and did not get up again. I do not know how many miles we made today. I have lost track of all Creation, while Sophie shivers in the wagon with its stifling, sickened air.

All those graves we passed on the way . . .

August 28, 1869

By God, we have arrived! But I can't write now, here is the doctor.

Later

Sophie is resting. I feel I could close my eyes now and fall immediately into sleep, but something within me will not allow me to. I must stay up and watch over her.

My only solace now is that our privation must be at an end, for there can be no privation like that of the trail, and its lonesome, endless movement. Hardly the adventure it was made out to be. I believe it was only the expectation of meeting John Henry's brother, Emery Cain, and the prosperity he promised in his letter, that pushed us onward. Only now hardly any of that seems to matter. Emery is nowhere to be found.

The doctor, an older gentleman whose mustache seems in the process of devouring his ample mouth, was called for at once on our arrival, and we brought our wagon around to his house, warmed within by a fire even as its walls without were besieged by the gray wind. John held Oscar aside while I fretted my handkerchief to pieces. Sophronia looked so thin and pale, but for the fever in her cheeks. Her body lay limp as a fish; at eight, she looked all of six.

Oscar asked, "Will she die?" John Henry held him firmly by the shoulders while the boy looked on with neither fear nor sadness but a kind of curiosity, and asked again: "Will she die, like Charles?"

For him to mention Charles and Sophie in one breath stilled my heart. The boy, who can be so dear, in his young five summers, is also predisposed to voicing such unintentional cruelties.

"That isn't for us to say," said the doctor, a man called Ira Hartsworth. "We will have to keep a weather eye on her till the fever breaks." He folded a cool, wet cloth over her forehead and told us she would remain here in the house. "The rest of you will find a barn out yonder with enough hay for beds."

There was such kindness in his voice, the heart was liable to melt. Perhaps it is being so long on our desolate trek, through endless vistas of wilderness, which softens the soul. The doctor fixed a pot of tea as John and Oscar went to bring in the horse and prepare the barn.

He brewed it strong, for which I was grateful. I have always preferred strong tea, the way my mother used to make it. It went down bitter and warm, and it calmed me to sit with the fire at my back. If I closed my eyes, I could almost pretend I was drinking it from my mother's silver tea service, the one she gave to us on our wedding. It is now packed away in the wagon. John Henry didn't want to bring it. Sentimental foolishness, he said, and added weight to boot. Yet it is all I have of my mother, who seems now so very far away.

I asked him if this entire journey wasn't sentimental foolishness, but he wouldn't hear it. "There is nothing foolish about twenty thousand tons of silver ore," he'd said to me. A land full of riches, indeed! Then why is it so drab and dry?

By and by, I came to ask the doctor how long he has lived here, and he said, "Nigh on five years now. Since it was just a camp with a few tents."

When I asked him further, what he said left me only with ill feelings. He told me that some months ago, Virgil was bustling with a flood of new miners and folks like us. "But things change," he said, nodding to himself, "Oh my dear, things do change." He grew quietly contemplative for a long while, consumed in his thoughts, then smiled and said, "What were we talking about?"

I cannot but wonder if age has begun to loosen the man's mind. I do not like to think what it must be to get old; I am already so bone-weary, sometimes, after twenty-six years. Still I resented him for not being in the sharpness of youth, and for my being made to trust this specimen of the dusty frontier with my child's life.

In spite of the tea, the fire is making me drowsy. Sophronia has been restless, though still insensible. I will not leave her side, but I must stop writing, for now.

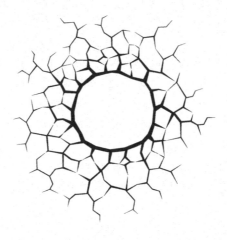

THE DUST DEVILS

AUNTED BY THE IMAGE of the little girl lying on her sickbed, Waynoka rubbed her eyes, found them drawn to Mads, who had slipped into the depths of a black slumber on the pile of rags.

Her eyelids seemed glued shut by the force of exhaustion; her mouth hung slightly open. Yet even in sleep, pain etched lines of tension across her forehead.

Setting aside the book, Waynoka moved closer to check on Mads, to make sure her breathing was even. She placed the back of her hand gently on Mads's forehead, trying to tell if it felt hot, but unable to distinguish between the regular warmth of a human body and a fever.

Poor little Sophronia, she thought. *Poor Lavinia. Starting a new life only to be met by illness.*

Waynoka rummaged through the rusty tools in the room, found a pick-ax, and used it to prod the fire back to life as its flames grew low and sleepy. Jarring the wood rekindled it nicely, and she sat down again, fanning the smoke to the room's exits to keep the air as clear as she could.

She fought back a compulsion to wake Mads, even though she had only been asleep for a few minutes and needed her rest. With Mads asleep, Waynoka felt alone.

After her apartment burned down, and she had nothing left but what she'd taken with her to the evacuation center, Mads had been there—offered her whatever food she'd managed to scrounge up; protected her from predators when they'd ended up at the overcrowded homeless shelter; hot-wired a second motorcycle for Waynoka when they'd decided to set off on their own.

Waynoka had been reminded of her mother giving her the keys to the family car for the first time: her mother's eyes filled with pride after she'd passed her driving test; Waynoka weighted by the gravity, the responsibility to live up to the gift. That's how she'd felt when Mads had presented her with the stolen motorcycle.

"We can go anywhere we want now," Mads had said, eyes gleaming with the thrill of it. "You and me. Yeah?"

But the gift had brought with it that terrible weight in Waynoka's chest, the need to prove herself equal to Mads, who had all kinds of survival tricks that had saved them time and again. Waynoka came to learn that Mads had spent months camping and fending for herself even before the fires—that she'd lived off the grid in Slab City for a time, that she'd roved from one place to the next taking odd jobs, gently skirting the law when she had to.

Next to her, Waynoka felt sheltered and useless. What street smarts did she have? What did she know about survival? She tried to imagine having to live in Lavinia's day but could hardly fathom it.

What it came down to, really, was that Waynoka had been suited to the modern world; could fancy herself independent because she lived alone, paid her rent, cooked her own meals, paid her taxes. But when all the trappings of that life were torn away, the naked truth beneath lay bare: Waynoka didn't have what it took to fend for herself.

And if Mads wasn't okay—if she was too injured from the fall, or if the leg got infected—

No. She couldn't think like that.

She would take care of Mads, now, the way Mads had taken care of her in those early days when Waynoka had spent nights shivering off the day's sweat, hungry and afraid. She would take care of Mads until she was well, and they would get out of here together.

They had to.

Her hands felt fidgety. Just being down here in this claustrophobic darkness put her on edge. She picked up the book again and found the spot where she'd left off.

How did Lavinia's diary get from the town—Virgil, she'd called it—all the way down here into the lower levels of the mine? Had Lavinia come down here at some point? If so, how had she gotten out?

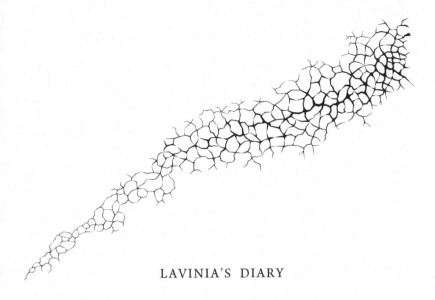

LAVINIA'S DIARY

Later, again

I'll write this quickly, for I am filled with relief—her fever has broken!

I woke stiff in my chair at the doctor's rousing to find Sophronia alert, gleaming with sweat by the unstable light of the kerosene lantern. "Mama," she said, reaching out for me, and I took her small hand and held it tight until she fell asleep. Just before she drifted off, she said, "Have we made it to Eden?" I told her yes, we had—I did not tell her how very far from Eden this place truly is. In those last few weeks on the trail, I told her we were going to a place of bounty and riches, and she read her Bible and said it must be Eden where we were headed, and I hadn't the heart to tell her otherwise. Those eyes as blue as the ocean make a body want to tell her only sweet things.

In a while, when the sun begins to rise, I will tell John Henry the news, but for now I shall let him rest—he has been sleeping hardly at all on the trail, and I fear he is worn nearly as thin as Sophronia. Sometimes I feel as if it is my duty alone to keep this family chugging along like a well-oiled machine. It isn't John's fault; he simply does not notice the things I do, the subtle change in the children's temperaments when they are tired or falling ill. I knew before she did that Sophronia was not well, by the way she irritably refused food when she must be hungry, and by the dull gleam of her eye as she listlessly watched the forsaken landscape roll by—the flat gray clouds, the strange vistas of scrub and distant twisted rock. John refused to believe it until her skin was hot as a skillet, tears making riverbeds of her cheeks. He was adamant that all would be well.

I am not convinced. The people we met on our arrival acted so oddly when we asked about John Henry's brother. As we came into town and set about finding the doctor, a young couple came to our aid—I briefly caught their names, Olive and Chester Blackburn. They brought a jug of water to our wagon, and as I bade Sophronia to drink, I heard John Henry ask them where he might find his brother. He described him—"not a very tall man, but stout and robust, with a jovial sort of face and a coarse brown beard with a small white patch just here at the jaw." He called him by name, but they shook their heads and would not look at him. "Emery Cain?" he said. "Please, Emery Cain? He has lived here for more than a year. Surely you must know him?" The looks on their faces seemed that of alarm, but they only shook their heads and retreated.

And now the last of our cattle has perished, as if it had only to see out the rest of the journey before returning to the Lord.

Perhaps it is premature of me to take this as a bad sign, but I feel a premonition in my bones, the way I felt Sophronia's illness coming on. Though I know it is colored by our initial experiences, which have not made for the pleasantest start of a new life, already I can feel that something is not right in Virgil, Nevada.

August 30, 1869

Yesterday was too full to write. In the evening I brought out this book and stared at the blank page, for though I find it calming to sit by the light of a candle and spill the world onto paper, I was paralyzed of thought and washed of language, so I put it away before I could make the slightest mark, and instead held Sophronia's hand and told her fairy tales until she fell asleep. She is stronger, but only just. I shall be glad when I no longer fret at her every labored breath, though a small voice in the corner of my mind asks if I ever will.

As soon as my dear one sat up and ate a bit of porridge, John Henry donned his hat and coat, and when I asked where he thought he might be going, he said he was off to see about meeting the mine's owner and securing himself a position.

"Now?" I asked him. Right this instant? What could he be thinking of?

We are staying with the doctor another night yet; Sophie has not moved from her sickbed while I have been sleeping in a chair beside her, ragged and unkempt. We have nowhere else to stay but our wagon. Our next step must be to file a claim for land and find Emery so that we might stay with him while we build a house. I had believed John Henry would desire to accomplish these important tasks before he set himself to work the mine.

Yet he asked me, "Why did we come here, then, if not for my employment?" When I suggested that we must at least see to Sophie right now, he told me, "The doctor is seeing to her. If we are to make our home here, we will need to purchase land, and how do you suppose I will do so without a wage? We have nothing." On looking at me, he softened somewhat, and became tender. "There is no time to waste," he said gently, and called me his rabbit's foot, as he does, and reminded me he is not one to sit about idly when there is something he can do to improve the lot of his family. "We came here for a reason, and I intend to see it out."

These were his exact words as I write them, verbatim. I remind you, Diary, that I have a keen memory for language, and I would not quote unless I was sure just what had been said. There is no sense, after all, in writing down speculations. My own mother taught me that. If you are to keep a diary, she said to me, once, when I was young and she had discovered my very first little book, in which I'd written quite juvenile poetry, then at least you ought to write an accurate account of your day. I won't have a daughter taken to whimsy, or next thing you'll be writing novels! She is a fair and diplomatic woman, my mother, though I don't see what would be so wrong with writing novels.

But here I am, taken to writing about my mother, instead of what lies before me, which is riddled with problems. First, the matter of where we will stay when Sophie is well enough to leave the doctor's house. For, if we cannot find Emery, then where shall we go?

When I asked John Henry where he thought his brother might be, he only shrugged as if the matter did not concern him. "He has always taken to wild flights of fancy, going wherever the wind blows him," he told me, as if this concluded the matter.

Yet it is strange to me that he did not write to tell us he was leaving—especially after he told us we should come! Unless, perhaps, his last transmission arrived after we had already left Boston. But then, wouldn't someone in town know of his whereabouts?

And what of the way that young couple acted so oddly when J. H. asked after him? They seemed spooked and made as if Emery had never been here at all. Only we know he has been here for a year, from his letters. When I asked Doctor Hartsworth what he knew of Emery Cain, the doctor only shook his head and said the name did not ring a bell—but his face blanched the color of flour, and he excused himself.

There is one thing that I am glad of, and that is the way Doctor Hartsworth has taken Oscar under his wing. The boy wanted to go out and explore his new surroundings, but I was unwilling to allow him to stray far on his own. Thankfully, the doctor has taken him about town and has set him to small chores, such as milking his cow.

When John Henry returned yesterday evening, he bore triumph in the set of his shoulders. He kissed me on the top of my head the way he does when he is pleased with himself and set his pipe in his mouth when he sat. "I knew the West was a true promised land," he said as he lit his tobacco and began to smoke. "You know, Lavinia, there are two sorts of men in this world: the kind of man willing to go out and seek his fortune, and the kind who is content with what he has. Truly the West knows just who ought to hear its siren song, for it is only the Seeker who will reap its bountiful rewards."

"These are pretty words," I told him, "and I suppose you've something you'd like to tell me?"

John Henry has an aversion to forthrightness, preferring to talk his way around a subject before arriving at the point. I had to needle him to get there sooner, but by and by he did.

"You are looking at a man employed by the Virgil Consolidated Mining Company," he said at last. He grinned as he puffed on his pipe. "It is all coming together, just as we'd hoped. Do smile, Lavinia. You needn't fret so—Sophie is getting better all the time." I told him I was very happy for him and inquired if he had asked after Emery at the company.

His eyes darkened at once. When John Henry loses his mirth, the dour set of his heavy brows, the long arch of his nose, and the way the corner of his left eye sags, as if looking at you sideways, puts him all in darkness. He can transform from a handsome gentleman one moment to a fiend in the next.

John Henry told me the man he had spoken with had never heard of him, and this despite what Emery told us, which is that he had been employed by the very same mining company, and therefore ought to have been known to them.

"It's clear, isn't it?" John Henry said when I voiced my doubts. "Emery hasn't the commitment to stay in one place for very long—or why else do you think he hasn't found himself a wife yet? I doubt he paused here for more than a day before he was off again, wandering far and wide to avoid stable employment. He's a bad egg, Emery, and probably somewhere's town bummer by now. And he has a strange sense of humor, indeed. So it seems clear he told us a thumper, just to have us on."

I couldn't believe it, and I told him just so: "But to have us come all this way, merely for a joke? Doesn't that seem awfully cruel?"

"The thing you must understand about my brother, Lavinia, is that he cares for no one but himself. When we were children, he would do whatever he pleased, even when his carelessness had us both beaten. Nothing I said could have persuaded him to think of his own brother before he shirked his duties, and not even my father's punishments dissuaded him from doing whatever he had a mind to. I know it may be hard for you to believe, for he has a charming nature that puts him in easy favor, but that is the truth of it. My brother is a son of a bitch, only he is very good at hiding it."

It was about this time that Sophie began to stir, and I preoccupied myself with tending to her. When Doctor Hartsworth returned with Oscar, we sat down for supper (I brought Sophie hers afterwards), and our boy prattled on for some minutes about the men he had met outside of the feed store who sat sharing a bottle of whiskey between them, and how they had told him stories of strange creatures in the tunnels of the mine, frightful spirits that swept through town, and all manner of terrible things.

And all this, before we could even say grace!

Our baked beans and cornmeal grew cold on the table. "Had they nothing good to say about this place, or was it all ghost stories?" I asked him, but Oscar only gave me a fiendish smile. So I told the doctor that I hoped the next time he took my son to town (if I should let him!), he will not allow him to listen to those sorts of stories, for I shouldn't like to put such dark fancies in his head.

Yet the doctor said the queerest thing: "It's just that one cannot escape such tales hereabouts." When I asked him why that is, he picked up his knife and fork and began to eat, chewing ponderously.

"Now, Lavinia," John Henry said, "I'm sure you're likely to find such tales anywhere you go in the West. Isn't that right, Doctor?"

"Well," he said, still chewing slowly, "I allow that might be true. But the tales here are of a particular nature. That is, it's said the mine is cursed."

"Cursed?" I'm sure I said, with some surprise. John Henry chortled. I did not share his amusement. I turned to the doctor and said, "You sit here, talking of curses! Aren't you a man of science?"

He nodded, his white beard twitching. "I am." He lifted his napkin and dabbed it at the corner of his mouth in a delicate fashion. "But there are things here, Mrs. Cain, that are more ancient than our medicine. That are, perhaps, more ancient even than us."

John Henry began talking of how we had come to an ancient place— how old the mountains and the land, how unsullied the caves and depths of the mine—as if to explain the doctor's unnatural words with clarity and reason. I held my tongue and ate, allowing John to wax about the wilderness and its bounty for the duration of our meal. Yet I will be glad when Sophie is well and we may leave Doctor Hartsworth's house. I do not think I trust him.

September 1, 1869

John Henry told me it was a fool's errand—that I wouldn't find hide nor hair of him if I looked, that Emery is surely long gone from here, if ever he were here at all. When he asked me why I was so interested in finding him, I could see in his eyes he was thinking of that unfortunate time five years ago, as if to imply that my desire to find Emery were something more than it is. And I felt all at once ashamed, even if it is a shame over something that never happened but which John Henry insists on believing. The bottom fact is Emery came to my aid in my time of need, and if something has indeed happened to him, I would never forgive myself for abandoning him. I simply cannot believe he is as callous as John Henry says he is.

I decided I ought to keep quiet about it in front of John Henry and temper my eagerness to find the answer to the mystery, if only so that he does not read too much into it.

It all seemed to happen quite by luck. John Henry was at the mine learning his duties, Sophronia was resting, and the doctor had Oscar quite occupied with milking the cow or feeding the chickens, so I found myself walking into town for the very first time. Its brightness startled me. That is, there is no shade anywhere, and not even a wisp of cloud, so that the sun beams all through the sky, turning it the purest blue, and glares over the earth, to make all its colors lighten and fade. Without any barrier between me and the sun but my flimsy bonnet, I could feel the sun as if it were inches above me. There is but one tree in town, a dead and blighted thing of a most ominous sort, with nary a leaf on its limbs.

My hope was to find the assessor's office, not to make a claim but to find the parcel of land which Emery had purchased when he came to Virgil. He had told us as much in his letters: I have bought a tract of land and am building my cabin upon it. Though it is not the type of land that will bear fruit, being more rock than soil, it will do. I like to live simply, and do not require much. This he wrote more than nine months ago.

Unable to find such an office, however, I contented myself with exploring the town. Main Street proved to be much what I had expected, with a kind of rustic charm: a dirt road lined on either side by close-set wood buildings, grocery store, feed store, restaurants, an inn, a tailor shop, a blacksmith, a bank.

One side, however, was unfinished, and I wondered at the abandoned construction, for I saw no laborers. Perhaps this was where the doctor's office was meant to be. Doctor Hartsworth had told me there was to be a small hospital, or office, that had been in the works for some time, but that construction had lately stagnated, which is why he has been practicing out of his own home.

Just off Main Street, I came upon a two-story building (one of only two in town) emblazoned with the moniker MISS SHAW'S in letters partially worn away by the wind. A woman sat on the veranda. Her sweeping waves of black hair bore a contrast to my own dusty brown tresses, spooled and tucked away beneath my tattered bonnet. She sat smoking from a pipe, her lively colored skirts fanned out about her limbs, which were propped up on another chair as casual as you please. The dark gems of her eyes found me as I approached. Thinking her the eponymous Miss Shaw, whom I assumed to be the proprietor of this establishment, I said hello and asked if I was right in my assumption that I had found a boardinghouse.

She looked me up and down and said, "New in town?"

I told her we had just arrived, and that I would be happy to find room and board for me and my family, if there were rooms available here.

Claudia—for that is her name, she introduced herself later as Claudia Montaña—glanced behind her at the door, then sat up straight. "No, not here," she said, her dark eyes searching me. "Would you like my advice?"

"Please."

"Go back where you came from."

The wind took up her words and hurled them into its howl; I held my hand over my bonnet to keep it on my head while my dress whipped around me. Yet it wasn't the wind that floored me so. Already it seems we are not wanted here. It is as if our shame from Boston has followed us.

"My daughter is ill," I told her when the gust of wind moved on. "Are there truly no rooms? We were to stay with my brother-in-law, Emery Cain—he promised us a place at his cabin, but we cannot find him—"

She drew in a breath and stared at me. "Emery Cain?" she repeated.

How relieved I was to hear someone say his name as if she had heard it before! "Yes," I said with relief. "Yes, Emery Cain is my brother-in-law. Land sakes, I was growing concerned when it seemed no one here had heard of him. Do you know him?"

Instead of answering, she stood abruptly. Claudia seemed the kind of woman who makes decisions quickly and commits her full confidence to them. "*Vamos*," she said. "Come with me."

She came down the steps and continued past me—I had no choice but to follow. She walked briskly, purposefully; she did not seem to care that the hem of her skirts whisked through the dirt. I raised my own skirt to hurry beside her, the air stinging my eyes and tickling my nostrils. I have never seen such a cacophony of dust as chokes the throat of this town, as if the earth should strangle it. A species of dread lives here, perturbing the wind with its howling. Yet when the wind blew eastward, it caught Claudia's spicy scent of anise and tobacco, a welcome reprieve from the smells I have grown so accustomed to: the sour odor of sweat, of sickness—and on the trail, of horse dung and the musk of unwashed bodies crowded together in our wagon. There is a thing to be said for kindly smells. A foul odor can make a foul mood.

We must have walked three miles through increasingly bleak desert before we arrived at the cabin. Its walls were composed of crude logs bearing up a roof of sod, but it looked in better condition than some of the others we had passed on our way—one fashioned from adobe brick, and another of barrels that appeared to be splitting open, which even so seems a clever construction, as I have heard it is expensive to freight lumber here, where the largest flora are sage-brush and cacti. The cabin before me, at least, was pleasantly sized, with two little windows that had shutters to close them. I wondered at first why Claudia had brought me here, and she further surprised me by saying, "This is yours." I thought perhaps I had misunderstood, or that maybe her English wasn't as good as it had at first seemed. When I asked her who the cabin belonged to, she said, "No one," with a grave look on her face. "Not anymore."

Still I was confounded by the idea of simply taking up residence on someone else's property, but Claudia explained further: there are many empty cabins now. People are packing up and leaving all the time, and this one she knew to be vacant.

Strange and stranger! In a boomtown, no less, why on earth should people be leaving rather than coming? It is the very opposite of what one might expect.

We entered the quiet abode, which spoke of emptiness and abandonment. A threadbare, musty bed lurked in the corner; metal tools hung along one wall below a series of yellowing animal skulls. There was a blackened hearth with a cast-iron pot and candle mold set on a makeshift mantel; a dining table set with two stools, a tin plate, and a half-burned tallow candle; a crate that I suppose contained some of the former owner's possessions; and some clay jars on shelves that revealed themselves, upon inspection, to hold stale coffee, cornmeal, and dried beans. The windows admitted a modest pallor of sunlight, though they will have to be shuttered when cold nights come on, as there is no glass and they are open to the whims of nature.

Claudia touched the jars and candle with a gentle sort of sweetness; a familiarity, as one returning to fond memories. We sat at the table, and

I found myself enjoying the society of another woman at long last. I came to find she worked at the establishment owned by Miss Rosemary Shaw, a shrewd woman with iron-gray hair and a keen aptitude for business. Miss Shaw was said to have ears all about the town, though she kept her secrets to herself. Claudia has ears too, though, and she picks up on things. If I wanted gossip, I had only to ask her.

Well, I did ask her—of course I did! I asked her what she knew of Emery Cain.

A haunting recognition came over her face. She listened attentively as I explained that we could not find any trace of him here, that he seems to have vanished, and it is terrible strange that no one seems to know of him. I have become suspicious, and I am getting ominous feelings from his disappearance. Claudia nodded and said, "Yes. He is gone now."

"But he was here?" I implored.

She hesitated, twisting her fingers about in her lap, and afforded me a curt nod. I could make neither heads nor tails of the look on her face, the nervousness that emanated from her. I asked her, as no one else has heard of him, how she knew he had been in Virgil.

"Because, Mrs. Cain," she told me, "you are sitting in his house."

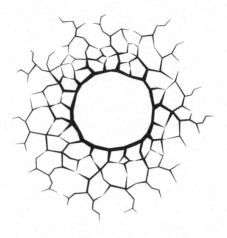

THE DUST DEVILS

"W HAT?" WAYNOKA SAID OUT loud, unable to stop the word from slipping past her lips.

She had to set the book on the ground beside her and stand up just to get away from it. The air, rich with smoke, tickled her dry throat; her skin itched and crawled.

A sudden jab of pain behind her left eye reminded Waynoka that she might have a concussion from the fall. She longed, in that moment, to curl up with Mads and sleep, but she knew she shouldn't. Wasn't that what they said about concussions?

Trying to stay awake, she turned over what she'd read.

Cursed. That's what the old doctor had said—that this mine was cursed. Waynoka fought down a burst of anxious laughter. Just their luck to wind up trapped in a cursed mine! What did that mean, though? What was the curse?

"Stop it," she snapped, shaking her head. That was a ridiculous question. It was just the superstitions of people from the nineteenth century who didn't know any better, people who didn't have the scientific and worldly knowledge they had now. Probably every frontier town had a ghost story. That didn't make it real.

Lavinia seemed like a rational-enough person. Surely she would offer some explanation for this superstition later in her diary. Along with—Waynoka hoped—some idea about how to get out of here.

A sound—like a grunt or a snort—sent Waynoka flinching back against the wall. She looked around, attuned to every whisper in the underground silence, and realized it was only Mads snoring, her neck craned back against the pillow of old rags.

Waynoka rubbed a hand down her face. She had to calm down. She'd let the foolish beliefs in the diary get to her, and now she was jumping at shadows. She longed for the wide open desert. She was horrified to find herself, impossibly, missing the scorching sun—that blistering ball of flame they took such pains to avoid. It seemed so far away, beyond this wretched place.

She looked at Mads and said, "Isn't that fucked up?"

Mads continued to snore.

At least Sophie was getting better, thought Waynoka. And if Sophie could get better, then Mads could too. She just had to let her rest a while longer.

Waynoka drifted back to where she'd been sitting and picked up the diary again, compelled by the cramped handwriting that filled its pages and the wide open spaces of Lavinia's world.

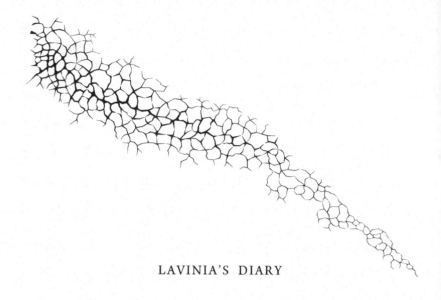

LAVINIA'S DIARY

September 4, 1869

We have begun settling into our new home: unpacking the wagon, cleaning the stale musk from the cabin, setting up beds for Sophie and Oscar. The cabin is imbued with the simple rusticity of the frontier. It is quaint and comfortable and almost pleasing. This respite, a place at last to call our own and rest our weary heads, will be worth the drudgery of the trail and the toil that lies ahead, without the amenities of civilized life that we enjoyed in Boston. It is simple and quiet. I walked a ways from the cabin to see what was there of the land, until I was far enough away that I seemed wholly surrounded by nothing but the desolation of nature and the sublimity of its lonesome beauty. The rocks exhibit shades of color I fancy come from the Heavens themselves.

I concluded at once that this was not an empty place as it at first appears, but that a divine presence lies just behind each crevice and cactus. In the seeming emptiness of this place, when the bustle of civilization is far removed, one can truly understand the Spirit that underlies all Creation, and that this land cannot belong to us in any but the most superficial sense, because it belongs only to itself.

When I told John Henry of the land and the cabin, he was surprised and pleased. At first he thought I had managed to purchase a parcel of land on credit and grew angry at my having attempted to do so without his consent, yet when he discovered that we were indebted to no one, he seemed not to care why the land was ours, only that it was. And though I told him it was ours only because it had belonged to Emery, this troubled him only briefly, for soon he was smiling again at our good fortune for landing in this hospitable place. "I always knew you were my lucky rabbit's foot," he said. He has hardly been around, however, for his work is long at the mine.

I admit I was shocked to my core when Claudia told me where she'd brought me. Some rummaging turned up the land deed, and as she handed it to me, she said, "This house once belonged to Emery Cain. Your name is Cain. Take it. It is yours now. This land is worthless, anyway. You could not sell it for peanuts."

I wondered at that. As it happens, a strangeness has plagued Virgil for some months now. Ever since an accident up at the mine, many residents have pulled foot and cleared out of town, leaving empty cabins and a dearth of workers for the company. When I asked Claudia of the accident, rather than give me a straight answer, she said only that we should avoid going out after dark. Before she left, she crossed herself and told me there are dangerous creatures about these parts. I can only imagine there must be, in a wilderness such as this.

To-morrow, the children begin their schooling with the twelve or fifteen other children who attend the schoolhouse in town. Sophronia is improving by the day; her growing restlessness tells me she has had enough of lying down. Just this morning, as I was beating dust from my mother's beloved quilt, I saw the children chasing each other around, their laughter almost continuous. When they ceased their activities, Sophie's hair wisping free of her bonnet, Oscar with dirt on his knees, I found myself feeling terribly fond of them both. My heart has lightened with seeing Sophie's smile, the way her pink tongue presses through the space of her missing tooth and the sparkle of her deep blue eyes. I cannot imagine what I would have done—!

So much of our nourishment is dried and salted, we elected to trudge into town and assess what victuals are to be had in the grocery store. I was plumb delighted to find Sophie hungry, for once, and thought her hard knocks must be at an end. Oscar dashed about ahead of us, kicking a rock across the ground, while Sophie held my hand primly. "Mama," she said to me as we passed onto Main Street, "why are there bells on all the doorways?"

Indeed, she was right. I had not noticed it before, but it is just as she said. As soon as I saw them, I could not imagine how I had missed them: little silver bells hanging not just from the doorways of the shops, the boardinghouse, the post office, the two-story stone courthouse, but also from the doorway of each cabin and residence we had passed. Every last building had a bell over its entrance.

Why this should disconcert me so, I cannot say.

On the edge of town, rugged hills and mountains carve up the pale dusty sky. One can see the buildings of the mine from here, it is so close; it is, after all, the town's lifeblood. Virgil would not exist without the Virgil Consolidated Mining Company. And out beyond the edges of Virgil loom strange rocky hills, toxic plants, and evil cacti. Nothing here is familiar. Indeed, Virgil seems to be a lone outpost amid a vast wilderness.

I suppose the bells are so that they can hear when someone is coming, yet it seems strange to me why there should be one on every building. Perhaps the people here do not like to be caught unawares. Sophie asked me if we would put a bell on our door as well, gazing up at me with those eyes of deepest blue, wide and guileless. I do not think I would like having a bell on our door, jangling intrusively every time one of us goes in or out. It seems a dreadful intrusion on the quiet.

Claudia will know what it means. I must ask her of the bells, why they are there, though I fear I may encounter her reticence once again.

September 6, 1869

Today I secured us a goat and two sheep. I attempted also to identify what sort of crops might grow on our land, only to be stymied by the grocer's laughter. "All hardpan out here," he said. "You won't get naught but weeds." Even the sheep seem resentful of the lack of good eating; their eyes seem to accuse me so! If only I could explain to them in a language they might understand that we are all making the best of things. Perhaps my stroking them puts them at ease. I often find the company of animals a balm unlike any other, a contentment one simply cannot find among people. Animals have an utter honesty and sincerity about them; they are incapable of the lies and manipulations that contaminate human society.

It is too late in the season, besides, to do much planting. Winter will be upon us in short order. Yet the days remain hot even now, as in the thick of summer, and excessive dry. There is but little rain and nary a cloud to blot out the overbearing sun.

By this time of year, Boston would be cool and rainy, the air ripe with the soft moisture of the sea.

I filled my bucket with water from the pump outside of the grocery store and my arms strained as I lumbered back down the street with it, as well as the sack of feed thrown over my shoulder. Others were about, and I heard hushed conversation as I passed. Perhaps they did not know I could hear them, or perhaps I have acute hearing.

"Help the poor girl out," said one.

"That's one of the new ones. The Cains," said his companion, and they turned away from me.

I lowered the bucket and set myself down for a spell, the sun hot on my back like all-fire; I swatted flies from the sweetness of my sweat. I felt alone as a body can feel. It was just as if the other people about town were only flies buzzing away from me.

It reminds me of Boston, in the latter days of our shame, when we had become pariahs. If it had only been the bucket or the feed, I wouldn't have had such trouble, and perhaps I ought to have made two trips, after all. But now that I had both I was determined to get them back to the cabin, and as I was all on my own, it was a double burden upon me.

Just as I was beginning to gather myself to continue, I found that I was in sight of the boardinghouse, and I wondered if Claudia was in. It took me another few minutes to bring myself to its porch—not because the way was so very far, but because I was continually and stubbornly convincing myself that it was more prudent to simply continue home. Yet the notion of a brief respite from the toil, to call on the one person in town who has shown me an ounce of kindness, seemed to me a merry prospect, so I set down my bucket and feed on the porch and went inside.

The parlor was more lushly appointed than the building's exterior suggested: there sat a scrolled velvet sofa against elegantly patterned wallpaper which appeared in a French style to my unworldly eyes. Two young women in scandalously little clothing sat there with drinks in hand. Behind a counter stood the woman I took to be Miss Rosemary Shaw. So used to plainness, I was quite struck by this woman, who I can only describe as *adorned*: fur on her shoulders; a pair of miniscule spectacles on her delicate nose; a feathered hat on her silver curls; striking jade earrings dangling from her ears. Though heavyset and imposing, she was nevertheless a handsome woman.

She turned to me on my arrival and appraised me quickly, then said, "Looking for work? Don't worry, dear, there are so many men in this town and so few women, no one will bat an eye at those homely looks."

I told her I was looking only for Claudia.

"Bernadette," Miss Shaw snapped at one of the girls lounging on the sofa, "Up with you! Go and retrieve her." Miss Shaw's keen eyes turned sideways to me as the girl leapt from the couch and bounded up the narrow staircase. "You're lucky we're slow this time of day. Claudia is quite popular."

She came down, just as lovely as ever, wearing a plain white gown. Her hair was pinned up today, with loose curls hanging around her rouged face. She seemed surprised to see me here. Miss Shaw went off somewhere else, and Bernadette returned to her companion on the sofa, who had been holding her drink.

With a tilt of her head, Claudia indicated that we had better step out onto the porch, so we did. My bucket and bag of feed became quite apparent at our feet, so I told her I had stopped for a short rest before carrying my burdens the three miles back and had desired to thank her for bringing me to Emery's cabin.

She glanced behind her though we had shut the door on our way out, then looked back at me and said, "Let me help you."

I attempted to decline—it would be far too generous of her to help me all the way back to the cabin, although she was at work, but she told me she was not busy right now and she would very much enjoy a walk out of doors. So Claudia took the sack of feed while I hefted the bucket, and slowly we made our way down the dusty road. There was nothing to do but talk as we went. I didn't want to trouble her or frighten her off, so I did not ask her again about what happened to Emery, though I very much wanted to.

To my delight, after correcting my pronunciation of her name, she taught me a few Spanish words. Let me see if I can remember them: *mantekeeya* is butter, *grasias* is thank you, *amore* is love. She offered to teach me more if I ever came round again.

"Miss Shaw is a strange sort of woman, isn't she?" I said, thinking back on the peculiar way she had greeted me.

"She goes about the world with dollar signs in her eyes," said Claudia, who then proceeded to tell me about some of the other people in town. There is the minister, whose name I am sorry to say I have quite forgotten already; the tailor, Mr. Branson, who could frequently be found sitting outside of his shop with his hat pulled over his eyes so that one could not tell whether or not he was snoozing; Mr. Warrant and his family, one of the more powerful about town due to his high position in the mining company; Mr. Faraday, the postman, who was the friendliest sort of man you could meet; Mr. Pavlovsky, the grocer, and his wife, Josephine. I asked her of the schoolteacher, whom I had met only briefly when bringing the children round to the schoolhouse, and Claudia told me that Miss Delilah Barnes was well-known for being charitable and accommodating, though, perhaps due to spending her time in the company of children, given to flights of fancy.

The walk was so much pleasanter with Claudia beside me, sharing the load. The cabin lay not far ahead of us when the distinct jingle of a bell shrilled nearby, as a woman exited her home with a bundle of washing.

I couldn't help myself: "May I ask—why are there all these bells?"

She said the most peculiar thing: "The bells are so that we can hear when spirits are approaching. When you hear the bells at night, you know *los fantasmas* are about."

This must be the quaint superstition of the town. It reminds me of those awful stories I have heard about poor souls who are inadvertently buried alive: how some will install bells above the grave, with a string that goes down to the coffin, so that if one awakens to find himself wrongfully interred, he may tug on the string to ring the bell and signal whoever might hear.

The thought sends a horrible shiver all though me. How awful, the notion of waking in the dark of a little coffin, closed in by six feet of dirt, hoping that someone will hear your ringing before you truly perish.

When we arrived at the cabin, I invited Claudia in for tea, but she regretfully declined, intimating that she must return to work before Miss Shaw discovered her missing. I couldn't begrudge her this, though I was sad to see her go. I do miss the society of other women and the long conversations I once shared with my sister and cousins, so very unlike the brief and efficient conversations I share with John Henry of late.

By the time I had tidied up the cabin, fed the sheep, milked the goat, and churned several pounds of butter, it was just at the hour to retrieve the children. I walked to the schoolhouse overcome with the realization that this was the longest I had been without my children in shouting distance for many months, after being on the trail in such close quarters. Making sure no one was around to see, I lifted my skirt and ran the last half mile to the school, wondering if Sophronia was still feeling well, wondering if Oscar was behaving himself.

But all was well. Sophronia and Oscar both were lively and pleased with their new school. The grip of dread that clutched my heart loosened.

Miss Delilah Barnes, a young woman of perhaps twenty-two years, with a comely face and wide-set eyes, her gait somewhat hindered by a limp under her calico dress, came over and told me I have "two very bright children."

I bade the children thank her and told her we regularly practice reading and writing with our Bible. She seemed pleased to hear this and encouraged us to continue these studies.

As we walked home, I asked Sophie what she thought of the school and the other children she had met there. She said that Peter Warrant in particular was a perfect gentleman to her (the boy is thirteen or fourteen, I believe), and I told her that the Warrants are said to be well-to-do, and she could do worse than the Warrant boy. "But that isn't something for you to think about just yet," I reminded her. "What you ought to think about is what you would like to do with yourself when you are an educated woman." This sent Sophronia into a period of quiet contemplation. She is a most thoughtful child.

All the while, Oscar was ahead of us, calling out, "Watch me!" as he walked with his arms outstretched at his sides and his eyes closed. Every so often, he turned back to see if we were watching.

I regained Sophie's attention: "And Oscar? Did he make any friends today?"

She seemed hesitant to respond but said this: "You know how he likes to play by himself."

I called Oscar to come back beside us and bade him tell me the names of the classmates he played with today. He tucked his lips in and rolled his eyes around as if he was thinking very carefully. "I don't know any of them," he said. If he was to be spending each day in their company, though, I knew he must get to know them soon enough. I said, "Miss Barnes let you out to play between lessons; with whom did you spend your time?"

He grew still and sulky, and said, "I played with Charles."

Now I grabbed the boy roughly and demanded he tell the truth, which is that if he did not play with the other children, he played with no one, for Charles is dead. He has been dead since the moment he came into this world, and no amount of pretending will change this. At times I find I cannot even stand to look at Oscar, for he looks just as Charles would have had he ever grown. There would be two of them, as twins. Instead, there is only one, playing the part of them both and insisting upon his dead brother's presence as if he were still alive.

The boy was punished for his lies, though guilt troubled me through the rest of the evening. When John Henry returned, I felt I had not seen him in an age. Though we had spent so much time together on the trail, it is remarkable the distance now between us. We have hardly spoken here. The trail has led to a vast wilderness of silence.

Yet we did talk at last when he returned. I shall try to render our conversation as accurately as I can, but there was a great deal we talked about, and I fear I will leave some of it out of this account.

We sat on stools outside, enjoying the cool night breeze. In the thick darkness there were but few lights making orange glows of the cabin windows in our view, like strange beacons out yonder. It was quiet and peaceful. The stars left their dazzling mark overhead. John Henry smoked his pipe, releasing a warm tobacco smell, and I asked him what it is like to work in the mine.

He thought about it some, and I could tell he was composing his words in his head.

"I'll tell you what it is like," he finally said. "Dark. Hot. Narrow. Not the sort of place you would ever hope to find yourself, Lavinia, and if you did, surely you would lose your way in those many tunnels. One must be careful of that—and of falling rocks and unstable supports. But that is saying nothing of the labor itself. Demanding work, grinding away at that mountain. What sustains us, however, is what may lie hidden right under our own noses. They've found silver here before, twenty thousand tons if you can believe it, and they find more every day, though often in such small amounts as to hardly matter. Traces, that is. Merely traces. All we need is to find another large strain of ore. They say this could be the next Comstock Lode." His eyes gleamed as I bade him explain to me what the Comstock Lode was—also here in Nevada, with many bonanzas under its belt, and tens of thousands of tons in gold and silver.

"Nothing worthwhile comes easily," he said as he refilled his pipe, moving carefully, as if all movement pained him. I reached out for his shoulder, but he flinched away from my attempted ministrations. Still I could see in the pinched lines of his face, the hunch of his back, the way he rested his elbow on his knee to hold the pipe, the effects of his suffering.

"All that danger and toil," I said, "and you don't even know whether you'll find silver or just more rocks."

"We *will* find more silver." The tone of his voice brooked no argument. "There is plenty of silver here. It is only a matter of finding it, removing it, and refining it. And I plan to be the one to find it. Some of these men, for all their bravado, don't have much adventure in them. They sweat in their corners of the mine, never considering what a little initiative could result—" Here I did not favor his tone overmuch; his eyebrows had drawn together and the curve of his mouth soured as if disgusted by those he believes beneath him. He continued: "There are tunnels they avoid—for superstitious reasons, if you can believe it. I told them, how do you expect to find the mother lode if you're not willing to look very hard? They may not be willing, but I believe I may find a ready strain of ore if I try one of these unspoiled tunnels. I could have that find all to myself."

"And you believe you will be the one to find it?" I asked him with a little smile. "A man with no mining experience, who comes right in and whisks away the silver from under their noses? Doesn't it sound a touch idealistic?"

"You laugh," he said, "But look: it is quite simple. I will ascertain the layout of the mine and identify the places most likely to remain as yet untouched, and thus most likely to contain strains of undiscovered silver. Before I declare my discovery, I will pluck out the largest nuggets I can find and safely bear them home with me. Only then will I share my find with the company, and receive a pretty penny as a bonus, I imagine. By then we might abscond with our fortune to less unpleasing lands, where no one will ever know where our silver came from."

"It sounds like stealing," I said.

He flicked his hand through the air as if to wave away the thought and said, "The company will have all the rest of it and will never know any is gone. They cannot possibly miss what they never truly had, can they? Why should I give over all of it to the company if I am the one who discovers it—if they wouldn't even have it without me? Rightly it should be mine, and I am generously allowing the company to take the lion's share while I divest them of some small scraps for myself. I fail to see how that is stealing."

"You fail to see a good many things."

"What is that supposed to mean?"

"You like to see what you like to see, that's all. If it is good for you, then you see it. If it is not, you find yourself mysteriously blind."

John Henry laughed and said, "I see as sharply as an eagle. But I do not act on all that I see. One must be shrewd about these things."

"One must, mustn't one?" I said playfully.

"You are mocking me."

"Perish the thought!"

His eyes twinkled, and somehow there was laughter in my voice, even as I spoke my misgivings about this serious business. He has the habit of turning things around so that I myself make light of the very matters that trouble me most.

He laid a kiss upon my brow and said, "All will be well." Such is his mantra when he is so sure of himself: All will be well, all will be well. How easy it is to believe him!

Still, I asked: "Isn't it dangerous? Going off on your own in the mine?"

"That isn't for you to worry about," he said, taking my hand and kissing it gently. His whiskers tickled my knuckles. "It is a dangerous business, yes. Must be why Emery ran off. He couldn't handle the work. Won't he be sorry when I strike it rich?"

I opened my mouth then, I knew not what to say—but he continued, almost to himself, before I could speak. "It will all be worth it," he said. "And if it isn't?"

He pulled away from me as if I had slapped him. "You don't trust me?" I pursed my lips. It would not do to argue. If this is just another of his get-rich-quick schemes, then like the others, when it falls apart, we will move on somewhere else and try again—always reaching for something forever out of reach. It is nice to think about, even if I know it is a fantasy.

He turned away from me and looked out into the darkness as he smoked. I remembered Claudia's admonition not to be out after dark, and I found myself prickling with unease. Even with the cabin's open door at our backs, I felt immediately exposed to all the unfamiliar elements of the desert.

I stood up, but John Henry's voice stopped me from going inside: "You know what makes us different? From them?" I did not ask who he meant by 'them,' but I surmised his implication. "We are willing to do what it takes, whatever it takes. I spend each day in the dark, underground. The narrow tunnels echo with endless clanking. We are all of us covered in a layer of grime and sweat, and at all times, we are aware of the mountain of rock just over our heads, liable to collapse on us if it pleases the devil. I begin to forget what the sun feels like on my skin. But I am willing. For all that, I am willing. I will go to the farthest reaches of the mine, into the deepest tunnels, where no man would dare to go, to provide for my family. And I should hate if my own family was ungrateful for that."

A sick feeling of shame coursed through me. But beneath it, somewhere as deep inside of me as those distant tunnels in the depths of the mine, I could not help but wish he had found some other form of work, though I knew it was a selfish thought, for wasn't the work he was doing now, finally, honest? Was that not what I had wanted of him?

Fearing if I remained out there any longer some of this awfulness would come spilling out of my bone box, I left him out there without another word and came inside to sit and write.

Later

What is the time? Late—all is dark, John Henry snoring beside me. A waning moon sits in its sea of stars beyond the roof. I woke to the sound of bells, somewhere to the north, if my ears do not deceive me. Though I try not to let Claudia's words disturb me, I cannot help thinking that *los fantasmas* are about, and I have had to settle my mind by lighting a candle and writing before I can fall asleep again.

After our conversation, John Henry and I lay in bed for a while before we slept. I curled into his solid presence beside me and found myself wanting to remain like that for eternity, in the warmth and dark of him. He spoke softly, his breath brushing strands of hair over my ear. I told him I was concerned for him in that mine, and that is only why I am so agitated. I had heard of an accident that occurred some months ago . . . but he shushed me, running his calloused fingers over my cheek in a gesture of intimacy that I had not even realized I had been craving dearly. He told me not to worry, that I was prone to upsetting myself when I worried, and he hated to see me like that. He confessed he had been worried for me these last weeks, worried I might fall into that same despair that took hold of me after Oscar was born and Charles born dead, should something have happened to Sophronia. We clung to each other, there in the dark, in the wide and unforgiving desert of the frontier.

The bells have gone quiet. I wonder who has been about, this late.

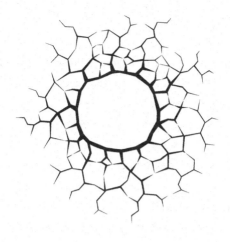

THE DUST DEVILS

WAYNOKA SET DOWN THE diary. Her hands were cold. She rubbed them together close to the fire as she looked up at the bell that hung, still and silent, beneath the red-painted figure.

Superstition, she told herself, *nothing but superstition.* She watched the flow of smoke leak out into the tunnel behind the bell, filling it with a gray haze. Anything might lie in the darkness beyond. Might come creeping out of the depths.

Stop it, she told herself. And yet she couldn't take her eyes from the painted figure—the sharp lines that radiated outward.

Rather than finding answers in the diary, Waynoka felt she had even more questions. What were the phantoms that Claudia had spoken of? What was she not telling Lavinia?

Part of Waynoka wanted to tear down the bell from where it hung, its very presence seeming to invoke whatever had plagued the town of Virgil back in the 1860s. But another part of her—the part that hissed in the shadows of her mind—feared if she took it down, they would have no way of knowing if the phantoms were approaching. She laughed at herself to relieve some of the tension.

Her head throbbed. She swallowed dryly, checked how much water she had left. Maybe two swigs, probably just backwash.

She had the sudden desire to crawl onto that moldy bed with Mads, wrap herself around her partner, bury her face in that wild frazzle of hair, let the curls tickle her nose. Like the time someone had broken into the burned-out apartment they'd been squatting in, stolen all the tools they'd managed to collect. Mads was on him like a rabid dog, might have bitten him in the jugular if Waynoka hadn't woken and cried out, fumbling around in the dark, distracting them both. The guy threw Mads off of him, trained his gun on Waynoka. Mads backed off. He punched her and fled with his loot.

Later, lying on the bare floor wrapped around each other, Waynoka asked why Mads bothered to keep her around. She wasn't clever; she wasn't athletic; she wasn't quick on her feet. She had always played by the rules, colored within the lines. "I'm dead weight."

"I needed someone to talk to," said Mads. "You're good for conversation."

"I'm not even that talkative."

Mads patted Waynoka's cheek roughly and sat up. The deep socket around her eye was already turning black, giving her the look of a skull. "That's why you're so perfect."

"Great. Thanks."

"Hey." Mads trapped her gaze and held it. The lid of her blackening eye drooped heavier than the other. "I'm not lying. Chatty Cathy is not a good conversationalist. A good conversationalist knows when to shut up."

"I guess that's what I'm good for, then. Shutting up."

"*Hijo de puta,*" Mads grumbled under her breath, then lay back down, and they both shut up for a while. But they had huddled close together to protect each other from the world and all the gun-toting assholes in it, an intimacy that didn't happen often but that Waynoka craved.

She wished she could wrap herself around Mads and offer the same kind of comfort, but she felt she had no comfort to give, not when she could barely calm herself.

"We'll get out of here," she murmured to Mads's sleeping form. "You and me. Just like Lavinia."

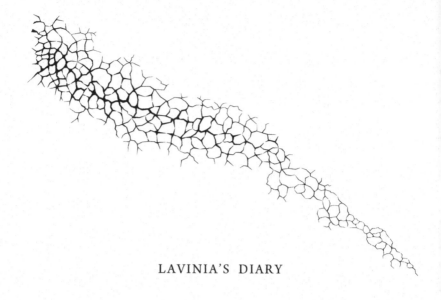

LAVINIA'S DIARY

September 7, 1869

Having thought we had left all those trail graves behind and found ourselves in a place more suited to life, I could not have imagined death marking Virgil so soon after our arrival. At every turn, the trail promised to make an end of us, yet we prevailed.

Now a man is dead, and not in any natural sort of way.

It was Olive Blackburn who first intimated to me the news. Our paths crossed going and coming, as she returned from town and I went toward it. She and Chester are our nearest neighbors. I was at first delighted to find that another woman lived so close to us and had determined to find a friend in her, but I fear, after our strange conversation, that this is not to be.

She was white as a ghost, so I called over to see if she was quite well, and she told me that Jeremiah Frost, a miner, had been killed. By what? By whom? I asked her, but she would not, or could not, say. She said he was killed in a most horrible way, "just like the others," and was found this morning all bloodless and cold. By and by, the color returned to her cheeks, and she grew more angry than shocked, her eyes alighting on me. "We are still being punished," she said with venom. "All for *his* foolishness. You and your lot will be the end of us all." Before I could ask her meaning, she hurried away from me with a sort of mad fury in her eyes. The shrill of the bell above her door as she slammed it shut sent a bolt of lightning down my spine.

I was rather more confused by her reaction than upset, so I was undeterred in my trek to town. Though I knew I could not continue wasting time walking to and from town each day, with so much yet to be done at home, I have been steadily acquiring supplies that will hold us over for a longer stretch.

What I heard in town, however, only added to the mystery of Olive's unsettling claims. The grocer, Mr. Pavlovsky, said that Mr. Frost's body had been found utterly drained of blood, "white and withered as a skelyton," and he crossed himself as he said it.

"What could do such a thing?" I asked him, to which he only shook his head and mumbled something about the curse of Virgil, this haunted town. By now I was growing quite uneasy and ever curiouser about the matter, yet still I thought this was but wild fancy, the same sort of superstition that brings one to ornament his doorway with a bell. If he was killed, then surely we should find what man or beast has done it, and hold him—or it—accountable.

Yet Mr. Pavlovsky was not alone in his spooky superstitions. All others I passed whispered among themselves such phrases as, "Not another one," and "Death be on us all." When I stopped in at the post office to send a letter to my sister informing her of our arrival, I asked Mr. Faraday, the postman, what news he had of the unfortunate Jeremiah Frost. "Was he killed by man or animal?"

"Neither," he said, and the sincerity and honesty in his voice oppressed me with dread.

"Then how did he die?" I asked him. "It's been said he was killed."

"Aye. Killed by what it is comes out of the dark. We have no name for it. Man or beast, it cannot be. More like a devil. All I know is this: it comes out of the dark and leaves men all empty and covered in strange wounds, like they been used for a pincushion."

Forgive the messy writing. My hands will not stop trembling.

It was Mr. Faraday's words that convinced me this was something more than superstition. Whatever had happened to Jeremiah Frost was a phenomenon that had previously occurred in Virgil, and that has no explanation. Can it be the Devil lives here in God's country? Or is it the work of some dangerous beast that hunts by night? The sort of creatures that survive in this desolate place must be frightful, must be the sort that could kill a man. Like a scorpion.

It is the unknowing that I find unendurable. If one could only identify the animal who hunts in this manner, or the madman whose weapon is a thousand poisoned darts, then I might at least put my mind at ease in understanding the nature of the death. Yet the answer is inscrutable as Emery's whereabouts, mysterious as the aether.

As I was making my way down Main Street in the direction of the boardinghouse (that I should call it that, even now knowing its true nature!), I stumbled across the tailor sitting outside of his shop with his hat low over his eyes. Yet he sat up straight as I passed and said hello, as if he hadn't been sleeping at all. He wore a trim gray suit and occasionally pulled out his pocket watch as if he had forgotten the time he only just checked, or perhaps he only wanted to show off the beautifully engraved backing and gold chain. His mustache was carefully groomed, curled up at the corners so that it looked as if he was always smiling. Indeed, his pond-green eyes twinkle merrily as if he *is* always smiling, even when he is not. His name is Rutherford Branson. He seemed delighted to meet me: "I do love to see a new face about town, especially one as lovely as yours."

His words were so kind, I cannot help but write them here. I have never been the sort of woman men fawn over—that's my sister, Emma. She has always been the beautiful one. I have been described as somewhat plain, with a hard jaw and a long chin. My mother used to tell me I had an unfriendly face. This distressed me when I was young, for I tried so hard to be pleasant and friendly, but my efforts always seemed in vain if my very face contradicted my behavior. Once, I remember my mother telling me that no man wants to marry a woman with an unfriendly face, and I will have to settle for whatever suitor comes around. Luckily, John Henry was that suitor, and I happened to fall in love with him.

I quickly found that Mr. Branson likes to talk. He told me about all the rips and holes these miners manage to work into their clothes, and how all the unmarried men must come to him, for they have no wives to mend their clothing for them. It is a good business, he said. Talking with the lively and peart Mr. Branson raised my spirits some, yet still I could not shake my distemper, and I asked him if he had heard news of the dead man this morning.

"Oh yes, nasty business," he said, no longer seeming to smile. "But we ain't so easy to run outta town, huh! Whatever it is killing them miners, I'll be danged if it gets to me. Mayhap these men ought not to be meddling in places they ain't welcome. But, well, the work is good, and I cannot complain. 'Tis only in a place like this that such a middling tailor can get so much business!" He laughed, and I tried to share in his mirth, but a black dread was creeping through me like a tangle of vines, reaching up to strangle my heart at the very thought of "whatever it is killing them miners." I bade him farewell, and he said he hoped I would stop by for a chat whenever I was in town, as "I would be happy to see your lovely face again and hear your musical voice."

Despite the pleasantness of Mr. Branson's words, I remained utterly chilled, but I did not immediately set off for home. Once more, I thought if anyone should have some answers, it must be Claudia, who had so far provided me the clarity that no one else has, clarity that Emery had existed here once, clarity about the bells. If I am to be perfectly honest, her presence comforts me, and if nothing else, I thought that calling on her might soothe my ill feelings. Well, when I called on her, what I discovered there distracted me quite from the matter of Jeremiah Frost, even if it only added to my present discomfort.

How horrible it is, to sit here alone with my sewing as I mend John Henry's clothes, thinking of that dead miner, picturing all manner of terrible things which might have happened to him—no, I must not dwell on it, or I will go mad. But I have spent too much time in writing already, so I shall continue my tale after I have finished my mending.

Later

I hadn't thought I would write of it, but I feel I must, if I am to keep an honest account of my experiences. What I discovered when visiting Claudia makes me feel quite the fool, that I should have missed something so obvious.

The visit began well enough. Claudia was less surprised to see me today, even pleased, though the same cannot be said of Miss Rosemary Shaw, who harrumphed when I came in, as if she'd been hoping for someone else when she heard the bell above the door. Certainly she was hoping for a client. I should have found it strange how quiet the boardinghouse is during the morning and early afternoon hours—for it isn't a boardinghouse at all, of course.

Claudia and I had tea in her room. The warmth of it stole into my body through my fingers, and through the sweet vapors as I inhaled them. When I asked her if she had heard of what happened to Jeremiah Frost, she nodded gravely and said, "I told you it was dangerous after dark. He is not the first." I asked her if she knew what had killed him, and she told me that she did not know for certain, though once, when the same tragedy happened before, she had managed to glimpse a strange shadow moving through the night: a shadow she had not been able to convince anyone else she had seen, but which she believed to be proof of the existence of *los fantasmas*. She told me: "I notice more things than those whose work does not keep them awake at such hours."

I asked what sort of work she did that should keep her up such hours, and at first she did not answer but only gave me a coy sort of smile, as if pitying me that I did not know. How could I have been so blind? I had assumed all this time that she did laundry for the boarders. Here I thought I was having tea in a boardinghouse when it turns out I was enjoying the company of an adventuress, in a brothel!

She seemed most amused by the red flush that came over my cheeks as I babbled in flummoxed embarrassment. I nearly spilled my tea in my haste to rise from the little table at which we sat, as I looked about me with fresh eyes and saw Claudia, my only friend in Virgil, for what she really is. I managed to stammer an apology before dashing away, passing Miss Shaw as I bolted down the stairs—or, rather, Madam Shaw!—and hurried home.

Later, again

I seem to be unable to quit my diary today. It is only writing, I suppose, which can calm a disturbed heart.

When John Henry returned from the mine, we supped in good humor so as not to upset the children—though Oscar told me he heard at school of a gruesome murder in the early hours of this morning before dawn, and I persuaded him it was only rumors (from the way Sophronia looked at me, I believe I did not quite convince her of such). Later, when the children were abed, John Henry and I finally had a chance to talk about Jeremiah Frost. He said he didn't know the young miner well, and that the others were solemn and quiet today, which was to be expected after a tragedy involving one of their own. "But didn't you ask them what has done it?" No, he told me. John Henry is not curious enough to ask them such a thing. He doesn't want to know. He wants only to get on with his own business. If anyone truly knows the nature of his death, I imagine it would be Frost's fellow miners. I only wish John Henry would pursue answers as vehemently as he pursues silver.

As darkness fell around us, closing us into our little cabin until morning, I felt I should have listened to Claudia when I first met her. "We ought to leave," I said. "This place is cursed."

John Henry stubbornly refused the idea: "Where would we go? When we have only just arrived? The idea is pure madness. And how do you think

Sophronia will fare, back on another long journey so soon? Do you want to get back on the trail?"

That gave me pause. The very notion of resuming those rough, dreary days in the hot, stuffy air of the wagon, jostled constantly from one side to the other, made me ill. I looked to Sophie, her narrow chest rising and falling as she succumbed to sleep, and I kept my voice a whisper so as not to wake her. "How do you think Sophronia will fare if we should be killed by some . . . rabid creature?" I decided it would be better not to call it a devil or a phantom, lest John Henry think me truly mad.

At this, a look of anger came over John Henry's face; he balled his hand into a fist, and with his skin still covered in black grime from the mine (he hadn't bothered to wash up before supper), he was quite a sight, almost feral. "Isn't that why I'm here?" he said. "Isn't it my job to protect you?"

"How can you protect us when you're always away in the mine?"

He slammed his fist down on the table, and the children stirred. "We need money," he said, his eyes wounded. "Money we don't have. Money I make to provide for us. Do you begrudge me that?"

As I went to the children to urge them back to sleep, John Henry stepped away. The children were still half asleep anyway, and drifted off again quickly; I turned to find John Henry pushing a long gun into my face. "Here," he said. "Take it. This is all the protection we need. One good shot will take down anyone, man or animal." Reluctantly, I took the gun. It was heavy in my hands, the weight of life and death residing within it. "I won't be like my coward of a brother," said John Henry. "I won't turn tail and run."

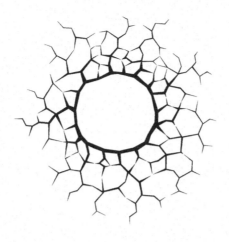

THE DUST DEVILS

 SPASM OF SOUND—SHARP, metallic, echoing—threw Waynoka's heart into a lurch. The bell's peal crashed through her sleep and flushed her cold, awake.

Her eyes sprang open as the bell slowed to a gentle sway against that black entrance.

Something had disturbed it.

She hadn't even realized she'd fallen asleep, the diary open on her chest. A red-tinged light was fading: the fire in its death throes, burnt to embers.

She stared into the darkness as the bell went still, willing herself to go long intervals between blinks. Something had made the bell ring. She thought of the man who had died in Lavinia's time, and her heart lurched again. That ache bloomed into a swell of panic, which she forced down like a rising gorge. Panic would not help this far below the earth.

But panic had followed her down the broken ladder into this warren of narrow tunnels where the darkness closed in like the tightening of her own throat as she tried to remember to breathe.

With a quick crank to give it a little burst of juice, she aimed the flashlight into the tunnel. The bell flashed and the walls turned white as they receded into nothing. Trembling, Waynoka convinced herself to step toward the entrance, and then through it.

Twenty steps in, her beam of light stuttered. She hurried to wind the flashlight as its flicker caught something moving or turning, caught what looked like two gleaming black marbles that made Waynoka think *eyes*. But by the time the light steadied, there was nothing there except for a dark lump on the ground.

Cautiously, she drew closer, not understanding the shape, which she realized was distorted by the long shadow the flashlight threw behind it. When she recognized the shadow, she understood she was looking at another dead bat.

She looked behind her at the bell, which by now had fallen still. Could the bat have rattled it when flying through the tunnel? And then it . . . dropped dead all of a sudden? What, had the ringing given the bat a heart attack?

She drew the flashlight beam back toward the bat, and then all around, training it on the crevices in the walls to be sure there was nothing else here. Nothing with black marble eyes. When she felt she had been as thorough as possible, she returned to the little room and watched the dwindling embers, trying to convince herself of the plausibility of the bat-heart-attack narrative.

She considered rousing Mads but thought better of it. Her knee had swollen, a grisly eggplant-purple through the rips in her jeans, clotted blood turning black. Waynoka winced just looking at it, and then winced again when the throbbing in her head intensified.

She missed pills. Ibuprofen, acetaminophen, aspirin. The stuff of gods. That warm rush as a headache magically receded after a couple of Advil, or when an extra-strength Tylenol suddenly took the edge off a stomach-churning bout of menstrual cramps.

Mads would have to do without painkillers for the knee. Waynoka thought about Lavinia Cain, who knew no pharmaceuticals. What did she do when she had cramps? Toughed it out, Waynoka guessed, the way they had to now as well. Nothing but a rag and a lack of sympathy. What a waste of suffering, and for what?

Her heart, by now, had slowed to a calmer rhythm. She kept the flashlight aimed at the tunnel entrance presided over by the painted ochre figure and the mercifully still bell.

So much of history—and all its advancements—was about the alleviation of suffering, no matter the cost to the world around them. As if they had forgotten that humans were a part of that world; as if they could divorce their own suffering from everything else. What was it her grandfather had once told her? *When the air suffers, the ground suffers. When the ground suffers, the trees suffer. When the trees suffer, the birds and the squirrels suffer. And when the birds and the squirrels suffer, so do we.* Why birds and squirrels? He had never said. But by now, she thought she knew why the air suffered in the first place.

Smoke burned her eyes and sent needles into her lungs. They were lucky they hadn't asphyxiated themselves. That meant there was enough ventilation, which might mean there were other ways out of the mine nearby. But it wouldn't do to relight the fire now and risk breathing in more tainted air—the kind of air that made her throat a rusty pipe.

And even if there *was* a ventilation shaft nearby, who was to say they had any means of climbing it? Who was to say they could make use of it at all, except to shout impotently up into nothing, into the emptiness where no one would hear them?

It reminded her of those Chilean miners, years ago, who, famously, had been trapped in the darkness for, what, two months? Except here, the world wasn't watching; here, no one knew or cared who they were or why they were in this long-disused and dangerously forgotten mine; here, no one was coming to help. They were on their own, and those are the ones you never hear about. You hear about the boys' soccer team trapped in a flooded cave in Thailand because of the daring rescue, the various nations that pulled together to send elite teams swimming down flooded tunnels. You hear about the resourceful ones, too—the rock climber who sawed off his own arm after being trapped in a narrow fissure, who survived through his own stubbornness, to have a movie made about him. You don't hear about the ones no one comes to save or who can't save themselves. The ones who disappear in the desert, never to be heard from again.

Waynoka moved the flashlight around the room, livid shadows twitching in its wake, as if the room all around her was alive and crawling around just outside the focus of her beam. Her skin crawled in response.

Lavinia had been down here at some point. There was nothing to indicate she'd died here—no body, no bones. That must be proof there was another way out. Waynoka wondered how long it took for bones to turn to dust. Her eyes danced around the chamber, sharpening on the grit that lined the floor, waiting to spot a tooth or some other telltale sign of death. But there was nothing.

Nothing in here, at least.

How long had it taken those prospectors to dig out this vast labyrinth? All that work for a bit of gold and silver. Even if it meant burying themselves in earth, digging their own tombs, trapping themselves away from light and life. All for some useless silver.

Gold hadn't stopped the drought's desiccation from turning green plants to dead sheaves of kindling; gold hadn't stopped the fires from scorching the hillsides and filling the blue sky with smoke; nor had it stopped the wave of newly unhoused from dying of heatstroke when summer hit hard and long, or the riots that followed, or the empty grocery store shelves when the supply chain broke down. The rich and powerful threw obscene sums of money at the problem, but it didn't stop any of that from happening.

Waynoka stared at the dangling bell. Her ears strained to make out any hint of sound in the abyssal chasm beyond it. Did she hear a scrape, maybe like a pickax dragged against stone? It was too indistinct to make out its sharp edges. Or maybe she was only imagining it. She couldn't tell. But she stared at the bell, a silver beacon against a void, and she hoped the bat had had a heart attack.

She shook Mads by the shoulder and said her name until her partner roused, sniffing sharply as her eyes popped open.

"Oh, damn. Being awake sucks. How long have I been out?"

"Not sure. It's been a few hours."

Mads sat up and dragged her bad leg stiffly to the edge of the bed, wheezing. "Ah, fuck."

"Can you walk?"

For a moment she didn't answer. Then she shook her head.

Waynoka swallowed a burst of panic. She was starting to get pretty good at that.

"We need to bind it," she said, and started tearing strips of moldering cloth from the bed, silently thanking Lavinia for the cloth. When she tightened it around the knee, Mads sucked in air sharply and made a high whining sound like a train whistle. Waynoka tied a few more strips to create a thick, tight wrap that made it impossible for Mads to bend her knee.

Finished, they sat for a bit while Mads got her breathing under control. Eventually, she lowered her leg off the bed and gingerly tested her weight. Her teeth gritted together as Waynoka pulled her up, and she leaned heavily to one side. A sheen of sweat slicked her face.

"That'll teach me to go spelunking," she said, but her voice was too strained for the humor to land.

"We could stay here for a while longer, rest up."

"No." Mads tentatively stepped away from Waynoka. "We've got to keep moving."

They both looked at the bell and the strange depths that lurked behind it. Waynoka felt her stomach lurch. There was only one direction for them to go.

"It rang earlier," she said.

"No shit?"

"Woke me up."

Mads frowned. "Sure you didn't dream it?"

"Don't gaslight me." Waynoka sighed. "I found a dead bat."

"So the bat rang the bell?"

Waynoka shrugged. Mads powered up her flashlight and said, "Look at me," then blared the light into Waynoka's eyes, which made her shrink back.

"The hell was that for?"

"One of your pupils is dilated."

Waynoka touched the dried blood on the back of her head. "Guess that explains why I'm seeing double. I thought it was the smoke." She tried to make it a joke, but it was the truth: she found herself blinking more frequently to clear her vision, especially after having spent all that time reading in the low light.

"Probably have a concussion," Mads murmured as she sat down again, keeping her bad leg stretched out straight, bundled in rags. "No wonder you're hearing things."

"I don't think that's one of the side effects of a concussion."

"Sorry, didn't realize you were a brain specialist."

Waynoka sighed and conceded. She really didn't know. She'd never had a concussion before. Maybe Mads was right. Maybe the combination of reading a ghost story and the head injury had made her dream the sound of the bell so vividly she'd thought it was real.

"Actually, that used to happen to me." She remembered. "When I was maybe seven or eight, I would wake up in the middle of the night—a few times a week—thinking there were spiders on the ceiling. I would jump up out of bed in a panic and run to turn on the light, then spend ten minutes searching every corner of my room, convinced I'd seen a spider descending toward me on its thread. But I never found any spiders. It was so *real* though—it was like I'd really experienced lying in bed and seeing them coming down from the ceiling, even though I knew I couldn't have seen such a thing in the dark, and even though I never saw any when I turned on the light." She shuddered. "Haven't thought about that in years. Pretty sure it started after I found a big hairy wolf spider hanging out under my pillow one day before I went to sleep."

"Nightmare fuel," said Mads, her voice strained by pain. "Once something like that gets in your head, it lodges there like a damn tumor."

"Yeah," Waynoka murmured, picking up the book. "I've been reading this diary, which is . . . kind of creepy."

"Let me guess. Psycho? Axe murderer? Someone who liked to make skin suits out of their victims?"

Waynoka shook her head. "No, not at all. But—the people who lived here, they said the mine was cursed."

"Cursed?" Mads snorted.

"I know, but—" Waynoka shrugged, feeling a little foolish. "That's what she says in the diary. *Los fantasmas.*" She looked carefully at Mads. "Do you believe in ghosts?"

"Hell, I don't know. My mama believed in all kinds of stuff. There were always prayer candles burning at my apartment growing up. Pictures of Jesus on the walls. She talked to the saints just about every day. But I don't think it's that simple. I think humans are idiots if we think we've got all this figured out."

Waynoka nodded. "'There are more things in heaven and earth, Horatio, than are dreamt of in your philosophy.'"

Mads paused for a moment, frowning. "Shakespeare?"

"Since when are you a reader?"

"Jesus, give me a break. I went to school. Plus, a name like Horatio kind of gives it away."

Waynoka slipped the diary into their one remaining pack, pulled it onto her back, and helped Mads limp to the entrance. She ducked around the bell, not wanting to touch it, as if it was cursed.

"Cursed or not, here we come," she murmured to herself.

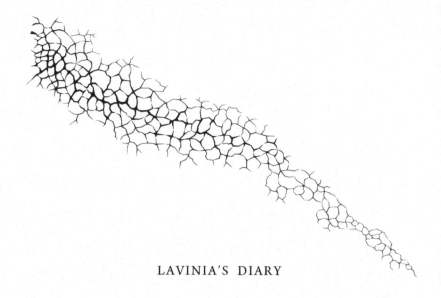

LAVINIA'S DIARY

September 12, 1869

How I miss the sea breezes of Boston, landing with a salty mist on the lips; and the screech of the gulls, the rush of waves, the clatter of horse hooves and wheels on the cobbled streets as carriages rush past; even the maritime stink of the fishermen hauling in the day's catch; the way the sun sparkles on the harbor and the little white boats that dot the horizon. The air here is nothing like Massachusetts air, which was thick with humidity. Here it is thin and dry, with nothing to wash away the dust.

Virgil is the kind of place where the cruelty of the desert comes knocking at the rough-hewn cabins and even the brick courthouse and post office—even in these bastions of society, where law is maintained and communication sent out and brought in, the frontier has infected with its blistering heat, the sun like a great white eye bleaching lumber that does not belong in this arid landscape and drying one's skin to the point of cracking. Virgil is not a friendly place; the harsh environment seems hardly fit for human habitation. And yet we have inhabited this place and built this town where the mountains begin to make hungry jaws of the horizon, and we have dug down into the earth in search of wealth to plunder and take from it, as if we could take from God Himself.

John Henry has promised me our own rags-to-riches story many times, conjuring it like a spell for my ears—though we have always remained closer to rags than riches, clutching the barest wealth from each of his endeavors. Yet one cannot help but believe in his next great plan. John Henry has always been charming—and dashing too. Though his face is long and his eyes brooding, there is a twinkle in them, as if he is faintly amused by all around him—amused and a little scornful. He is clever, but he knows it, and that makes him the less sincere for it. Yet there is such confidence behind those twinkling eyes that hold all the night sky within them, that one cannot help but be captivated and want to know their secrets. And he will tell them—oh, yes!—for a price. I suppose in my case the price was rather a bargain. It was only marriage. Or it was marriage where lay the promise, and it was our shameful retreat from civilized life that turned out to be the price. Oh, but John Henry can convince one to do just about anything. He could convince a lobster it requires a new set of knives if given enough time to explain how dull that lobster's claws have become.

For all of that, it was John Henry's powers of erudition that so enchanted me in the first place, and that grew his little scheme into a successful business. He charmed me, as he charmed them all, peddling his cure-all medicine, called Darling's Elixir, which was some horrid concoction of opium and spices colored with wine, meant to soothe stomach ailments of all kinds, rickets, stones, distemper, gripes, cholic, ague, and more, as I recall—though it did not really do any of these things.

Yet he sold it all the same. He charmed the money from their pockets and the trust from their hearts—big bugs and beggars alike. And by the time it was discovered he was nothing but a fraud, no one in all of Boston would do business with him any longer (no one likes to be played the fool), and we had no choice but to turn tail and run, quite disgraced. The name Cain bears the curse of he who betrayed his brother Abel.

It is one of those things one must force down, deep inside of himself, for wasn't I the pretty hypocrite? All the while I thought myself a person with high morals—one who values honesty and loyalty above all. Though I enjoy a clever turn of phrase as much as John, I never lied to him, nor to anyone, at least not in matters of any circumstance. And I have tried to instill these morals in my children too, most particularly in Oscar, who is wont to tell a fib (Sophie, at the least, is both discerning and true of tongue). Somehow I convinced myself of all this while standing idly by what John Henry did. I knew from the start it was bunkum. Though his words were sweet and persuasive, it seemed to me no potion could exist that could cure all such ailments, or wouldn't a physician have come upon it first? It was I, too, who enjoyed the consistency of hearing each of his various speeches whereby I noticed the minor discrepancies among them that his typical audience would have no hope to catch, as they heard his pitch only once. It was only commonsense and these discrepancies that bore out the truth, for John Henry never did breathe a word his elixir was anything but what he claimed, adamant to the end, even as we ran away, first to Illinois, then, when we had acquired what we needed for the journey, west to Nevada. We both know it for a sham, but I think to say it aloud would be a kind of defeat for him.

Still, I did nothing. Even knowing he was stealing the money from those poor people's pockets and selling them an ineffective mix of liquor and spices, I said nothing. In that, I suspect I may be just as culpable, and not at all the good person I like to think I am. Even with honest intentions—the intention to have food for my children and to stand by my husband—even those good intentions do not overshadow what has been done.

At least the work he is doing now is honest, even if he has high notions of what will happen if he strikes silver.

Yesterday I did not have a chance to write, as the children called for my attention most constantly. I set them first to their study of the Bible, and their chores, and finally sent them out to play, but I felt I had to keep my eye on them, for when I turned away my heart lurched into my throat at the thought of bells even though the sun blazed down at the bright midday.

Last night John Henry reeled home from the doggery at half past two, quite corned, and has slept straight through this Sunday morning, when we ought to have risen for church. At last he roused for coffee, and as I set it to boiling I could hear Oscar outside talking, so I went out to see if there was someone here. He was alone with the sheep, digging hills in the dirt. Sophronia had taken to her bed, for the poor thing has most certainly over-extended herself these last few days as she has improved, thinking she was all better even as she continues her slow recovery from illness. I ventured out after the boy, for the sight of him speaking to no one at all pricks at my nerves, especially when he will not make friends with other children but insists on talking to himself.

Here is what he was saying as I approached: "It's in the earth, the silver. That's why Daddy goes down underground, to get it. But he has to face the bad spirits in there." He paused. "Well, you're a *good* spirit."

I interrupted him at once, and his wide, innocent eyes met me, dark as two pools of coffee; his tousled sandy hair moved with the wind; his pale freckled face bore smudges of dirt. I asked him who he was talking to. The sheep? He shook his head, quiet now in my presence. I took him by the ear until he admitted in his flat little voice that he had been talking to Charles.

Something black came over me, and I said things to the boy that now make me ashamed: "Charles is dead! *He* wouldn't say such things, were he alive. *He* would have been a good boy!"

Then I raised my hand and came at him full chisel, my blow making his mouth run red. He started to holler and cry, while Sophie came hurrying outside at the ruckus and saw what I had done. Without delay she went to comfort her brother, who cried as she used his shirt to wipe at his face.

"You done what you needed to do," said John Henry. The coffee had near boiled over by then. "Boy's got to learn. My father used to tan my hide. He set me to rights."

I could not but think over Oscar's talk of bad spirits underground, for the death of Jeremiah Frost still hangs heavy over this place like a black cloud. Wherever could he have gotten such notions? Is it from the time he'd gone out with the doctor and heard those tales from men in town? Or have his child's ears picked up more than they ought to—though from where he should pick up anything I couldn't say, for all his time is spent here at home or at school. I must speak with the schoolteacher, Delilah Barnes, about his behavior. Perhaps she will help me to understand what drives the boy to his dark fancies.

But perhaps he has only inherited them from me, for haven't I been finding myself all wrapped up in the curse of Claudia's *fantasmas* and Mr. Faraday's devils? Perhaps there is only something bad inside of me, like a pomegranate seed, which I have unwittingly passed on to him—something bad that made Oscar come into this world without his twin. Something in my womb that strangled Charles before he could see the light of the world.

I must resolve to be more levelheaded in all matters, and to find sound explanations for all of these strange phenomena, as my mother would have me do, lest I become just as superstitious and affrighted as those others here who believe in curses.

This evening I walked about for a while as I dwelled on these thoughts. There was a cool breeze that sighed over me. One becomes aware of a great quietude at night here, and I felt surely alone, or I would not have strayed far. I walked a ways, far enough to see the Blackburns' sod house come into view, Chester and Olive setting on two stones that were good as stools, with a bottle of Old Orchard between them and a fire going at their feet, over which it looked like they were about to cook up supper. Olive is pretty, even in the dark. She wears her hair in a long, neat braid that the wind must slowly pick apart over the course of a day. Her eyes are inscrutable, hidden behind long spidery lashes, and she never does seem to have a smile upon her face. Their clothes are thin and scrubby, worn and washed and worn again.

I waved, feeling neighborly, but when they saw me, they only stared and did not return my friendly gesture. Chester spat on the ground while Olive wore her stony frown, which seemed particularly livid and cruel by the red light of the flames. Their gleaming stares unnerved me so that I turned and went immediately back home.

Well, I feel quite wrung out and admit I shall be glad when the children are back at school to-morrow.

September 13, 1869

Something else I miss in Boston is the library. This town is starved for books. I could sit me in a library and watch the day go by with nary a thought to leaving. Yellowy pages at my fingers and myself surrounded by castles made of books. A body never felt so free and alive as in a library. Books can take you away from here into somewhere new and romantic, and if anyplace should need some romantic sort of escape, it is Virgil, Nevada.

But there is no escape, is there? Maybe that is why everyone around me goes about with hunched backs and hard eyes, their bodies muscled with toil; why the ladies, too, are not the soft sort of ladies back East, but rigid, their bones askew on emaciated frames, showing their crooked teeth with nasty smiles, some wearing trousers and riding horses just like men, and carousing with all the Johnnies about town—you can hear it in their laughter, even, which is cruel and brittle as animal bones.

I have settled into a pattern of drudge: Mondays are laundry, Tuesdays are for ironing and mending, Wednesdays are for baking, Thursday is for scrubbing the kitchen, Fridays are for shopping: flour, sugar, cornmeal, coffee, beans, and rice. As such, Fridays have become my favorite day of the week, the only day in which I am able to enjoy the society of other people. The rest of the week, my comfort consists of the fire burning at the stove, my company the goats and sheep. Saturdays I sew garments for the children, who are ever growing out of them, and I teach Sophie her stitching while Oscar goes out to collect buffalo chips. Sunday is for rest, though there isn't hardly any of that.

Today, after I fed the animals, I scrubbed the laundry—particularly the children's grubby clothes and John Henry's blackened attire—wrung it out, and hung it all to dry. I did my other daily chores, stoking the fire and curing salt pork, and then I sat down to write and rest before the children return and it is time to cook supper.

The days are filled with silence.

Later

Though I have been allowing the children to find their own way home of late, now that they well know the way, I went to collect them this afternoon so that I might speak with Miss Barnes about Oscar's peculiar disposition. She seemed to believe that he wishes terribly he could have had a brother to play with, and that every reminder of this loss of companionship has resulted in his imagining his brother's spirit, which is quite easy for him, as all he has to do is look in a mirror. She suggested I ought not to worry overmuch, and that the boy will very likely grow out of this fancy in short order. I thanked her for setting my mind at ease but said, "I fear his dark imagination has his mind conjuring all sorts of things. Just yesterday he was talking of bad spirits."

Now Miss Barnes sat me down (the children were off playing and could not hear us). She took my hand and looked hard into my eyes with earnestness and solemnity. "Mrs. Cain," she said, "he is not alone in this talk. Many of the children have said such things. They talk mostly amongst themselves, but I hear what they say." Her words disturbed me, but I bade her tell me more. She told me this: "The children have said they see ghostly figures in the desert. There is one which they call the Strange Lady. Strange, they say, because she has whiskers, like a man, and hair all over. They say she is thin and thirsty, and that sometimes she sneaks into their homes at night and pricks their parents' feet while they sleep."

I smiled and told her it sounded like a fairy tale that the children's parents had told them, perhaps to frighten them away from wandering off into the desert. Miss Barnes let go of my hand, and though her eyes never lost their earnestness, she offered me her own sad little smile in return and told me that none of the children had heard this tale from their parents. In fact, when she had relayed this story to the other parents, they all laughed and told her it was probably a story that the children had heard from someone else. "Yet I have been unable to find out who that 'someone else' might be," she said. "Every mother thinks it was another child's mother who created the tale. But you know, Mrs. Cain, I believe that children are quite keenly aware of their surroundings, and sometimes they see things that may escape our notice."

The sun was westering, so I took my leave, but the schoolteacher's words do linger inside of me even now.

September 14, 1869

Spent the day mending. Decided to see if Mr. Branson had any spare scraps of cloth that he might sell me for my patchwork, so this afternoon I went into town and found him in his shop. He did have some cloth, which he sold to me for a fair price. We talked some, of this and that, and then he produced a small flask and imbibed a drink, right then and there, and gave me a wink. I think now I understand why he always seems so cheerful.

I ventured to ask him, quite casually, if he had known my brother-in-law, Emery Cain, while he was here, and he fairly choked on his liquor before shaking his head, which I had expected by now, saying he had "barely known the man from a mongoose" and that he'd "had nothing to do with any of it." Any of what? Mr. Branson merely waved me off as he caught his breath. So much for that.

It is fortuitous that I was in town buying cloth, for I also happened across Mrs. Mary Warrant, who invited me to a quilting bee next week at her home.

September 15, 1869

Can't sleep. I tried, for a few hours, listening to John Henry snore beside me. Thought about sitting outside, but the idea of being out after dark sent a shiver through me. I worried, then, that lighting this lantern might rouse John Henry (which would undoubtedly irk him) or the children, but they all remain fast asleep as I sit here writing. Their little faces smooth and content in sleep, though even in her deepest dreaming, I can still see those darkish rings under Sophie's eyes that remind me she is not all well just yet.

As I write, I've turned my attention out the open window. A crescent of moon hangs in the sky buoyed by its bed of stars, leaking just enough light onto the land below for me to make out some distant shapes beyond our animal pen: the hills rising into sharp mountains and the strange scrubby landscape.

I cannot help but wonder about Claudia's shadow, and about the Strange Lady, and all manner of frightful things that infect a mind in the dark and loneliness of night.

Just now, I needed to relieve myself, so I went out to the privy after trying for some time to convince myself that I might wait until morning. The terror I felt closed up in that little outhouse! The lantern light was close and the wooden walls around me even closer, and I began to fancy all sorts of ghostly presences just outside where I could not see them, so that I feared both to remain within and to open the door! When I was finished, I waited for some long moments, listening carefully for any footfalls or rustling out there in the dark, as if I would open the door and see the Strange Lady just there, covered in whiskers, waiting for me.

Of course there was nothing out there, and I fled back inside quickly as my feet would carry me. Now I feel downright foolish for giving into such childish frights. There is no Strange Lady. It is only a children's tale.

And yet, I am now entirely awake and fear I shall not fall asleep again any time soon. I will need something else to occupy my mind.

I wonder if there may be any clues as to what became of Emery, that I should at least find out what befell him and put my mind to rest. This was his home, after all. Surely there must be something here that could help me find the truth. My mind is all abuzz and awake now. I shall look around to see what I can find.

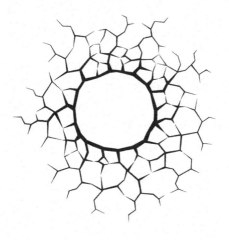

THE DUST DEVILS

T HEY HAD TO STOOP, the tunnel so narrow and low at times that Waynoka had to focus on her breathing, in and out, in and out, so that she didn't lose it. How did those miners do it? How did they spend hours and hours, day in and day out, crawling through tight spaces that might crush them?

Maybe the mine wasn't haunted. Maybe the whole mountain was alive. And they were only descending into its entrails. It needn't even swallow to consume them. It just had to wait for them to get deep enough to digest.

At least the closeness of the walls gave Mads something to cling to, so that she didn't have to put any weight on her bad leg. She used the crags in the wall to drag herself forward, her body jerking unevenly as she limped. They stopped periodically, moving at a painstakingly slow pace, which somehow made the mystery ahead of them even worse. They passed the dead bat, which Waynoka was oddly relieved to see hadn't moved. (Why she'd even think it would have moved remained a mystery. It was dead. Dead things didn't move.) Eventually, they reached another chamber, smaller than the one they'd left behind, maybe the size of a bathroom or a large closet. Hardly big enough to really be called a chamber, but at least it was a widening of the narrow tunnel. Mads paused, leaning against the wall, pale and sweating. Waynoka pulled off her pack and dug around for something to eat, but there was so little there she decided instead to save it for later.

If there *was* a later.

While they were stopped, the thick silence of the cave pressing in on them without at least the shuffling of their footsteps, Waynoka tried to ignore what her ears kept trying to convince her she was hearing in the silence. Was that a footstep? Something shuffling around? An animal?

While Mads rubbed at her leg, Waynoka shined her flashlight to see what lay ahead of them. Just beyond this little spot, the pathway forked in two directions.

"Which way, you think?"

Mads frowned and looked up, eyeballed their options. "Flip a coin."

Waynoka walked ahead to the point at which the two tunnels branched off, debating with herself, shining the light down one and then the other. If only they *did* have a coin to flip. Her hesitation revealed the terror gripping her heart that she would choose the wrong path, lead them farther into the maze of darkness with no salvation.

The path to the left was a straight shot into the darkness, with a ceiling that dipped low. The path to the right veered steeply down—walkable, but likely rougher on Mads's bad knee. And as she stood there, gazing to where the light receded, she thought she heard, again, a kind of scraping noise that clawed at the back of her neck the way nails on a chalkboard do.

She turned her flashlight away from the sound, back to the leftmost path. "This one."

Leading the way into the tunnel, Waynoka had to pause a few feet in to wind up her flashlight after it dimmed, sending her heart into her throat. She got the light bright enough to guide them farther, picking her way over uneven ground scattered with shards of fallen rock. The debris slowed her pace, as did her constant awareness of Mads shuffling along painfully behind her. She could hear her partner's breathing, amplified in the confined space.

"How far do we keep going before . . . I mean, how far do you think—?" Waynoka's fumbled question cut off abruptly; she leaned her full weight onto her right foot, where something beneath her, very unlike stone, groaned. The wooden boards splintered and gave a rending crack as they collapsed and dropped away.

For a moment, she was weightless; then she felt herself pitch downward as the ground disappeared beneath her feet, sending her plummeting toward the abyss.

Her other foot caught on the shattered remains of the boards, and before she could fall below the edge of no escape, Mads had her by the arms, her face taking up Waynoka's vision like a beacon. Her dropped flashlight rolled across the floor, framing her mane of hair in a pale halo. Panic closed Waynoka's throat as she kicked her legs in empty air that seemed to suck at her, trying to pull her down. She held tightly to Mads's forearms and thought she heard herself murmuring a mindless litany: "Don't let go, don't let go, don't let go."

The murky greenish-brown eyes bore into Waynoka, wide with alarm, and her brain whispered to her that Mads couldn't hold on, that she was going to let go, that in a moment Waynoka would be in free-fall down the vertical mine shaft.

Then Mads groaned as she heaved backward, pulling Waynoka with her. Inch by inch, her clammy grip slipping just as slowly as Mads attempted to pull her up. One accidental slip, one bad move, and there was nothing to stop her from falling.

"The pack is weighing you down," Mads grunted. "You have to let it go."

"No, no, no," said Waynoka. Its straps were around her shoulders. There was no way she could release its weight without also letting go of Mads, and there was no way she was going to let go of Mads. The flashlight that had been in her hand when she'd stepped onto the shaft, however, was long gone, fallen away below her. Her feet found the side of the shaft and tried to identify some sort of purchase, a crack, a ledge, but just ended up scrabbling vainly against the wall.

Mads pulled and pulled, and at last Waynoka found her torso over the edge, able to bend ninety degrees onto the ground. Adrenaline kicked through her system, driving her to lean as far forward as she could—she just had to hang on to Mads and slide the rest of the way out—

And maybe because they had disturbed the rocks around them with their scrambling, a spider the size of her fist darted out of a crack in the wall and toward them, its spindly legs crawling over her outstretched arms. She cried out. The sensation almost made her let go, and despite the panic clouding her brain, she knew, and she told herself, that she could not let go, that to let go was a death sentence.

The spider's legs sent a shiver through her body, and then it was on the other side, scampering away, uninterested in these large beasts that had disrupted its habitat.

Her skin crawled as her old arachnophobia flared up. For a wild moment, she thought the spider would be the death of her—and wasn't that just fucking perfect? After all those times as a kid, thinking there were spiders out to get her while she slept?

Mads hauled her up the rest of the way, and they lay on their backs panting by the slanted beam of the fallen flashlight. Neither could stop shaking, either from exertion or misplaced adrenaline or outright panic. The terror of the blind drop was so abstract to Waynoka that all her senses narrowed on an echo of the spider's legs creeping over her flesh, the tangible sensory experience of it, making her shudder anew in revulsion.

Miraculously, she still had the deflated pack, which was yet heavy enough to have made her think she'd never get over the edge, but she thought of what they would have done if she'd let it go, and it made her shiver even more than the spider's legs.

Somewhere in one of the packs was a spare flashlight, and she wondered if it was this one or the full pack they'd left behind at the entrance to the strange living quarters where she'd found Lavinia's diary. She hoped it was in this one.

"So you mentioned you were afraid of spiders ..." Mads wheezed.

Waynoka swallowed dryly. "Goddammit."

Eventually they found the energy to get up and shuffle back to the cozy little spot just past the fork, where they collapsed again, still breathing heavily, still trembling from the near miss.

"What the fuck are we doing?" Waynoka said after a while, her voice coming out a whisper. She mentally berated herself for being frightened by the idea that the mine was haunted. There was a lot more to be frightened of down here than ghosts.

Mads's hands were at her knee, and she looked as if saving Waynoka had taken the last of her energy. Her skin was tight against her face, every inch of flesh pulling taut. "We're resting. Just for a bit. Then we try the other path."

As the adrenaline continued to leak out of her, Waynoka felt her body grow leaden. She was so tired, but there was still enough energy rattling around in her head that she knew she couldn't rest. But Mads had to. She couldn't continue like this.

If Waynoka had to sit here in the dark waiting for Mads to feel up to moving again, she'd go crazy.

She took the flashlight from Mads and used it to dig around in the pack, searching for the spare, growing more frustrated the more she dug, eventually realizing that it wasn't there. They only had the one, now, to beat back the darkness.

As she gave up, ready to shove the pack aside and sit and stew in her own fear, the light found the leather cover of Lavinia's diary. She pulled it out of the pack and flipped it open.

"Maybe there's something in here that will help," she said with desperate hope. "Right?"

Mads sat against the opposite wall, her eyes squeezed shut as she fought off waves of pain, and Waynoka felt utterly useless. She couldn't help her.

"Let me know when you feel ready to move on," she said.

"I'm just going to lie down," said Mads, stretching out on the rough ground and closing her eyes. Her voice was thin as pulled taffy.

Maybe reading more of the diary could be useful to them, somehow. It was the only way she could rationalize the desire to transport her mind away from here, into another time, another world. It was one way to escape, at least.

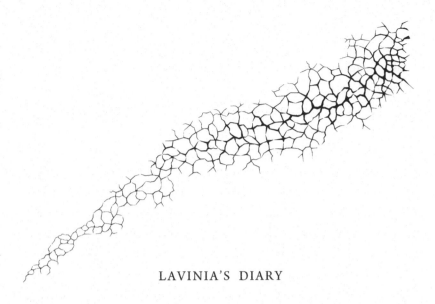

LAVINIA'S DIARY

September 16, 1869

Tried to confront John Henry about what I found last night; now I fear I've driven a further wedge between us.

When I showed him, his face was impassive, deliberately uninterested, though I could see his sharp eyes working furiously beneath those knotted, heavy brows. He tried to tell me it didn't mean anything, that this was no proof Emery hadn't simply run off, just as John Henry had suggested.

So adamant was he that when I tried to put the letter in front of his face, he shoved the paper away in aggravation while he fixed the buttons of his shirt, and I had to read it aloud to him until he cut me off with a quick rebuke.

There was again a certain accusation in his words which stung me: "You love my brother so dearly, perhaps you ought to have married *him*."

My response to him was fierce: "I love *you*, John Henry Cain. I have only *ever* loved you. Your brother came to my aid in a time of need—"
At this, he cut off my words with his own: "While your husband was busy

taking care of our livelihood, minding the finances and the children, and even the household, and you lay abed at all hours."

"Lay abed!" I cried out, wounded at the very thought he would consider my period of grief in such frivolous language.

"And you criticize my every word!"

John Henry's words are quite important to him, of course. I cannot help but think of all those times he'd stood before a crowd rattling off the wonders of his magic elixir. And think, too, of all the ways he had promised our lives together would be filled with wonder, with riches, with everything we could ever desire—oh, when it was just us, before the children, so young, leaping from one opportunity to the next, spending our evenings in the company of boats in the harbor, while he whispered all the beauties of the earth in my ear.

How things have changed.

He left for the mine without saying anything more, and I was glad for it. But here, I never said what exactly it was I found in the house: Last night, as I was opening drawers and cabinets, searching out anything I hadn't noticed when we'd moved in, anything that might give me a glimpse into what happened to Emery, I found two intriguing artifacts. One was a photograph taken at the mine, with a group of miners assembled against the grainy gray backdrop of what looks to be the mine's entrance. The men are wearing headlamps and holding tools, as if they are just about to go in to work. I do not believe this was taken after they emerged from the mine, for they are not quite as covered in soot as John Henry is when he returns at night, and their eyes are bright with excitement, not the dull exhaustion I see in John Henry's face after a long day of work.

And sitting among them, the second from the left, sure as anything, is Emery. It is unmistakably him. There is no trace of worry in his face. He bears an eager disposition; perhaps this was taken when he was new to the work and hungry. He does not look like the kind of man who would run off as soon as he realized how difficult the work would be. At least, not yet. I turned over the photograph but could find nothing written on it to document the date. I wonder who in this town has a camera—or was it an official photograph taken by the company?

The other thing I found is a half-completed, hastily scribbled letter addressed to John Henry. Instead of trying to summarize its contents, I will copy them here as they appear on the page, in case I should lose the letter:

John,

I know in my last letter I told you what a grand opportunity was here for you—I hope you have not yet begun your journey west and that this letter catches you before you make a grave mistake—something awful has happened that has changed things utterly—I do not know how to explain—you and Lavinia are better off where you are, and I say this thinking of your own wellbeing, do not come—do not come to Virgil—I fear I may not have

Here the letter cuts off without finishing its thought, as if he stepped away from writing and never returned. Perhaps he stowed it in the drawer to finish later, needing to attend to some other pressing matter, and forgot he had been writing. But how can one forget such an important warning, especially when he knew, from John Henry's own letters, that we were planning on joining him this summer? Surely it would have been imperative to finish and send the letter as quickly as possible if he truly did not want us to come? Unless, of course, something terrible happened to him before he could finish writing it.

I fear I may not have . . . How had he been planning to finish that sentence? May not have been entirely honest in his previous letters, about what Virgil was really like? May not have time? May not have . . . what? The question drives a bolt of curiosity and dread through my brain.

If only John Henry would talk to me, truly and honestly, the way he used to; he is the only one I want to talk to about what happened to Emery, yet each time I mention his brother's name, he scoffs and tells me not to worry myself over him. He calls his brother a dog and a whoremonger and says he's glad Emery took off; that we're better off here without him. Sometimes I fear the mine is pulling him away from me in his hungry quest for silver. As if finding silver will prove, once and for all, that he is the better man. Maybe then he will stop feeling always in Emery's shadow, and we can finally move past these trivial resentments. I want my John Henry back. I want him to speak sweet words into my ears until my fears are calmed.

Instead, all I have are Emery's hasty, inscrutable warnings and a feeling of dread in the pit of my stomach.

September 17, 1869

Willie Ray Randall, she said. Ask Willie Ray Randall. I write it here so that I do not forget the name, though how should I talk to such a man?

Yesterday I worked out all my frustrations with scrubbing and cleaning, until I was too tired to write. Today is Friday, when I go into town for the shopping. Before I went to the general store, I decided to pay Claudia a visit. At first I thought I might not be able to look her in the eye, but by and by, I began to think, Who am I to judge one's moral character? When my own is questionable itself? Only the Lord will judge, and if He sees fit to condemn one so lovely as Claudia Montaña, then I suppose that is His will.

Knowing that I was entering a brothel and not a boardinghouse, however, greatly discomfited me, and I near turned and went right out again. Miss Shaw glowered on my arrival and sent me up to Claudia's room, which I admit has the most calming effect. Colored fabrics drape the window such that the light comes in a warm orange, a hue shared by the half dozen candles she has lit about the small space, concentrated upon an altar that holds a rosary, a thin bouquet of drying yellow flowers, a decorated clay skull, a thimble of whiskey, and a piece of hardtack. She called these her *ofrendas* and said they were for Rebecca.

"Rebecca was another working girl here," she said. "She was out one night with a miner named Otto. He was a frequent client. A brute, but with deep pockets. I told her it wasn't worth it, a man like that—not after he beat her so many times. But she was his favorite, he always came to see her. He had a liking for redheads, you know? She told me she wasn't going to see him again, but he lured her out for a drink, said she would feel differently after some whiskey. They went out, I don't know when, and they never came back. Miss Shaw found them the next morning, both dead and drained of blood."

I wondered then exactly how many had died in this manner, and I suspicioned that it was more than just Jeremiah Frost, Otto, and Rebecca. There was a note of sadness and fear in her voice when she spoke of the tragedy. To distract the both of us, I asked her to tell me more about Rebecca, at which she grew wistful and nostalgic with a soft smile on her ruby lips, and I could tell at once that she loved Rebecca, and it made me love her too.

She pronounced the delightful mirth of Rebecca's laugh, which had a husky note that belied her delicate features; her talents at drawing; the way they pretended with one another that someday they might run away with a wealthy prospector, and what they would do with their lives when that happened; the knowing sadness in the bottomless wells of her eyes.

How strange it is to speak of ghosts. She comes alive on Claudia's lips, but I shall never meet her. That husky laugh is only an echo on the wind, as gone a sound as what my children made when they were infants, now babes no more. Why should we always long for those things we can never get back, and forget what sits right in front of us?

I told her it was a shame what had happened to Rebecca—to her, and to Jeremiah Frost, which sent chills all through my body to think of it—but oughtn't the law be doing anything to discover the source of all this tragedy? Oughtn't any of us be doing something to discover its true nature, and to stop it from happening again? Would not Rebecca have desired someone to solve the mystery of her murder?

"You do not know what she would want." Claudia's eyes glittered with resentment. "All she wanted was someone who would make her feel safe. She wanted what I had with Emery." I asked her what it was that she'd had with my brother-in-law, and she told me after some hesitation: "I was beginning to love him. I thought maybe he was going to make me his wife. I don't know that I wanted to be his wife—I don't know what I wanted. I liked being with him, though. He was a good man, a kind man. He didn't deserve what happened to him." She looked at me, her eyes sharp again. "I had no part in it. You must believe me. I had no part in it. I cared for him."

Her words reminded me of a similar sentiment I'd heard from Mr. Branson, and I grew to believe something terrible must have happened to Emery. I asked her, filled with dread at the answer, if he had died like Rebecca and the others.

I cannot say whether I was relieved or unsettled by Claudia's answer: "No, not like the others."

Yet something did happen to him, I knew from the tone of her voice. Something terrible, which Claudia did not want to speak of, which nobody wanted to speak of, it seemed, as if the town had decided it were better to forget that Emery had ever existed than to remember what had happened to him.

"I do not know the full story," she said at last, after much cajoling. "I fear I would make some mistake in telling, and—and it was a terrible thing. I do not want to think about it."

Even more of my prodding did not sway her to speak more, at least not until I was preparing to leave, and she relented.

"If you want to know what happened to Emery," said Claudia, "then go ask Willie Ray Randall. Ask him what he did." And she would say no more.

As I was going about my shopping then, I ran into Doctor Hartsworth, who asked me how Sophronia was faring, and I told him quite well. At first he insisted on making a house call to check on her, but the thought of that old man bumbling about our cabin made me ill, and I convinced him otherwise. Though she is tired at times, Sophie is rapidly returning to her old darling self.

Besides, there is something about a relative stranger intruding on what is meant to be our own space that disagrees with me. It's as if he might leave some part of himself behind, and it will change things. I don't know why else I shouldn't like the doctor to come round, but sometimes I feel as if I never have had a place entirely of my own, and while I know this cabin isn't exactly all ours, being that it used to belong to Emery, well, it is starting to feel like home.

Mr. Branson was out in front of his shop with his flask, and he noticed me conversing with the doctor. "Now I don't care beans for gossip," he said to me, "but you know that doctor was a border ruffian for some long while before he came to Virgil. I heard tell he didn't have so much as a tent over his head for so long you'd mistake him for a savage." Mr. Branson leaned back in his chair and took a contemplative pull from his flask. "Can't say I know where that man learned medicine, but I heard also that it ain't no real medicine, if you follow me, that he stayed with some Indians and picked up their witchery. I'm a healthy horse of a man, but I tell you, if I ever take sick, I'll tough it out on my own before I try some pagan remedy."

Mr. Branson started in on more town gossip, about which I cared very little, my mind so caught up in wondering who this Willie Ray Randall fellow was that Claudia mentioned. I decided to ask Mr. Branson if he knew where I might find the man.

Immediately his face grew dark and cold the like to chill you. "Now whyever would you want to find a man like that?" I wasn't quite sure how to answer, but I needn't have worried. He said: "That's a man you'll find in jail."

Jail? I asked how he had come to be there. "Don't ask me about it," he said. "I had no part in it, I tell you. I was just here in my shop, minding my own business." He waved me into his shop, where he picked up a scrap of fabric and handed it to me. I stood politely near the dressmaker dummy, admiring the jacket upon it as he picked out a few more fabric scraps, telling me to take them to the quilting bee. He is altogether too kind to me. When he saw me admiring the jacket he said, "Yes, ma'am, I do believe that is some of my finest work. Take a look at the stitching here. This hem is a huckleberry above a persimmon, I tell you."

I graciously took the fabric scraps, paid him a small sum for his trouble, and made my leave, all the while wondering, What did Willie Ray Randall do to earn himself a place behind bars? Did he rob a bank? Shoot someone? Is he a violent man?

Once home, I returned to my endless stream of trivial tasks: hauling water, feeding the livestock, keeping the fire, cooking, cleaning, mending. I am plumb tired. Life here is a constant toil, its joys small and dim, its drudge most continuous. Even the strange beauty of the rocks and all their myriad colors seem to lose their luster, and I begin to wonder if God has abandoned this place.

September 21, 1869

Last night I dreamt that John Henry came home from the mine and his mouth was filled with silver, and his eyes, too, were coated over with silver, and it was a frightful thing to behold, as if he were some horrible cousin of Midas.

September 22, 1869

Today was the quilting bee. This morning I rose with the sun and tramped to Mary Warrant's abode, a well-built house both larger and cozier than the little cabins endured by most hereabouts, with enough space in the living quarters to accommodate the ten or so women present, who had assembled their hoops and frames and sat with a heap of fabric scraps at the center of their circle.

Mary introduced me to the others present. There was Josephine, a country woman married to Cecil Pavlovsky, who owns the general store; Virginia, skeletally thin (she ate ravenously when we broke for lunch, as if she hadn't touched food in days); Willa, stout and wrinkled, with gray running all through her hair, her hands deft with a needle but calloused—her husband runs the saloon, to which she said, "Men will always need a drink!" with merriment; Tabitha, a young thing who cannot be more than fifteen, with perpetually downcast eyes, whose husband drinks away what little he makes from work in the mine, leaving them always hand to mouth; Bedelia, a pretty miner's wife; Gertrude, or Trudy, as the others called her; and of course, there was Olive, who barely acknowledged me. Early on, feeling still the newcomer, I was content to sit and sew and listen. Even the banalities of trivial conversation were a balm to me. Such trite things as Bedelia's, "It's been powerful warm, too warm for quilts lately," and Trudy's response, "But you know what they say—hotter the summer, colder the winter." Then Josephine told me I ought not let this Indian summer fool me. "Come a month from now," she said, "the cold will arrive, and you'll be wanting a thick quilt for the winter." This was followed by a general chorus of: "Don't I know it?" and, "You can say that again."

After we enjoyed a bit of quiet, Willa filled it: "At least our winters ain't quite like those in the north. I've a cousin up in Montana territory, who tells me in her letters the snow piles so high she plumb lost her dog in it last year. Don't you worry none, for she found the rascal sure enough, but for a time she thought he was gone for good." And all nodded solemnly, grateful we were spared from the severity of such weather, even with our own to contend with.

Presently Bedelia asked whereabouts I had come from, and I told her Boston, at which Willa made an appreciative sound and said, "Now ain't that a journey? Why on God's green earth would you want to leave a place like that to come all the way out here to a place like this?" At their growing interest, which discomfited me somewhat, for perhaps I have gotten used to being alone where one need not bear the scrutiny of so many eyes, I started to say, "There was a bit of trouble. My husband's brother—" but stopped myself upon growing conscious of something dangerous brewing behind those eyes. So I gave the most direct answer. "My husband thought he'd get into mining and heard tell of the Virgil Consolidated, so we found ourselves here." This seemed to satisfy them, but I felt uneasy.

Then the tide turned to Bedelia's buffalo berry jelly recipe, which Josephine praised highly, and everyone else's favorite recipes, which they swapped amongst one another, and then it turned again, to the best remedies for miner's cough, which so many of our husbands bring home in their lungs, and other such conversation that filled my spirit with a tender feeling of companionship. It was the very feeling of lifting one's burdens and discovering they are shared, and therefore need not be so heavy. I begin to believe that the isolation has infiltrated my soul with its landscape of lonesomeness. To have another know and understand you is like the world acknowledging your existence. It is to say, yes, I am a part of this world, and this world is a part of me. One can never truly be alone, then.

By and by the conversation turned to temperance and politics; it was Willa started in on the women's suffrage movement, revealing a general enthusiasm among our group for the idea. Mary said, "If women ruled the world, we wouldn't make such a mess of things as them. I wouldn't tell my husband that, but I'll eat my hat if it isn't true." Virginia replied with quiet lament, "It's always the men, isn't it?"

All of a sudden, the atmosphere of the room seemed to darken, and I felt again whatever had been brewing behind their eyes coming to the fore. Olive gave voice to it: "It's them that brought down the curse on us all. Fooling around in that mine where they shouldn't be fooling around." Willa admonished her not to go passing blame around, which never does any good, but Josephine said, "Blamed if Olive ain't right though. Now look. It's happened again, and we can pretend all we want it hasn't, but we all darn well know that it's still going on and what happened didn't fix anything."

I became aware that I lacked some vital information. "What's happened again?" I asked, even though I felt they must be talking about that miner's death.

Only a heavy silence followed, and our sewing was threaded with this awful unease that seemed to swell in the air. "Never you mind," Willa said. "Let's not ruin a nice day with such talk."

"Not talking about it won't make any difference," Olive said as she glowered over her stitches. "Any one of us could be next." Then she turned those dark eyes on me, and her mouth curled into a wicked little grin. "Maybe it'll be you."

"Well, who else is ready for lunch?" Mary cut in before I could think how to respond.

Thankfully, the introduction of food improved all. By the time we returned to our work, we were in better spirits, and the conversation returned to trivial matters and compliments of one another's work. Trudy said to me, after looking over my quilting, "Lavinia, what a beautiful design! What do you call that pattern?" I had no name for it, but I eventually settled on the Cactus Trail, and the others looked over to admire my patchwork. Josephine called it beautiful stitching and added, "It's no wonder I've seen you spending time over at the tailor shop, talking to Mr. Branson. I'll bet your work is much better than his!" My gratitude at her kindness came abruptly to an end when Olive eyed me up and down with an unpleasant sneer on her face and said, "He doesn't want to talk to her for her stitchwork. You know he only likes unattractive women; they're easy to spoil."

"Pshaw, Olive!" said the others.

Her words slapped me with physical cruelness, so I said to her, "Mrs. Blackburn, if I've done something to offend you, I truly do apologize. You seem to bear me an endless tide of ill will."

Her response surprised me, for she cried out, "Mrs. Blackburn!" and then, burning with indignation: "My name isn't Blackburn. Mrs. Blackburn is dead."

Well, by now I was plumb confused and a little worried for her sanity besides. I've heard it said that one can go mad from the loneliness of frontier life, particularly if one has given up on faith and prayer. When she said, "First my cousin's wife was killed. And now my husband . . ." I felt a wash of dread and asked if he was all right, if something had happened to Chester?

Olive's stare was cold and dead-like when she told me the truth: "Chester is my cousin."

Despite her cruelty, I felt somehow ashamed. It was a mistake anyone could have made, with the two of them living together. How was I to know he wasn't her husband? "Come now, Olive," said Willa. "It isn't Lavinia's fault."

"No, it was his fault, the cussed fool, and he deserved what he got," she said savagely. "He opened a gate to Hell, and he deserved what he got."

The others had started talking all at once, trying simultaneously to quiet her fussing and to comfort her, and in the commotion I wasn't sure I had heard her correctly. What surprised me even more, however, was when Olive finally corrected my mistake about her name and told me who she really was: "So that you're not mistaken again, my name is Mrs. Randall."

Well, by then the bee was quite over. The others began quickly to say their good-byes, and Josephine ushered Olive out by the shoulders, for Olive had settled into a brooding manner. I think I begin to understand now why she is such an angry woman. Tethered to a town she clearly despises, unable to leave with her husband locked away. Only I wish she had said what exactly happened. I seem to have even more questions now than ever.

September 24, 1869

I did it. I went. I know, now, by God. I know the truth.

Poor Emery!

Let me tell it all, and tell it true.

Just past the stately courthouse sits the jail, tucked back from the road like a thing of shame. Today was blustery and clouded over with a most ominous shade of gray, darkening the little jailhouse: a one-story brick structure with an air about it already of ruin, its bricks prematurely scarred by the pummeling dust and wind as if it were made a monument of destruction. Something about it, lurking there, gave me a frightful feeling: knowing it was meant to house evil people, meant to lock in the sickness of criminality. It's as if that selfsame disease infects the very walls of its captivity. Or perhaps it was just that I knew what it was, and Hamlet was right that there is nothing good or bad but thinking makes it so.

My entrance gained the attention of the guard, who was leaning back on a wooden chair as far as it would go with his boots up on the table, balancing his head in his hands with a pipe wedged between his lips. He startled, the chair dropped to all four of its proper feet with a bang, and he looked up at me with the brightest green eyes. He was a young man, small and lean, and his hat sat askew on his head at an unintentionally careless angle.

"Ma'am," he said, standing in my presence, surprise still bright in his eyes, I think, to see anyone here. "What brings you?"

There was only one cell in the small building, set off with heavy iron bars in a crosshatched pattern. The unwindowed cell's shadows all but obscured the figure that sat on a bench against its brick wall.

I said I would like to speak with Mr. Randall, "if such a thing is permitted," and my saying so surprised him again, for he said, "Certainly it's permitted, but can I ask why a lady such as yourself would be interested in talking with a brute like Willie Ray Randall?"

I wondered if he would be amenable to my questions—or if he would shut me out as soon as he knew what I had come for, just like everyone else in this town. It was a moment of sheer inspiration that made me blurt out, "I have word from his wife, Olive. She wanted me to come by and check on him and pass along her love."

The man wore a slight frown but accepted this. "Certainly, Mrs. . . . ?"

"Cain," I supplied. "Lavinia Cain."

I detected something of a crestfallen expression on his face when I did not correct his assumption of my marital status. Poor Mr. McCullins seems like a lonely fellow. For that is how he introduced himself to me, when I gave him my name—Abernathy McCullins, sheriff's deputy, given the most tiresome position of watching over Virgil's one and only incarcerated criminal.

He allowed me to go up to the iron bars, cautioning me not to get altogether too close, then stepped out the front door to finish the tobacco in his pipe, giving me a respectful modicum of privacy with the man in question. The bell above the door chimed on his way out, and its sharp peal sent a shiver all through me.

I could hardly see the prisoner in the shadows of his cell: what I made out was just a dark figure, sitting with his legs apart and his arms resting on his knees.

"Good day, Mr. Randall," I said, feeling then a thrill of nervousness. Now that I was well and truly alone with the man, my heart froze up in my chest and a dreadful feeling came over me.

It was hardly a relief when he finally spoke from the shadows. "Cain," he drawled, chewing over the name. His voice was a deep grumble, like a train roaring through a mountain tunnel. He chuckled, and it, too, was a coarse, unpleasant sound, as if his throat were filled with sand.

"You don't know me," I told him, "but I know your wife, Olive."

"How is the old lady?" he asked. "She don't visit me much anymore. Suspect she's tired of this damned cell. Lord knows I am."

I couldn't stop myself from muttering, "You speak of the Lord behind bars."

"The Lord knows I'm here, and He knows why I'm here too. Ain't no use keeping nothing from Him. He done worse than me, anyhow. Or ain't you never read the Bible?"

Such crude and uncouth words! I disliked him immediately, yet I cannot pretend I wasn't drawn to him in some way, intrigued, despite myself. He bore a dangerous air like a brewing storm, even behind bars, and he spoke like one who knows things, terrible things, which could turn one's blood cold. I told him his wife seems distraught at his predicament, and he said, "Olive can take care of herself. Her cousin's a good-for-nothing lout, but my Olive's resilient as steel. Now what's it you came here for, little lady?"

Listening to that voice come out of the shadows, I wished he would come forward into the light; yet at the same time, I was glad he didn't. He remained but a silhouette, and when the light behind me shined just right, it showed the gleam of his smile. He had a broad mouth and crooked teeth, and that was about all I could tell of him.

I told him I was trying to discover what had happened to my brother-in-law, Emery Cain—did he know him? And he laughed, that dark unpleasant chuckle like the sound of scraping rocks, and said, "You come here to talk to me, and you don't even know why I'm in jail?" At my silence, he laughed again, the sound grating at my ears. "Well why don't you set on down for a spell? It's quite a tale and I expect you'll be wanting to set down by the end of it."

Loath as I was to obey the man, I found Deputy McCullins's chair, dragged it closer, and perched myself upon it.

I do not know that I have it in me to replicate Mr. Randall's peculiar drawl though I can still hear his voice in my ears, ringing there with perverse clarity. Instead I shall retell the yarn he spun for me, which is thus:

Willie Ray Randall and Emery Cain were partners, of a sort. By which I mean they worked in the mine side by side, looked out for each other, traded tips, felt obliged to keep each other's secrets in the event one found a nugget of silver he wanted to keep for himself. They both worked hard, with the promise of fortune on the horizon, and even off the job they sat together in the saloon, drinking themselves into ever-grander visions of the future. Maybe more than partners, even. I suspect by his telling that Willie Ray Randall and Emery Cain had been friends.

But as they found themselves deeper in the mine, working those remote tunnels far beneath the surface, they came upon a certain closed-off section that piqued their interest. Sometimes there were these little pockets where the mine collided with an ancient cave system the likes of which one often encounters in the depths of a mountain, and this was one such area. It was closed off, however, because some years ago, when the Virgil Consolidated Mining Company was in its infancy and the mine still unfurling itself through the mountain, whoever first broke through into the natural cave found bad air and decided to block the entrance with some wood planks and rocks to stop anyone else from entering. It was more than bad air, though, if you listened to the way the seasoned miners told it: that chamber was cursed. There was something evil in there. And, so the stories went, if you found yourself deep enough in that evil cave system, eventually you might come upon the very gateway to Hell itself.

Willie Ray was content enough to leave it be, but Emery wouldn't let it go. He became increasingly fixated upon that sealed-off cave, getting it into his head that they might find a vein of silver ore in there, seeing as how the mining company had left it foolishly untouched. The rest of the mine was getting picked clean, with the most recent strain all but removed by then, making it necessary to find another large strain soon—and where else could one find a decently-sized silver nugget but in a chamber that the miners hadn't set foot in? That remained pristine, unravaged, a natural bounty just waiting to be plucked free?

With this singlemindedness driving him, the very same singlemindedness that he shares with his brother, I would add, Emery conscripted a few other miners to help him break through the barrier. Lafayette Albers and Phineas Cartwright eagerly obliged, and even Willie Ray Randall was unable to ignore the call of fortune, though he claims now he cautioned against it mightily. Together the four of them made their way into those remote recesses of the mine to that barrier of wood and rock, which they broke apart to make an opening into the cave.

This is where Mr. Randall's tale becomes queer: bereft of detail, the man turned cagey. Still, I could not see the look upon his face as he remained in the shadows at the back of his cell, as if, having worked so long in the mines, he has come to prefer the darkness.

What I could tell though, and which set my nerves on edge, was that this dangerous man—this fearsome, hulking shadow of a man—was afraid. He was afraid of what they had found in that cave, which he would not describe to me. All he said was they'd found a chamber, and there was something horrible in it. Something that convinced him this cave system was, indeed, a gateway to Hell, for whatever they'd found could only have come from perdition.

As soon as they'd discovered the chamber, and whatever horrible thing resided within, they hastened out—not just out of the cave system, but out of the mine entire, desperate for the daylight they so rarely saw anymore. But even the daylight was unable to wash away their terror at what they had found. Mr. Randall looked around at the other men who had seen what he had seen. "I saw them and I knowed I looked just the same, as like looking in a mirror. You've never seen such a look of fright on a man's face before." There was a note of buried terror in his voice that struck me deeply, for what could make a man such as him feel this great fear?

At first the men thought they'd left behind whatever it was they'd found in the cave, and they refused to go back into the mine, even though it would cost them their livelihood. Only Emery ventured back into the mine the following day to resume his regular work, while the others stayed home and as far from that mine as they could.

"Wasn't long though, afore we realized by leaving that chamber open, we'd let out what was in there."

And he said that's when the killings began.

First Nathaniel and Tabitha Conrad, then Edgar Howell, then Otto and Rebecca. All found covered in a frightful percussion of inexplicable sores piercing all through their flesh, which was left white and bloodless. And of course, there was Chester Blackburn's wife, a woman named Margaret who was dearest friends with Olive, and who was found by Olive herself, her jaw hanging open as if in some perpetual death scream, her skin pocked and ruined.

"It was him what done it," said Willie Ray, his voice turning angry. "It was Emery what opened up that gate to Hell and damned us all, for that's what it was, I swear it on my own grave. The Lord don't exist down there. If Emery hadn't been so determined to get into that place, if he hadn't've led us in there to see them things . . ."

And it was here, at last, that Mr. Randall leaned forward into the light, and I beheld his grizzled face, with its growth of shaggy beard shot through with gray, and the bright, piercing blue gray of his round and staring eyes, which penetrated me like a shock of cold water thrown over my head. And with those wide, wild eyes striking me like silver blades, he said with all conviction: "Emery destroyed everything. I saw, clear as day, we was all going to die. And it was all because of him, because of the gate he opened. I ain't proud of what I done, but I would do it again. I would do it again and again, and let him rot in Hell."

He punctuated this by spitting on the floor.

A sick dread filled me, and it was all I could do to choke out the question, "What did you do?"

"Wasn't just me," he said. "They was all on my side. They knew what I told them was true, that it was Emery who brought death down on this place and it was up to us to bring justice. When I found Emery in his house, I wasn't alone, mark me. I had half the town at my back, calling for blood. We done strung him up good, too. Brought him right to the center of town, where that old tree stands. And we hanged him till he was good and dead."

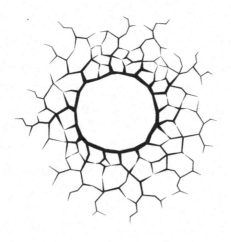

THE DUST DEVILS

MADS NUDGED WAYNOKA, AN act that shocked the diary from Waynoka's fingers and sent it dropping to the ground.

"Didn't mean to startle you." Her voice was gruff. "You were absorbed."

The diary lay splayed open, naked and prone.

Murder in its pages.

"Any new ideas from your book?" asked Mads. Her voice moved with the rhythms of attempted levity, and Waynoka wondered why they had to pretend with each other—pretend that they were not as frightened as they really were. Perhaps it was because if one panicked, the other would too, and then they would never reach the surface.

She shook her head.

Mads pushed herself up, still holding the wall with one hand while she winced, trying to keep the weight off her bad leg. "All right, let's get going. I'm sick of this place."

"You feel up for walking?"

"Well, I don't feel up for dying."

Waynoka put the diary back in the pack and slung it over her shoulders, holding out her arm at an angle for Mads to take, which of course she did not, instead taking the flashlight from her and pushing ahead, toward the fork and this time, to the right-hand path that sloped downward, half dragging her bad leg along at an angle that looked extremely uncomfortable.

Of course, the discomfort was probably nothing compared to the shard of bone poking out of her knee.

Waynoka felt sick and a little dizzy. She tried not to think of that. For the moment, Mads was moving, and as long as she was moving, everything was okay.

Well, as okay as it could be in a place like this.

This place wasn't meant for people. Though it was people who had carved this maze out of the rock, people who had drilled down into the earth to plunder it of riches, people were never meant to crawl around in these dark endless tunnels. The earth belonged only to itself.

It reminded Waynoka of a documentary she'd seen years ago about the Paris catacombs, down past the section that was open to tourists, the deeper part, the miles and miles of unmapped tunnels in which amateur spelunkers often got lost. What happened to them when their flashlights died, and they couldn't find their way back out? Did they wander those black tunnels, blind and terrified, as they slowly died of thirst or starvation? At what point did panic give way to hopeless acceptance of death? At what point did they stop running deeper and deeper, toward their own damnation?

That would be their fate if they lost their one remaining flashlight. Waynoka mentally willed Mads to cling to it with a firm grip, willed the ground not to suddenly give way under their feet into another open mine shaft. The flashlight was all they had left to maintain their sanity. One little beacon of light that had to be periodically wound up by hand.

It wasn't exactly comforting—especially when it began to flicker.

The ground sloped downward at a gentle decline and the ceiling dipped low, forcing them to crouch. The bent angle did no favors for Mads's knee, and she moved with agonizing slowness as she tried to limp forward without putting any weight on it. Every so often they had to stop for a brief rest, and though Mads kept the light aimed down the tunnel ahead of them and not at her face, Waynoka could tell she was in terrible pain.

How much longer could they continue like this?

Mads slid down to sit, her legs stretched out from one wall of the tunnel to the other; her body folded over itself. She held out the flashlight for Waynoka.

"Take it."

She did.

And when she only stood there looking dumbly at Mads, her partner flashed hard, flinty eyes at her and said, "Keep going."

Waynoka shook her head.

"Just go up a little ways, see what's ahead, and then come back."

"And leave you here alone? In the dark?"

The horror of that thought crawled up her throat.

"I'll be fine," said Mads, the strain in her voice sounding anything but. "I just need to rest my knee."

"I'm not leaving you."

"Then we'll both die!" Her voice, high and wild, echoed off the walls around them, startling them both with the sudden, vicious volume—with the bubble of panic that emerged from a throat normally low and gravelly with ease.

"I'll be back soon," Waynoka said quietly, then turned before the pale beam of the flashlight could linger any longer on her partner's grimace, on the blood that had seeped through the ragged bandage around her knee. She started down the tunnel, Mads's words still echoing in her head if not in the mine any longer.

We'll both die. We'll both die.

Every step took her deeper, left Mads farther behind her and farther behind the light, which shook in Waynoka's grip—from fear, perhaps, but also very likely from dehydration, from the dizziness that plagued her, compounded by the head injury she had sustained in the fall, from the constant gnawing hunger in her gut at the pitiful rations of food they allowed themselves. Somehow, as she moved away from Mads, her own weakness seemed to manifest itself more strongly. She noticed herself more, noticed the way she stumbled slightly when she wasn't dragging one hand along the rough wall, noticed the way she had to constantly swallow to try and work up saliva in the desert of her mouth.

We'll both die, her lonely footsteps echoed back to her. *We'll both die.*

To her right, another tunnel split off from this one, but the opening was narrow, only a little wider than the width of her body. Briefly, she shined the light inside, but it didn't go far. Probably a dead end. Probably a patch of cave. Jagged rocks lined its edges.

She kept going.

The ceiling dipped so low she had to crouch, as if the earth would swallow her. Then the tunnel widened again, made a sharp turn, dipped. The air felt different. Cold. There was a yellowing, rusty color to the rock here. Evidence of heavy metals.

Realizing what that meant, she aimed the light down at her feet and saw just ahead of her a strange, murky reflection.

Water.

At first she couldn't believe what she was seeing. She couldn't move. She stood frozen with the light on the surface of the muddy sump. Then a cry ripped from her throat, a cry of desperate joy, and she surged forward until she was up to her ankles in the icy water. She dropped to her knees and splashed it on her face, the shock of the cold and wet hitting her like a slap. Her body leaned forward irresistibly, wanting to drink, to open her mouth and lap it up, but some latent caution buried like a nugget of wisdom reminded her she had to boil it first. Could she wait that long?

As she sat, scrubbing dust from her skin until she was cleaner than she had been in weeks, in months, the flashlight died away. With a jolt of panic, she went to wind it back up but hesitated with the sudden morbid urge to know what Mads was experiencing.

The darkness was unlike anything she had ever seen before. It was like being blind, she imagined. She was nowhere, floating in a void. She could feel the water around her, but it was like there wasn't anything there, not really. Sensation without form or substance, without meaning.

Then she heard a gentle splash, like something emerging from the water. She froze, sensing a presence beside her. She tried to convince herself there was nothing there, there was nothing in the sump, there couldn't be, she was alone.

The water sloshed with movement.

Waynoka clutched the flashlight to her chest in the pitch-blackness, not knowing whether to wind it up and reveal herself or to remain here with that sensation of something nearby, blind to whatever it might be. She didn't dare move. She held her breath.

Then a rusty, high-pitched voice whispered, "*I like to swim too.*" Right in front of her, the voice like a soft breath on her face. Unable to inhale, her throat freezing up, Waynoka desperately fumbled with the flashlight, winding it erratically, and the beam stuttered to life against two dark, gleaming eyes too close to her, in something that was less than a face, which darted away immediately at the sudden light. Waynoka nearly dropped the flashlight into the water, her hands were shaking so badly. By the time she steadied the light, whatever she had seen had splashed out of the water and run off behind her.

She stood up out of the water and turned so fast a wave of dizziness overcame her, nearly sent her off balance.

Mads.

Without thinking, she started back the way she'd come—but she didn't make it far before her flashlight found a figure crawling down the tunnel toward her, its hands like claws reaching out as it dragged itself forward.

Thinking of those dark eyes, that withered and rotten face, Waynoka shouted.

The figure lifted its head so she could see the face behind the mane of hair. For a moment she was confused. She couldn't make sense of what she was seeing. Then her vision cleared and she recognized the person crawling toward her.

"Mads!" Her heart skipped and tried to find a rhythm. "What the hell are you doing?"

"I heard you scream a little while ago . . ." Mads panted, pulling herself up. "I thought . . ."

"Did you see something? Just now?"

Mads looked at her like she'd grown a second head. "What?"

"A figure—it came this way. It must have passed you." Then she remembered, Mads couldn't have seen anything. She didn't have a flashlight. But surely she would have noticed, heard, felt . . . ?

"No. Jesus, what's going on?"

Waynoka put her hands on her knees and bent over, tried to make sense of the last few minutes of desperate panic, which had become a jumble in her head that she could hardly keep straight. What exactly had she seen? No real details, nothing she could accurately describe. Just a flash, a glimpse.

Spiders on the ceiling, she thought, and for a moment she wanted to cry.

Instead she stood up straight, remembering the more important thing she had seen, the thing she knew was there, just down the tunnel. "You were right," she said, helping Mads up. "I found water."

They returned to the sump, where Mads delivered an excitement-hastened prayer of thanks peppered with plenty of swear words, and Waynoka dug the pot out of her pack and dipped it into the water.

"We'll need fire."

Mads nodded. "The room?"

"Quite a ways back."

"Well, I don't see any fire fixings here, do you?"

Waynoka conceded. They would have to backtrack to the little room where she'd found the diary.

She couldn't help Mads and carry the pot of water at the same time. She offered to help get Mads back first and come back for the water, but Mads said fuck that, she could make it on her own if they took it slow. There was no way they were leaving the water behind, even for a minute.

With painstaking slowness so as not to spill even a drop of the precious liquid, Waynoka started the laborious climb back up the tunnel, flashlight in one hand, pot in the other. The muscles of her forearm strained from the need to keep it level. Mads half limped, half crawled along beside her, and she tried not to think about how it was seeming more and more as if, once they made it back, Mads wouldn't be able to go any farther. She was at the end of her limit. Waynoka concentrated on the water, on not letting it spill over the edges.

It was strange, how precious water had become. Only a few years ago, she could have turned on the tap in her kitchenette and stuck her face under it, let the cool water flow over her. She'd had a pitcher of drinking water in her fridge. It was so easy, so accessible. Even in that tiny studio apartment, she'd had it so good. How had it all gone so wrong? How had people managed to screw up such a golden age of luxury?

A part of her wished she could leave humanity behind altogether. Good riddance. At every moment she expected to come upon the thing that had been in the sump. At every moment, she felt the simultaneous agony of relief that they were alone and the terrible anticipation of a figure appearing out of the dark.

It seemed to take forever to get back to that little room, and by the time they did, they were both shaking with exhaustion. Waynoka set down the water reverently while Mads dropped onto the bed, then worked on getting the fire started. Once it was blazing bright, throwing their shadows crazily against the walls and making the red stick figure seem to come to life and dance against the stone wall, she rigged up the metal stand for cooking over the fire and set the pot on top of it.

Waynoka joined Mads on the bed, and they sat together, clinging to each other as if, at any moment, one of them might suddenly drift away into the darkness. They stared at the pot in awe. Here was the evidence of their salvation.

After a minute, Mads turned away. "A watched pot never boils."

"A cliché never gets any less cliché," said Waynoka. Then she shook her head. "I can't fucking believe it."

"You can't believe I was right?"

She gave Mads a playful shove.

"This is gonna kill me," said Mads. "Boil already, you fucker."

"Waiting for it to boil is like waiting for traffic to start moving in LA."

Mads barked out a laugh. "Back when traffic was your biggest problem. That was a time. Everyone wanted to be on the road. Everyone wanted to be there." She looked sidelong at Waynoka. "Hey, what made you come out to LA in the first place?"

"What?"

"You're not from there."

"I never told you that."

"I can tell."

"What, do you have some kind of radar that tells you who's a native and who's a transplant? An LA-dar?"

Mads leaned in conspiratorially. "Don't tell anyone I told you, but everyone from LA has it. We're born with it. Like a little antenna, in the backs of our heads. Actually, if you shaved my head—"

"I came with my boyfriend," Waynoka said, then amended: "Boyfriend at the time."

"That's not really a reason."

"He was an aspiring director. Is. I don't know. I haven't spoken to him in years, obviously. He might be dead, for all I know. I came out with him because he wanted to get into directing."

"Sure. You didn't come because you wanted to get into Hollywood. You're just . . . wannabe Hollywood adjacent. And I say 'wannabe' because I assume he did not, in fact, accomplish his dreams of directing. But . . . I could be wrong?" She raised her eyebrows. The firelight flickered, making her face seem to jump and twitch.

"You're not wrong."

"That Hollywood fantasy." Mads barked a laugh. "The good old American Dream."

Waynoka leaned back and closed her eyes, grateful for what Mads was doing, despite her obvious pain. Grateful for the distraction. She forced herself not to open her eyes to see if the water was boiling yet. "Didn't stop him from trying, even long after he realized he wasn't going to make it. He started bringing it all home with him though. I don't know. It started to feel like he was . . . directing our lives. Like I was just playing a role. Like nothing was real."

"So why didn't you go back to . . ."

"South Dakota."

". . . South Dakota, after you broke up with him? And I say that because I hope you dumped his ass and not the other way around."

"Still not wrong," said Waynoka with a shrug. "I don't know. I just stuck around. By the time we broke up, I was already hanging with this environmentalist theater group in NoHo—"

"Excuse me?"

Waynoka opened her eyes to see the incredulous look on her partner's face. "Yeah, they were actor activists . . . 'actorvists.'"

Mads snorted. "Gentrification is a hell of a drug."

The more she talked, the more the saliva built up in her mouth, and she was grateful for that. She felt like she could keep talking, knowing that soon she would be able to take a drink. The promise was like a drug; she felt almost high. "I was into it at first—the environmentalist part. I was never an actor. I just tagged along, helped them learn their lines. Sometimes I couldn't tell if they wanted to save the planet or if they were just playing the part of people who wanted to save the planet. Not that they were that good at acting."

"So you just . . . stayed, to hang out with your weird little theater group?"

Waynoka shrugged. "Yeah. I also . . . don't laugh, okay? I also had this stupid idea that I might write a screenplay."

"I don't think that's stupid," said Mads.

They sat in silence for another minute, each savoring the promise of an imminent drink, talking of the past as if it were another life that no longer had any place in this world. A curious and distant artifact that no longer held any real meaning, like an episode of a television show.

And maybe it was. Waynoka thought now how naïve she'd been, back then. Thinking she could save the planet. If only there hadn't been so many people determined to let it burn.

Then a strange little sound broke the quiet: a burbling. Hardly daring to look, Waynoka peeked over the edge of the pot to see the water bubbling sporadically, and in that moment she felt calmer than she could remember feeling in ages. They would let it boil for ten minutes once it really got going, then they would have to let it cool, but each minute that passed was another minute closer.

Mads interrupted her thoughts.

"So did you ever write your screenplay?"

Waynoka kept her eyes on the pot. Now that it was boiling, she could watch it. Her old desire to write a screenplay felt very far away right now. The only thing that mattered was the pot of boiling water. "I couldn't even get past the first line," she admitted. "I guess I didn't really have a story to tell."

"Maybe you'll get a story from all this." Mads cracked a smile, but it was forced. "Getting trapped in an abandoned mine seems like pretty good material to me."

"Yeah." Waynoka found it hard to imagine that she might ever again do something as mundane as sitting down to write a screenplay. Even the idea of getting out of the mine receded further and further from the realm of possibility in her mind. She tried not to let that hopelessness infect her. "When we get out of here, I'm going to write all of this down, like Lavinia did."

"It'll be an indie hit," said Mads. "Wouldn't even need a big budget. Just two actors. One location."

"Maybe I could include snippets from the diary." Waynoka dug through her bag to pull out the little book, the feeling of its cover and thick pages somehow a comfort. "You know, have scenes from it interspersed with the scenes of us in the mine?"

"Oh," Mads added with excitement, "and then the stories will come together, you know, like the scenes from the diary will give clues about how the 'us' characters eventually get out."

Waynoka nodded as she tried to keep the glimmer of warmth alive inside of her. "That would make a pretty good movie. I'd go see it."

"Hell yeah," said Mads. "Red carpet premiere and everything."

They fell quiet again, watching the water boil. Time dripped slowly.

Eventually, Waynoka couldn't help but ask, "What if it's a horror movie?"

"Hmm?" Mads grunted.

Waynoka swallowed, trying to fight down the gnawing sensation that they were not alone down here. Lavinia's diary had just revealed that Emery had been murdered because he'd let something evil out of this mine—at least, according to Willie Ray Randall. What if she'd encountered whatever Emery had released?

Despite the fire's warmth, she felt a chill run through her skin, tingling her fingertips. It would be useless to try to convince Mads of this notion— because Mads hadn't seen anything, and she was the kind of person who dealt in absolutes, in reality.

"Never mind," she said, realizing Mads was half asleep. "I'm going to keep reading until the water's ready. Find those clues, you know."

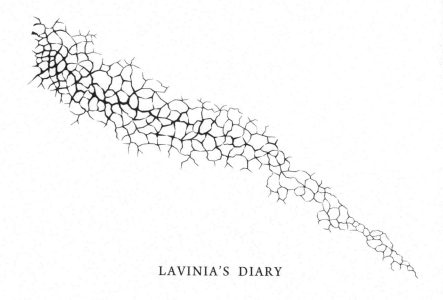

LAVINIA'S DIARY

September 25, 1869

What I told John Henry was exactly the truth as I had heard it. Willie Ray Randall killed Emery, and now shame hangs over this town like a cloak, for no one bothered to stop him. Even Mr. Randall's accomplices, Lafayette and Phineas, supposedly ran off into the desert, unable to stomach their complicity. Who knows what became of them after that? I told John Henry that this town, which he believes to be our future, has let his brother be murdered—and though anger and agony clouded his features, and he sat heavily to process this terrible truth, after a long silence he said, "Good that the criminal is behind bars. He will hang for what he has done."

Diary, from the way our conversation turned—I think he hadn't truly accepted his brother's death in that moment. I think it was still an abstract thing to him. That it wasn't real.

I decided not to press him too much on the subject of his brother. But what about the others involved? The whole of this town is rotten! And I said as much.

"What would you have me do?" John Henry said. "Abandon everything we are building here? If this account is true, then I will be glad to see justice delivered to this heathen."

"But what of his story?" I continued, unable to help myself. "The gateway to Hell he says they opened?"

John Henry scoffed. "It's quite the tale. But if he thinks that load of hogwash will stand in a court of law, he's got another think coming. The man is an imaginative liar, I'll grant him that. Can you even be sure what he claims to have done to Emery is true? He might have been taking you for a ride."

I shook my head, even knowing that without proof I had only my gut to tell me that Willie Ray Randall had told me the truth about all of it. And I knew nothing could convince John Henry of a thing if he has already set his mind and snapped it shut. If my problem is that I am perhaps too gullible (according to him), then his problem is that he is altogether too much the skeptic, thinking all Creation is just as deceitful as himself.

When I tried to articulate my fears to John Henry, his grim countenance, like a demon erupted from burning all-fire, turned to one of smug satisfaction. "My darling, you have spooked yourself by listening to a criminal's wild story. But believe me when I tell you there is no such thing as a gate to Hell, or demons, or whatever it is he's claimed. You're liable to believe things easily, Lavinia. Even when you shouldn't."

Is it possible he's right? That I've simply allowed myself to be spooked? But then what of those mysterious deaths—I did not imagine those!

I ought to have said something smart to John Henry, something which could convince him I am not a gullible little girl, but instead I said what came into my head just then, and it wasn't very pretty. I asked him why I should believe anything *he* says. "You've hoodwinked people to sell them that worthless elixir. You knew exactly how to make them believe you. And now you say I shouldn't believe too much."

Oh, but did his grin turn sour then!

"My business is my business," he said. "But you ought to know better than anyone that I would never lie to you."

Diary, there was an ache in my heart then, for I knew, deep in my bones, that it wasn't true. It wasn't that he'd ever downright lied to me, no, but that he told what he wanted, he promised impossible dreams, and nothing he's done has ever quite lived up to what he said he would do. He talks a lot of talk that never manifests as anything else. I shouldn't like to think that makes me terrible, but the more he talks, the less I believe him, it's true— and one too many promises now leaves me cold.

I believe that was when the children ran into the house, laughing and cavorting, Oscar giving chase and Sophie pretending to run away full tilt. I sent them back outside with a word, and they retreated, mollified. There was a long moment as John Henry and I held each other's gaze and didn't want to say anything as we waited for there to be distance between us and the children.

So I tried a different tack and said it only seemed as if he didn't care, after all, what had happened to his brother—he didn't seem to care one way or another, whether Emery really did absquatulate and clear out, or whether he had been murdered, and why. Surely, even if John Henry holds a grudge against him for making their lives difficult as children, surely he could still find it within himself to care about his own flesh and blood?

The look John Henry gave me, red-eyed from dust, was of such pain that it became fury. "Of course I care," he said. He turned from me then, as if a tether was broken, and stomped away to pick up his cup from the table and take a long drink. When he finally did turn back to me, he appeared more composed, but I was still shaken from the look of such raw despair I had glimpsed in him, reminding me that he feels things deeply, and maybe that is why he so resents his brother, who allowed things to roll off him easily as water from a duck's feathers. He took his cup out to sit on the front porch, and I shut pan on the subject and let him be. I figure, by and by, he'll acknowledge the corn, but until then it just won't be any use needling him about it.

That was yesterday, what I have written. Afterwards we went to bed in silence. I rose early this morning and found myself with you, my trusted diary, in my lap as I watched the sun creep over the horizon, and by the time the sun had fully shown its face I had fixed us all breakfast, and we went on with the day.

I should like to find some proof of Mr. Randall's story, but now that remorseless man is the only one left who saw what they had found. What they unleashed. Not wanting John Henry to think me just a silly, scared woman, I did not tell him how Willie Ray Randall had crept forward in the cell and drove a hand through the bars, grabbed me by the wrist and locked me in the bruising tightness of his grip. How I could smell his foul breath as he pulled me near enough to see the lines around his eyes and the yellow of his teeth. Nor what he said then:

"Killing Emery didn't stop them things," he whispered to me. "They're still coming, up from Hell. These fools think they're punishing me, keeping me locked up here." He laughed. It was a harsh sound—almost insane. "Don't they know! I'm the safest of all. Them things can't get in here."

Yes, he scared me, Diary. The deputy had to run in to pry his hands from my flesh, and I still bear the faint marks of his fingers, though I have covered them with my sleeve.

But even Mr. Randall could not say exactly what "them things" were. He said what they had found in the mine appeared to be a sort of burial chamber . . . "only whatever was buried there, it wasn't quite dead."

The thought gives me the shivers.

So I've finally done it. I've acquired a bell for our door, and I've already affixed it to the top of the frame so that if anyone should come through that doorway, we will hear its jingle. It will wake us, should someone try to steal inside at night. And we will know when *los fantasmas* are about.

September 27, 1869

It is so quiet, but for the wind and my washing. My mind has so much room to run away from me while I work. I should like to be able to turn it off and focus on the steady movements of my arms, but these repetitive motions seem to free my brain from my body. I can think only of Emery.

September 28, 1869

I wonder what it feels like, to be hanged? What a horrible thought. My throat tightens even considering it, as if a rope is closing around it. Poor Emery!

September 29, 1869

Do you know something strange, Diary? I am almost jealous of the children and John Henry. They are all out of the house, the children among other children, John Henry among other men—and here I am, alone, alone. When all the days stretch emptily around in their vast and yawning silences, one almost forgets that other people exist in this world.

September 30, 1869

What a horrible rhyme! I've gooseflesh all over me. It gives me a creepy feeling. Reminds me what Ms. Delilah Barnes said, how the story of the Strange Lady had not come from any of the parents, but that the children came upon it all on their own, these children who claim to see apparitions in the desert.

Perhaps the children are making it all up. They are children, after all, and children do enjoy their make-believe—and yet, and yet!

This was the rhyme I found Sophronia and Oscar singing together while they played, and which chilled me to the bone:

Strange Lady, Strange Lady,
What do you eat?
She comes in the night
And pricks Father's feet!
Strange Lady, Strange Lady,
Why do you thirst?
She'll never be slaked
For she has been cursed!

When I caught them at this song and bade them cease their awful singing, they looked at me with surprise, and why shouldn't they? It is just a childish rhyme, like any other. My anger must have startled and confused them.

Yet when I heard these words, my heart leapt into my throat the like to strangle me, all manner of foul and frightful thoughts driving through my brain: thoughts of demons and phantasms, of things that ought to be dead but are not, climbing out from the depths of the mine, even from those ancient caves and wherever they lead, and coming out to bring death on this town, to slake their endless unquenchable thirst for the lifeblood of the soul!

When I asked the children if they had ever seen figures in the night—if they had seen the Strange Lady of the infernal rhyme they had learned from their schoolmates—their eyes grew round and solemn, and they nodded and admitted they had heard that adults did not believe the other children, and therefore they had expected the same of me. But they said yes, they had seen the Strange Lady, and Oscar even said that once he had seen her come into our house at night! Come creeping in to crouch at our feet and go away again.

I could not stop myself from slapping the boy for voicing such a horrid thing. Oscar cried out when I hit him, saying, "But you asked! I only told the truth! Charles saw her too!" And these protestations convinced me not to believe a word the little liar said, with his dark fancies. Of course the boy who claims his dead brother as an invisible friend would claim also to see the phantom from this children's rhyme, doing exactly what the rhyme promises: "She comes in the night / And pricks Father's feet!" It is a fairy tale, merely that; I would be mad to think it anything more. You see, John Henry, I do not believe everything I hear.

I am not so gullible as you think.

But, oh, whether or not I believe, I forbade the children from singing the rhyme again, for I cannot stand to hear it; yet it rings in my ears even now, like a bell, like a demon's song laughing up from the pits of Hell.

October 1, 1869

There is a constant distemper that lives in my chest. I fear it may begin to gnaw my heart till it is no more than a withered fruit. An ache reaches up into my skull and down my limbs, uniting in some deep well within the chambers of that vital organ.

Should I speak to John Henry of my affliction, I fear he will call me hysterical. The look he directed toward me tonight at the saloon, with disgust at my behavior, seems to float before my vision still, like a photograph my eyes must carry with them.

There was a minor collapse at the mine, nothing serious and no one injured, but with the dust in the air and the need for a crew to bolster the supports, the rest of the men had to clear out rather earlier than usual. And where else should a bevy of misplaced miners go on a windy afternoon but the saloon? That is where they went, and that is where they stayed till candlelighting and after. I didn't mind that he was drinking—I do not consider myself a particular advocate of the temperance movement; it isn't drink that makes men act with violence, it is but their own inclinations and willingness to abandon themselves; John Henry drinks a good deal but has never raised his fist against me, for he knows restraint—but when I saw dark falling fast in the desert, falling like a heavy quilt, my distemper, sleeping and quiet thus far, awoke in my breast such awful feelings that I could not sit but had to move most constantly to quell the dread that began to chew on my heart.

Oscar even asked me, "Why are you moving like that?"

It was my pacing, my fiddling with my hands, that he referred to, but his question struck me irrationally as condemnation. I calmed myself and put my hand on his head, petted over his soft golden hair. I knew I could not continue pacing about in this manner, so I told Sophronia to watch her brother while I went out to fetch their father: "Do not let him leave this cabin. Neither of you are to leave, do you hear me? You must both stay put right here. Do not take even one step outside."

She was eager to be put in charge, which made me smile. Sophie likes to prove herself a little adult these days. She has long since given up those childish, undisciplined ways; now she behaves like a little lady. My heart swells with pride, yet I cannot help but also feel a distant sort of sadness that she will never again, in that unruliness of youth, cast off what the world expects of her, will never be a little girl again. And when I look at her, I see how young she is still, how small and fragile.

In that sweet, high voice of hers, she asked me, "Is that why you put the bell on the door? So you will hear if we go outside?"

Well, I could not think of any good answer to give that would not frighten her, so I told her, "Yes—and no matter how far I go, I will hear it, and I will come hurrying back to you. This bell has its own unique voice that I will recognize, the way a cat recognizes the mewl of her kittens. No matter why the bell rings, I will come back for you."

Sophie nodded, her face set in thoughtfulness, and, gathering up my courage, I went out into the night.

All was black, but the stars shone exceeding bright. The moon gave its half smile, lighting the way in pale shades. The heat of day had fallen away and a chill crept up from the earth and shivered me in my heavy shawl, which I wrapped tight about my shoulders, but not tight enough to keep the ghosts of desert night from breathing cold down my back. And how the shadows seemed to shift as cottony clouds passed over the moon! And how the distant shapes of sagebrush and cactus seemed to creep about in those shifting shadows!

By the time I had arrived on Main Street I was fairly running, my skirts flying up behind me as the wind bayed its endless hollow cry in my ears— but then I saw the saloon just ahead of me, with warm light behind its doors, which swung open to allow bursts of sound into the night, laughter and voices and music spilling free into the deadly dark and silence like drink from an overfilled cup.

Pushing my way inside was like emerging from the depths of sleep into the brightness and motion of midday. Of course the lanterns did not shine as bright as the sun, but their warm light shocked the eyes after the vast, oppressive dark outside.

Men surrounded the tables and sat on barstools—more men than I expected in the wake of such mysterious deaths. The bartender poured whiskey and slid small glasses across the bar, wiped down spills. Tobacco smoke filled the air with a warm, leathery smell. Standing at the bar were two women who I could only assume were adventuresses, color high on their cheeks as they leaned in close to the men who sat hunched over the surface. An old man sat at a piano against the far wall, plinking out a jaunty tune.

I saw John Henry at a table with three other men engaged in a card game. Each had a beer close at hand—what was clearly not their first and likely not their second, either—and each time they threw their hands down on the table a cry rose up, either despair for the loser or victory for the winner, who reached in to slide the pile of coins that sat at the table's center toward his own lap.

Weaving my way through the room, I arrived at his side, but he did not notice me until I raised my voice to say his name. Then he did look up with a measure of surprise. I thought perhaps he would ask me what I was doing there or tell me to go home, but instead a crooked sort of smile came over his face (and that was how I knew he was further in than three drinks), and, sliding his arm around my waist, he pulled me onto his lap.

"Come to see your man make paupers of these gentlemen?" he said with a twinkle in his eye. His black, grizzled beard was grown unkempt over his ruddy cheeks, and I wondered when he had shaved last. I felt his hands on me, and it reminded me of when we were young, when he had just brought home enough money to last us two months from selling his elixir. Those times seem far away now—now that we are raising a family—but for a moment, I must admit, it gave me a thrill. Still, I gently pushed his hands away and tried to stand, but he held me firm upon his lap.

Then he leaned in close and whispered very softly in my ear, his voice the merest brush of breath, "Next hand, go round and flirt a bit, get a look at their cards."

As I jerked away, his friends jeered, "Are you going to forfeit? Does the missus have you by the balls?" They laughed at their own searing wit.

John Henry joined in their laughter, though I could tell it was only for show, for it was a defensive sort of laugh. He relinquished me and I stood up, both missing the closeness of him and also glad to be on my own feet again instead of held like a child.

"John," I said. "I would like you to come home."

"See!" the men laughed.

"Lavinia," he said to me in that patronizing way he knows I so despise.

"Please come home," I implored. I held his gaze and tried to communicate my concern without words. When his eyes refused to take my meaning, I said, "It isn't safe to be out after dark."

"Then why have you come out?" he asked.

I told him I worry for him, and the other men guffawed. Now John Henry looked almost angry; he turned to me with affront and said, "You worry for me?" as if it ought to be the other way around.

"Please, John!" I said. "These men might pretend bravado, but they know as well as I do, there is something evil that comes out after dark."

Their laughter rose about me hideously, drowning out all else yet just another part of the audible landscape of the saloon.

"Helmuth, didn't you say what it was?" One man had turned to another beside him, a man with stringy blond hair, his nose ample and fleshly, his skin pocked with sores.

Once he spoke, I took him for a German fellow. The man who nudged him, however, had said this all with the kind of lightness of one merely joking.

Yet the German fellow looked dour; his laughter had not been as loud nor as jolly as the others, though he had laughed all the same. "The bogge-mann," he said in his accent, one of many I heard in the saloon, which rang with melodious Spanish, sophisticated French, vibrant Italian, and other manner of languages I could hardly decipher.

"You see, Lavinia," John Henry said to me, "it is a town legend, and a good one at that! This bogeyman comes round at night to drain the life from poor unfortunate souls, and that is why the bells are strung on all the doorways—to pay respect to this legend and appease the bogey!" He laughed, as if it were all in good fun.

I could hardly believe him. "And what of that young man? The one who died? Jeremiah Frost?"

"Bats," said another of the men, this one profoundly tall—the sort of man who would have to stoop through every doorway—and of sufficient chin beneath his growing beard. "Vampire bats. They live in the mine."

"Tragic," said John Henry, in such a way (oh, but I had half a mind to slap him!) that took none of it seriously at all. He raised his cup. "A toast. To Jeremiah Frost!"

They drank.

The room seemed to tilt about me. I found it difficult to breathe, a heavy weight settling into my chest—a familiar sort of weight. I recognized its terrible leadenness from just after Oscar was born. Yet I was not finished with John Henry. I asked him about the others, then: Rebecca and Otto? Margaret Blackburn?

The German fellow, Helmuth, glowered into his beer and shook his head even as the man beside him slapped his back in merriment, and they returned to their game, almost as if I hadn't spoken at all. "Tragedy," they said to themselves as they were dealt a new hand of cards.

Men must be the most foolhardy and single-minded lot. It is just like when John Henry would get it into his head that he could sell that damned elixir to all without consequence; by the end he even seemed half sure, himself, that it did work, after all! He'd touted its miracles so many times that even in private he spoke as if it were all true. I never knew if he was starting to believe it himself or if he thought that I believed it and was trying to keep me convinced.

It wasn't until the cold truth arose, until those he had sold to came after him, angry and demanding their money back, that his face turned pale and he lost the righteous vigor that had driven him forward, right up to the edge of destruction. By then, of course, it was too late, and we'd had to quickly make our plans to leave—and come here, to this dreadful place, where he has now regained that shine in his eye, that foolhardy belief in the promise of silver, willing to discredit all else.

I stood at his side, feeling quite useless. He dealt me hardly a glance, merely raising his brow, which seemed to suggest he still hoped I might go round and cheat for him. Instead, I remained rooted in place until he angrily folded, and then I begged him to come home with me. But all my begging, all my pleading, only served to make him more irate and ashamed of my behavior.

Eventually—I am somewhat ashamed now, myself—there had been tears in my eyes, and my voice had taken on a wheedling tone like a child's, and I had become so distraught that they tried to put a glass of whiskey in my hand to calm me down. I refused to take it, not wishing to dull my senses for the terrible walk through the dark back to our cabin. Yet now it is what I had feared: John Henry himself, and the rest of the men at the saloon, saw me as no more than a hysterical woman who must not be believed for all her foolish wailing. It upsets me so, I feel tears burning my eyes even now, but I cannot give in.

Why must I be so emotional? They would say it is in my nature, but my mother was the most stoic woman I have ever met. She brought me up to keep hold of myself, never to give an inch of my sorrow away. But I have been weak. All I have ever wanted is to be like her—like that clever, haughty woman always in control, with never a single hair out of place. Yet I will never be like her. She was ashamed of my weakness after Oscar was born, and she would be ashamed of my weakness now.

At the very least, my own hysterics eventually convinced John Henry to take me by the arm and lead me home, his hard grip communicating his disappointment and anger all the way there. Once inside, though, and safely out of the dark, I sank onto a chair, feeling faint with the effects of dread, and John Henry grew softer, as he sometimes does when we are alone. He made me a cup of tea and sat beside me in stony silence until I drank it all down.

The children were nearby, quiet as lambs. I gave Sophronia a thin smile to show my appreciation of what a big girl she has become, watching her brother all on her own. At long last, in the quiet closeness of our home, a somnolent calm came over us all. The children crawled into their beds and closed their eyes.

"I will not abide such behavior again," John Henry said to me. "You're smarter than this. You know our reputation here has not yet been settled. This could ruin Virgil for us." He shook his head. His voice was soft and low but firm. "You cannot let your emotions overcome you—you know what will happen if you do."

"I know," I murmured.

He reached out and took my hand in his. "There is a devil inside you that would see you suffer needlessly. If you need to rest, then rest. If you need to pray, then pray. I cannot bear to lose you to this darkness."

He let go of my hand and stood up, loosening the buttons of his shirt. My throat felt tight, as if a ball were wedged inside of it preventing me from speaking. With all my heart I wanted him to take me in his arms and hold me. I felt my love for him unspool from my chest, large as a warm blanket. And I was thinking, just in that moment, that I too would undress and go to bed with him, where we could hold each other close, but he had to speak once more.

"Besides," he said without even looking at me as he removed his shirt and started on the laces of his boots, "my brother is not here to pick up the pieces this time."

He went to bed without another word.

October 2, 1869

Very early this morning, before the sun crept over the desert's fine edge, I heard a musical tinkling. At first, I drifted slowly out of sleep, unable to identify whether the sound was only in my dreams. Then all at once I came fully awake, my heart leaping into my throat with the realization that the bell above our door was ringing.

The cabin was dark, and I slid out of bed in a panic. I stumbled into a chair, nearly falling over myself; with all the shambling slowness of a fool,

I grasped around in the dark for a candle and a match, and it took two tries to light the wick. It all seemed to take so long, I thought for sure an intruder would have had all the time in the world to come slit my throat or drain the blood from my body. And though I am ashamed now to admit it, my mind did alight on the notion that it was the Strange Lady, and she was stealing inside to prick our feet, or worse.

These wild notions set my hands trembling, but when I lifted the candle to see—why, it was only Oscar standing beside the door, a mischievous smile on his face! The candlelight caught the gleam of his eye as he scampered back to bed.

He has taken to jingling the bell at odd hours, that little devil, but never in the middle of the night like this. I admonished the boy that he was not allowed to do that, keeping my voice low so as not to wake the others.

He threw the covers over his head and his muffled voice emerged: "It wasn't me. It was Charles."

That was it.

The little devil thought he could get away with mischief by blaming it on Charles—on the child who couldn't be disciplined. I pulled his blanket down so roughly his hair stood up in fine disheveled strands. Surprise stood out on his face. We gazed at one another for some long moments, and then I smoothed his downy hair.

I could hardly explain to him what I find difficult to articulate for myself. The terror for the fragility of their tiny bodies—their skin so soft and tender, their bones as thin as twigs, the way their thin chests rise and fall in sleep. The question of what my other son would look like now, had he ever had a chance to grow, had he not died from the sickness of my own womb—and the knowledge that I will never be good enough, even if I have six more children, that Charles will still be the one who never was, came to mind. How could I explain to him that there are strange and mysterious things in this world that we do not understand, and if the bell rings in the night, it might mean that we will be killed and bled dry by one of those strange and mysterious things?

So this is what I said: "Please tell Charles that if he rings that bell again, his dear brother will be punished. I'm sure he wouldn't want that to happen, would he?"

Oscar shook his head. He went back to sleep at once, but I remained wide awake, so here I sit, watching the bell hang in silent stillness.

Later

I must tell you another thing that happened today, Diary.

I did not do the shopping yesterday, so I went into town today instead, and I brought myself to look up from Main Street and identify the hangman's tree on which Willie Ray Randall had strung up poor Emery. It is a tall but pitiful thing, with broad branches that have been sawed off and deprived of leaf and proper growth; the bark is pale and knotted, and you can see precisely which overhanging branch must have been used for the hanging, although thankfully now there is no noose tied to it. I stood and looked at that tree for some time, trying to imagine all the folks I have met here in Virgil standing around, cheering on as Emery's neck broke, or if not, as he dangled there choking to death. I cannot imagine but that Willie Ray Randall was exaggerating somewhat. The people in this town are not animals. Surely most of them would have opposed his actions, tried to stop him, but Mr. Randall, so intent on his murderous mission, must have imagined that all were on his side. It was a long while before I was able to take my eyes from that skeletal tree.

As I returned down the dusty road with a sack of flour (which I hope is not infested with weevils, as the last batch), I passed the Chester Blackburn residence as I always do, and there was Olive, leaning on a long gun as if it were a walking stick. Her dark hair was uncovered and flying free in twisting, ragged threads; a smudge of dirt marred her forehead, and her eyes bore into me. The wind nipped at her well-worn dress no longer white, clinging barely to her bony frame.

She watched me as I passed and said, "Heard you went to see my Willie Ray."

I did not pause but kept steadily on, and she moved to block my way, lifting the gun to carry with her although not pointing it at me. I was forced to stop, but I refused to speak.

"You're just like him," she said. "A meddler. Always meddling in others' affairs."

I bristled at that. "He told me what he did to Emery."

She leaned in closer, and I could smell the staleness of her breath when she spoke.

"Emery Cain deserved every bit of it. Willie Ray only did what everyone else was thinking, and they all went right along with it, didn't they? This whole damned town went savage, calling for his blood. They all wanted to see it done. Only now they think themselves so civilized. You want someone to blame? You'd best blame everyone." She took a step back though still did not move aside to allow me to pass. Her gun leaned ominously against her shoulder. "Stop your meddling. That's what got us into all this. Don't you go seeing my husband again, or I'll have something to say about it."

I looked at the gun, which rested significantly where it lay, and I took her meaning. Why Olive should hold such animosity toward me, I hadn't understood, but I suppose it must be my connection to Emery—she seems to blame him for her husband's incarceration, as if it were his own fault for being murdered!

Still carrying that bag of flour like a babe in my arms, I shifted to keep it from slipping, and I admit, I found myself becoming angry. Though at the time I hadn't identified exactly where her animosity came from, I felt it was unjustified.

"You're in my way," I said. "Who's meddling now?"

The scowl that came over her face! At last she moved out of my way, and I was free to continue. It was all I could do not to turn back when I'd made it a significant distance, just to see if she was still standing there, watching me, with that gun at her side.

This town is filled with devils. I see now how it has hardened Olive, and how it will have to harden me too.

October 5, 1869

Thankfully, Olive has left me quite alone since our confrontation.

I have been working with Sophronia on her stitching, which is coming along quite nicely (I think someday her skills shall surpass mine).

I've also gotten a letter back from my sister, Emma, which lifted my spirits considerably. It was so lovely to see her small, neat handwriting filling the page with news of Boston and of her children. I read that letter three times before I could put it down. How dearly I miss her.

What is there to say? Perhaps all the ugliness is behind us now. Yes, I cannot quite forget the horrible thing that happened to Emery, but after all, the man responsible is rotting in jail, exactly where he belongs. The mystery is solved. Willie Ray Randall is paying for his awful deed. What more should I want? Even John Henry seems satisfied. Perhaps, in time, he will grieve, but he exhausts himself daily in his work so that I think he has become quite numb.

No one else has perished. The bells remain quiet and still in the night. Olive has kept her distance from me. A bad start, but that is ended; yes, perhaps now all will be well.

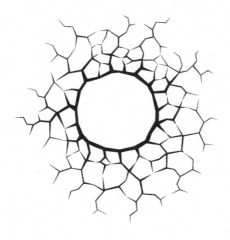

THE DUST DEVILS

"I THINK IT'S READY," SAID MADS.

Waynoka looked up. The water must be cool by now. Mads lifted the pot to her lips and took a brazenly large sip, paused to swallow, then thirstily tipped it again so she could drink with abandon.

Waynoka shuffled forward on her knees as Mads tipped it toward her, and she caught it with her hands and her tongue, which was met by lukewarm water with a fetid smell and a bitter, metallic taste. The complaint of her taste buds almost made her spit it out, but thirst won handily, and she swallowed, pausing only to gulp in air.

They passed the pot back and forth until it was half empty, each pass slower than the last, until it ended up sitting between them while they stretched out their legs on the cave floor and fell into an almost hypnotic trance at the relief of liquid in their dust-ravaged throats.

"Oh my *God* is that good," said Mads.

It was only after drinking that Waynoka fully understood just how bad off they had been. It was not the kind of thirst that occurs after a few hours

in the heat, leaving the mouth and throat parched; it was not even the kind
of thirst after more than a day, and the dizziness, the lack of stamina; it was
that period of thirst close enough to reach out and touch death, just before
the organs begin to shut down, when all the world is a funhouse and your
feet seem oddly distanced from your head—when lying down to close your
eyes might draw you away into a deeper darkness from whose boundary no
traveler returns.

What a miracle was water, in a drought-ravaged place. Something unspoiled and cool in a warming world choking on its own pollution. Waynoka marveled at the idea of an endless source of potable water so close by.
It did not require a trek of unknown length and rationing bare sips once a
day; all it required was a trip back and forth to the sump, and time to boil
and cool. Only that, and they would have as much water as they could drink.

They lounged with their backs against the makeshift bed. The fire was
pleasantly low, so the air was not as smoky just now, and it cast a warm,
gentle glow over the little chamber.

Waynoka felt her stomach churn, and she had to physically push herself away from the pot to stop drinking the water, which now roiled and
sloshed inside of her.

"Don't drink too fast or you'll puke," said Mads.

Holding a hand over her mouth to force down the nausea, Waynoka
waited until it passed. She leaned back again with a sigh. "Still worth it."

"Luck is on our side, my friend," said Mads. "We've got water. We've
got fire. And you've got your little pioneer friend in that book to tell us more
about this place."

Waynoka didn't want to admit how little the book actually said about
navigating the mine, not when Mads looked so satisfied. Instead she nodded, telling herself she just hadn't gotten there, that Lavinia would enter the
mine yet. She was very meticulous and detailed in her writing. She would
eventually describe the mine. And hopefully reveal the way out.

For the moment, Waynoka felt safe in this little room with Mads. But
as the water dwindled, her thoughts drifted closer to that lonely trek to the

sump, and then carrying the pot of water all the way back here. On her own. In the dark. With whatever it was that existed down here in these tunnels. She tried to make the water last.

⬚

IT DIDN'T LAST FOREVER THOUGH.

And soon, they found it would no longer last in their bodies either. The urgency of their bladders, a feeling that had until then grown numb and distant, hit them with such force that they bumped into each other as they quickly decided the best place to relieve themselves, found a little nook a few paces down the tunnel with the bell over the entrance, and urinated. When it was done, Mads swayed, trying to keep her balance, and Waynoka had to grab her and help her pull her pants back up.

One arm around her partner's shoulders, Waynoka felt her way back in the dark as the embers popped and lowered. The flashlight changed that, but rather than diffusing a soft glow throughout the air as the fire had, it merely cut a beam of light through webs of stifling darkness.

"I wonder if your pioneer friend ever walked from here to the sump," said Mads. "She write about it?"

Waynoka shook her head. "Not yet."

Mads lay down on the bed. Her eyes drifted closed. "Well, you let me know if she does."

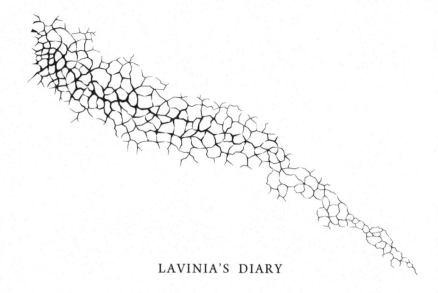

LAVINIA'S DIARY

October 6, 1869

I knew that John Henry would come round.

While rummaging for his tobacco, he came upon that photograph I had found, of Emery and the other miners. I was kneading hardtack dough and watching him from the corner of my eye, trying not to let on that I had seen him lift the photograph to his eyes and pause like that, his back slightly hunched.

It was a long moment—I must have turned the dough four or five times before he spoke—but at last he said, very quietly, "He is dead, then."

"I believe so," I said as I folded and pressed the dough.

He finally put down the photograph. "Well, that is that."

"I don't believe he ever had a proper funeral," I told him. And I started to say something like, "Wouldn't you like to—" or, "Shall we consider—" but he cut me off as soon as I began to speak.

"Who would come? What's done is done. I expect he's buried now in boot hill, just as likely unmarked, although they well and good know his name. If I should find where he is, I will make a marker myself. He deserves at least that much." He looked up and his eyes met mine, and I could see the anger that he uses as a cloak over his anguish. "Willie Ray Randall, you say?"

I nodded.

He said nothing more to the matter, but in a little while, he came up behind me and enfolded me against his body. At first I was annoyed, as I hadn't quite finished kneading the dough, but then I let myself be taken in his arms. He held me tightly.

"Forgive me," he said softly in my ear. "I have behaved like an absolute brute these last weeks. This mining business is a beast. I should much rather prefer to make my fortune with my powers of persuasion than with my arms."

I could tell, as he held me, how much harder and more tightly muscled his arms have become from all his toil.

"Mining is honest work," I said, and bit my tongue before saying anything more.

He said nothing either, though his arms grew stiff around me. *Stupid Lavinia*, I thought then, *putting your foot in your mouth as you always do.* I know just as well as he does that he is not cut from the same cloth as miners. His constitution isn't one for such work, although he holds himself well, and there is a certain robustness to his nature. He tries not to let me hear him coughing, but I do, most every night.

"It's savage work," he said at last, not a little bitterness to his voice.

What is a man to do who is clever as they come but has had only a meager education? He was made for a life that he was not born to, and that, I think, makes him bitterer than anything.

"In any case," he continued more lightly, letting me go to pace away as I continued at my dough, "once I have my prize, I will not need to engage in such brutish work. We will be gone from here. Someplace green, perhaps. I think I may have identified just the spot most likely to bear untold treasures. Fools and their superstitions shall soon be parted from these riches."

He went away from me then, but now that I have time to sit and think on it, I cannot help but wonder—fools and their superstitions? Where is it he plans to excavate in that mine?

It is only when I am writing that I have time to think things over. At the time I was busy enough that his words flitted into and out of my head. After all, I had to resume my work to finish making extra hardtack for the winter, lest we find ourselves hard up and starving. The cold months are coming on, and there is much to prepare for the challenges that will be upon us in this remote environment. More candles must be made, as ours have near burnt themselves to nothing; more food must be preserved; there is butter and soap to make; the sheep must be sheared for wool, and then I shall commence sewing new trousers for Oscar who has quite grown out of his.

But none of that—this writing ought to be my leisure, not another reminder of my labor. Enough!

October 11, 1869

It has been days since I've seen another soul, apart from my own family. There is an emptiness that calls across the wildlands. You can hear it on the wind. One might almost forget there is a whole town here, how sparse its inhabitants remain. It is almost as if the land itself is haunted. No, I ought to scratch that out—but there, it has already been written down. My eyes deceive me sometimes, for again in the night . . .

If any place should be haunted, I thought it must be some old European castle with its crumbling turrets, like one reads about in novels. Not here, in the new land, the new frontier. Of course, we are not the first ones here, are we? The natives have lived here for how long, who can say? And who before even them? One thinks of this place as having no history of its own, a pristine wilderness, but that is not true. Just because there are no old castles here does not mean the land has not seen a thousand years of life and death . . . And perhaps it is all the more unsettling because we do not know what was here before us, because there are no structures to inform us of religions that have come and gone, no abbeys, no ancient ruins—there is only the land and its great unbroken silence, unwilling to share its secrets. The great empty wild: that is the most haunted place of all, haunted by beings of whom we have no knowledge or understanding. Haunted by virtue of its seeming emptiness.

My mother would disapprove of such ideations, but so be it! This is my diary, and I will write what I like. I am not some fanciful girl reading novels and getting carried away with notions of ghosts and grand romances. What I believe are the things that I see with my own two eyes.

And this is why, when in the night I glimpsed a figure moving through the emptiness of that land in the moonlight, like a person grown stiff, one whose limbs move as if locked at the joints—my heart almost leapt straight from my body! When I looked again, I could not find the creature, but shortly thereafter, as I continued to strain my eyes on the black horizon, I heard that most distant musical sound of a bell echoing in the vast reaches of the desert . . .

And did my ears deceive me? For nothing came of it, after all. I would have heard if something had happened. Wouldn't I?

October 13, 1869

My doubt must now go find a dark little hole in which to hide itself away. Perhaps he was right after all, and I was believing all the wrong things, when I should have been believing him—but now believe him I must, for I have seen the silver nugget with my own two eyes, and I have felt its weight in my hand!

When he presented it to me, he looked just like the cat that has caught the canary—there was that self-satisfied smile on his face that he used to get after a particularly good day of business, the one so pleased with himself it is almost bursting free. And as he allowed me to hold the cold rock and marvel at its mysterious shine, he told me there was more where he had found it.

"Took me some time to wrangle this little nugget free," he told me as he took it back and tucked it away in a handkerchief. "I think I may be able to chip away three or four more of almost this size before anyone is the wiser."

"What will you do with it?" I asked him. "Won't they know you've taken it?"

How pleased he was as he took my hand and squeezed it in his own! "Don't worry. I will take the raw nuggets to the nearest town, where no one will know where they came from, and I will be able to exchange them for more money than we have seen in all our lives."

My heart swelled with joy. I must admit I did not truly expect John Henry's promises to come to fruition, and I thanked the Lord for, at long last, after much suffering and hardship, rewarding our efforts. This is a happy day. I should have known the Lord was smiling on us when I beheld at dusk the most wondrous sunset: a cascade of jubilant magenta and orange, layered in lusty streaks like a painting—and these shades the more pronounced for the wideness of the sky and the simplicity of the land shadowed beneath. The sight brought to me a profound sense of peace and tranquility, as if in witnessing His majesty I held Communion with all of Creation.

October 14, 1869

They say it never rains but it pours, but perhaps the opposite is also true: when the sun smiles upon you, it offers a dozen splendid smiles. For even after beholding the silver nugget, and reconciling with it my former cynicism, I still never imagined he would bring home a second silver nugget—which he has!

I begin to imagine what lies before us: windows with glass in them; fancy shawls that have not grown threadbare. We will travel somewhere new by locomotive, and in the dining car we will feast on roast turkey with cranberry sauce, or lamb with mint, and on other such delicious morsels. The children will have new shoes and their own bedrooms with beautiful four-poster beds.

For this second nugget's significance lies in more than its worth and weight. John Henry had told me that once he had found his fortune, we might leave this place for greener pastures. I reminded him and suggested we might begin to think of where we should like to go.

John Henry only guffawed and directly dismissed the idea: "Leave? When there are so many more riches waiting to be plucked from the earth right here? As long as no one is aware of my taking a bit extra for my trouble, why should we leave? There will be more for us if we stay."

I must not allow my joy to be twisted up in misery. Yet this is what happened in Boston, isn't it? He kept taking and taking, until finally we had no choice but to leave. And I fear now the same will happen here. I fear ours is an ill-gotten joy, and like the Strange Lady herself, John Henry's is a thirst that shall never be slaked.

October 15, 1869

Can it be that good fortune is always met swiftly by tragedy?

Another death—and it is altogether too awful to think—for who should the victim be this time—but an innocent child!

Worse, worse—unlike with Jeremiah Frost, whose death I only heard of, this time I saw the body, and it was even more horrible that I could have imagined. I saw the tiny puncture wounds scattered all across the flesh like stars across the night sky; I saw the bloodless white of that selfsame flesh; I saw the cadaverous skull, withered as if aged beyond its meager years, teeth showing in a rictus of death.

Horrible! Horrible!

After our own little celebration last night, John Henry and I fell hard to our beds and slept deeply, until I awoke with the sun and set off to town for sugar, salt pork, and coffee. John Henry and the children remained abed, as it was quite early yet, and I hoped to return home before they awoke, but I was halted by Mary Warrant and a small search party sweeping through town. Her son Peter was missing. He was a disobedient boy who liked to sneak out at night with his father's gun, and they discovered that he had done so again, only this time he had not returned.

They called his name as they searched—Mrs. Warrant and her husband, along with Josephine and Cecil Pavlovsky, and several miners who worked under Mr. Warrant. I offered to help look, and we conducted ourselves down Main Street, passed the horrid hanging tree, and there we split down several paths to widen the search.

All along we called and called his name, and though our voices were nearly drowned by the wind itself, I was sure if he were hereabouts, he would hear us and respond. Yet we kept up calling and calling as we went. I found myself together with Mrs. Pavlovsky near the post office, and as I came around and looked to the stable that lay just behind the building, I noticed something peculiar—a foot protruding from the stable's opening, as if someone had lain down just inside the cool shade and fallen asleep there.

I knew at once this was not the case, and a dreadful foreboding filled me as I stared at that still foot, which, as I looked, I ascertained could only belong to a youth. I ought to have called out to Josephine nearby or to the others farther along, but my voice was restrained by a thickness in my throat, and I could hardly croak out the barest sound.

Knowing that I had to see for myself who that foot belonged to, I approached the stable, my own feet carrying me with trembling slowness as if my body could tell I did not, truly, want to see what lay within that structure. Yet continue I did, and there, upon the floor of the stable, limbs strewn about the hay, lay the poorest creature I have ever seen. A boy of no more than fourteen, dead, flesh white, pocked with innumerable tiny holes as if stung a thousand times by a thousand deadly hornets!

I might have cried out at the sight—I cannot say whether I voiced my distress, as the moment sent all feeling rushing from my body with the horror before me—but I know that when I dared pull my eyes from the tragic sight, I became aware of an odd silence and stillness within the stable, where there ought to have been the postal service's horses. In spite of the sick fear coursing through me, I stepped farther inside to peer into each one of the stalls and see what had become of the horses.

Dead! All dead!

And in the same disturbing and unexplainable manner as the child—covered in small puncture wounds. Their black glassy eyes stared through the walls, unseeing.

How I managed to stumble out of that scene of death and how I managed to come across the rest of the search party escapes my memory; all that remains is a blur of awful feelings that threatened to consume me. Yet I did gain their attention and led them to the stable, which the postal operator had not even come by to check on yet this morning, and the men went in to see while Josephine and I clutched at each other, and while Mr. Warrant held his wife, whose screams and sobs choked the air as she strained against him to see her son.

They found the gun nearby, and a bullet hole in the stable wall, though what the boy had been shooting at remains a mystery. His presence here, too, remains a mystery. Perhaps he was sneaking into the stable to steal a horse and go for a midnight ride. Just before I left to hurry home and inform John Henry of the fresh horror that had befallen Virgil, Doctor Hartsworth came to examine the body. I nearly scoffed at the sight of him, remembering what Mr. Branson had told me of how he had learned his trade from Indians. What sort of witchcraft had he learned? Did the others know? I wondered.

I left Josephine who went to join Mr. Warrant in consoling poor Mary, and just before I found myself steady enough to walk, I heard the doctor speaking with the men of the search party. He held in his hand a most peculiar object, which he claimed to have found embedded within the flesh of the dead boy: some sort of spine, perhaps five inches long, almost like one may find protruding from a cactus.

October 17, 1869

This morning's church service was a funeral for the Warrant boy. Yesterday the coffin was built, and the Warrants saw visitors in their home, though poor Mary spent her time dabbing hopelessly at her streaming eyes under a veil and was too inconsolable to make a coherent utterance.

When I returned home on Friday morning without any of the goods I had gone to purchase, John Henry and the children were up. He was showing them a silver nugget, which each wanted to pass back and forth to the other, and he was explaining to them the process of removing it from the mine. When he looked up over their heads to see me entering, he knew at once that something terrible had happened, for he stood immediately to see me to a chair and sit, and he put before me a flask of whiskey which I ordinarily would push away but, in that moment, took gratefully and sipped until I had recovered myself somewhat.

Then I told what had happened, with as little detail as possible—I saved those gruesome details to write here instead. John Henry had to go to the mine, but I decided to keep the children home with me, to keep them close. Sophie and Oscar read quietly from the Bible while I sat down to put to paper what I had seen, and then I did something I never do, which is lie back down in bed and sleep again until the morning was through.

All that day passed as if in a dream.

When John Henry came home, the children peppered him with questions while I cooked supper. "Is he in Heaven?" asked Sophie, and, "Is he with Charles?" asked Oscar. "Yes, to both," said John Henry. "But why is he dead?" asked Oscar, and, "How did he die?" asked Sophie. John Henry said it was a tragic accident, and they must never disobey us, for we will protect them from such things, yet we cannot protect them if they disobey us the way Peter Warrant disobeyed his own parents. Then Sophie, clever little Sophie, said, "What about the bell on the door? Didn't they hear him leave?" I did not hear what John Henry said, but I pondered the question, thinking the child must have crept out the window or exercised some manner of caution so that he would not be caught—and yet, if only his parents had caught him, indeed!

It might have saved his life.

This morning we attended the service, where they had the boy's body laid out so beautifully in his coffin, and he wore sleeves so that his wounded flesh would be covered, and the only bit of him one could see was his face, which had been smeared with some sort of cream to hide the worst of its unsightly wounds.

Sunlight streamed in through the church's windows, lighting dust motes that danced across my vision, and our singing carried up to the Heavens on angels' wings, yet the air was heavy with mourning. As the minister commanded the boy's soul to God, I sat in that rough pew trying to listen while my mind whirled away to the horrible image of his body before he had been dressed and laid in his coffin; and as I sat trying to focus on the minister's beautiful words, I could not help but allow my attention to be torn in twain, listening also to the men murmuring quietly in the pew behind us.

At another time I might have turned around to shush them, but as it was, I remained frozen in my state of horror and grief. Behind me came the voices of two men—miners, without doubt—talking in such conspiring whispers that I could not help but try to make them out.

One was saying that "something must be done." The other countered him by suggesting that "what was let out was let out" and "we can't well put it back, can we?" Then the first came back with something about putting a lid back on the bottle, closing it off for good, even if no one else will do it. "We will do it ourselves," he said with some conviction, "at the very first chance. We cannot allow this to continue, not for a moment longer."

I wondered what these men were planning to do. Could they really put a stop to these deaths? Wasn't that what Willie Ray Randall tried to do? A chill ran through me.

When I looked to John Henry to see how he'd reacted to this murmuring, I saw only his eyes closed and his hands clasped in prayer, and I saw him nodding along with the minister's words, enraptured by the persuasive appeals of a righteous sermon—and I thought, then, how similar his own speeches are to that of a clergyman, except of course with altogether different content, but the compelling tone of voice and eagerness have such strong similarities that I realized in that moment why John Henry becomes so engrossed in a good sermon whereas I find my own attention wandering to every little distraction. I let him be as he listened, and I tried to listen too, to put my attention where his was, and to forget the men behind us, whose business was obscure to me anyway. And if the men behind us were planning on trying to stop these horrible deaths from occurring, then I wish them all the luck.

We followed the procession to the cemetery, a small plot of land with several markers carved with dates and names, and to the grave, which had been dug yesterday evening.

While the coffin was lowered and Mary threw the first handful of dirt down over it, my eyes wandered over the headstones to see what manner of death has plagued this town. Here I found several names I recognized from those I knew had been killed in the same manner as the Warrant boy, and as Jeremiah Frost; and I saw another name I did not recognize, someone who had died of ague, and I continued observing each marker as the crowd began to disperse.

At last I came upon a very crude wooden marker with hasty, near illegible carvings on it, as if the one who made it did not want it to be read or did not care whether it ever would be. It was the marker, surely, of someone who would not be missed, or who had no family to mourn him.

Indeed, when I bent down to examine the words more closely, which declared this year of eighteen hundred and sixty-nine as the year of death, I saw that above this year it bore the name: E. CAIN.

I called John Henry over to see, and he stood for some minutes staring at the grave. The children came over as well, and Sophie asked if Uncle Emery was dead too. I could only tell them yes. Oscar asked why some people were dead and some were alive, and I found I could not answer, but Sophronia leapt in to say, "Everyone is alive first before they're dead. They're all just ahead of us. Someday we'll be dead too."

The answer sent a chill through me, coming through her rosy child's lips, chapped by the wind, as if they brought another pall of death over us— and here we all were, only waiting our turn.

What dreadful times. I had almost forgotten about John Henry's two nuggets of silver until we were home again, exhausted from the lengthy service even though all we had done was sit and kneel, sit and kneel. I brought out the Bible for the children's reading while John Henry took out a silver nugget and moved it from one hand to the other, as if holding it reminded him that it was real, that it was ours. He took it with him outside to smoke, and it bulged in his front pocket as we sat down to supper. Perhaps he finds it a comfort.

I cannot begrudge him this token of joy, in such dark times. The nugget of silver reminds us of what we have, and what we may yet gain. To-morrow he will return to the mine to bring home more silver, yet a part of me wishes he would stay with us and take us far from here.

October 18, 1869

Everyone is alive before they are dead—that is what my dear Sophie said. And she was right. He is ahead of me now, hopelessly ahead of me, forever.

Oh, he is dead. He is dead. He is dead. John Henry is dead!

Let me die too!

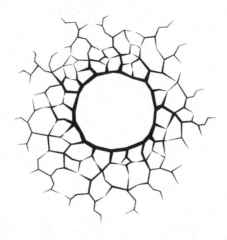

THE DUST DEVILS

"**N**o!"

"What?"

Waynoka closed the book with a measure of embarrassment. What would Mads think if she knew her partner had gotten so emotionally caught up with the story unfolding across those brittle pages? It was almost as if Waynoka and Mads were living two different experiences, both branching off from this central shared reality: one entirely present in the mine, in its dark confines, and tuned into the present through pain; the other only half there, half seeing a different world through Lavinia's eyes and living her life through her words.

"Sorry." Waynoka glanced down at the diary, which sat closed on top of the rucksack. "It's just—Lavinia's husband just died. I mean, he was kind of a snake, but . . . still."

"Oh, that's a shame," Mads said with a degree of lightness that nearly stung Waynoka. "But by *just died* I think you mean, like, two hundred years ago. How did he die?"

That gave Waynoka pause. "No idea."

"Okay," said Mads. "What do you think? We finished off the first pot. Should we fill another, get it boiling?"

Waynoka nodded slowly, remembering she would have to face that walk alone. Even though she knew she needed to get them more water, a part of her wanted to stall. The dark of this little room with Mads was so much better than the dark of that long, narrow tunnel.

She felt oddly fuzzy. Coming out of the story and back into the cave was like wading in from a dream. The flashlight hit the craggy walls in sharp relief. Somehow both the light and the dark were worse than the diffusion of sunlight or moonlight on the earth above.

As she looked around, she noticed more details: the rough-hewn walls, the way the tunnel expanded and contracted in size, like an esophagus. The question popped from her mouth in a burst of panic: "Are we in a cave?"

Mads gave her a bemused look. "Pretty sure it's a mine."

"I mean—have we entered a natural cave that was connected to the mine? Or is this still the actual mine that was carved out?"

"Hmm." Mads looked around critically. "Well, there was that patched-up mine shaft where you almost fell to your death."

The memory made her stomach jolt the way it had when her foot had slipped through into the void below. "Thanks, I'd almost forgotten." The flashlight's beam lit up a jagged roof of gray stone and walls the same. Trying to shake off the grip of dread, Waynoka released a slow, measured breath. "I'm starting to think they were right about this place being cursed."

"If this place were really cursed," said Mads, "do you think we'd have been so lucky to have found water?" She handed the empty pot to Waynoka. "I'll have the fire stoked by the time you get back."

Waynoka looked at her. In the flashlight's unforgiving glare, she looked wan and ill, with unhealthy blotches of red rising in her cheeks.

"Let's check your bandages first," said Waynoka. Worried about infection, she bent down to carefully unpeel the rags. Mads hissed as the last sticky layer came away.

The knee was black and bulbous, making strange terrain of her flesh; blood and pus had dried into a putrid cast. Waynoka wet one of the rags with the remaining dregs of water in the pot and tried to wipe away the crustier portions to see the wound beneath, but as she did a scream ripped from Mads's throat.

She passed one of the rags over. "Here. Bite it."

Mads stuffed the rag in her mouth and bit down.

Now there were only muffled groans as Waynoka worked, trying to be gentle yet needing to exert enough pressure to clear away the dried blood. By the time the wound beneath appeared, Mads was sweating and panting through the rag, her head leaned back, her eyes wide, rolling, delirious.

The dented part of the knee caved in on itself and gaped open where shards of bone protruded like teeth. The rest was bruised and unnaturally spongy.

Suddenly lightheaded, Waynoka looked away and breathed slowly. "It's not so bad," she said as she started wrapping it tightly in fresh strips of cloth that she mined from the bed. "It's really not that bad."

Spitting out the rag, Mads leaned over and vomited a thin yellowish bile, followed by hiccups and a sort of wretched sobbing.

"We just need to let it heal," Waynoka found herself babbling as she finished tying the cloth. "I'll get more water. You rest."

Flat on the bed, her eyes pinched shut, Mads said nothing.

Before she left, Waynoka stoked the fire. Then she picked up the pot in one hand, flashlight in the other, and turned to the doorway where the bell winked in her pale beam.

"I'll be back soon," she said, and started down the tunnel.

※

THE TREK BACK TO the sump felt interminable. Waynoka tried to keep her focus on her feet so as not to stumble over the uneven ground, and on the way ahead so as not to crack her skull open if the ceiling lowered. This was good, because it kept her attention on navigating the tunnel, which was the only thing that mattered right now, and not on how Mads would go on with her gruesome injury or on the figure who had emerged from the sump ahead of her.

As she passed a branching tunnel—barely a tunnel, barely wide enough, she thought it was the one she had seen last time she'd come this way—she froze. It was cold here. Was that movement, the barest breath of air against her skin? She couldn't tell if it was the lightest of breezes or her imagination wanting it to be a breeze, wanting to turn and find a tunnel open to the outside. She waited there, begging her skin to confirm what she thought she had felt, the feeling so mild, however, that she couldn't be sure.

The beam of light crept around the jumble of rocks and disappeared into the small recess. She could not tell what lay within—another tunnel? Only darkness deep enough to swallow her light. She tried desperately to feel a more definitive breeze. It was maddening not to know. What if this led to a way out?

She considered taking a few steps into it but thought once she found where it was leading, she would want to keep going. She would keep going and going, and Mads would be waiting for her. Even the thought of it sent a sick feeling into her throat.

Then another thought hit her. What if it wasn't another tunnel, but . . . a chamber?

She had to fix her grip on the pot where her palm had grown clammy.

No. It was not the burial chamber Emery Cain had found.

She turned and continued to the sump, trying to push the haunting thought from her mind.

As she lowered the pot into the dark water, the flashlight balanced in her lap, she wondered where the sump led. It was clear that the tunnel dipped lower here and became fully submerged at the far end of this pool—but what if it continued beyond? Where did it go? Could she swim it? Sure—and drown, enclosed by a world of solid rock. They might have died for lack of water; ironic, then, to die from too much.

She set aside the full pot and shined the light on the water anyway, but it was too dark for the light to penetrate whatever mysteries lay beneath. Her beam moved over the surface like strange moonlight. The murk returned a dull greenish reflection.

The flashlight was waterproof, though.

Could she risk it? If it wasn't quite as waterproof as it should be, what if it shorted out and left her stranded here in pitch darkness? Could she find her way back to Mads without a light?

On the other hand, what if the tunnel emerged from the water and led to a way out, just on the other side of this rock? An open stream, maybe—a river in the desert?

Could that be possible?

She had to at least try.

Taking off her shoes, Waynoka waded into the water. Its coldness made her gasp as it climbed up to her waist. As the ceiling lowered, the water deepened; cranking the flashlight again just be to be safe, she took a deep breath and dove.

The light filtered through water made cloudy by her disturbance, but she couldn't wait for it to settle. Blinking away the sting of dirty water in her eyes, particulate matter floating like dust in the beam, she swam until she saw the way forward—the tunnel continuing into darkness. She would just go a little way, then turn back. It was all her lungs could manage.

The muffled burbles of her movements punctuated the water's thick silence. With each stroke, she urged herself on just a little farther. Her lungs began to ache, but not enough to turn around, not just yet. As she went forward, she kept reaching her free hand up to the rocky ceiling, guiding her. If she got lost and couldn't find the way back—

She was reaching that critical moment, her lungs urging her to turn back, when the rock disappeared, and her fingertips met open air.

She pushed forward and burst up, surfacing from the water with a huge inhale. The flashlight had survived the swim. It zigged and zagged as she waved it around this new space.

It was wider than the tunnel. To the side of the sump, there was a dry patch of rock that she was able to climb up onto as she caught her breath.

But this little patch of rock wasn't empty.

What she found here was dry, which told her it had either been here long enough to dry out after a swim, or that the passageway hadn't always been submerged. That might explain why the walls here were slightly blackened with old soot.

It did not, however, explain the rotting doll, woven together with wood and hay, with nails sticking out of its head; nor did it explain the pile of tiny bones, as if from some small, winged creature; or the little collection of rusty bells nestled in a very old woven blanket, or the corroded lantern that lay on its side, shattered, almost fused with the rock.

Least of all did it explain the writing on the wall, in that same red ochre as the stick figure in their room, that read, SECRET HOLLOW.

Waynoka moved her flashlight over these strange tokens, a hideous fear rising in her. She didn't want to touch any of these things. Who did they belong to? What if their owner came back?

The secret hollow instilled her with dread.

Someone had been down here—even here, in this deep, impossibly remote enclave. The idea that someone had been living here seemed unnatural. People did not belong here, not this far below the earth. Not in this impenetrable, enclosed darkness.

She looked at the water, which seemed to continue ahead, though the tunnel lowered and submerged again in its icy depths. Who knew how far it went?

The cool air drying her wet skin made her shiver. She thought about trying to swim a little farther but wondered what other secret hollows may lie deeper in this cave system. She didn't want to find out.

Her skin crawled. This wasn't just spiders on the ceiling.

Someone had been down here. Might still be down here.

Without hesitation, she slid into the water and swam back the way she'd come. Dragging herself out of the sump, she took a moment to lie there clutching the flashlight, resolving not to tell Mads anything of the secret hollow. Somehow, it was too horrible to recount—especially the totem with nails in its head—and she didn't know what it meant. Mads didn't need to know.

She needed to heal.

Still, she was trembling as she picked up the pot full of water, and she had to refill it again after she'd taken two steps and spilled half of it. She just needed to make it back to the room with the fire, with Mads.

Wedging the flashlight into her armpit, she set off back the way she'd come as quickly as she could while holding the pot steady, her eyes on the warbling water, filled so high it threatened to spill over with every step.

Anxiety thrummed through her. She felt she was being watched. A figure somewhere behind her, rising out of the sump from its secret hollow, which she wasn't supposed to have found. It was secret for a reason.

She did not look back.

She passed the narrow opening where she'd hoped she'd felt fresh air and could not help but turn her body so that the flashlight's beam grazed the edges of the entrance and offered a muted glimpse of cave floor and not much else.

Waynoka bumped into the wall, spilling a few drops of water that plinked to the ground. A tickle ran up her sinuses, dust in the air, and she did her best to hold the pot steady while a sneeze ripped its way out of her nose.

And then a voice in the dark—whispery and close, so close that the hair on the back of her neck stood up straight—said, "God bless you."

Waynoka bolted—without looking for the source of the voice, spilling water here and there.

The flashlight flickered. She set down the pot, wound up the light as fast as she could, picked up the pot hoping nothing was following her, hoping no one could catch up during this brief pause, then continued. And it went like that, until she made it, at long last, back to Mads.

"Took you long enough," she grunted. Waynoka could not express her relief at hearing coherent complaints from her partner's lips.

"You try carrying a pot of water with a flashlight that sometimes goes out through a long, narrow tunnel," she replied, her teeth chattering, trying not to give away how terrified she felt. In the pitch dark, she didn't add; with every echo of movement seeming to indicate strange life lurking just out of sight; with something creeping around in the tunnels.

"Did you go for a swim?"

Waynoka realized she was still wet. Her shoes squelched. Even though she hadn't pulled them back on until she had emerged from the sump, water had dripped down her legs. Her hair clung to her neck in a matted mess.

The fire was roaring. Mads must have regained enough strength to sit up and stoke it while she was away. The air was already thick with smoke. Waynoka set the pot over the flames, feeling much less urgency now for it to boil. They had drunk so much water that Waynoka had had to stop again to pee during the trek, reveling in the relief it brought even as it left her feeling vaguely queasy, and left her also wondering what might catch up with her in the dark. Even now she felt satiated from the drink. She could wait patiently for the next pot to boil.

"Do you think anyone else might be down here?"

"No," said Mads. "I don't think anyone else has been down here for a long, long time. What were they mining, anyway?"

Waynoka blinked, remembering Lavinia's diary. "Silver."

Mads snorted. "Water's a lot more valuable these days."

"Hey," said Waynoka. "Do you think we're fucked?"

"I think the *world* is fucked." Mads leaned back, watching the pot of still water. "Us?" She shrugged.

It did not exactly make Waynoka feel better. "Why don't you rest for a while?" she said. "You need to rest as much as possible before we try to find a way out."

Even as she said it, she knew no amount of resting would save Mads from an impending infection or would magically heal her shattered knee. Waynoka just needed time to think of what to do. Come up with some plan. They couldn't get out by navigating the flooded tunnels beyond the sump—that much was obvious. They couldn't climb back up the vertical shaft with the broken ladder.

She knew that at some point she would have to go off alone, leave Mads behind to venture into the unknown darkness in search of a way out, in search of help . . . but what help could there be out here? They were in the middle of nowhere, deep in an abandoned mine, next to a ghost town in the Nevada desert that had been deserted since the start of the decline. She needed to breathe fresh air. She needed to see the sky. The rock closed in around them, too close. Haunted.

The crackling static of panic crept in at the edges of Waynoka's vision, and she held it at bay, trying to remember the calming exercises her mother used to do with her when she was an anxious child: breathe in for five beats, hold for seven beats, exhale for eight.

"Are you doing that breathing thing?"

She froze. "What breathing thing?"

"You do it when you're stressed out."

Waynoka forced herself to breathe normally. "Everything's fine. Look, we've got water. That's what we came here for, right?" She nodded to herself. "Once you're better rested, we'll find a way out. Everything's fine."

The look on Mads's face told her she did not believe a word coming out of her mouth. Her silence told Waynoka that she was too exhausted by pain to talk. Which only made Waynoka worry more.

A moment passed. Two. Mads reached out and grabbed Waynoka by the wrist, their eyes finding each other. When Mads spoke, her voice was soft, vulnerable, and tinged with desperation and fear: "Just . . . don't leave me behind. Promise you won't leave me."

Waynoka's breath caught in her throat. A part of her knew she could never leave Mads—couldn't imagine going on without her. Mads was her beacon, her guide; without her, she was lost. "I promise," she said.

But she knew she would break that promise to try and save them both.

Mads nodded and lay back, closing her eyes, and as soon as her breathing evened out with sleep, Waynoka felt immediately and powerfully alone.

She found herself missing Lavinia, who must have felt that same loneliness now that John Henry had died.

Scrambling for the book, Waynoka grabbed it and flipped it open.

"I need your help," she whispered to the sheaf of old paper. "Help me, Lavinia."

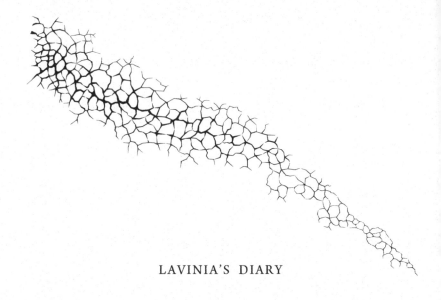

LAVINIA'S DIARY

October 22, 1869

When I fell in love with John Henry, we were both so young, it didn't matter that he hadn't means. He came along with his lofty ideas, his eternal optimism, his promises . . . with his old and worn but perfectly tailored jackets, and with his shirts that were slightly too loose, as if he could never keep on weight because he simply had too much energy.

Marriage came easily to me. Even when his work turned cold; even when we were in dire straits; even when out on that harsh and lonely trail, I was proud to be his wife.

Motherhood, however, has never come easily to me. I have had four miscarriages: two before Sophie, one between Sophie and Oscar, and one after him. While I will never forget the pain of what was almost there disappearing within my own flesh, and the empty ache it left behind, none of that compares to the mingled joy and calamity of Oscar's birth—and Charles's entire life, lived in the merest blink.

For so long afterwards, Charles haunted me.

I would look at Oscar and see him double, as if he wore a ghostly shadow: as if the world knew there ought to be two of him. It didn't help that as soon as he started to talk, he would get into mischief and claim it was Charles, or claim that *he* was Charles, and give me a wicked little grin as if he were fully aware of how he taunted me. I would tell John Henry and he would remind me that Oscar was only a child, that he didn't know what he was saying, that he heard us talking about Charles and that was why he invoked him. He must have grown up thinking he had nearly had but lost a mysterious and wonderful brother who was just like him, his very doppelgänger, and he could not have fully understood what it meant for Charles to be dead.

At least Oscar had Sophie, as I had Emma. My sister and I were inseparable as children. Pretty little Emma! We looked almost nothing alike, but anyone could tell we were sisters. Whereas I was long-faced and mousy, Emma was a doll of a child, soft and light as sunshine. Three of our siblings died. Perhaps that is why we grew so close. Our brother, Arnold, is ten years older than I, twelve older than she, and always seemed distant and impenetrable, more like an uncle than a brother. We never spoke of our other siblings because our mother did not speak of them. Once they were dead, it was as if they had been erased from her life and no longer existed. She must have thought of them, but she would not speak their names, so we did not either. To invoke their names seemed like bad luck.

We spoke of Charles though. We must have spoken of him enough to lay the seeds of Oscar's mischief in his mind. When Oscar was a baby, I could hardly even stand to look at him. It was just as if I were looking at a corpse.

That was when I fell into my black period.

It seems rather like a dream now. Each day a repetition of lying in bed, and every movement required efforts beyond compare, as if to rise were to scale a mountain. A quiet lived in my ears, in my mouth, and in my soul.

J. H.—it pains me even to write his name now—tried to make me care for Oscar. Didn't he? He would put the babe at my breast to nurse, but I would only sit there in a blank sort of state, allowing Oscar to latch without moving to aid his hungry, toothless mouth in its quest, allowing him to take from my body as I drifted somewhere beyond the physical realm.

He tried to help me; I believe he tried. I remember him pleading with me, weeping, kneeling at my bedside; I remember him carefully pouring liquor into my mouth as if to revive me. But I also remember his anger and his stony silences. For after all, one can only plead and cajole for so long, to an unresponsive creature.

It was in the time of angry silence—past the weeping time and even past the shouting time—that Emery came to see me. It is funny: when Emma visited and held my hand and spoke soft words of comfort to me, I felt nothing. But when Emery came, he pulled a chair to my bedside, sat in it, and said, "Well, are you going to get up?"

For some reason, his words fairly startled me out of my stupor, though I remained where I lay. I believe I must have said something like, "Why should I?"

He leaned back in his chair, casual as you please, and said, "Whatever you like, then," as if it were really no matter to him whether I got up or not. He began to pack tobacco into his pipe, paying me no mind, and I watched as he smoked. We remained there, in silence, for some time, and I found his quiet presence a strange sort of comfort. There was no need to talk. We could simply exist, in a room together.

The next time he came to visit, he brought with him a little notebook and a beautiful pen. "I thought you might like this," he said, quite nonchalantly, as if he had come upon the notebook by accident and was only giving it to me so that he might not throw it out. At this I sat up and took these small tokens.

Previously I had kept a diary, but I hadn't written a word since Charles—I could not bring myself to lift pen to paper, and J. H. certainly didn't encourage it. He thought it best if I rested and kept away from such intellectual work as writing or reading. Such was the recommended cure for hysteria, as he had heard it from a doctor friend of his.

Well, I ignored that. I took the proffered diary, and I began to write.

Once I did, I found the words pouring out of me, and I managed to purge myself of all that was rotten at my core. Emery continued to visit; he sat quietly with me while I wrote, and sometimes we talked, but more often we didn't. We came to enjoy one another's quiet company. We hardly ever conversed, but we seemed to understand each other all the same. And he never coddled me, or pitied me, or grew impatient with me. His silence was acceptance.

J. H. never saw any of that though. He was busy—understandably so!—caring for the children, working to support us. All he knew was that his brother (whom he had always envied, it is true, though he had nothing to envy; he simply always wanted more than what he had, which is a kind of eternal envy in itself) and his wife were spending an immoderate amount of time in each other's company, and once or twice he saw us embrace, when I finally allowed myself to shed tears for Charles, after I had kept it all rotting inside of me for so long. It was upon Emery's shoulder that I spilled those tears. It should have been John Henry's. But it wasn't.

And now—now, he is buried beside his brother. Their rivalry is over, and they have ended up in the very same place.

As have I . . . I know I must write and keep writing, or that darkness will creep over me again like aether, to smother me, and this time I will have no one. These last few days have lasted an eternity, and though the people of Virgil have brought me food and offered their support in the face of my tragedy, I have never felt more alone. The Virgil Consolidated Mining Company has even offered a small payment of recompense, though it brings me no comfort.

Who could have foreseen a collapse in the very place J. H. had gone to chip away at his secret strain of silver? I think of him, crushed by all that falling rock, trapped in the rubble, suffocating . . . the hours it took to pull his body from the caved-in tunnel . . . what it must have been like to die in that darkness below the earth . . .

And for what? All I have left now are these two little silver nuggets.

October 23, 1869

The children are handling it as well as one might hope. Sophronia bears herself with such dignity and grace, although she cries easily now. At first Oscar did not quite understand what had happened, not until he watched them hammer the lid shut over the coffin and lower it into the earth, at which point he began screaming at the gravediggers to pull it back up and let his daddy out.

He was terrified at the idea that J. H. would be trapped in there, and it took several of us to calm him down and tell him that J. H. was not really in that coffin anymore, but that he was with God.

When he stopped his wailing, he tilted his head, the way he does when he is thinking something over, and at last he concluded, "So Daddy is with Charles."

"That's right," I said, wiping tears from his cheeks. "Daddy is with Charles now."

"But I want to be with them," he said, and my heart nearly broke.

I tried to comfort him: "Someday you will be. We all will be. But that will be in a very long time."

This only seemed to upset him further, for he cried out, "I want to be with them now! I want to be with Daddy and Charles!"

How his words ring in my ears still! Now he is angry, as if I am stopping him from being with his father—as if it is my fault for keeping them apart.

How can he be gone? I keep expecting him to return from the mine covered in soot and embrace me despite the dirt. He will wipe a black smudge on my nose, his eyes laughing all the while, and he will carry me to bed telling me all the wonderful things we will have when the world is ours.

But the world will never be ours. John Henry is dead, and I am alone as a body can be, in a place lonelier than a graveyard.

October 25, 1869

Claudia came by today. I seem to have lost all track of time. One minute the sun was just angling forward into morning, and it seemed the next it was on the other side of the sky, and there she was, bearing a chokeberry pie and a handsome frown.

"*Los ninyos?*" she asked, and I told her the children had returned to school today, both eager, it seemed to me, to resume whatever routines they had made before—before . . .

We sat outside in the afternoon's lethargy of golden light. She sliced up the pie and handed me a piece, but I could only stare at the jelly oozing from its crust and think of J. H., his body, where his insides would have gone when he was crushed.

She asked if I had eaten, and I found I could not answer. I had lost all sense of time. When the children were here, their appetites reminded me when it was time for lunch or supper, keeping me constrained to the movements of the day, but today I feel all adrift, with only the empty wind for company.

I did eat a little of the pie. It was good. Then—for I had no one else to share it with—I took out one of the silver nuggets and showed it to Claudia. Her eyes became very round. When I handed it to her, she took it reverently and said, "He found this?"

I told her there was another as well, and that "he was going back for more. That's when—" Yet I found I could not get any more words around the lump in my throat.

Her eyes turned to me, and they were hard, like obsidian. She handed back the silver as if she no longer wanted to touch it despite its value. Clouds reared up to the north and blew down to us until her dark hair lifted and fell back around her shoulders. Her voice was strange when she said, "They say it was an accident?"

"Of course," I told her, a little unsettled by the question. When she kept looking at me, I felt compelled to rattle off some inane explanation: "I imagine those tunnels are dangerous—unstable—sometimes there are collapses. There was one not long ago, though no one was hurt—he was simply . . ." I had been about to say, "in the wrong place at the wrong time," but that felt queerly naïve in my mouth.

I looked away from her, at the hazy horizon in one direction, at the hulking shadow of the mountains rising in the other. She took my hand and leaned closer to me. "Lavinia. I have something I must tell you. I have news. About the collapse."

It was a frightful feeling, to tense up in wondering what she might have heard of John Henry's untimely death, and my skin prickled over unpleasantly, though it may only have been the burn of dirt in the wind. I felt it in my eyes, but I dared not blink, and I was afraid of the answer, but I asked anyway what it was she had heard of the collapse. She took my hands; hers were warm and dry, where mine were strangely cool and clammy, unusual for the climate but telling, perhaps, of my surfeit of feeling.

She took a breath and said, "It was no accident."

Her words cut through me like the wind through my skirts. I let go of her hands quickly, and she let them drop. Something terrible was in my heart and I had to stop it from crying out.

She had been spending an evening with that German fellow, Helmuth, who she said was quite distraught and wanted rather the comforts of a female presence than any sort of physical gratification. He got to talking, and here is what came out:

All miners are rather more spooked than they let on in public. One can feel an atmosphere of dread as soon as one steps into the tunnels of the mine, for they all know there is something evil in there, even if they laugh about it in the warm comfort of the saloon with drinks in hand. And they know, too, that whatever it is—the bogeyman, as Helmuth called it, or something else—is what has killed so many.

They knew, too, that whatever it was had come from the part of the mine that Emery had broken into—the part that connects to a natural cave system, which has been in the mountain for perhaps a thousand years, and which, according to the most superstitious among them, tunnels straight to Hell itself, if one only ventures deep enough. One might creep farther and farther down inside the mountain, and there they will find the host of demons that have come to terrorize this place.

"There were some," he said to her, "that could not abide it any longer —not after the Warrant boy. We could accept the death of men. But the death of children? Not if we could stop it."

And so, a small contingent of men crafted a plan to close off what Emery had opened—and they did so by deliberately triggering a collapse.

"John Henry?" I said in a trembling voice.

"I do not believe they knew he would be there," Claudia said. "No more than a terrible coincidence."

Now, why should that make me feel even worse? That Emery was killed for something he had done—but John Henry, innocent and unawares, was merely caught up in a mistake?

I am glad that Helmuth, at least, feels guilty. They all ought to feel guilty, for what they have done to us.

I could not look at her, so instead I looked again at the horizon, but that only told me how the sun was lowering dangerously toward twilight, and that the children were late in returning, and that darkness would swallow us as fast as a blink—but I saw, also, a narrow shape in the distance that I thought for one strange moment was J. H., that his ghost had returned to me. That he is haunting me now, like Charles did then. But it became immediately clear that it was only a cactus and not a man at all. Each shape on the horizon seems a figure, each twist of the clouds a face.

"So they have killed him," I said bitterly. "What scoundrels are men."

We sat in quiet for a time. Then she glanced up at the door, her eyes catching our little bell. "You are staying in after dark, yes?"

I nodded.

"*Bien*. This is good. *Los fantasmas* have been hungry."

"The children believe there is a lady who comes out of the desert to hurt us. The Strange Lady, they call her," I wanted her to know. Claudia looked at me curiously, and I understood that she had not heard this tale before, but that she believed it, which frightened me. "It's only something the children say," I told her, rather hoping she might laugh so that I could laugh too. Yet she only gazed at me with a wistful gleam in her eye.

I soon discovered that Claudia had always wanted children of her own: "*Una casa* filled with *los ninyos*," she told me, for she grew up with many siblings and always remembered the joy of a home filled with children. "They were happy times. Our home was alive with the mysterious joy of family. There is a sadness here, in this place, without one."

I had never thought to ask her before. "What made you come here?"

"We had no money. We had nothing. Still, banditos came on horseback through our little village, which had nothing, and they took the nothing we had. But they wanted more, so they took our joy. They shot my father, raped my mother, and they took me. These men were wanted by the law. They had robbed and killed—and they brought their stolen money to towns with saloons and brothels to spend it. But in the very first place they took me, they were recognized, and shot for the bounty on their heads. I stayed in that town for a time, but there was nothing a girl could do for work. Then I found transport to another town, an even worse one. There was a brothel there, run by a lecherous *gringo*. Finally, I ended up here. Miss Shaw took me in and gave me work. So I stayed."

"You never tried to go home?"

She looked at me sadly and admitted, "I would not know how to find it. And if I did, I do not know what I would find there. Home is gone, for me. But I carry *mi familia* in my heart, and maybe one day I will have *una familia* of my own." She even told me that, though she'd thought it foolish, she had hoped that she might have a family with Emery.

We shared our comingled grief over our men, gripping each other by the hand as if to make up for their loss. And I vowed to be better to the children, to cherish them.

I told Claudia she ought to sup with us some nights. To make this place more alive, with the mysterious joy of family. She agreed and stood to leave, pulling her shawl more tightly around her shoulders.

As soon as she had disappeared down the road, I gathered myself and hurried toward the schoolhouse, though I met the children on the way, who had already been heading home hand in hand.

My dear, good children. I held my arms around our little family of three, tightened them closer to me, and urged them on faster as the sun set quickly behind us.

October 26, 1869

Dear ones, dear ones, we are all alone.

The goat's black eyes do watch the horizon, and the sheep baa plaintively, for all the world has forgotten us. And the rocks make faces in the distance, and the shrub and cacti do seem to walk about.

Maybe it is we who are *los fantasmas*.

October 29, 1869

I should strike out that last entry. I feel I have not been in my right mind these last few long and lonesome days. I do not know what was in my head. Yesterday there seemed to be nothing at all inside of it, nothing but a vast well of silence.

I have taken to breaking the interminable silence by opening and shutting the door to make the bell ring. It is my only music. I used to hum and sing while I worked, but my throat is all dried up. Now I only have the song of the bell—a song of death.

There is a crushing weight on my soul.

October 30, 1869

Strange Lady, Strange Lady, what do you eat? Perhaps I am the Strange Lady; or rather, the children look at me as if I were. I am the Strange Lady who discovered Oscar was not inside and burst into the dark calling his name to the emptiness of the desert, which only swallowed my voice. I am the Strange Lady who shouted "Oscar! Oscar!" at the top of her lungs as if he were miles away. I am the Strange Lady whose panic sent her tripping and sprawling, her gingham dress flying about. Yet I am not the lady he spoke of when we met in a fierce embrace (for he had not, truly, gone far); when I asked him what he could be thinking, running off like that, when I asked him this three or four times, shaking him by the arms, until he gave up his answer: "I was going to help the lady!"

"What lady?" I demanded.

And he told me there was an old woman who said she was thirsty, who took him by the hand, which tingled in a funny sort of way. He told her he knew where she could have some water. "But Mama," he said, his voice all grave and serious, "I don't think water is what she wanted to drink!" For she disappeared, didn't she, before he could take her for a cup of water.

I told him not to make up stories, that there is no lady here, that there is no one here but us. "But there was!" he insisted, "You must have frightened her off."

Though there was no one anywhere near, his words chilled me; I looked around us, peering into the dark for signs of life. I felt a crawling sensation all over, like the scratch of insect feet pattering across the skin, and I took him by the hand and dragged him back inside, where the fire was warm and bright. The bell rattled angrily as I shut and latched the door. Once inside I felt calmer. I turned to the boy and said, "All right, Oscar. Tell the truth, now. What were you doing out there?"

"I told you," he said. "I was with the lady."

"There is no lady," I told him, and I must have made some wild movement, as if to strike, for the boy raised his arms defensively, and that's when I saw his hand. I pulled it closer to examine it, asking, "What is this? What did you do to your hand?" As I always must do with him, I demanded several times before he would let an answer pass his lips. He said he was only holding hands with the lady, "but she was all funny."

The sight of those tiny puncture wounds all over the palm of his hand revolted me, and I let go of him as if his flesh had delivered me a shock. They were strange and unnatural, those red marks all over his soft child's flesh—and I was cold, dreadfully cold.

"Little Oscar," said Sophie as she came to him gently and asked to see his hand. She tutted and fretted over him like a mother hen, took a rag and some water from the bucket, and gently patted the wounds, though it was rather more for the sake of pure tenderness than healing, for any amount of bleeding had already ceased.

I was so cold, I was all a-tremble. I sat beside the warming fire, but it seemed to have no effect. Sophie finished her ministrations and sent Oscar to bed, and he dutifully obeyed, though he kept throwing me small angry glances, as if I were the one who had hurt him. Even Sophronia looked at me with something like shame. And she did not speak to me at all afterward!

Is he to turn even my sweet, dear one against me? Is that what he wants?—to use his mischief and cruelty to make my Sophie believe me a villain? He is rather too clever for a boy of five summers. Yes, he is far more devious than I had believed. What if he is doing all of this just to spite me? For I am certain he has hurt his own hand on purpose. What else could he have done out there except lay his hand upon a cactus so that when I saw it, I could not help but be reminded of the children's song: "She comes in the night / And pricks Father's feet"? To scare me with that rhyme? He wants to drive me mad! It is why he pretends that Charles's ghost plays with him, why he rings the bell in the dead of night! There is something of the Devil in that boy.

I will not let him succeed, though his manipulations have already affected me. For when I looked out into the night and saw him coming toward me—it was only my tortured imagination that made me believe for a moment he was not alone. The sky was bright with stars, and the moon writ large—for I could see its subtle cast in that otherwise black abyss. And in that light I thought I saw (only because Oscar has insinuated this idea into my mind) another figure standing just beside him, holding his hand. What I thought I'd seen had so startled me that I'd tripped, and when I regained my feet, I found Oscar quite alone, as he had surely been the whole time.

October 31, 1869

This morning the tiny wooded church was full. I took Oscar's hands and clasped them together where we knelt, and I told him he must pray for forgiveness.

The church's interior is dusty and dim, like twilight, even in the full of morning, and shadows dwell in the rafters of its peaked roof. The minister spoke, his voice now high and emphatic, now low and measured. It is stuffy in that church, and I grew warm and somnolent as I listened to the rise and fall of his voice, like the ocean tide lulling boats in and out of the harbor. Yet the salt on my lip was not sea spray but only perspiration. It felt just as I imagine the inside of a coffin would. The wooden walls stifling the air, closing us into the darkness with the dead. Poor John Henry, shut up in that coffin for all eternity, in this forsaken town! If I closed my eyes, I could just imagine I were there with him, buried in the churchyard.

Oscar's hands had begun to fall slack as he shifted, his knobby knees chafing where he knelt, so I pushed his hands together again and whispered, "Pray, Oscar. You must pray harder."

Sophronia was already praying, her eyes squeezed shut and her lips moving silently. I wondered at the time what she was praying for. Did she pray for her father to find peace in Heaven? Did she pray for her health, which at times seems fragile as glass? Did she pray for her brother and the wounds on his hand? I know her so well—I knew her inside of my womb, the most intimate way one can be known—yet her mind remains, like all minds, a mystery. It is strange, sometimes, to think of her becoming her own person, separate from myself and unknowable.

After the service, I asked her, "What did you pray for?"

She looked at me queerly and said, "I prayed for you, Mama."

I do not care to report the conversations I shared thereafter with Mary Warrant and Josephine Pavlovsky. Suffice to say there were condolences spoken, tears shed, and tight embraces given. I believe Mary and I are bonded now through our shared loss. We may be of different status, but we understand each other. She continues to wear black with a veil over her face and carries herself as if she will break like fine china. One almost hates to look into her sorrowful eyes.

We parted ways, and do you know what we found when the children and I returned home? As soon as we walked inside, Sophronia hesitated and said she'd heard something. I did not know what she could possibly have heard over the jangle of the bell as we opened the door, but she narrowed her eyes, listening, and said she heard it again. She described it as "a hiss . . . a rattling hiss."

Now I really looked, and there directly before me was a snake slithering across the floor.

Sophie screamed and took Oscar's hand. I ordered them both away as I slowly approached the beast. Its black scales undulated when it moved, and it emitted a menacing rattle from the end of its tail. I knew its fangs must be full of venom. When I crept closer, it turned its reptilian eyes upon me, appraising me with its own alien intelligence, and I knew what I must do. I had to get it out of our house that instant.

Diary, I cannot say what came over me then. Was it fear for my children, now cowering together in the far corner? Anger, at our lot, that J. H. is no more and cannot protect us? Despair?

Without giving it a moment's thought or hesitation, I snatched up that snake by its tail and turned to throw it out the open front door.

It curled its body toward me, and I saw its vicious fangs as it reared back its head to strike. Given even a moment's clumsiness, it would have sprung through the air at my face, but I released it in one swift movement that sent it sailing out. It landed some distance away in the dirt, immediately curling around itself as if for protection.

Sophie leapt from the corner and shut the door with a musical shriek.

After that, the children laughed and spoke together at once, admiring my brave deed, but I stood frozen there, for it was only afterwards that I had time to think about what I had done. What if it had, indeed, bitten me? Should I have left the children orphans? What if my aim had not been true, and I had flung it straight at them?

And though it has all ended well, I cannot but shudder. A snake appearing in our house on the Lord's Day? It is a bad omen, like that skull we found on the trail, etched with its strange poem. We may be rid of it for now, but what if the Devil returns? What if the Devil is already here?

Jo Kaplan

November 4, 1869

The days grow shorter and colder. I begin to wonder for what purpose we remain here, but that we have nowhere else to go. These two silver nuggets stare at me like bulbous eyes, useless shiny rocks. I must find a way to sell them—yet they remind me of J. H., and I do not want to part with them. They are a defiance of the company and its men, who killed him. I imagine them like talismans, warding against evil. And so perhaps I ought to keep them, at least until we become desperate.

I have been sitting here staring at them for hours. They hypnotize one so! How easy it is to sit without thought or deed, in the quiet. Yet our clothes grow dirty and tattered, for I did not launder them this Monday; and nothing has been scrubbed today, and the kitchen is covered in grime. All I do now is keep the fire burning and feed the animals. It is difficult to do much else.

Perhaps I will let the fire go out and we will freeze to death.

November 5, 1869

Fridays are for shopping in town. Formerly my favorite day of the week. Now I think I shall despise Fridays, as I have come to despise this town. All its strange beauty has turned bitter and ugly. Even the sunsets take on terrible dimensions of color.

It is all because of what happened at Rutherford Branson's tailor shop. Looking back now on all the times he called me over for a chat, with that merry twinkle in his eye and his laconic way of speaking, as if to an old friend . . . now it makes me shudder.

He invited me into his shop to show me—well, now when I try to recall what it was he said he wanted to show me, I can't even think of it. Some nice calico, perhaps. No matter. No matter at all. I went into his tidy little shop, with its dressmaker dummy and its spools of thread and measuring tapes, and with Rutherford Branson all as cheery as you please in his brown jacket and vest, and his hat canted at such a jaunty angle one could not help but find him friendly. And find him friendly I did, Diary. Each time I passed, each time we spoke, I found in him a friendly and voluble spirit. If only I had known the truth.

The truth will always come out, and I am nothing if not an honest woman. I tell all truthfully here, and I will write the truth. Though it may be ugly and coarse and though it pains me, I will write it. I have no more use for pleasant euphemisms. The truth is as harsh as the desert, and what use is it to try to make it pretty?

The desert does not care.

He invited me in, and we found ourselves beside the dummy, which wore a handsome jacket. He wanted my opinion on some color or the stitch. "Sometimes one simply needs a lady's eye," he said, ever the gentleman. As I leaned in close to the unfinished jacket, he stood behind me until I could feel the warmth of him and smell the liquor on his breath.

I must have given him my opinion—one hardly remembers such a thing, and I was distracted by his heavy presence so close behind me—but as I straightened, I found his chest at my back and a bulge in his trousers.

There was no room to reel away, although I tried. Mr. Branson grasped me by the arms and held me with his laughing eyes and said, "Why are you affrighted, my dear? You are excited. Whyn't you come into the back room and set down a spell? It'd do you some good, I wager."

He gestured to a door at the back of the room, and the sight of that door made me as queasy as the sight of the snake in our cabin, for at once I had the notion that if I should step through that door, I would be giving over to whatever Mr. Branson wanted to do with me.

I tried to resist him—I tried to pull my arms free, but he held them tightly. I most expected him to hiss like the rattler and bare poisoned fangs that he had been so cleverly concealing beneath his veneer of joviality.

"Come now, Lavinia. None of that," he said, pulling me closer to him. His breath was hot and sour, as he enwrapped me in his unyielding arms. "We have been getting on so well. And now it seems you're all alone. Won't you let your friend comfort you in your time of grief?"

"Let me go," I told him.

"You'll be wanting a husband I expect," he continued, as if he hadn't even heard me. "A woman like you, all alone in a place like this? And with them children of yours? Try to see," he urged, "I'd like to do you a favor."

I saw a figure walk down Main Street outside. My attempts to call out were stifled by the meat of his palm clapping against my face.

"It will be nice," he said in my ear, his voice like rotted silk. "It will be very nice, my dear, not vulgar at all. I promise. I'm very good. You'll like it."

With his sweating hand pressed so tightly over my mouth, I could hardly draw breath—so I bit down on the tender meat of his finger, which sent him howling as he let me go. Still, he stood between me and the door, and he recovered himself quickly enough that I knew I had missed my opportunity to run.

Scowling in a very un-Rutherford-Branson-like way—or perhaps in the most Rutherford-Branson-like way of all—he pulled out his flask and, without taking his reptilian eyes from me nor even blinking, took a long draw. He continued to hold my gaze as he capped it and tucked it away in his inner pocket.

As soon as he took a step closer to me, I said, "Why don't you go to the brothel if you're feeling lonely? I expect Miss Shaw can take care of your animal needs."

This elicited a hearty laugh from him, a glimmer of the jolly man I have conversed with these last weeks. "My dear, I am a man of principles. I never pay for it, and I won't start now," he explained—and I won't mince words, this is just what he said: "I never fuck a whore."

By then my back was against the dummy with its unfinished jacket, and my hands flew behind me, patting against the fabric for what I knew must be there. By the time he took another step toward me, I'd found what I was looking for.

Let that snake bite me?—I would bite him!

I can hardly describe the sound he made when I stabbed that pin into his ear.

The drum must have ruptured, for he doubled over as blood ran from the injury, the pin still protruding from within the caverns where it had lodged. I had not been aiming for the ear, particularly—I had only swung toward his head—but it seemed a fortuitous place to land, for it pained him a great deal and must certainly have done some damage.

I dashed out of the shop and down the street toward hope, without any of my shopping. But as I hurried away, I found myself laughing at what I had done. Laughing! I was free and fleet as I flew down the road. Had I the chance, I would do it again, to anyone with such a filthy soul as Mr. Branson.

The feeling left me, though, when I arrived home, and now I sit here, trembling with my cup of tea, all my words unsaid, as silent as the desert sky. Yet I have decided that next time I must go into town, I will bring my gun. For a gun is indeed more potent a weapon than a pin.

November 7, 1869

Yesterday I tucked Sophie and Oscar into bed and took myself to the saloon.

Why do I feel no shame? I would have felt shame in writing this only a fortnight ago. Yet I feel none.

I despise them all! Had I a pin for every one of them ...

No, none of that. None at all.

Am I so terrible? Let me write it out and read it back, and then I will see.

I went to the saloon, though it was dark and impossible to see what may lurk out there. I went by moonlight and the sky's puncture wounds of stars. No one paid me any mind as I came inside and found the man at the bar, Willa Carver's husband, who seemed surprised to see me but only in his manner; in his words, which were all of politeness, he asked me what I would like to drink.

I ordered a whiskey and turned from the bar while he poured, looking out over the room full of men—and a few women, though mostly of the sort one finds at Miss Shaw's—trying to pick out familiar faces from the crowd. The light was mild and the shadows long, and their hats obscured their eyes. The piano player was warming up on his keys to some eager shouts and requests.

"Mrs. Cain," said Mr. Carver as he slid me the glass. I took it in one swallow, which sent the liquor burning down my throat, but I slammed it back onto the bar and indicated for him to pour again.

"What brings you here, Mrs. Cain?" he asked as he poured a thin stream into the waiting glass.

"Can't a body come for a drink?"

As the whiskey worked its way through me, I found myself feeling fine—fine, or at least careless—and I began to understand why men so enjoy sitting in such loud and bawdy company, in this hot and stuffy room, with the piercing piano plinking out its strident tune and the air thick with tobacco smoke.

The liquor makes it all go down just fine.

Around the tables I went, with a few men turning to eye me up and down, and one even daring to reach out for me as if I were a prostitute; but I merely swatted him away and kept along until I found myself beside the piano, and the music drowned out all else. The man at the instrument grinned with a gold tooth as his fingers went tapping along the discolored keys.

When I had found my familiar faces, I pulled up an empty stool and sat myself at their table, much to their surprise.

"What is this?" they cried out at first, before they recognized me. Then it was, "Beg pardon, Mrs. Cain," and "Condolences, Mrs. Cain."

These men were miners—from John Henry's crew. That German fellow was not among them, but these others I recognized. Their names were Gregory, Adam, and there was also a dark-complexioned man I did not recognize who called himself Joe.

I emptied my glass, and Adam whistled before offering to get me another. I obliged.

The drink made me bold. I looked seriously at Gregory and Joe and told them I would like a job working in the mine.

Both men laughed in my face!

I had heard there were some women known to work in mines—not many, perhaps, but what does that matter? If John Henry could do it, so could I.

"Oh sure, I've heard the same, but not here in our mine. Any woman who dares take on such work is of another kind," said Gregory in a most patronizing way. "You . . . I'm sorry, Mrs. Cain, but you do not seem that kind."

Adam returned with my drink and I knocked it back before another word was said.

"The work would destroy you," Gregory continued.

"I am no stranger to work," I said. I spied the cards on their table. "A game, then. If I win, you three will go to your supervisor and tell them John Henry's widow requests her husband's former position."

They blanched as if I had suggested they ought to bite the heads off a few rattlers.

"Don't be affrighted," I told them. "I know Mr. Warrant, and I'd wager he'll be keen to hear the sad tale of a widow in need of work."

Without another word, they dealt a hand. I took up my cards and found there a most unfortunate series of mismatched numbers and suits, with only a queen high in the bunch.

We played with money, though also with the understanding that this was not what was really at stake in the hand. Gregory raised; Adam and Joe called; not wanting to give myself away, I raised. Gregory called my bluff; Adam folded; Joe hesitated, then called.

As we sat, each of us was eyeing the other, trying to ascertain what lay hidden in the other's hand. I said over the tops of my cards, casually as you please, "I'd also like to know, who set the collapse?"

"Excuse me?"

"You heard me," I continued, just as casually, rearranging the cards fanned out before me as if they would look better in a different order. "John Henry died in a collapse that was deliberately set by a handful of miners. I want to know who it was."

"It was none of us, if that's what you're letting on," Adam protested.

"I suppose that it was also none of you who dragged my brother-in-law Emery to his death at the hanging tree?"

None answered, and that was as much answer as any voice they could give to the matter. At last we had to share our hands. I had only the queen high; Joe set down a pair of jacks; Gregory, a nice two-pair: threes and aces.

I had lost. As they gathered up the cards for a new hand, I said, "No matter. I'll find my way into that mine one way or another."

"For what? What answers do you think you'll find in there?" asked Adam.

I folded my arms and stared him down. "Another drink."

"You hope to find another drink in the mine?"

What small minds some men have. I had only to raise my eyebrows, though, for him to realize my meaning, and off he went to fetch me another whiskey from the bar. I need hardly write here, I think, exactly how fuzzy and off-kilter my world had become by then; something about the lanterns and the music and the jumble of voices seemed to mask it though. I felt high and invigorated.

"All I want is the truth," I told Gregory and Joe as they dealt a new hand, excluding me this time.

"Mrs. Cain," Joe said, turning fully to me and giving me his earnest look, "I don't know what you expect from us. Ain't we told you the truth? We never had no quarrel with your husband, and we're sorry to see him dead. What more is there?"

Adam returned with my drink. This one I sipped, aware I was dangling over an edge far past sobriety.

"You know who did it," I said.

They gave me no names. I slammed the glass down on the table and stood quickly, the stool scratching across the floor beneath me. Against the din of the saloon, I raised my voice, not caring who else might hear me.

"Who killed my husband?" I demanded. The men at tables nearby turned to look, but I hardly paid them any mind. "Who killed John Henry? Out with it! I want the names of every last man who set that trap."

More and more looked over at us until I was horribly aware of the eyes upon me, yet still I did not let that deter me. The drink had made me fearless. The men at my table attempted to cajole me and tell me they did not know, they had no idea, but I was not having this. In fact, I hoped that the men around us heard me; I hoped that one of them might speak up, since these men were either truly ignorant or else—cowards.

When I paused, waiting for answer, I did hear someone else in the room say, "Ain't that the dame who maimed the tailor?"

I could not find the man who had given voice to this, so I called out to the room at large, "Yes, and any man who defies me stands to get a pin in his ear!"

This pronouncement was met by some hooting and hollering; many seemed excited by the threat of violence from a lady. I noticed the piano man had ceased his playing to watch, his gold tooth gleaming in his grin, and the few other women crept away to the corners of the room to whisper amongst themselves.

"Now I have your attention," I said, raising my voice for all to hear—for now I truly had a captive audience. I had become the most interesting thing in this saloon, which until then consisted of the usual activities of gambling and drinking. "Which of you killed my husband? Come now! There is no Willie Ray Randall for you to cower behind this time! So which of you was it? What, are you afraid of a woman?" I laughed. "And you call yourselves men!"

Those at my table stood to escort me out of the room, but surely they did not dare manhandle me, and I refused to move. Someone elsewhere in the room said laughingly, "Beware the Widow Cain!" to snorts and jeers.

Almost as soon as I'd captured their attention, they lost interest in my shouting. The piano man took up his playing again, and many of the gruff and dirty fellows turned back to their tables, their game, and their drink.

"You are all cowards, then!" I shouted even as Adam took me by the arms and tried to coerce me toward the door. "You all sit and drink while your children die in the night, and you pretend you're not afraid!"

I heard some grumbling at this, but I continued even as I found myself pulled inexorably toward the exit. But, as I say, I was high and filled with the vigor of Old Crow.

"But you are! You're all afraid—that's why you set the collapse, isn't it?"

By now the cool night air was at my back; Adam spun me around so that I gazed out the swinging doors at the light spilling out from the saloon, and the darkness beyond.

"Go home, Mrs. Cain," Adam said gently. "Go to your children."

I fairly tore my arms free of his grasp, unwilling to allow him one moment more of forcing me out of this domain of men.

"You are all to blame," I said to him as I straightened myself, took one last look behind me at the men resuming their former activities in the saloon, and stepped out into the night.

I did not make it far before I heard footsteps hurrying up behind me and Joe's voice telling me to wait a moment.

Reluctantly, I did.

"Mrs. Cain," he said—but that is all he said. Whatever else he had been intending to tell me was swallowed by several more men spilling out the saloon doors, hollering after him. He reached toward me, in the same manner his friend had, in a supplicating sort of way, as if to convince me of his innocence. Yet as he did so, more men approached, shouting at him to get away from the lady.

"You see that?" one of them hollered. "He touched her!"

And another came right up and jeered, with a finger in Joe's chest, "Think you can touch a white lady?"

Joe's moonlike eyes turned to the man as the group surrounded us, each one as eager as the next, though for what, I could not say. Blood sport, perhaps. They wanted something, and they wanted it from the man who stood before me.

"He didn't touch me," I said, though it hardly mattered, for no one listened to my words.

All that whiskey hit me hard then, and I swooned, unable to do much but try to keep my balance as the men set upon Joe with a terrible eagerness in their faces. I imagined these were the same looks they'd worn when they came for Emery: looks of pure animal savagery, of creatures who want nothing more than to tear another creature to shreds, not for survival, but for enjoyment.

It sickened me, the way they dragged him to the ground and beat their fists into his face. I must have shouted at them to stop, but in truth the entire scene is a hazy blur. They stopped short of killing him, at least—that much I do remember.

The scene so disturbed me that, I must admit, I turned and fled.

Guided by the moon alone, I hurried down the dusty road, a cool and gentle breeze pulling at me with a hint of winter bitterness. I had only the faintest notion that I was even heading in the right direction. My skirts rustled as I went, and I remember I thought in that moment that I would begin to wear bloomers instead of skirts, for it would be much easier to move about.

Or perhaps that thought did not come to me until I was already running through the desert in fright?

For it was when I looked out into the moonlit landscape grown strange by darkness that I saw a figure lurking out among the scrub and stones, very like the figure I thought I had seen holding Oscar's hand. At first I hoped to see it better, to make out who it was—yet it thwarted my sight, seeming to vanish into the shadows and appear elsewhere. The further I drew from the faint lights of town, the darker the night, and even the nearby mountains rose to such height that they blocked out a swath of stars.

I turned in the direction I thought was home and quickened my pace, eager to escape the strange figure lurking in the dark. Then I saw it again, just ahead of me, drawing closer on stiffened limbs, and I fled in the other direction. It followed, just the same.

My skirts twisted about my limbs, and I stumbled over rocks and small round cacti that shocked me with their sharpness and stuck through the

Jo Kaplan

fabric to pin me in place until I could tear myself free. The bottom of my skirts grew ragged and dirty, but I kept on. The drink and the sick fear possessed me to dash off madly, impetuously into the night, away from the creature that followed.

The wide-open desert surrounded me, and I lost all sense of which direction was home. Delirious with drink, I had to slow my pace, for the stars spun above me. When I turned to assess where I was, there stood the figure, so close my heart leapt with terror: tall and narrow, emaciated, yet moving with startling swiftness. The moonlight swept over us as a wispy cloud pulled away, and I glimpsed its horrible face.

Deep-set eyes gazed out from within something withered nearly beyond recognition, and a mouth gaped like a black gash in flesh that was more like leather or dried fruit; and there were whiskers, of a sort, but they grew out all over the face rather than only at the chin, and they protruded in vicious, spiked clusters.

Then it grabbed me by the arm with a shock as pins sank into my flesh, and it seemed to draw from me some vital substance. Horror pulsed through my veins, which I could feel beating intensely in my ears; and with revulsion and wonder I said, "You are the Strange Lady." Had my spirit not been dampened with liquor, I might have been shrieking. My fear seemed to hold me frozen and hardly able to draw breath.

A rustling voice like old dead things emerged from the horror of that face: "You taste of poison."

The figure let go of me, and the sudden release sent me reeling backward over a weedy shrub. My back met the earth with a hearty smack that sent the wind from my lungs, and I had to lay there a moment to catch my breath. By the time I was able to look again, the creature was gone. It was only then that a tingling sort of pain rushed over the flesh of my arm.

It took me longer still to pick myself up and regain my wits, for what I had seen, Diary, was not remotely human. Though it bore something like a human face, if it indeed was a man (or woman), it was rather more like one long dead—desiccated, mummified—only it was as if it had forgotten it was supposed to be dead, and continued to roam the night. It was not until I had finally slowed the gallop of my heart that I was able to ascertain where I was—which is to say that I had no idea where I was.

The lights of Virgil were distant enough to have vanished, and in the darkness, it was difficult to tell even which way, exactly, the mountains were facing, which otherwise would have been my marker for direction to find my way back. As it was, the desert stretched around me like an alien wasteland, and I worried that if I chose a direction and tried to walk it, I might only be venturing deeper into the wilds with its unknown creatures, its haunted land.

I could not remain where I was, though, so eventually I set off in the direction I thought I had come from. Yet the farther along I drew, the more I realized that I was moving away from the mountains, not toward them, which was surely the wrong direction; and I had to turn back, retrace my steps, and continue.

Diary—I wandered that desert all night long.

After hours of circling, I was so lost that I sat and wept. The night had grown bitter cold, and I had to wring my hands to keep warmth in my stiffening fingers. My feet grew sore from walking, and the alcohol was fleeing from my body, leaving me tired, remorseful, and aching in both my head and my heart. After resting I stood, I walked, I ran, I shouted, but I remained lost in the wilderness.

For a time, I lay myself down and slept. I could do nothing else. When next I opened my bleary eyes, the sun was cresting the horizon and diffusing enough light into the air to offer me a clearer view of the mountains. Rising on my aching limbs, I trudged home, shivering. The children were fast asleep, thank God, and did not see their mother, with hair falling loose and knotted around her filthy face and her clothes all torn and dragged through the dirt, come slouching inside, smelling of the outdoors and the sourness of the saloon.

This was last night. Since then, I have cleaned myself and rested some, and the children are none the wiser of my eventful evening at the saloon and nighttime journey through the strange desert. Am I mad? But I was drunk. I hardly know what I saw. Pieces of the night flee from me like distant memories, and even that which I remember seems fuzzy and strange, like a dream. I feel I cannot trust my own memory. Did I truly see those men brutalize Joe outside the saloon? Is it possible that my fierce shouting over the whiskey was, in fact, more like the incoherent rambling of a drunk? I cannot help but think it so. And if that is the case, then how can I trust what I thought I saw in the desert?

Oscar had frightened me. Only this time, I let it get into my head, and when I was drunk and lost and afraid, I allowed my mind to conjure the images he'd engendered in me. What I saw must have been a dream, after I had fallen asleep. And who could blame me for having a nightmare out there? After all this—it is no wonder I thought I had seen a demon!

And yet, my arm is covered in pockmarks!

November 8, 1869

Sophie has hardly been out of bed today. At first, I thought it was mourning. She seemed sad and listless; her eyes looked wet. I thought it must be her grief making her ill, and I clung to this thought.

"You miss your father," I said as I sat her up and brushed the tangles from her hair. "I do too."

"Why did he have to die?" she said with a hiccup in her voice; tears brimmed in her eyes. "Do you think he's in Heaven?"

I ran a hand down her silky locks and thought of all the times John Henry had lied, had cheated, had manipulated to get his way. "Of course," I said, and resumed brushing.

Her words then sent a haunting shiver through me:

"Oscar says he thinks he might be lost in Hell. He says he got lost underground when he died and now he can never get out again."

"That's a horrible thing to say," I told her. "The boy likes to scare us. The Lord knows why, but he's only trying to scare you. He makes things up, terrible things—like seeing Charles, and that lady in the desert."

"There wasn't a lady in the desert?" she asked.

"Of course not." My voice became harsher as I grew more firm in my conviction that Oscar was playing games with us. A boy of five, clever enough to unsettle both mother and sister! If only there were someone to talk to, someone to allay my fears about him. What am I to do with him? Is there a problem with his mind, his soul? Did he come into the world only half a person, having lost his twin in the womb?

I must stop these thoughts—he is only a boy, he is my boy!—but they creep up on me.

When I tried to bring Sophronia her lunch, she only turned over in bed and went back to sleep. My hands shook as I carried the plate back to the table. I twisted my fingers together to give them something to do other than tremble, and I fairly worried the dry flesh from the edges of my nails.

No. She is not sick again. I refuse to believe it. She has been well for many weeks now.

I tried to busy myself with the laundry, scrubbing until my arms were sore, until I realized I had spent the last twenty minutes scrubbing one of John Henry's shirts. Tears came to my eyes as I brought the wet garment to my face and used it to briefly smother myself. I had to take it away when I could not breathe through the damp fabric, and I choked up again when I realized I had cleaned it well enough that I could no longer smell him on it. I wanted to put it on. After all, it was a perfectly clean shirt, and now who was to wear it? I found a pair of his trousers, too, and set about washing them, wondering how I might pin them to fit me instead. I know these were silly thoughts, the idea of putting on my husband's clothing—goodness, what would the children think of me?—but I admit them to you, Diary. I wanted to put on his clothes and dissolve into his memory. He may have lied and cheated and manipulated, but he loved too. He loved me, and was tender with me, in his way. And when he wrapped his arms around me—

Anyway, when Oscar returned home from school, he took one look at Sophronia and diagnosed her with all the confidence of a little boy: "She's sick again."

"Shut your mouth," I told him. "Go wash yourself."

He went to the bucket outside that we kept for washing and rinsed his hands while I checked on Sophie, who lay sleeping. I even lifted the bedcovers and checked to see if she had begun bleeding, if that's what this was. I was a little older—I must have been twelve or thirteen—but I remember my first time quite clearly: the aches, the embarrassment, the excessive emotions that passed through me. All I had wanted to do at the time was sleep, though my mother wouldn't let me.

Of course, Sophie is still young. She hasn't begun bleeding yet.

All day long, I have worried and worried. It gnaws at my belly like an intensely queasy form of hunger.

November 9, 1869

This morning when I woke the children and it was clear that Sophie was no better, Oscar looked me straight in the face and said, "What if she dies?"

The question rang through me with the sharpness of a bell clanging in my ears. I slapped him, hard. It left a bright red mark on his cheek and his mouth hanging open in shock.

"She isn't going to die," I told him.

The boy backed away from me as Sophronia tried to sit up, her face dreadfully pale, rubbing sleep from her eyes. As he backed away, shame came coursing through me.

"Come back here," I said firmly. "Please, Oscar. You know I didn't mean it. I'm sorry. Let me put a balm on your cheek, make it better."

But he held his hand over his face where he had been struck. "You're wicked!" he said. "You're mean!"

"And you are insolent!" I snapped back at him (God, why must he rile me so? Why am I never cool of head around him?).

"Mama, he didn't mean it," Sophronia said feebly, her voice sounding younger even than her brother's.

"I want Daddy!" Oscar wailed. "He would never hurt me! Daddy is nice! You're mean!" I lurched toward him to take hold of him and calm him down, but he slipped away from me and shouted, "It should have been you who died!"

It hit me as if Oscar had slapped me right back. I froze. The boy turned and ran right out the front door, the bell jangling wildly as the door banged on its hinges. He took off down the dirt road, and he was a long way off before I made it to the doorway to call after him, but he never slowed or turned. He was running toward town though, so I thought he must be going to the schoolhouse.

So be it, I thought! He had forgotten to bring his pencils, but he could face the consequences from the schoolmistress, and he could spend the day stewing over what he'd said to me.

That's what I thought, then. I was so convinced he had simply gone to school that I did not bother worrying about him while I went about the day caring for Sophie, trying to get a little tea and broth into her.

But as the day wore on, my heart grew sick. I should not have laid a hand on the boy. Such violence is intolerable. I would never lay a hand on Sophronia. I decided that it was I who ought to apologize, as soon as Oscar came home.

He didn't mean what he said, after all (even if I knew he did—even if I knew he had always favored John Henry over me). I would tell him that I have been under a great deal of strain ever since his father's passing. I would tell him I was sorry for hurting him, and that I have been horrible.

But the afternoon passed on into evening, and he never came home.

Now I am sitting here staring out into the cool blue of twilight. There is snow on the mountains and a chill in the air.

Where is he?

Is he safe? Is he lost out in the desert somewhere? Oh God, if he is lost, if he roams all night as I did, if he dies of exposure—

Stop. Stop it.

I must find him.

Sophie is resting anyway. I will go out into the dark and call his name until he comes home.

Later

I searched for hours as night fell into blackness, all the dark shapes of the desert looking like him everywhere I turned. First, I went to the school-house, but it was empty. I passed the saloon but did not go in; it was not as full as it had been last time I was there, and a quick glance through the doors confirmed that Oscar was certainly not inside. Then I went out into the open cactus-studded plains, calling his name, a ghostly howl in the night. He wasn't there.

Eventually I had to come back home. I was too exhausted to continue, and I thought perhaps he would have returned after all, perhaps I had been out all this time and I would find him sitting next to Sophie, his eyes accusing me for not being there. So convinced of this was I that I turned and dashed home as fast as I could, only to find Sophronia in bed and no one else. He wasn't there.

He isn't here.

And now I have wept and prayed, and I fear there is nothing more I can do until morning. But I will not sleep, I cannot sleep, no matter how tired I am. If he comes home, I will be waiting up for him.

November 10, 1869

What good will these silver nuggets do me if I am all alone? John Henry died for nothing! Oscar is gone—Sophronia is ill—

What am I to do?

I must have drifted off at some point last night, for I woke this morning with a start, only to find that Sophie and I remain the only two inhabitants of this cabin. The horror of it wracked through me again.

I am trying to get Sophie to drink some water, though she is reluctant even to take the smallest sips (I think her throat pains her). And then I will go out again. I will find Oscar. But I cannot leave Sophie until I am sure she will be all right. I am worried to leave her. What if I leave her and—and something awful happens?

And now I grow angry at Oscar all over again.

Why should he do this to me? Run off like that and worry me sick when he knows I must stay here to care for his sister? Always, always, he makes things more difficult than they need be!

"You need to go find Oscar," Sophie said between sips of water.

I told her I needed to stay with her, to make sure she was all right.

"What if he's hurt?" she asked.

"I don't know," I confessed. "I don't know what to do."

"It's okay," she told me. "You always do your best."

And this made me feel even guiltier, for it made me wonder—do I? Am I doing my best? Why am I not a better mother? Why is my best never good enough?

I knew I needed to unscramble my thoughts by writing them out here before I decided what to do. I must go find Oscar. I must take care of Sophronia. I fear that in writing out these thoughts, I am still just as mired in doubt and confusion and fear as I was before.

What if I

Later

I stopped writing abruptly, Diary, for there was a knock at the door, and who should it be when I opened it up but Doctor Hartsworth.

Though I had been planning on calling for him to see to Sophronia, I hadn't yet been able to, between her sickness and Oscar's disappearance, so his appearance quite surprised me.

"Doctor," I said bluntly when I opened the door, "what are you doing here?"

Then I noticed a child lurking behind his legs, and I peered around until I saw who was hiding there.

"Oscar!"

"This fellow showed up at my door last night," said the doctor amiably, stepping to the side so that Oscar became visible and patting him on the head, which tousled his sandy locks. I opened my arms to receive him, hoping Oscar would run into my embrace, but he remained where he was.

"He claims to have been mistreated," said the doctor, his voice very carefully neutral—not directly accusing me, but neither discounting what Oscar had told him.

"I have not been myself," I told him.

"Understandable," said the doctor. "You've been through a great deal. All the same, when he arrived yesterday, and I told him I had to take him straight home to his mother, he was quite adamant about not returning here. Just about refused, he did. So I said he could stay with me the night, and I would come talk to you in the morning. I do hope you haven't been too terribly troubled over it. He was quite safe with me."

I nodded dumbly—what else is one to do?

The doctor continued: "So I got to thinking, and—well, the little fellow and I might have an idea that suits everyone. You have been overburdened, Mrs. Cain, by the untimely passing of your husband. Allow me to help. Oscar can stay with me as long as he likes, and in return I will teach him. He will be my apprentice. Though he is young, there are things he can do for me that will be a great help, and he seems to enjoy learning about medical science, even at his age. He's a very bright boy!" The doctor's warm eyes met mine. "Well, Mrs. Cain? What say you?"

What could I say? Oscar was watching me with eager apprehension, and the doctor was offering me an opportunity—the chance to put all my attention on Sophronia, to not have to constantly fret over Oscar and his lies, his mischief.

But how could a mother agree to such a proposition? Agree to let go of her own child?

"I say . . ." The words came out slowly, but at last I relented: "I say, if Oscar wishes it, then so it shall be."

"Well, young man," the doctor said, turning to him. "Why don't you go on in and gather your things?"

Oscar darted around me into the house to pack his bag.

"Now, the boy also said something about his sister falling ill again?" Doctor Hartsworth said, turning back to me.

I bade him come in and see to her as Oscar packed away his clothes, hovering over the doctor as he knelt by Sophronia's side and checked her pulse and temperature, and peeled back the lids of her eyes to get a better look at them. She tried to pull away irritably, but she was too weak. I held my breath as he conducted his assessment, terrified that he would tell me all hope was lost—but he only stood and said to allow her plenty of rest and fluids.

"That's it?" I asked.

"She's come down with fever again," he told me. "It's like last time. It will be up to her to fight through it."

"But . . . there must be something you can do?"

The doctor shook his head and said, "'Fraid not."

Oscar finished packing his bag and darted out the front door, clearly not wanting to be in my presence for a moment longer; I reached out to touch his shoulder as he passed, a gesture of intimacy, but he cringed and slunk away from my hand before I could so much as graze him.

The doctor also stood to leave, but I situated myself between him and the door. "You're absolutely sure?" I asked him. "What about . . . I heard from Mr. Branson—you know, Rutherford Branson—"

"Ah yes. He has mended many a pair of trousers for this old bachelor. He came to me t'other day with his eardrum all burst. Accident with a sewing needle, he said. But I heard tell that might have been your handiwork?" He raised his thick white eyebrows at me expectantly, and I resented his turning of the subject.

All I said was, "So what if it was?"

The doctor shrugged, as if it made no difference to him. "He's deaf in that ear now."

Enough of that. I got to the point: "Mr. Branson told me you learned medicine from an Indian tribe."

"He did, did he?" Doctor Hartsworth grinned, showing crooked yellow teeth. "Well, I'll grant you, it's part true. Now don't you get me confused, Mrs. Cain. I did have the requisite formal education, I assure you. And I did, as well, stay for a time in company of a native tribe, where I was privy to a great deal outside the realm of traditional science, and studied at the feet of a shaman."

At another time, I might have scoffed at this. But I was—I am—desperate. I will do anything, anything, to make Sophie better. So I was not ashamed to ask him—"Is there anything you learned from them that might help her?"

He scratched at his tangled white chin hair. "Nothing that I can do, I believe, but you could go to him yourself."

"Go to whom?"

"The shaman himself."

I looked at Sophie—at the fever in her cheeks, the sheen on her forehead, the glassiness of her eyes.

"Then it is a nearby tribe?" I asked, and the doctor told me their village was not altogether far from here, if indeed they were still there—it had been some years since he had last been there. On horseback, it was a journey of a little under two days, if he remembered correctly. Once they had been a nomadic people, but the land on which their village sat was said to be sacred to them, so he believed that at least some of them would still be there, if they hadn't been killed off by settlers. "Most men are cowards," he told me. "They feel threatened by the Indians, so they kill them. But the time I spent with them was perhaps the most enlightening time of my life. We may know things about science and medicine that they do not—but they, too, understand things about the world that we are utterly ignorant of."

The doctor left with Oscar, left me and Sophie alone in this cabin. I cannot imagine making a two-day ride to find some strange tribe, but I fear—I fear, if I do nothing, Sophie will continue to get worse.

November 11, 1869

I cannot do nothing. I cannot sit here and watch her suffer.

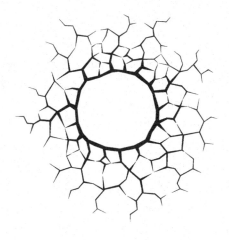

THE DUST DEVILS

THE WATER WAS COOL. It had been cool for some time, but despite her headache, Waynoka had been unable to stop reading. When she did at last look away from the page, she found the fire dwindling in the gloaming of underground night.

Once she'd wound up the flashlight, it burst to life over Mads's sleeping face. She looked pale. Gaunt. Sweat slicked. Waynoka moved the flashlight down to her leg, hoping to inspect it before Mads woke. But when she tried to peel the rag from the wound, she found it stuck fast as with glue, and her heart shivered with dread.

She tried again. The cloth peeled away with a grotesque ripping sound, but Mads did not so much as stir.

The rag pulled dried blood from the wound and set it freshly weeping. Mads whimpered in her sleep. The flashlight revealed a butchery of blood-blackened flesh, swollen with lumps standing out at unnatural angles, and a large patch of yellowy skin oozing pus. Waynoka covered her nose against the foul, ammonia-like smell, and she knew the wound was infected.

Hands shaking, she rewrapped the knee, moving slowly and carefully to not wake Mads, who continued to shift and grunt, her brow creased. The pain had followed her even into sleep.

They had no antibiotics. They had nothing to stop the infection from spreading. Mads couldn't walk. They were trapped underground. In the middle of the ruined desert.

Waynoka tried to breathe slowly, in through her nose and out through her mouth. Sick with panic. Was this how Lavinia had felt when she'd feared Sophronia would die? *That must have been worse,* Waynoka thought, being that it was her own daughter.

But Waynoka loved Mads. She loved her with a starved, desperate affection. Maybe it was only because they had spent so much time alone together, but they had become a family, the two of them. Mads was the gas that fueled their motorcycles, the starlight that guided them through the dark.

Now she would die. From a simple infection—something that could have been cured in a hospital back in the civilized world. Although come to think of it, Waynoka was pretty sure Mads had never had health insurance, so maybe the "civilized" world wouldn't have done her any good anyway. Maybe rubbing mummy dust on it was as good a remedy as civilization had ever had, in its stupid arrogance.

When she shook Mads awake, Waynoka had to bite back the words in her mind—*you're going to die, there's nothing I can do to stop it*—as she watched her partner blink groggily. Once she had woken up, Mads said, "I was dreaming we were swimming in a lake. Surrounded by these big leafy trees."

"Sounds nice," said Waynoka, choking back *you're going to die.* "Water's ready."

They sipped slowly, ponderously this time. There was a heavy weight in the air.

"We were baptized in the lake," Mads said—soft, meditative.

"What?"

"In my dream. You know how sometimes you know things, in dreams, but you don't know how you know them?"

"Sure, okay."

Mads looked wan as she sat there, gazing inward, back into the dream. She looked old, tired. A melancholy calm lived in her words, so unlike her typical demeanor. "We were baptized. That's why the animals in the forest were leaving us alone. We had become like them. But everyone else— everyone else was dead. There was an invasive species in the forest, and the trees were trying to strangle it. But it turned out that *we* were the invasive species. They left us alone, though, because we had been baptized in the lake."

"We were saved because we were baptized. How religious of you."

Mads looked away. "It wasn't religious. It was . . . spiritual."

"Are you thinking about what happens after?"

"After what?"

Waynoka looked at her and could not answer.

"Shit, I don't know," said Mads. "Probably nothing happens after. Look, it doesn't matter. We're not gonna die down here, so don't even think that."

Waynoka wanted to believe her. But hearing Mads say they *weren't* going to die was confirmation that Mads, too, believed the opposite. When she thought they had a fighting chance, she never failed to remind Waynoka of the direness of their circumstances.

Hearing this brought a hopeless chill. Part of her wanted to mention the infection. She found she could not seal Mads's fate like that. There had to be another way.

"I found another tunnel," she said, "or . . . something. An opening. I don't know where it leads." She hesitated but could not help adding, "I think I felt a breeze from it."

"A way out?"

"I don't know."

"We should go investigate," said Mads, taking a sip and passing the pot to Waynoka. When it was out of her hands, she reached into the bag and rummaged around, pulling out what was very likely their last stick of jerky. They longed, each of them, for a can of beans, thinking of their early days when they had complained of such a meal, which now seemed an extravagant feast.

"We?"

Mads carefully unwrapped the jerky. Her face was bird-like in its angularity. Her teeth tore off the smallest bite and she exchanged the package with Waynoka for the pot of water.

The embers reddened the dark air which broke around the lone eye of the flashlight, lying on its side.

"I'll go check it out and come back," said Waynoka as she chewed the dry, salted meat. She wondered when her stomach had stopped grumbling and taken on, instead, a cavernous, unending ache.

There lay between them a vast thread of silence. They were ants in an anthill; they were Theseus in the labyrinth, lost, waiting for the Minotaur to find them.

Going back that way would bring her near the secret hollow. But it was just a place. And it was on the other side of the water—long abandoned, probably.

Still—what secret hollow lay within that narrow opening she was going to explore? Was it yet another place made toxic by the presence of something vaguely human?

She almost wished *she* were the injured one so Mads could instead go investigate the dark, mysterious recesses of the cave. She knew this was unfair. Unthinkable. But didn't Mads deserve to live, more than herself?

"Come *right* back," said Mads.

They stoked the fire; Waynoka took the flashlight. Mads hugged the half-filled pot to her chest as if it would protect her from the ghosts of the cave.

And then Waynoka went.

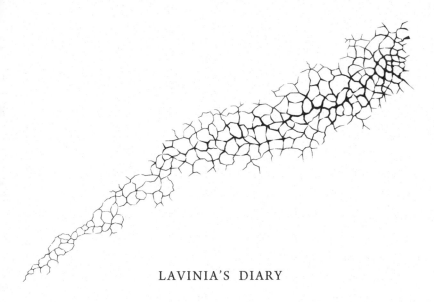

LAVINIA'S DIARY

November 14, 1869

It was two days' ride, as he'd said—two days of dread and exhaustion on the open plains, ensuring Sophronia was secured against me so that she would not slide off the horse in her delirium. The sun beat down on us by day, and by night the cold and dark crept in toward our fire. Animals called to the moon with voices that echoed over the desert, and when I tried to close my eyes, I fancied a terrible face was looming out from the shadows, twisted and withered like a tanned hide, with ghastly thorns protruding in all directions—some curving up from the forehead in the manner of horns.

Yet these were only fancies, for we were quite alone where we camped. And yet the emptiness around us, in a land abandoned by God, promised such awful possibilities that I could not dash them from my brain.

Sophie was restless, too, when we camped—she tossed and turned in her discomfort. "I'm scared," she said once, when she seemed not to know where we were, and she begged to go home as I held her against me. It tore my heart to tell her we could not go home, not yet, that I hoped where we were going would help make her better. She did not understand, reverting to a younger version of herself that wanted only comfort, a version devoid of all curiosity and thoughtfulness, driven only by the maladies of the body, by suffering.

And she seemed to accuse me, too, for she reminded me: "You said we were going to Eden." The notion I had given her a false promise was a bitter one to accept, so I told her, "Eden is wherever you make it. We will make our own Eden—you and I. When you are better, we will leave behind this suffering and forge a life in harmony with all Creation, just as Adam and Eve did in their garden. And we will never be wanting, for the Earth will provide; and we will never be lonely, for we will have each other, and all of Earth's creatures beside us; and we will have no need of God's mercy, for we will be masters of our own domain, unbound by His cruel whims; and neither will Fate direct our course, for we will be masters of our own lives."

It sounded like a prayer, a blasphemous prayer, that poured from my lips as if with its own intention, yet it was a prayer that soothed Sophronia, who finally settled and went to sleep. I kept watch in the dark—the crackling fire sending shadows lurching all around us hither and thither, like creatures cavorting just out of sight—waiting to see whether the dancing shadows might peel back from the face of a barbed Devil and cast its visage into the hellish firelight. Each movement of sagebrush in the wind sent me flinching; each snuffle of the horse momentarily stilled my heart, for the creature was still a stranger to me.

Before we left, I traded the sheep and goats in town for the horse, thinking, *What need have I of these dutiful creatures anymore? What use is any living being if Sophie should sicken and die?* The horse is lean, with mottled brown fur and oily black eyes that crawl occasionally with stray flies, yet it is a dutiful horse that rides obediently and at a moderate pace, which suits me for I am still unused to riding like a man.

All the way I worried that Doctor Hartsworth's map might be insufficient to guide us, or that the village might no longer exist—but when I saw the smoke from their fires billowing into the sky ahead, I nearly wept with relief, and then their huts came into view, some made of wood or straw, and others like tents pitched from animal hides.

Here again was a repetition of experience as we arrived at the village, just as when we had arrived in Virgil—tired, hungry, sick, in a strange place filled with strangers. When we approached the village, we were met with a small contingent of Indians who held bow and arrow on us, and I thought they might turn us away and send us back out into the desert, where I knew we would not survive. When they saw it was only a sick child and a haggard woman, they lowered their weapons.

For perhaps an hour we remained where we were, held at bay in spite of their lowered weapons, wondering whether they would admit us into their village or whether they would consider us hostile and send us away. The wind blew smoke from the fire toward us, which made me cough, but it took the smoke away again when the wind turned. Trees here shaded us from the worst of the sun despite their autumn denuding; their limbs blazed with varicolored strands of rust and gold, unlike Virgil, which seems an interminable dusty beige. A mountain rose steeply to the west, cloaked in the warm colors of autumn bloom.

At long last, a young man who could not have been long past childhood emerged from the village and came toward us; he crouched down beside me and asked, in clear English, why we had come.

I explained our situation and asked if there was a medicine man here who might help, for a man called Ira Hartsworth had directed us here for his aid. The boy's eyes watched me with striking intensity; his long dark hair was pulled behind his shoulders, and his face was smooth and unmarked by the trials of age.

When I was finished, he stood and vanished again into the village. I closed my eyes, and sleep had nearly overtaken me by the time he returned. "We will provide you and your daughter food, water, and shelter for the night. It will be dark soon. In the morning, you will be on your way."

I begged him to help us—to help Sophie, that is, and he asked me, "Why should we help you?" which left me silent, for I had no good reason to give him. I had come here in a state of sheer desperation, but presently I thought: *Why should they help us, indeed? Why should they help us, when our people have trampled their land to take what we like—plundering gold and silver from their sacred mountains, claiming their home for ourselves?* This moment of clarity reminded me of the two silver nuggets in my satchel, and I swiftly produced them and urgently pushed them into the boy's hands, saying, "Take them, please. Take them, if only you will help us."

He was obliged to take them, as I had fairly shoved them at him, and he spent a moment inspecting them to determine if they were genuine. Then he stood and went back to the cluster of Indians behind him, who each inspected the silver nuggets in turn; and when their translator returned, he said he would present my offering and if it was accepted, then their *hatali* will heal my child.

I must have offered him thanks ten or eleven times as he stood and walked from me, but I was so delirious with exhaustion by then I hardly knew up from down. We were brought into the village, where an older woman and a girl brought us water to drink, and where all around us cast suspicious looks in our direction, for we are strangers here. They wear garments made from animal skins and are adorned with all manner of beaded jewelry; we remain clad in our dirtied dresses, aprons, and bonnets.

They brought us then to a small, warm dwelling that smelled of sweet smoke, and there I was unable to stop sleep from coming on. When I awoke, golden afternoon had fallen into night. An elderly woman with skin creased around her dark eyes sat beside me by the light of a fire, weaving. When she noticed I was awake, she brought a cup to my lips, and I drank eagerly. This was not water but some kind of tea, and it revived me enough to sit up and call out for Sophronia. The woman patted my hand and said something in her language, what sounded like a reassurance, but I could not understand. I tried to let her words reassure me, even without knowing what they meant.

An urgency to find Sophie filled me; I was filled with terror that they had taken her away and—and I knew not what they might do with her, but it feared me all the same. Outside of the old woman's hut I was met by a huge crackling fire that lit up the night, where far above, innumerable stars pricked the endless darkness. Around me, inscrutable faces looked at me with surprise; I called out to them, asking where they had taken Sophronia, but none answered until at last I found the young translator, who assured me that my offering had been accepted and that she had been taken to the *hatali*. "Now we must let him do his healing," he said.

I demanded to know where that was, but he refused to tell me; and I tried to remind myself that this is what I had wanted, after all: for their medicine man to heal my daughter and make her well. Still, I could not stop myself from fretting. Who is this *hatali*, and what will he do with her? What manner of strange medicine do they practice here? I know nothing about them, and my ignorance only fuels my fear.

Thank goodness I thought to bring you with me, Diary, for I knew I must record this journey. Writing has helped me to pass the time in waiting. Several small children scurried past me not an hour ago, curious at what I was doing, but they were chased away by a stooped older woman and scampered off into the night. The firelight now begins to strain my eyes.

A peculiar surmise has come over me—that even if (*when*) she is cured, Sophie and I will return to Virgil, and we will feel no more as if we belong there than we do here. An unsettling thought. I do not know why I should have it.

November 15, 1869

Last night, despite my bone-weariness, I hardly slept. It was as if the gravity of night weighed me down with a heaviness too terrible for sleep. When the cool, gray light of dawn alit on the craggy mountains, I rose with a kind of insomniac sensitivity to each breath of wind and went to the nearby creek to splash water over my face.

By and by I found the young translator again—Tsela is his name— and asked for any news of Sophronia. He only told me that we must not interrupt the healing, and that my presence, as non-Navajo, could ruin the ceremony.

Is it foolishness to have come here? Is it madness that I have brought my daughter to this mysterious medicine man, expecting a miracle?

My mind is either unraveling or opening like a flower. For if Virgil is haunted by strange spirits who drain the blood, spirits or demons that have escaped from a mine that leads to Hell, and now those creatures roam the desert—then why should I not believe in magic?

What would my mother say? Land sakes, if she could see me now! A disheveled mess, skirts torn and bonnet lost somewhere to the wind, begging at a tribal village for tricks. Perhaps I am just as gullible as John Henry believed me to be. I am a mind at war with itself, wanting both the hope of belief and the steady practicality of the skeptic.

Later

This afternoon I helped some of the women with their weaving, though my work was shoddy in comparison to their tight weave. At sewing or knitting I am expert, but weaving is another matter entirely. Yet they were kind, and though they did not speak English, we communicated by nods and smiles, and occasionally one of them came over to tighten my work.

It put me at ease, though I was in company of strangers and still have not seen Sophie. Nor will anyone tell me where, exactly, the medicine man is. I believe he is in one of these huts, but I have no way of knowing which one.

They have treated me well—better, I must admit, than the people of Virgil, with their suspicion and their hostility. Though I sense some hesitance and distrust, they have welcomed me and let me share in their food. Tonight we dined on rabbit and squash, and though I tried to eat little and make myself unobtrusive, Mosi—that is the old woman who has been sharing her hut—shook her head and pushed an extra piece of frybread upon me. It was delicious. I thanked her, and I think she understood.

After we supped, I found myself away from the crackle of the fire, near Mosi's hut, with tears springing from my eyes, which I could not stop. I sat in the dirt and cried until my eyes had dried, and when I was finished, there was Mosi. She draped a woven blanket over my shoulders and shuffled back into the hut.

It is too cold to stay out tonight. When I finish writing this, I will join Mosi in the small warm space and hopefully sleep until morning.

November 18, 1869

What is this accursed flesh of mine, that all I bear are withered fruits? That I am to love, only to lose? It cannot be my lot in life to suffer, but it seems so. No. I will not allow my daughter to die. Bring me Hell and damnation, but I will save her if I can.

It is only now upon returning that I feel able to give an account of what happened with the medicine man, who I was able at long last to see when Tsela took me to his hogan. We arrived at a hut of tree bark and mud supported by wooden poles, its east-facing doorway hung with an old blanket, like a curtain.

Tsela nodded for me to enter, though it was clear he did not intend to follow me inside. I meant to ask him how I might communicate with the medicine man, but I hadn't even the chance before Tsela was on his way back into the village.

With some wariness, I pulled the drapery aside and entered.

First I saw him: the old man, his skin tight over a skeletal frame, his eyes deep set and his movements like the sinuousness of smoke. Then I saw her, and at first I imagined something terrible had happened, for Sophie was black from head to foot, lying on the dirt floor, which had been intricately designed with colored sand or dirt.

I believe I must have cried out in shock at seeing Sophie all blackened in that manner, but the medicine man spoke to greet me, and he did so in English. Then he told me that she was only covered in charcoal, and that he had summoned me to help clean her of it. Sophie remained asleep, or unconscious.

His young assistant approached with a bucket of water and some rags. We soaked the rags and began to wash the charcoal from her fevered flesh, with the medicine man occasionally singing and chanting as we did. As I wrung out the rag in the darkening water and rubbed it gently on Sophie's tender flesh, I observed the colorful dirt beneath her, which seemed a sort of painting. There was yellow, white, and red that I found were ochre, gypsum, and sandstone: "a re-creation of the world," as he described it. When I asked him the purpose of the charcoal, he called it the Blackening Rite, which is used to ward off evil spirits.

I asked him if he believed she had been afflicted by evil spirits. Perhaps it is so; perhaps our whole family has been cursed.

"Contact with witches or spirits of the dead can lead to ghost sickness. The seer who diagnosed her believes she has been cursed by contact with one such creature."

Before I could stop myself, I murmured, "the Strange Lady," with horror and wonder. Yet I dashed away this thought at once, for if she were real, then she had been closer to Oscar than to Sophie—she had been closer to me than to Sophie.

Still, his words thrilled me with fear, and I looked again at my sweet child, at the flush of her freshly washed cheeks and the sallowness around her eyes. "Did it work?" I asked him. Even then, I knew the answer. I could feel it in the pit of my stomach.

"The ceremony is less potent for an outsider," he explained. His assistant continued cleaning Sophie's feet, and I wondered if he spoke English and if he could understand us; he seemed not to pay attention to our conversation at all. The medicine man continued: "White man is cursed with sickness."

"But she's just a girl," I insisted, "just a young girl. Can't she be spared?"

"No one is spared," he told me with darkness in his voice. "If it is an affliction by evil spirits, then the ceremony will work its healing. If it is some other sickness, then she must fight it on her own." He placed a hand on her hot forehead, covering it easily from hair to brow. "There is not much strength left in her, but she is fighting her battle for life. Every living being wants to survive."

His words clanged in my skull like the tolling of a knell. All my strength left me, and I sat back heavily on the dirt. In that moment I felt dull and distant from myself, and I seemed to speak words welling up from inside of me: "These witches—or spirits—where do they come from?" Instead of answering, he gave me a curious, knowing look, and I explained, "There are creatures in the night where I've come from. A town called Virgil. Spirits, who are said to have emerged from a doorway betwixt our world and Hell itself, deep inside of the mountain. They feed on our blood."

The medicine man grew very still. Then he nodded to his young assistant, who gathered up the rags and the bucket of filthy water, now that Sophie was clean, and left the hogan with these items. Then it was just my sleeping child, the medicine man, and me in the dim, warm hut. The man said, "Yes, I know this place."

My heart threw itself against my chest. "What are they?" I hardly dared whisper.

At first, he said nothing. His calculating eyes raced over me as if inspecting every inch of my skin. I felt as if he were peeling it back to reveal the dark sticky evil that lives in my heart—as if John Henry's lies have infected me and made me, too, untrustworthy, or else I am untrustworthy of my own merit. Or I am cursed; we are all cursed.

But at last he said, "They are not like us. They are an older kind of life, from an earlier world."

"What do they want?" I asked.

"They want only to survive, like every other living being."

For a time, we sat and I watched Sophie's chest rise and fall in measured breaths, feeling pitifully helpless. Imagining her fighting demons on some other plane of existence, trying to rip herself from the evil spirits and return to us. And here I sat, useless.

"They killed a child," I told him, remembering Mary Warrant's boy: his bloodless, punctured flesh, his staring eyes.

When next he spoke, his voice was filled with bitterness: "Some people come and trample over other life as if it has no meaning. Tear up the trees, slaughter the bison, destroy the earth itself. They think some life means less than theirs. When you disrespect life, do not be surprised when your life is disrespected in turn. Violence begets more violence."

In that moment, I recognized his meaning with absolute clarity. The people who had slaughtered his kin and stolen their land were of a kind with those who took women's bodies by force, or who spoiled the earth in their quest for wealth and comfort. It is perhaps the worst impulse of the human spirit, but deeply inherent: the centering of self above other, and the willingness to cause harm, as long as that harm is brought upon the other and not oneself.

These creatures are not fully human, yet I believe we share this impulse. They are human enough for evil.

It seems at last I can admit that the creature I beheld was not some figment of my overworked nerves but as real as my own self. The thing with the hideous, withered face, like a dried apple. I described this to the man, and he explained to me how the remains of his ancestors in the caves nearby have been preserved by the dry air.

I believe he was describing natural mummification. John Henry told me once about how Egyptian mummies may be ground into a powder and used as medicine, though I never did understand how the consumption of ancient human remains could cure one of much besides appetite. He always said if he ever got his hands on one, he would make it the key ingredient of his elixir.

Yet even if mummified, the beings in this cave do not succumb to death. They wither, yet they live. They sleep for long periods like some animals in winter. He told me, however, that like any other living thing, they harm primarily for survival. He warned that we need only fear the creature who harms for sport. "What creature does this?" he asked.

I feared I did not know enough about animals to give the correct answer, but I suspicioned what he aimed to disclose: "Men. It is men."

And I have been thinking on this ever since—during the wearying ride back through the desert, clouds of dust from the horse's hooves prickling my eyes, enduring the ache that grew in my legs from so many hours of riding, and the hunger and thirst that plagued me during those two days of our journey. Despite the immediacy of the physical world encroaching on me with all its discomforts, what troubled me the most was this realization, whereupon I began to have funny thoughts out there alone but for my delirious Sophie, thoughts about the creatures from the mine, thoughts about the kind of men who perhaps deserved that unspeakable fate. We do not begrudge the hungry bear killing a caribou for its meal; we only assign moral depravity to humans, perhaps because we are the sole species capable of electing to commit immoral acts with the full consciousness of their immorality and with no other reason than sport and self-gratification.

But what of self-preservation? For, Diary, as sickening as it may be, I believe I would slaughter men and women alike were I only able to save my daughter! What vile creature am I?

When the shaman told me again that every living being wants to survive, but "some realize that the cost of survival is simply too great," I wanted to tear him limb from limb. I refused to accept that Sophronia will not get better, to accept that she might give up. I grew livid and lashed out at the man.

"Perhaps it is you who wants to survive," he said. "At what cost? What are you willing to sacrifice for survival?"

"Anything," I hissed, as I have said countless times before, and I threw the blanket over the doorway aside so that I could breathe the fresh air, crisp and sun kissed, outside of the hut. I told him I would ready the horse, and then we would leave.

Only, as I made my way back to Mosi's hut for my satchel, I was met by a man with a warm smile who stood in my way and tried to put something into my hand. At last, I took it. It was a silver crescent moon threaded on a length of twine. Bewildered, I tried to ask the man what it was for, and it was only by the grace of Tsela's appearance that I learned it had been made from one of the silver nuggets, and the man trying to give it to me was a blacksmith.

"He learned silverwork from Atsidi Sani," said Tsela with some amount of pride. "He wants you to have it, as protection for your daughter."

I pulled the necklace over my head. The silver pendant knocked against my chest, cold at first, but warming against my skin. It is a beautiful piece of craftsmanship. I hadn't expected such a gift, and I admit this token of kindness brought a lump to my throat. I thanked the blacksmith directly, and even without Tsela's translation I think he understood.

When we set off on our ride, I was still trembling with emotion, thinking again of those creatures who wither but do not die, and my Sophie, so young and unwithered, who will die. I can feel her soul slipping out from the crevices of her body, a body losing the will to fasten tight and hold it in. Had I but some magic elixir that delivered all the promises John Henry once made! Can such a thing exist? My mind began to turn over that medicine made from mummified remains. I have never believed in such strange miracles, but I thought, *Now I am willing to believe anything if only it will save her—for I know in my heart, I cannot continue without her.*

If her soul should fly, then, sin or not, I will destroy myself.

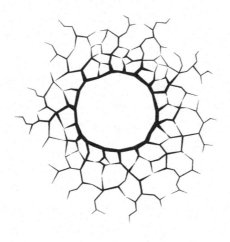

THE DUST DEVILS

THE WALLS SEEMED TO close around her as Waynoka stepped into the tunnel. When she was perhaps ten paces in, the jangling of a bell set her nerves on end. She turned, shined the flashlight back toward the room, and hollered for Mads—there was something down here, there was something with them, something Lavinia had warned would *drain your blood*—but Mads called out, "For good luck!" And Waynoka realized she had tapped the bell.

She couldn't have known what the bell signified to Waynoka. Not good luck at all.

"Don't do that again," she shouted back to the distant bulb of reddish light that was the room with the fire. Her feet led her on.

WHEN SHE MADE IT to the branching tunnel, she hesitated at the jagged opening.

It seemed silly to fear this new place, when her very flesh was calling out to go somewhere—*anywhere*—that wasn't this same narrow tunnel and that same tiny room, somewhere that wasn't an abandoned mine or a cave carved into the heart of the mountain by some ancient geological phenomenon, a cave never meant to see the light of day. So deep in the interior of the earth, it was fathoms below where even the dead luxuriated in their six-foot-deep coffins embraced by moist soil. This was the stony depths of, if not Hell in the religious sense, then perhaps something like it, something as unfathomably bleak and horrifying. Hell was, after all, only a human conceit. Whatever this was went far beyond the simplistic ways that humans attempted to understand the world.

She shined the flashlight into the opening and stepped inside, desperately hoping this could be their way out.

Right away she surmised this was not just another tunnel. The narrow walls opened up into a wide chamber. Jagged fangs reared down from the ceiling like icicles made of stone.

Her breath seemed too loud as it dragged in and out of her throat.

She turned the light about the chamber, thinking, *No, no, no.* At first, it seemed as if oddly shaped rocks had been fashioned into some sort of design, an artistic pattern. It was not until she examined the lumpy wall, with its series of nearly identical rounded shapes, that she understood they were not rocks, but bones.

A wall of crumbling skulls stared out at her, as if to say *Abandon all hope.*

Waynoka nearly turned and ran back the way she'd come. She would have, were she not frozen with recognition that she had stepped into a burial chamber.

The burial chamber.

When she stepped backward, her foot sank into something soft, something very much not stone. With a vivid flash of nearly falling to her death through the rotted boards covering up that hidden mineshaft, she leapt away on instinct and shined the light down to see what it was she'd trod on, what had squished unpleasantly beneath her foot.

A dead bat.

She moved the light over the floor, not having noticed at first, for the shapes looked just like uneven rocky ground when not in the full glare of the flashlight; but now she recognized them with something dreadful climbing up her throat: the floor was littered with dead bats.

These were not bones, nor ancient mummified remains. These were freshly dead.

The light jumped and trembled in her grasp.

Still, she was determined to find what she had come for: an exit. There *had* to be a way out. She had to get them both out of this nightmare.

When she reached the far wall of pure rock and discovered no immediate egress, she began tumbling immediately over the precipice of panic. Her body churned like disturbed sludge. She lay her hands on the wall and leaned against its unpleasant warmth.

"No!" she shouted, pounding her fist against the solid rock. Her eyes burned with unshed tears. "Please." Her breath shuddered. "Please. We need to get out."

She steadied herself and swept the light around the room, disturbed all over again at the dead bats on the ground, the skulls embedded in the walls. Part of her felt as if she could not return to Mads with more bad news.

But who had created the secret hollow? Surely that person had gotten out?

Or perhaps not. Maybe that person had died down here long ago. Maybe that person had drowned in the sump, or gotten lost in the endless tunnels, or . . .

. . . *or maybe that person was still haunting the cave*, she thought, the back of her neck prickling; maybe that person was the one she had glimpsed in the shadows, the one who had spoken in that dry whispery voice.

She felt along the wall, desperate for some semblance of a breeze, any sign at all that this wasn't the dead end she knew it must be. The empty sockets of the skulls along the wall seemed to watch her hungrily. Black holes for eyes.

And then she saw it.

Wedged between two stalactites that bore a passing resemblance to a pair of tusks hung loosely on a dripping jaw: an opening.

She shined her flashlight into it to be sure it wasn't some illusion of light on the cave wall, and she found a set of crude stone stairs—manmade perhaps, but so eroded they almost looked like a natural accident—leading down.

How long ago had they been carved from the rock? Hundreds of years? Thousands?

Whatever it was, she knew it could not be a way out. It led only deeper into the cave.

But what if—by some strange miracle—there *was* an exit down there?

She could not turn back now. Not without knowing.

Still, the darkness below raised gooseflesh on her bare arms, and she wondered how far she would be willing to go before she'd inevitably have to turn back.

She took one step down, and another.

The stairwell enclosed her like the shaft they had descended on that rotten ladder. The craggy walls hugged her, and the ceiling lowered with the stairs, tight as a tomb.

Once, she paused to turn and look back up to see how far she had come down the stairs, but her flashlight only glanced the distant opening to the burial chamber above.

She kept going.

Every crunch of her boot on the crumbling stone echoed with ghostly reverberations. Her breath sounded loud in the enclosed space.

And then, at last, she made it to the bottom.

There was no breeze. No opening. Only blackness.

Her flashlight beam shone straight ahead, one lone unbroken band in the steady darkness, like the singular eye of a lighthouse casting out to the alien milieu of the crashing sea—not knowing what it will find, if it dares sweep across that undulation of repeated patterns, but dreading, perhaps, the glimpse of a ghost ship hulking somewhere at the unseen place where sea meets sky. Thus she did not move, for if she swept the flashlight one way or the other, what would she find? The dark here felt inhabited yet desolate, like the abandoned town so far above.

What lay buried here?

For, she realized, what she had seen above had not been the burial chamber. There were no bodies. Only bats and skulls and bones.

It was with intense concentration that she forced her arm to move and sweep the beam across the room, where it caught, in brief glimpses—as if that was all the light could possibly allow, or all Waynoka could allow herself—a museum of figures.

They stood like waxworks, stiff and unyielding, distinctly human in shape, though of a particularly narrow and wasted sort, like a picture of starvation. And though they stood, they seemed like statues, or else deep in sleep.

Like some animals in winter.

Hibernating.

Her hand trembled, but she knew she had to steady the light on one of these creatures. She could not turn and run back now. She couldn't chicken out like at the secret hollow. She had to know. She had to see what Lavinia had seen. Even so, an instinctual part of her wanted to flee. She could run back, couldn't she? Back to Mads; she could tell her she had reached only a dead end, that there was no way out. And then? And then . . . there was no way out.

There was no way out.

She felt compelled to look but told herself if she caught any movement, she would not hesitate to flee. The figures stood frozen, catatonic. There was no sign of the ghostly creature who had met her at the sump.

Turning the flashlight to the nearest figure, she stared full into (what passed for) its face.

A face ancient and leathery, creased as the binding of an old book; lips shrunken back from the rotten teeth in a perpetual snarl; and the mummified flesh covered by a multitude of thorny spines protruding in all directions and from every bit of dermis, tips like deadly needles.

She thought of the doll with nails driven into its head.

Waynoka sucked in a sharp breath and flinched, her fingers letting loose the flashlight, which dropped to the ground, clattered, and went out. In that moment of pitch darkness—of wild, blinding fright—she flailed out her arms because it is better, perhaps, to encounter something strange in the dark with one's hands rather than feeling the breath of some unseen thing on one's face. But as she did, her right hand sank onto a bed of pins. Sharp pain sang through her palm. She pulled her hand back, dislodging the needles, and fell to her knees to find the light. As soon as she did, she wound it with her aching hand, stumbling at once to her feet.

When it came on, the beam swung wildly as she half crawled, half ran toward the stone steps—it swung around, once, behind her, and she cast back a glance, if only to see the figure on which she had injured herself. And see it she did, but this time she also saw the black gleam of its open eyes.

⬛

SHE RAN BACK TO the little room, bumping into the walls so many times she scraped her shirt at the shoulders and was sure she would end up with bruises, but could hardly care. She caught herself one-handed, smearing blood on the walls, dizzy with revulsion at the thing in the burial chamber, thinking only that it was the same sort of gnarled, twisted face she had glimpsed in reflection at the sump.

The face Lavinia had glimpsed in the desert.

⬛

WITH RELIEF SHE FELL through the tunnel's mouth into the smoky, firelit room where Mads sat, and the crash startled her partner badly enough that she cried out.

The flashlight rolled across the floor as Waynoka fell to her knees, gasping in the dry, wretched air and unable to stop the trembling fed by adrenaline and terror. She clutched at a stitch in her side, having run full tilt the entire way back along the narrow, winding tunnel.

"What?" said Mads. "What the hell did you find?"

"Not a way out," Waynoka gasped. "It's not a way out."

Her ragged breathing filled the silence. She turned around, horrified at the notion of having her back to the dark mouth of that tunnel, but instead found her eyes locked on the figure of red ochre, the one with lines radiating out from it like the sun, and she gasped, unable to get in enough air as she recognized what it was.

It took some effort to pry the old wheelbarrow from where it had glued itself with a crust of corrosion to the wall and floor. Heaving it forward so that it turned onto its nose, she propped it over the entrance to the tunnel, trying to lodge it in a steady position. It didn't completely cover the tunnel, and the movement sent the bell jangling, which buzzed through Waynoka's nerves like lightning.

Behind her, Mads was asking what she was doing, but Waynoka could not be bothered to answer until she'd covered the entrance. There were some old tools nearby, a shovel and a pickax, and these she added to the barrier, along with the remaining bits of wood from the broken-down crate. When she was finished, she sat back, breathing hard, then reached for the pot and took a long drink. Wiped its excess from her lips. Gasped again, air as precious as water.

"There's something down there," she said, and finally looked at her right hand by the light of the small fire. Mads leaned in close to see the dozen puncture wounds making a lotus seed head of her soft, bloodied flesh.

At the sight of it, Mads went very still. "What did this?"

"The—the *things*. Down there."

She tried to forget the sight of the open eyes like two glassy, dark pools. Probably the things hibernated with their eyes open. She must have been too focused on the spiky protrusions and the withered flesh to notice at first glance, and it was only at a distance that the light could shine on those staring orbs and make them glimmer and wink like black mirrors.

"We need to get out of here," she said, and almost laughed at herself for needing to voice such an obvious statement. "We need to get the *fuck* out of here" felt a little better, but still not vehement enough.

"How?"

Waynoka thought furiously. The fire crackled. She wound her brain like the flashlight, trying to get it to flicker to life.

"Back the way we came."

"We can't get back up that way," Mads reminded her.

"But there must be another tunnel! Some other way we missed!" Waynoka stood, walked to one wall, turned, paced. Her fear had made her agitated, and she felt compelled to keep moving. "Just because the way we came down is—just because that ladder broke, doesn't mean—there must be another one, another way—"

"Then we need to think strategically," Mads cut in. "Map out our options. See what we can find. We have to be smart about this. We can't just go running off half cocked."

"Like we did to get *here?*" Waynoka snapped.

"*I* can't go running around." The way Mads was hunched over her bad leg, her mane of curly hair haloing her like a defeated lion's, her eyes refusing to meet Waynoka's, it was clear she was reluctant to admit her incapacitation. "*If* we find a ladder somewhere, I won't be able to climb it if I've spent hours traipsing through miles of rough underground tunnels on this leg."

Waynoka knew she wouldn't be able to climb a ladder, period.

A long thread of quiet tension elapsed between them. The kind of quiet that bears no sense of peace or pleasantness but is so filled with every awful thought and feeling one can imagine that it becomes a kind of emptiness ripe for bursting.

What can one say that could possibly break that tension and tip it toward relief? No matter the words, a dam will break and secrete the poison hanging heavy in the air like a cloud of noxious gas into its victim's pores.

The words that come next will always be the wrong ones, the worst ones.

"I told you there was something down here," Waynoka said.

"Are you serious? You're really gonna 'I-told-you-so' me?"

The silence that followed then was even more disgruntled.

Mads finally broke it. "What was it, really?"

"Lavinia told me about it," said Waynoka, and Mads did not correct her strange syntactical choice. "They came out of the mine in 1869 and killed people in the town. Drained their blood." She didn't want to describe what they looked like. Obscene. Unnatural. As if humanity had taken a wrong turn in some dark corner of history. "The shaman said they're . . . an older kind of life. From an earlier world."

"The *shaman*?" Mads said incredulously.

"Yes."

A moment turned over as Mads chewed on this. She frowned. "Hmm."

"What?"

Mads stretched out her legs, massaging the muscular thigh just above the mess of her shattered, swollen knee.

"You ever heard of shadow life?"

Waynoka shook her head.

"Something I read about, once, before everything went to shit. Some scientists, you know. Speculating on another form of life that came about at the same time ours did, or even before, but with different—a different makeup, or something." When Waynoka continued to stare at her, Mads tried to explain. "Like, life that isn't made of DNA, or has just evolved in a completely different way than everything else. It kind of reminded me that people aren't, like, the end-all, be-all, you know? They said there probably wasn't just one origin event for life, that it probably happened in a few differ-ent ways, in different places, around the same time. One of those gave rise to us, and all the kinds of life we're familiar with. But what about those other events where life sparked in a totally different way? Just because we're the dominant ones doesn't mean we're the *only* ones. And maybe we *shouldn't* be, really, considering how much we've fucked everything up. It's almost hopeful, the idea that something better than us could be out there."

This did not make Waynoka feel any better. She sat down next to Mads, watching the bubbles of blood dry and crust over on her palm. "Shadow life," she murmured.

"Just a theory. I don't even know what you saw. It just made me think of that. I always thought it was kind of cool."

The way Mads said it was as if she were jealous that Waynoka had witnessed something so profoundly strange while she hadn't—but Waynoka would have given anything to forget she had ever found that burial chamber. She could understand, now, why those miners had wanted nothing to do with it, had wanted to close it off.

They had tried, with the collapse. Was it that pile of rocks they had wormed their way through in getting to this little room with the makeshift bed? Was that the spot they had chosen to block off, so that no one else could get through to the horror that lay at the end of the tunnel?

Was that where John Henry had been crushed to death?

"Did that book tell you anything else about them?" asked Mads, kicking the bag with her good foot so that it almost dislodged the diary which sat on top. "Did it say *anything* about it?"

Waynoka reached over and picked it up. "No. Not really."

Mads harrumphed. "Figure if you were going to read that whole thing, might as well give us an idea of what to do. Where to go from here."

"I haven't read the whole thing yet," said Waynoka. "There's still a bit more."

"Well . . ." Mads nodded toward the book. "Look through the rest of it, then, yeah? See what she says? I mean, it would suck if you read most of it and stopped before it finally told you something useful. Damn thing got down here somehow, right?"

Waynoka nodded. She creaked open the book. Lavinia's words, her familiar scrawl, fell into her lap. But she was still too keyed up to just sit there and read. She stared at the flimsy barrier she had erected over the entrance to the tunnel, willing it to keep them safe. Then she took a deep breath, held it, slowly released it. Breathed a few times like this, until her heart slowed its frantic thumping and she no longer felt the need to run until her feet bled. Mads was right. They had to be smart. They were safe here, for now. She had to believe that. They were safe here.

"As soon as I finish," she said, "We're getting out of here. One way or the other. Even if it doesn't tell us which way to go. We're going."

Mads nodded. "Read fast, then."

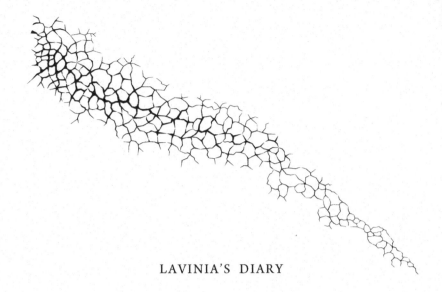

LAVINIA'S DIARY

November 19, 1869

The cold has come on with insensible swiftness. As if the day were only a warm exhalation, the twilight of vanished breath a suffocation of winter.

Sophie, Sophie. Still as a corpse, her skin like the very cold of winter. What will revive you? My life? You can have it! What need have I for it, anyway? What is my life, but a sad scrawl in the pages of a book, bound for some imminent end?

My world lives in your breast. Oscar—he has no need of me. I am no good to him.

When we rode into town, Doctor Hartsworth gave us a more enthusiastic greeting than even my own son. He relieved me of my burden and carried Sophie's limp form into his house to see to her as I stretched my aching limbs.

And he left me with Oscar and the whole world between us now.

I must have asked him if he was keeping up with his schooling, if he was learning from Doctor Hartsworth—such picayune questions that seem like they might have been important, once. He only pointed to my neck and said, "What's that?"

I had most forgotten the silver crescent about my neck hanging on its twine, and my fingers found it before my recollection did. I told him it was a gift from his father's silver nugget, the one he had prized out of the mountain. "Doctor says silver's good luck," he told me. "Doctor says, it's almighty powerful. Doctor says, it's good for healing."

"Is that right?"

The boy nodded. "You put it in your water to keep it fresh, and he showed me stitching skin with silver wire."

His words recalled to me the kinds of things John Henry used to say about his elixir and all its healing properties. I don't know that I set much store by what all silver is good for, but if it is true, then maybe it's what J. H. ought to have been looking for all the time, after all—maybe silver is his Darling's Elixir. If only silver could have saved him!

Yet it isn't just for healing, is it? The doctor (by way of Oscar) intimated silver is potent in other respects. And hasn't silver served for much superstition in the course of history? Hasn't silver been said to protect against evil spirits? I know I've heard that somewhere or other. Then wouldn't it make sense that a right smart grist of silver in that mountain might've kept the demons trapped in, where they were all this long while—and that it wasn't only Emery breaking through into their burial chamber (or their hibernating chamber?) that set them loose but also the whole of the Virgil Consolidated Mining Company, systematically plundering the silver that had protected all Creation from what was inside of that mountain for as long as life has lived, and in doing so, unleashing Hell just like one unlocking a door that cannot be locked up again?

Then it wasn't ever Emery's fault at all—and what they did to John Henry was for nothing too, like putting a bandage on a bullet wound. I'm glad that Willie Ray Randall will meet his maker for what he's done—but his punishment, too, is little consolation, for it wasn't only him that did this to my family, was it?

Now I'm all consumed with wild ideas, which didn't occur to me when Oscar and I brought the horse to the barn and sat together in the hay. I was too busy trying to gauge how much I had lost Oscar, who was eager to stay on with the doctor. When he told me all of the things the doctor allowed him to help with, all the things he'd learned already, my breast swelled with pride and filled, too, with a queer salt-laced sorrow for having lost something I know I will never get back. But if I am to lose one child, I will not lose the other.

Before I left the barn, I addressed Oscar carefully: "Do you remember that old woman in the desert, who injured your hand?" He nodded. "Have you seen her again?" Now a shake of the head. "Is there anything else you can tell me about her?"

He hesitated. I knew it was because of the way I had previously reacted to his claims, so I told him I believed him now, and he said, "Doctor says she's a demon from the mine and I oughtn't look at her because she will eat me."

I took his hand—he nearly flinched, which opened a profound well of darkness within me—and I told him, "I will *never* let that happen."

The desert creeps. It creeps around us with its own life. But I will not allow it to harm my children.

With cool, wet rags the doctor managed to bring down Sophie's fever, and she woke enough to drink some soup. Her delirium remained, though. Between sips she gibbered nonsense, said she heard bells even though none were ringing, and asked repeatedly for her father as if he were not in the ground.

The doctor implored me to keep Sophie there so he might tend to her. But what could he have done? He has already told me there is nothing but to keep her rested—he cannot help her, and neither could the medicine man. So I have taken her home with me, where she belongs.

If *they* cannot save her, I will find a way myself.

Silver. *Sophie. Sophie.*

Sophie.

Later

I fell asleep over my book before I could finish writing.

I fear—what has woken me now? In the dark? Sophie is asleep. All is still and quiet, but—

Oh God, there they are again! The sound of their ringing, like a death knell! It is the bells—it is the bells—it is the bells the bells—

Now they are stopped. Now they are silenced.

Now I lighted a lantern and saw at once the door swinging to and fro in the bitter wind, setting off the shrill peal of the bell again and again, as if to taunt me. When I went to close it, I paused over the darkness without, the hungry night, which creeps over and swallows the desert.

And I remembered, morbidly, that in one week hence, Willy Ray Randall shall be dead.

This was revealed to me as I brought Sophie back home—as we rode through town from the doctor's house to our own little cabin.

Evening purpled the sky in its frightfully beautiful blaze as we neared home. Yet as we passed, I saw Chester Blackburn and Olive Randall in the throes of agitation. Olive sagged like a rag doll and sobbed in Chester's stony arms as he tried to hold her aloft and console her.

I slowed the horse to a gentle trot and called over, for though I may dislike Olive, to see the biting woman with the firmness of an oak in such distress concerned me. What was it that could bring such a fiery creature into this sorry state?

"What is the matter?" I asked. Chester turned his black eyes to me and said nothing, as is his way. In spite of her tears, Olive managed to look up with dark hair tangled over her despairing face, her pallor acute and her mouth twisted into an angry and sorrowful shape.

"They've set a date for his execution," she told me, her voice hitching on the final word. "In one week."

I would have asked whose, but I needn't have—I knew the answer. And while this put my mind at ease, that he should finally be given the punishment he deserves, what came out of my mouth was congenial: "I'm sorry."

"Go to Hell," Olive snarled. Her eyes gleamed like cruel dark chips of stone behind their sheen of tears as she cursed me and mine. "May all the Cains rot in Hell! Damn you! Damn you all! The Devil take you!"

She continued to shout obscenities at me while I rode away, secretly smiling, for though I understand Olive's pain more acutely than I can express, the knowledge of Willie Ray Randall's imminent execution soothes my wounded heart.

November 20, 1869

Hibernating. Hibernating. Seems much pleasanter to sleep than to die. To sleep without need of nourishment. To sleep for long periods, years, perhaps. Sleep and sleep. I am so very tired.

There is death out there in the darkness.

Willie Ray Randall will die by the noose.

But these creatures—these things that live in the night . . . they do not die.

They hibernate, like bears, but they live far longer than bears. Somehow, they hold the key to long life. Is it in their makeup? If we grind them to a fine powder, could we take in their immortality?

How is it? Do they survive on our lifeblood? What is their secret?

Claudia tried to visit, having heard tell of our return, but I sent her away. She seems anxious for me. I told her I am no matter. My life is wrapped up in Sophie's. If she dies, I die. Be anxious, then, for dear Sophie, who lies fevered and delirious, soaking her bedsheets.

Perhaps Sophie merely needs to hibernate.

November 21, 1869

I have a strange tale to tell.

Hah! Now I read that back to myself, it seems unnecessary to say. What is this whole long yarn I have been telling but a strange tale?

It is strange, perhaps, how the mine has drawn me to it. At once dreadful and intriguing, I have resented its pull, its hold over this town since we arrived—the way it drew John Henry immediately away from us, the way it is secreted in the mountains that loom over Virgil. A mystery of rock and riches. It terrifies and compels me, and I see, now, why John Henry was so intent on going farther into its depths, exploring deeper, to find the beauty at the heart of its darkness.

Now that I have been there—no, let me go back and explain.

I woke in the night to the music of distant chimes. This hypnotic lullaby might induce sleep in those whose ears have not attuned themselves so acutely to the horror that attends the sound of bells, but upon recognition, I sat up at once, sleep torn away like fragile cobwebs to leave me starkly, abruptly awake. Again I listened, and again I heard bells, but these were not the ones above my own door and so echoed faintly from beyond. In the bleak desert, the wind carries music far, scraping it gently over the hollow landscape.

Instead of hiding here in our cabin and waiting for morning, I knew what I must do. The bells were calling to me. I donned my bloomers and absconded into the night with gun and lantern.

The wind blew the sound toward me, and I followed it with my ears. That open darkness pressed around the warm lantern light that carried me like a beacon through a black sea. I passed the cabin of Chester Blackburn and continued until I made a shocking discovery. At first I could not tell what it was I beheld in the muted light I carried. The moon was only a strange yellow leer in the Heavens and imparted little lucidity.

A figure stood embracing another—but it was a terrible embrace born not of love or anything like it. This embrace was born of hunger. A thick sucking sound emerged from the hugging figures, and with each inflection of the awful sound came a flexing and undulating, as if breathing.

I held my lantern aloft but could make out little detail beyond the shapes and movements. So I set down the lantern and fired the gun.

My aim was true (I have been practicing), and the embracing figure dropped the other to the ground. As I lifted the lantern again, I saw the figure limp away on swift but stilted limbs.

Hurrying to the more injured party, I dropped beside the abandoned figure and turned it over.

There lay a man I did not recognize, but who likely worked the mine; his dark hair was matted with blood, his stubble-peppered cheeks pocked, too, with puncture wounds that bled sluggishly, so that his face bore minute bubbles of blood all over it, little red beads dotting him all through. Spots of blood stained his nightclothes, too.

It was the deadly embrace—by a creature whose very skin was armored in sharp weapons!

But it had not finished its meal; this man was not white and bloodless, like the others, but still bleeding, still living. I felt his heartbeat, sluggish as it was, and his breath on my cheek when I leaned close to him.

He needed help. When I looked around me, I saw only the other figure stumbling off into the distance, heading in the direction of the mountain— the direction John Henry would take to the mine.

I had only a moment's hesitation. Ought I to have stayed there, helped the man? I did not think his wounds were the sort that would lead him to bleed to death, but it was clear he had already lost some quantity of blood— enough for his life to hang in the balance.

Instead, I called out at the top of my voice, "Help! Help! A man is dying! Help!" and ran off again, after the fleeing figure.

I chased it to the edge of town and up the steep road to the mine's entrance. The lantern birthed the desert from out of nothing where I tread, so that each step was upon me almost before I could see it. Clouds roamed over the stars, and the wind grew harsher the higher I climbed, snapping against me with such relentless cold it was like the devil's breath.

Ahead of me lay the entrance to the mine: a squared maw, a sore hole in the bowels of the mountain, like an open wound. A track ran into this mouth and disappeared, as all seemed to disappear into that gaping darkness. As if the darkness in which I tread, and which I thought to be quite deep and impenetrable, were in fact merely a precursor to the true and boundless dark that lay ahead.

Here is where I nearly stopped, for to bring myself through that entrance meant stepping into another world entirely—as if this were the gateway to Hell after all, and those who proposed its existence deep in the mine were only fooling themselves about where that doorway lay.

Yet, as I've said, the mine drew me, as if it breathed me in; moths do destroy themselves against an open flame, and perhaps it is people who do the same when they hear the siren song of darkness.

Within, the various sounds of the night—insects, the wheeze of wind—vanished into an abiding silence. The walls, rough and rocky, stood close. I gazed down a long, narrow tunnel, able to see only as far as the lantern allowed, and each step was like walking into the entrance, again and again, always moving blindly into the unknown. I lost my sense of where I was; my only path lay in the stretch of darkness behind me and the identical stretch ahead. Both sides, up and down—encased me in this stony channel. I could continue forward, or I could turn back.

These were my only options.

I continued.

Though I tried to keep my bearings, as I've said, it was impossible; for once I came to the first place of diverging paths, each one identical to the other, I could only pause and listen for the sound of the escaping figure's footfalls and choose the way I thought more likely. I had wounded it with my shot; it could not move as quickly as it would uninjured; and I intended to catch it and learn its secrets.

The fool I was, thinking it would be as easy as that!

Each time I thought I glimpsed the figure ahead of me by my lantern light, it managed to elude me again, until I was all twisted and turned around, hardly knowing up from down. These pitch-dark tunnels proceeding end-lessly into the earth had enticed me into a dizzying, inescapable warren.

The longer I moved, lost, through the mine, the more acutely aware I became that I had left Sophronia home alone and unattended, and I could feel my worry for her etch its way across my skin like a cloak made of bee-tles. The fear became intolerable. For it was not just fear that Sophronia was alone, but fear that I may never make it out of that terrible place, that it had sucked me in and would keep me there for all eternity.

Different, far different from the night I had spent lost in the desert. At least out there, I knew I could eventually find my way home, when the sun rose and lighted the way.

But when the sun rose in the mine, it would be just as dark and lonely, just as narrow and winding. There was no respite. And eventually my lantern would die and plunge me into eternal night.

I may have slept. Sleeping and waking both are a strange experience in those tunnels. If I did sleep, it was on my feet, in a continual shambling locomotion.

It was not the sun that saved me, but a miner. The fellow I knew from the saloon, Adam Scarborough.

He was horrified when he found me, and we spent several minutes each lost to our own emotions—him to his confusion and shock, mine to my great relief, which expunged itself as tears.

With his own light (my lantern had gone out hours previous, but I do not wish to write of what it was like, sitting in that perpetual darkness), he guided me out of the mine and then escorted me home. I fell into my bed, exhausted. Sophie was sleeping peacefully and awoke only at the brief commotion. Still fevered—for too long now, I know, it has been too long—she drifted off again.

Once he had seen to my immediate well-being, Adam left us to return to the mine, saying that he would call on the doctor so that he might check on us again later. He admonished me, too, about wandering into the mine the way I had. "It was just lucky I found you," he said.

Just before he left, I took his hand, remembering abruptly, when he mentioned the doctor—I asked for news of a miner who had been attacked the night before.

Surprise showed on his face. "Smith? Yes, he was found in the night and brought to the doctor's. As far as I know, he remains there." Then he eyed me shrewdly. "You know what happened, do you?"

"I saw it myself," I told him. "That is why I went into the mine. I pursued the attacker there."

Adam nodded slowly. "I suspect we will hear the full story from Smith, when he recovers. Then we will know who has been behind these attacks."

I almost laughed at him. "We already know. It is the demons from the mine."

He paled. "Enough of that talk."

"It's true. I saw it. It was . . . drinking him," I said.

"Enough!" he shouted, his fury silencing me. I remember, word by word, what he said next, for it is engraved in the sickness of my heart: "I said enough of this. I was willing to swallow your nonsense after John Henry died, but no more. You are deluded—drunk and shouting that your husband was murdered, riding off to meet with Indians, willfully abandoning your young child. The whole town thinks you a madwoman. What would they think of you now, dashing off into the mine on a whim? The Widow Cain, mad and hysterical! Your other child ought to be taken from you too. You are no fit mother."

With this, he left.

I have run over his words now many times, finding myself by turns shaking with anger and filled with the silent stillness of despair. To see myself from the outside—to see what the rest of Virgil sees when looking at me—how strange. But, by and by, it ceased to worry me. What does it matter what this foul little town thinks of me? The only thing that matters now is making Sophie well. Let them think me a madwoman. Their thoughts cannot harm me.

The next time I go into the mine, I will be prepared.

November 23, 1869

I have learned to find my way out again. Nights are best for searching the mine, when it is quiet and empty of its workers, and I am out before dawn. No one knows. I creep in, I creep out. So far I have found nothing, but at least now I can tell where I am going. I wear my silver necklace for luck, and to protect me from evil. As I map the tunnels, I know, truly, where it is I must go. I must find where John Henry was killed. I must find the collapse, the place they tried to close off—as if they could keep Hell out of our town! If Hell it is, then I will gladly make a deal with the Devil. Hell is already in the men of this place, and we only pretend it is not here, among us.

November 24, 1869

Violence only begets violence. I'm sure I've heard that somewhere.

John Henry may have had his own flaws, but he was never a violent man. His art lay in his tongue, his entreaties to envision a better world, a better life. If only reality had not disposed itself toward the worse. Even Emery, who was ever more the physical presence, short of words, believed in peace.

Had they lived long enough, would this be changed? Or are some men inherently inclined toward violence?

My hope, now, is that Oscar will grow to deplore violence, to value kindness. Where he is now, or where I hope he will be, perhaps this will come to pass.

My mind remains fixated upon the excruciating details, so I shall purge them here on the page.

The man I had found, half dead, recovered himself by the doctor's hand. Smith. A talkative fellow. Word from him spread through the town like a sickness: he had been attacked by a mysterious force he could not see in the dark, and found himself delirious and bleeding on the ground, with the Widow Cain standing over him holding a lantern and gun. Draw your own conclusions, he said of that.

This I discovered when I made a necessary trip into town—we had little food left, having sold the animals I could no longer keep—and I needed to replenish our stores. As I had vowed after what happened with Rutherford Branson, I brought the gun with me, but there I encountered the suspicious glances and swift condemnation of all who crossed my path, and it came out, by and by, what the recovering miner had said.

I could not hope to convince them that I had, in fact, saved the man's life. They were only too eager to believe the evil madness of the Widow Cain, who had become wild and unpredictable.

They whispered loud enough for me to hear: "They say she went mad with grief when her husband died," and, "What did she do with those Indians I wonder—learn some dark magic?" and "You know, she attacked poor Rutherford Branson, she did."

When I tried to ignore them and continue, I found myself barred in the doorway of the general store by Mr. Pavlovsky himself, who said, "That's far enough, Mrs. Cain. Turn around and go about your business, now."

"You've never had a problem with my shopping here before," I reminded him. He looked a mite uncomfortable at that, unsure of himself and his own actions; I know Cecil Pavlovsky for a gentle man, never ornery or confrontational. I even offered to leave my gun at the door, but he did not find that an acceptable compromise.

"I don't want any trouble, Mrs. Cain, and you do seem to bring trouble wherever you go. I've heard what Smith is saying about you, and I don't like it, and that's all."

Furious that I was unable even to do my shopping, beset by these accusations, I turned and made my way without hesitation to the doctor's house to confront the blasted man myself.

Before I could approach the door to knock, the doctor stepped out. He had seen me coming—and the trail of accusers who followed behind, curious to know what the Widow Cain might do next.

Betrayal upon betrayal—for this small crowd included those I had come to trust, if trust can indeed be bestowed upon anyone: Josephine Pavlovsky (they live behind the store and she had come out at the ruckus); Virginia and Gertrude, who I liked when we'd met; and even—I write with bitterness—Mary Warrant!

The men's anger did not surprise me. Anger is their regrettable domain. It was the women's righteous vitriol, their willingness to turn their backs so swiftly upon me, that hurt.

"Now, Mrs. Cain," said Doctor Hartsworth, holding up his hands at my approach. I stopped where I was, several paces away. "Whyn't you put down that gun and we can have a civilized talk?"

"You have allowed these slanderous rumors about me to go unchecked—from your own home!" I called out to him, the very sight of his calm face provoking my ire. "Let him who accuses me come out and tell me himself what he thinks he saw. Or isn't he a man?"

"Edgar Smith is a patient of mine, and he needs to recuperate. Coming here and waking snakes won't help any," he said.

But almost at once, as if to defy his own doctor's orders, the man himself came limping out the door. Bandages covered his hands, and his face bore traces of a poultice that had been smeared over the various scabbing pocks in his flesh.

He otherwise appeared pale and weak but stood his ground and turned his dark eyes at once on me.

"That's her!" he shouted, pointing an accusing finger in my direction. "She's the one done it! The Widow Cain tried to kill me! She pulled me from my bed, stung me with her poisoned pins—you heard what she done to the tailor!" There were some murmurs of recognition at this. "Then, after she'd nearly bled me dry, she picked up her gun to finish the job, but she must've realized she could never get away with such a sin, and she ran off into the night, like a coward!"

I was almost too infuriated to speak, though I did manage to tell him what a filthy liar he is.

His words, more than mine, held resonance with the stirring crowd. Mr. Pavlovsky stood back closer to his store, watching us; someone else peered out at the scene through the window of the post office; there were several women on the porch of the boardinghouse, drawn by the ruckus. And of course, there was the boodle of people who had unabashedly gathered to watch the scene unfold.

"Now, we don't have all the facts," said the doctor. "I've sent for the law, who will be here soon to clear all this up."

"There's nothing to clear up," said Mr. Smith. "I know what I saw, and you all know it's the truth. It's the Cains, the whole lot of 'em. You ask me, Willie Ray was right, what he did. They brought all this down on us. They're the devils."

I wanted to explain to them how absurd it all was. First, how many pins would I have to carry to puncture him all over in such a way? How could I have dragged him from his bed—what strength have I to do such a thing? And what about all the others, the ones who had died before we even arrived in Virgil? It did not make any sense, and I was prepared to articulate these points, but I never had the chance. When a crowd of sharks smells blood, reason becomes of little import.

It was Mary Warrant who grabbed me. She still wore her black mourning attire, and grief stained her face. "It was you who found my son," she said, her words wavering with emotion. "Tell me—did you kill him?" Preposterous! But her grip on my arm was fierce and unyielding. I recognized her grief and desperation, having felt it myself, and so I did not attempt to pull away. "Did you kill my son?" she cried into my face and grabbed for my gun.

Her sudden movement startled me; I held the weapon tightly as she tried to yank it from my grip, and then, suddenly, she was being aided by two men who also seemed to want nothing more than to part me from my only means of defense. I held firm, tried to push their grasping hands away—but it was Mary who gained possession of the gun at last. I tried to reach for it as one of the men held me back, and Mary swung its deadly barrel in my direction. I could do nothing but fall immediately to my knees to avoid her unhinged aim, and directly above my head there came a deafening blast. I pressed my hands against my ears. The men let me go and backed away.

The air sang; all other sounds vanished in the bright, high ringing that filled my head with almost a kind of peace; the moment seemed to freeze and stretch out into eternity as I came to myself and understood I was alive, I was unharmed, I had not been shot. The bullet had missed me. It had gone over my head. It wasn't until I turned around that the chaos of the world collapsed on itself again, and the ringing faded into the sounds of cries.

Smith stood with a look of unutterable shock upon his blood-spattered face. The doctor lay at his feet.

I must get the excruciating details out of my head. I must write it true.

The top of Ira Hartsworth's head had been blown clear off.

The white of his skull, broken into shards now, peeked through a brimming well of blood and dislodged tissue; a flap of scalp, still clinging with the old man's thin white hair, flapped free of the gaping cavern of his pate. One eye stared dully while the other had vanished somewhere in the bloody cavity which had opened his brain to the air.

Behind me, Mary dropped the gun; I heard her wrenching sobs but cared not for her. I could hardly comprehend the carnage before me.

Then Oscar came running out, likely to see what the shots had been about; the boy saw his keeper destroyed on the ground. I stood at once and raced to him, swept him up into my arms, trying to shield his eyes from the terrible sight, though I was too late. A blank, uncomprehending shock seemed to come over him. I carried him away from there, my feet flying without knowing their direction, until we arrived at the boardinghouse (here I am, still calling it that—excuse me, the brothel).

I pushed him into Claudia's arms and told her, "You must take him away from here."

The boy is too sensitive for this wicked town. Now I know the truth. It broke over me all at once, like sunlight breaking through dawn. He never invoked Charles to harm us; he never tried to frighten me. He is only a boy sensitive to the peculiar tragedies of life; a boy who has always been missing his other half, who has been lonely all his life because of it and has tried to make up for that loneliness by pretending he still has his brother. And I have punished him for this sensitivity. The best for him, now, is to get away from me, to get away from this terrible place.

So I sent Claudia and Oscar away. First, I retrieved my gun where Mary had abandoned it; we hurried back to the cabin; I gave Claudia the map the doctor had drawn for me, and I set them upon my horse with enough hardtack to sustain them for the journey.

This town is filled with a sickness that must be purged.

"They will shelter you there," I told Claudia, my dear Claudia, who always wanted children but who has instead spent years of her lonely life in the unloving arms of grasping men. "Ask for Tsela. Tell them the woman with the silver sent you."

And then I watched them ride off in a cloud of dust, until they were no more than a speck on the horizon, feeling a bottomless ache in my chest. I wished at once to call them back, but I could not. It was right to send them away.

They will be safe, far away from the horrors that have befallen Virgil—and the horrors yet to come, the horrors that I will bring down on this town. And perhaps in their loneliness Claudia and Oscar will find some solace in each other.

November 25, 1869

I went into the mine again last night, and, Diary—

I found them.

A turn, deeper than I had previously tread, took me to a collapse of rock. Yet there remained an opening, large enough for a body to pass. I crawled through and found myself on the other side of the blockage, where the air was stale. Down another long tunnel, I know not exactly how far I went, but I knew this must be the way. The rocks I passed had crushed my husband's body beneath their weight, and it must have been the shifting of the rock to extricate him that had left an opening. Even now, the way was precarious. The rocks trembled as if with another imminent collapse, and I had to move quickly lest they catch me.

Then, down that long tunnel—the deeper I trod, the closer I felt I was to what I sought. My heart thumped wildly within me such that I grew trembly and weak, so consumed was I with the excitement and terror of what I was about to behold.

What I was about to behold, Diary, was the very burial chamber that Willie Ray Randall had told me about though hadn't dared describe. I will rectify his error here as best I can, though I still feel wild writing it, as if my heart has never slowed its gallop since that moment.

Human bones adorned the chamber in a kind of macabre fresco: a menagerie of ancient skulls lined one side, all watching me through pitiless pockets and grinning at their own memento mori.

The opposite side bore intricate patterns of yellowed bones that reminded me of some patterns I had seen woven into blankets at the Indian village, and I was shocked to find a kind of mesmeric beauty in the designs so meticulously laid out in bone. Someone had crafted a work of art from the innermost structures of our bodies, of bodies long dead, and in seeing what lies inside us all arranged in such a way—it was beautiful and horrible to behold.

Yet there was no beauty to be found among the more recently deceased.

There lay upon the ground a corpse of some weeks or months, bloodless and withered, its skin gone sour and shriveling away to reveal the stark-naked bone underneath. Yet unlike those cleverly arranged ones divorced from any semblance of their former bodies, this bone was hideous in the way it peeked out from within the desiccated flesh, crude and unseemly. What little flesh remained was yet still pocked with those familiar puncture wounds.

And I had the sudden thought: how many of the men who were said to have left town did not, in fact, leave at all? How many were brought here to be consumed?

To be—savored?

Yet I will not go on about the chamber itself, for it is what inhabited this remote cave that is the subject of this writing. The demons that have plagued Virgil ever since Emery first broke through and set them free.

I met them with my gun, lest they be thirsty. The weapon kept them at bay; they perhaps remembered the one I shot the other night and did not care to experience my bullets; or perhaps it was my silver pendant that put them off, its mystical properties warding away evil. If this be the case, then I thank that skillful blacksmith for this recompense!

For there is not one Strange Lady, but many.

Not enough to number a quarter of Virgil's population, perhaps, but enough to make a body's skin crawl at being surrounded by them.

They might easily have overtaken me, but I made sure to announce my entrance by saying, "I am no enemy. I come peaceably and with good intentions." Though my voice shook as their shapes reeled back from the lantern light, and though my heart had most leapt into my throat the like to make me gag, I said my words loudly and clearly so that if they understood English, they would understand me.

Yet I cannot express the unspeakable fear of stepping directly into their midst—of stepping into the darkness where their shadows lurked and lurched outside of my swinging light, and knowing that I was surrounded by *los fantasmas* who had plagued Virgil with death. My life might have been snuffed out then, and quite easily, but I have found any thought of my own life rather abstract and unimportant, as the pointless lifespan of a mosquito. Either they would help me or they would kill me, and the first seemed worth the latter, and then some.

Or perhaps I am simply mad—the mad Widow Cain!

They did not, however, rush forward to deliver me the deadly embrace. No, they did speak to me then—though in archaic tongues and strange accents, they spoke to me!

Knowing, then, they understood me, I told them what I had come for: to save my daughter, "for you, who are said to hibernate for many years, must know the secret to everlasting life—where no doctor nor medicine man has been able to save her, I come to you, my last and only hope that she may not die."

I threw myself upon their mercy, Diary! I begged them impart to me their secret—or, no, not me, but Sophie, if secret indeed they held—and the Strange Lady (for I do not know her name, nor even if she has one, yet I recognized her, somehow, as the very same creature I had seen in the desert!) told me of how they had been driven underground long ago. And I came to understand the truth. These brittle things are not evil; they do not feed beyond their need and would prefer not to kill (most of them, at least) if only it were not so difficult to stop drinking once the sweet elixir flushes through them.

I remember my urgency when imbibing whiskey at the saloon, that night that seems so long ago—and I feel I can understand. When deprived for so long, how can one sip suffice?

They are merely trying to survive, as all beings do.

Well, I told them these people of Virgil are not worth saving! There is only one I care to save, only one who is precious, and I will do anything to prevent her dying. They could feed upon me, they could take my life—I could help them find better, heartier meals in town—if only they would help her!

By some sweet miracle—they agreed!

They told me the way to save Sophronia.

※

IT WAS A LONG AND difficult journey, bringing her into the cave; she was weak and could only walk part of the way. The rest, I had to carry her, with a bag over my shoulder to bring some food (and you, my Diary—I could not leave you behind), matches, and candles. I carried her and the lantern, both, to light our way, for dawn remained some hours distant. Sophie rested her fevered cheek against mine, her eyes fluttering, her little heartbeat rattling around in her bony chest. She had been fevered altogether too long for anybody to endure.

Her life was ticking ever closer to its end.

The cave dwellers took her for their strange ritual—I crept along to bear witness—though what I saw, I can hardly describe. What lies in the very depths of those tunnels is not like the creatures I met—it is something far older, and yet it lives a strange sort of life different from anything we can imagine—and Sophie partook of this unholy sacrament and was thus . . . transformed.

November 26, 1869

We rest, now, in a small chamber lighted by my candles; Sophie is in an agony of being stitched anew, like a tattered blanket mended by bolts of fresh thread. And I have fed her of myself, held her hand, and given her my own blood to drink, that she might be sustained. Blood of my blood, life of my life. I will give it all to her, everything. I will live underground. I will shun all civilized society. I will suckle her as she once did at my breast. She is all I have left. She is all.

It is warm in this little chamber, and the miners have not been near enough for us to hear so much as axe striking stone, which is a comfort; we are deep enough that we are safe from them.

I have been able to start a fire with some spare bits of wood from fallen supports in the mine. Sophie has begun to revive. She smiled at me, and though her appearance is no longer the sweet porcelain beauty she was, there is nothing more beautiful than to see her smile—and her eyes remain two pools of deepest blue, wide and intensely curious about her new state.

It only pains me that we may not embrace.

Sophie is weak, still, but she is regaining more than what she lost.

The brittle ones thirst and sleep, their voices like the sound of dry air through fallen leaves. They, too, require sustenance, and will need to feed soon. Yet I alone cannot sustain them all; soon, they must leave the mine to find a proper meal.

I have only enough of me to give to Sophie. But I fear she too will soon need more than I can provide. She takes but little from me, for she does not want to see me suffer.

These creatures were here before any of us. They are native to this place. Why shall we destroy them? Why not assimilate instead? Those men from Virgil Consolidated came, tore up the land, dug up their home, woke them from their slumber. The creatures have tolerated them. They have attempted to feed discreetly.

They have let them live.

Why should we let them live?

November 27, 1869

We emerged from the mine as the sun settled in the west. A cold wind blew, shocked me after so many hours in that warm little chamber, and sank through my skin to rattle my very bones.

Winter is upon us now. A thin, blue darkness stretched across the twilit wasteland, casting strange shadows over the craggy mountain: the strange hour when the earth begins to fall into darkness but holds still the faint magic of sunlight that hasn't yet let go. It is a between-things sort of time, a purgatory almost: between day and night; between wake and sleep; between life and death.

I felt between the two myself, in my weariness. I feared my strength would give out during the arduous climb from the mine, but my will and my love for Sophronia saw me out. It is a wonder, what a body can be brought to do for its children.

I saw the scene laid out before me as we came into town: The people of Virgil ranged around the gallows in anticipation, eagerness for blood in their eyes, expectant of their sacrifice; among them, recognizable faces— Rutherford Branson (deaf in one ear), Mr. and Mrs. Warrant, Josephine and Cecil Pavlovsky, Willa Carver and her husband, Abernathy McCullins (the sheriff's deputy), and all the rest. All those who had likely been complicit in the very crime for which Mr. Randall would now hang.

He stood upon the scaffold that had been constructed in the center of town, beside his executioner. A rope coiled about his neck. His hands tied behind his back. I recognized at once his dark hair and darker countenance, even from a distance.

Olive stood stoically in the grim crowd. To the last, she maintained her dignity. Her eyes were locked on her husband, obsidian dark, filled with damnation.

I wonder what it must have been like for her to witness her own husband's murder. It was unbearable enough to hear how John Henry was crushed to death under the weight of fallen rock—to hear, and not even see it happen! But Olive stood there, her cousin Chester at her side, to witness her husband hang from the neck until dead. To watch the light vanish from his cold, black eyes, and the preternatural stillness come over his dangling body.

They were all waiting for it. It was written in their faces; in their greedy, hungry mouths, satiated only by death. Was this how they looked when they were stringing up Emery? Did they shout their encouragement? Did they help Willie Ray Randall heave the rope? Were they hungry for blood, then as now? Did they all gather around the hanging tree to watch as his face purpled, as his eyes popped from his skull, as he choked on his tongue, as his legs twitched and then fell still?

I wondered, would Mary Warrant hang for the killing of Doctor Hartsworth? Or had they decided to blame that on me as well, and were only hoping for my reemergence in Virgil, so that I may join Mr. Randall upon the scaffold?

If they did hope for my return, they could not have known that I wouldn't come back alone.

I did not hear Mr. Randall's last words—but I did hear the last sound he ever made.

It was a terrible burst of laughter.

For he saw us coming before anyone else. He saw us from his vantage point up on the scaffold, for his eyes were the only ones not locked on the spectacle of death that held everyone else at attention. He saw what was coming for Virgil, and, knowing that he would be dead before it did, he laughed.

And then—he hanged.

They were all so busy watching, wanting to capture his very last moments and savor them. Wanting, perhaps, to witness the moment when a soul fled its host. They did not know that very soon, they would all get to experience this final moment.

They did not even notice us until the first of our number met them where they stood and enveloped them in the deadly embrace.

What chaos followed!

Those not touched by the demons raced every which way to escape their grasp, but I did not allow them to go far. Though I do not bear those savage spikes over my own supple flesh, I did carry my gun and enough ammunition to see me through. Those who ran were met by my bullets, and down they went.

Do you think me evil, Diary?

After all, it was I who asked the cave dwellers, Why do you care for the lives of these awful people, who would kill you for sport? Why do you take pains to only harm when survival necessitates?

Let us go, I said, and drink until our bellies are full!

Save Sophronia, I told them, and I will lead you to the grandest feast you have ever seen.

Oh, the people of Virgil were right to fear the Widow Cain!

More than a dozen of my new family moved through the crowd, slaughtering with impunity; drinking them dry with the swiftness of a man knocking back a shot at the saloon, knowing there were plenty more bottles behind the bar. And as I beheld their carnage, I could not help but find it miraculous: for with each drink, their withered frames plumped, like an old, wrinkled woman reversing her age back to the tender mercies of youth, and they grew stronger, more agile, more fearsome, invigorated—beautiful. The ruddy, vigorous flush of their feast rushed through their browned and leathery flesh. The more they drank, the more human they appeared.

By now the sun had gone as quickly as these people tried to flee; the moon grew swollen with silver light, soon joined by its brethren stars in the profound vastness of the sky.

I had my matches with me; I knew there was a cache of gunpowder at the general store, and I lit it.

The grocery and its immediate neighbors—one of them being, I realized with great satisfaction, Mr. Branson's infernal tailor shop—immediately went up in flames. An explosion rent them through like a crack of thunder, followed swiftly by an acrid smell that burned my nostrils and watered my eyes. The fire reared its livid edges upward, brightening the scene of destruction with its deranged, crackling light. Smoke billowed into the sky, obscuring the distant stars.

The blast of heat abruptly overcame the winter cold of the night.

The raging fire and its attendant smoke sent the rats scurrying, ever blinder as they sought escape. My beautiful *fantasmas* drank, and they left behind drained and papery corpses in their wake.

Among those frightened, scurrying rats, I saw her: Olive Randall, the side of her face blistered from the intense fire that raged over half the buildings on Main Street. She must have been caught too close when it went up; some of her flesh was blackening and bubbling.

She saw me as I caught sight of her. Our eyes locked.

I raised the barrel of my gun.

She put her hands up in a kind of supplication I had never imagined I would see from her, much less directed at me. "Lavinia," she said pathetically, "please."

I told her: "You all are the devils, not us."

By now the endless howl of the desert wind carried with it the screams of the dying; the nebulous expression of smoke; the strident peal of bells of different pitches and cadences ringing violently above open doorways, shrilling their dissonant hymns. And the body of Olive's husband, Willie Ray Randall, creaked and swayed over it all.

Perhaps thinking herself swift enough to outpace me, Olive made to dart away. I depressed my finger on the trigger—only to find that my last casing had run out, and that I was empty of ammunition. Triumph flashed through her eyes, but I was not about to let her get away!

Beside me lay the second weapon I had brought down from the mountain, in case I needed it: a pickax, nicked and dented with use but sharp enough to strike silver from rock. I pursued her even as she attempted to flee, and for a moment I thought she was too fast, that she would escape me and vanish into the night. I drew close, swung, missed; I reached out for her as she flew out of my grasp. In a blind fury, I swung my axe, and by luck or grace, it tangled in her hair and pulled her down. To be sure she would not get up again, I swung. My pickax caught her on the shoulder, pinned her down where she lay as blood came up, bright and inviting.

"Sophie!" I called out in the night.

Though I had wanted to leave Sophronia safe in our little chamber in the cave, I knew she needed to feed on more than I could give her. So I had allowed her to come out with us but told her she must hide herself among the scrub at the outskirts of town until I found her a satisfactory meal.

At my call she came out of the scrub, crawling toward us, the lambent firelight shining in her wide, eager eyes.

On seeing my daughter come crawling toward her, Olive let loose from her throat a low moan of revulsion. Behind us, the fire continued to devour the wooded buildings, spitting sparks and fallen timber like bones. Olive's dress had grown tattered, dirty; her face—the part that was not burned—was slicked with grimy sweat. Her eyes were like two saucers, wide and wild.

"Go on, Sophie," I encouraged her. "You are thirsty."

My dear one reached out tentatively even as Olive cringed away from her, but Sophie wrapped her small hand around Olive's and held it tight. For a moment they gazed into each other's eyes as if trying to understand each other. Then Sophie lay down beside her and pressed her cheek against Olive's, and with a sigh, she drank.

When she'd had her fill, she stood away from Olive's wasted form, her spine-tips shining red, and she smiled at me and said she felt well. She finally felt well, for perhaps the first time in her short life—strong, vibrant, alive.

What joy it brought me! I wanted so badly to embrace my girl but knew I never could again, and I felt the swell of grief and joy fit to burst in my breast. Together we surveyed the state of Virgil as the feast began to calm. Only a few townsfolk remained, trying to drag themselves, bleeding, to safety.

The fire continued to burn, but it seemed less malicious now without the symphony of screams. Even the bells seemed to have quieted, ringing out a gentler song into the night.

Above us, Willie Ray Randall's body continued to sway in the breeze, enrobed in smoke.

And at long last, when it was over, we returned to the mountain—me, my daughter, and my new kin.

December 21, 1869

Peace. All quiet, all peaceful.

They have all had their fill; they will be sated for years to come on the bounty that Virgil provided, able to store up sustenance within themselves like a camel stores water.

But there are those who have grown concerned. Now that we have killed off all the food, what happens when they grow thirsty again?

More will come, I told them, you'll see. More will come.

Yet on this winter solstice, on this dark, cold day of the year, I fear what should happen to me if I remain in their midst.

But I cannot leave Sophie.

There is plenty for us, still, in the remnants of this town; I have retrieved books from the schoolhouse to continue Sophie's studies; there is food enough for me, at least, which I am able to scavenge from the houses and the animals, which have all gone wild without their masters.

Yet this, too, will run out.

I fear there is only one thing for me to do.

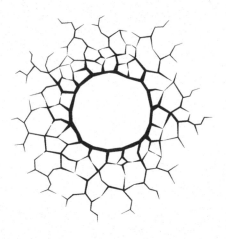

THE DUST DEVILS

WAYNOKA FLIPPED THE PAGE, only to find that the next one was blank. And the next. And all the remaining pages— blank. She'd reached the end.

She closed the diary.

Mads sniffed and startled at the movement, blinking out of whatever fevered reverie she'd fallen into. She cleared her throat and said, "Well?"

Waynoka shook her head, trying to untangle her thoughts. "Nothing useful."

Mads released a deep groan like a balloon slowly releasing air until it has become nothing but a shriveled bit of useless rubber. "Goddammit," she spat, and coughed. Dark bags hung under her eyes like half-moon bruises.

Waynoka set down the diary beside the dwindling fire. She felt as if she had come to know Lavinia, and though there lay a certain satisfaction in having reached the end of her story, she experienced, too, a species of grief, like saying good-bye to an old friend.

"I don't think she ever got out," she admitted. There was no way to save them. This, too, compounded her sorrow, so that a deep ache welled up in her chest. "I think they killed her, in the end."

They. The demons of the mine.

She curled her injured hand into a fist. Though the puncture wounds had scabbed over, she felt the mending flesh stretch and flake, reopening several of the holes. She imagined what it must be like, to embrace one of these demons; to be drained of blood. What must have become of Lavinia Cain, who had set them loose on Virgil, Nevada, and caused the death of the nascent town. If she had given herself to them willingly, to let her daughter live, or if they had taken her by force . . .

"All for nothing," Mads mumbled, picking at the fraying threads around the edges of the rags that enwrapped her knee. "All to stay alive just a little longer. What's a little longer?" She shook her head, her body swaying. "We need to go swim in the lake. The sump. It will baptize us. Save us. That's the way—"

"Hey," Waynoka cut in as her partner's voice took on a dreamy quality, her eyes hazy and distant. "You with me?"

Mads blinked, her eyes clearing, and nodded. "Yeah."

"Good," said Waynoka. "You've got to stay with me."

"Yeah," Mads said again, her voice whispering against the walls. "Hey, Way?" She swallowed. "I think we have to cut off my leg."

"What? No."

Mads started to chuckle: a dry, awful sound. "I can't move it anymore. It's numb. I can't feel a thing. It's like it's not even there. Like it's dead weight. I can't carry around dead weight. I won't make it anywhere."

Waynoka's stomach churned. "We can't cut it off. We don't even have anything sharp."

"There's a pickax behind you."

"No," Waynoka said again, sitting beside Mads and biting her lip to stop her eyes from prickling. There was no way—she couldn't imagine hefting that dull old pickax and driving it down onto Mads's leg.

There was no way. Even if the infection was spreading—there was no way. They were going to die down here. Their story would end as Lavinia's had. Except no one would ever know about it. At least, in reading the diary, Waynoka had met her, learned her story, and something of Lavinia had lived on in those words.

If they didn't make it out of here, who would tell their story? Who would know what they had been through down here? It would all be for nothing, somehow.

"We have to get out of here," Waynoka said. "To write the screenplay. Remember?"

"We can't make it out if I'm stuck with this leg."

"You won't be able to walk," said Waynoka. "How can you walk with one leg?"

"I'll hop," Mads gritted out.

Every bit of Waynoka fought against the idea. She shook her head. "I can't."

The look on Mads's face held wild desperation. "You promised you wouldn't leave me behind." She was rocking a little where she sat, eyes wide. "I can't walk. I can't go anywhere with this dead thing attached to me."

"You're not thinking clearly," said Waynoka. "I'll carry you."

Even with her diminished weight—the sharp cut of her bones growing more pronounced the longer they spent rationing insufficient food—she would be too heavy for Waynoka. She was broad where Waynoka was slender.

"You couldn't lift me if you tried," Mads said with tears in her eyes.

"We can still get out without resorting to . . ." But Waynoka couldn't bring herself to finish the statement when she didn't even believe it herself. She knew they had to do something drastic. They couldn't keep sitting around here waiting for a miracle to reveal itself in the diary.

Lavinia hadn't sat around waiting for a miracle. She had done whatever was necessary to save Sophronia. Even if it was dangerous. Even if it meant the end of her own life.

"I'll hold you back," said Mads.

Waynoka shook her head even though she knew it was true. She gave a wet laugh. "I've always felt like I'm the one holding *you* back," she confessed.

"You've never held me back," said Mads. "I wouldn't have made it this far without you."

Waynoka snorted, wiped at her nose. "Oh please. You would have survived just fine without me. I haven't done anything you couldn't do on your own."

Mads shook her head. Her gaze was hard.

Her throat bobbed as she swallowed. "You gave me a reason not to give up."

Hearing this, Waynoka felt a sweet ache in her chest. She looked at the barricade she'd formed in the opening beneath the red-painted figure, a hodgepodge of old tools balanced against the wall.

The pickax. The ache became a kind of queasiness in her gut.

She took the handle, picked it up. It was heavier than she expected. "You really want me to use this piece of shit? It won't cut through bone. Look, it's all old and worn down. And rusty. You want me to cut off your leg with a rusty pickax?" The words babbled free in an anxious stream. "And what would we use to stop the bleeding? Don't we need a tourniquet or something?"

Mads started ripping strips of cloth from the bed. "Use the sharp end to crack the bone and the blunt end to work the cut into a clean line. Then tie it off with a few strips. Or better yet, you still got that nylon cord? That should work." She shoved some cloth into her mouth and said around it, "Do it before I lose my nerve."

Waynoka checked the pack for the nylon cord, came up empty. She spent a few minutes rifling through their stuff, searching for it, positive it had to be there somewhere.

Eventually Mads told her to stop wasting time.

"Just use the cloth, then," said Mads, her voice muffled. "Do it! Please, just fucking do it!"

The raw anguish in her partner's voice made Waynoka lift the pickax, the entire situation surreal, her arms feeling as if they weren't even connected to her body anymore.

She aimed for a spot just above Mads's knee.

And swung.

Mads screamed through the rag as the axe pierced her flesh and hit bone. Terrified of what she'd done, Waynoka yanked it out, ripping open a chunk of thigh. The cavity welled dark with blood, which spilled over and ran down her leg.

"You need to break the bone," Mads slurred through the rag. Tears streamed down her flushed face.

Waynoka shook her head. "I can't do this. I can't do this."

But as she hefted up the axe again, trusting that Mads was right, thinking she had to finish now that she'd started—as she tried to steady her sweating hands on the rough wooden handle so she would have a good grip when she brought it back down on the terrible gaping wound she had made—she heard the tinkling of a bell.

She froze.

Behind her, the wheelbarrow tipped over, scraped against the rock, clattered to the ground.

Waynoka turned to see something crawling out of the darkness beyond.

She dropped the axe and picked up the flashlight. Saw the monster stepping into the room with the familiarity of one entering her childhood bedroom. Waynoka's cry was impotent, echoing uselessly off the walls, until it grew ghostly in its own ever-softer repetition and disappeared into the vast maw of darkness.

Thinking only of getting away from that awful thing, Waynoka stumbled back until she hit the wall.

Leaving Mads on the ground—moaning, bloody, defenseless.

The creature bent down over her, reached out its lonely limbs, and embraced Mads as if it were a prisoner having lived in seclusion these many years, longing for human touch. It clutched her so tightly, so fiercely, it looked as if it might never let go.

"Mads!"

Waynoka moved to push the creature off of Mads but encountered only thorny spikes with no safe purchase. She saw one of Mads's hands sink into the pins, which were sharp enough to pierce straight through her palm and emerge bloody from the other side. As the creature enfolded her in its deadly embrace, Mads's other hand flailed wildly, and Waynoka reached for it but could not grasp it. She realized that the hand with which she reached for her only friend, the only person in the world to her, was the one pocked with tiny puncture wounds, the one she had broken open on this very figure as she'd flailed in the dark of the burial chamber, the one that she had used to catch herself on the walls of the cavern as she'd raced back here, smearing blood, like a trail, all the way back to Lavinia and Sophronia's little room. And a wave of guilt and grief crashed over her, knowing what she had awoken, what she had led straight to them.

There was nothing she could do for her. She couldn't pull the creature away, not when it was covered in deadly spines. Maybe the only merciful thing she could do now was to let it happen.

She watched in horror as the creature held Mads as if with an excess of love; as it seemed to swell and deflate like one inhaling and exhaling, the swells drawing blood from Mads's body. From over that spiked shoulder, she saw the shock that colored the draining face of Madelyn "Mads" De la Cruz as her eyes locked on to Waynoka's first with horror, then a dawning peace. And then the final ruin as the creature sucked out the last bit of lifeblood and released Mads's body to slump, lifeless, to the floor of the chamber.

The flashlight's moonish glow trembled spasmodically over the bloody-spiked figure. Shaking, filled with a terrible grief, Waynoka turned and clambered into the narrow crevice of the collapse. She scooted through the horribly small space as fast as she could, but halfway through, her shoulders jammed against the rocks, her knees scraped as she kicked. She was stuck.

Like the eye of a hurricane, she experienced a moment of peace amid the chaos of panic. Maybe this was it. She was stuck, and she would either die here, trapped in the rock, or the creature would catch up to her from behind and suck out her blood. Either way, it would all be over soon.

The moment passed as her survival instinct kicked back in. She struggled, wriggled, contorted herself until at last she managed to worm forward again, inch by inch, until, at last, she slid out onto the rocks at the end of the passage—found herself in the tunnels of the mine—and ran.

▓

THE DIZZYING DANCE OF the bright spot on the walls conveyed her forward into the dark but gave her only glimpses of where she was going. At any moment, her foot might punch through into another mine shaft, might send her careening down into a bottomless pit. The mine drew her deeper into its treacherous labyrinth.

She had little sense of where she was and of how far she had come, but she had to slow, winded. Slowing allowed her to hold the flashlight beam steady, allowed her to avoid cracking her head open against the low ceiling. This passage was alarmingly narrow.

The close walls echoed back every ragged breath. She tried to fill the tunnel with some other sound, murmuring a mindless litany of, "My Very Excellent Mother Just Served Us Nine Pizzas," over and over into the dark, as if the sentence were a prayer, a chant to the planets like gods: Mercury, Venus, Earth, Mars, Jupiter, Saturn, Uranus, Neptune, Pluto. *Mother Mars will feed and protect us*, she thought deliriously. And all the rest would watch over Excellent Earth, to save it from itself. All nine of them, whether or not Pluto was a planet, because they were each a part of the sacred phrase, each called upon as Waynoka proceeded through the dark, bereft of Mads, alone but for the planets.

The tunnel widened. She thought this passage looked familiar, that she was heading back the way they'd initially come, but it was impossible to be certain. Everything looked the same down here. Slowly she picked her way forward, wherever "forward" led.

She mumbled her litany again, an invocation against the dark, and in its wake the dark burbled up a childish giggle, as if it found her phrase amusing.

The flashlight's white oval searched for the source of the sound, darting around until it juddered on the small crouching figure, the by-now familiar figure, who held in two spike-bristled hands a black bat, squeezing it gently, sucking through the palms while the withered face, somehow both old and young, twisted away from the piercing light.

She realized, finally, that the eyes were not black but a deep, rich blue.

Revulsion welled in Waynoka as she stared at the creature, the child. Finding her voice, she said, "Sophronia?"

Though still shrinking from the light, the creature-child tried to squint through it, dropping the bat. "How do you know my name?"

The creature-child scampered out of the light, and though Waynoka tried to follow with the beam, she kept ducking away. Knowing that she was skittering through the shadows somewhere like a giant spider sent Waynoka backing up, away from her. Let her go back to her secret hollow. But now that Waynoka was moving away, she had the sense that the creature-child was creeping closer. She glimpsed movement, the glint of eyes.

Then the creature-child's voice floated out of the dark again, in a singsong: "Strange Lady, Strange Lady, what do you eat?" And another giggle.

Waynoka turned and ran as fast as the tunnel would allow, so that she might put as much distance as possible between herself and what Sophronia Cain had become.

She only slowed when she felt she had gotten far enough that there was no chance of pursuit—slowed and tried to get her bearings.

She had come to a section of the mine that was bolstered with planks of old, rotted wood, and both ceiling and floor lay slanted as if time and gravity had been unable to hold the tunnel's symmetry. Wooden support beams stood precariously as skeletons, some with rusted nails sticking out at dizzying angles.

She took one hesitant step and heard the telltale rattle of pebbles and small debris coming loose somewhere, scattering onto the ground. Stopping again, she shined the light into the distance of the tunnel, which vanished into a black square, wondering if she could make it if she ran.

Don't be an idiot, Mads said in her head, and she choked on her own breath. Mads was dead. She was alone. There was nowhere to go but forward.

Only a few steps in, however, and the patter of falling pebbles became the rending creak of disturbed wood. As much on instinct as recognition of the imminent collapse, Waynoka turned back the way she'd come.

Behind her, the tunnel caved in on itself. A cloud of dust enveloped her as she ran, tasting sickness in her throat.

In the cloud of dust, with death grasping her from behind, she dropped the flashlight.

Unable to go back for it, she stumbled forward, free of the tunnel, into the dusty dark. Coughing wretchedly and thinking she had almost been crushed, like John Henry.

She turned, blind. The flashlight had disappeared somewhere under the collapse. A boundless black cloaked her eyes.

With her hands out against the walls to feel her way from nowhere to nowhere, she walked into the darkness.

Now she would know, she realized. She would know how those people who got lost in the catacombs felt, when their light ran out and they could only wander deeper and deeper into the endless miles of labyrinthine passageways until they died, slowly. Wandering alone—horribly, impossibly alone.

But the fact of her utter aloneness gradually became less potent than the unpleasant possibility that she might not be alone at all.

At every moment, she expected to reach out her hands in the dark and meet the sharpness of spikes. She went by turns faster and slower, feeling the urgency to move coupled with the terror of an unseen presence. When she put her hand against a particularly sharp jut of rock, she cried out, and in her mind the walls teemed with unseen presence, the undead creatures she had woken from their slumber with the taste of her own blood.

Panic welled up inside of her, ready to burst.

It was the darkness that sent her reeling between terror and despair. If only she hadn't lost the one remaining flashlight, like she'd lost the other one. She had lost everything. She didn't even have the spare flashlight, wherever it—

Waynoka froze. The spare flashlight hadn't been in her own deflated bag, which meant it had been in the other one. Mads's pack. The one she'd left at the collapse leading into Lavinia's room.

Waynoka didn't have to find her way out of the mine in the blind dark. All she had to do was find her way back to that collapse.

Mads's pack would have other supplies in it, too. That's where the nylon cord must have ended up, when they were digging through their packs for food on the long trek down into the mine. Accidental switches happened as they pulled things out and put them back in. Maybe she could even use it to climb up the shaft with the broken ladder.

Filled with renewed hope, she started in the direction she thought would lead her back there, feeling her way along the walls. She could still make it out of here. All this time they'd been together, she'd allowed Mads to take care of her, but maybe she could do it alone now. She could take care of herself.

She could make it.

The thought of freedom, fresh air, even the hot, harsh sunlight urged her onward. In the dark the future played for her like a movie reel. She saw her adrenaline-fueled climb out of the mine. The Zenlike peace of riding alone across the desert to the other side. Arriving in New York like they'd planned, where things were supposed to be better, where they had hoped to find a world not yet gone to shit. Sitting at a little desk while rain drizzled down the window, fracturing city lights in the distance. Typing out the screenplay with a mug of tea on the desk beside her, steam curling.

Mads's death didn't have to be empty. She could tell her story.

Ahead, the air seemed diffused with a strange cast of light. She could see, more and more, a warm orange glow, and an overwhelming joy flooded through her—somehow, in the dark, she had come upon an exit that led out into the open world, the blaring, blazing desert.

She would be free. She would be free.

She thanked the planets for watching over her, for bringing her to the sun.

With a burst of energy, Waynoka hurried for that distant light.

But after only a few steps she slowed, as with each closer inch she recognized it was not quite right, not quite the light of the sun shining through an exit. And when she was closer still, she recognized it for what it was: the rippling flame of a lantern.

She stopped.

But the light kept moving closer.

She could do nothing but stand and watch and wait as the figure behind the lantern approached, and as the light revealed the creature that carried it, casting its livid glow over the withered, ancient face like jerky, and the spikes over all the naked skin that was hardly, anymore, like human skin.

The creature drew closer, and Waynoka knew what was coming. She thought of Mads. At least she would be joining her soon. There was nowhere to run anymore, nowhere she could go to escape.

She waited for the embrace of death.

But as the creature spread its spiny arms, the light glinted off something the creature wore: though its profusion of spikes prevented the possibility of clothing, the figure, which now Waynoka began to identify somehow as female, wore a necklace of twine, its pendant a silver crescent moon.

"Lavinia?" Waynoka's voice released in a breath of surprised air. The figure stopped, made no further move to envelop her in those lethal arms. Perhaps she was surprised to hear her own name. It had probably been ages since anyone had spoken it. "I read your diary," Waynoka continued. "I know you. I feel like I know you." With wonder and horror she gazed at Lavinia, with even a tenderness for the woman behind this frightful visage, for the woman who came to Virgil so full of hope. "I feel like I know you," she said again. Then, remembering herself, she asked, "Are you going to kill me?"

Lavinia stared at her with those sharp, gleaming eyes but did not respond. Like she was considering it. Unsure.

"You found the secret," said Waynoka.

They hadn't killed her, after all. She had survived—she and Sophronia both.

As amazed as she was repulsed, Waynoka wondered if she would be able to escape before Lavinia got thirsty again. The future she had envisioned in the darkness crumbled and blew apart in a cloud. She might make it out on her own—or she might fall down a shaft while trying. She might starve to death in the desert. She might be turned away from cities already filled with refugees.

She might die anyway.

But she couldn't give up.

"Help me get out of here," Waynoka begged. "You know these tunnels. Help me get out. Please."

Lavinia observed Waynoka closely. Then she said in a dry, rattling whisper of a voice, through long-neglected lungs: "There is only . . . death . . . out there."

"I know," said Waynoka. "That's how it was for you, in Virgil. But—" She stopped. What had she been about to say? The town was even more dead now than in Lavinia's time. There was nothing up there but abandoned buildings and sunbaked dirt. She gazed upon the frightful visage of Lavinia Cain, realizing that she was right. "Why did you do it?"

"Death . . . is the curse of man," said Lavinia in that dry, scratchy voice. "The animal . . . does not fear death. The trees do not . . . know death." The lantern swung gently in her hand, throwing livid flares of light. "Man may wield death in his hands to feel strong . . . but even he knows what will become of him . . . in the end."

Hearing Lavinia's voice, even this withered echo of it, opened a longing in Waynoka's heart. A terrible impulse to reach out and touch Lavinia stirred within her. She swallowed it down, realizing with horror that Lavinia had killed Mads. Consumed her.

And it was Waynoka's fault.

For a moment, she wished Lavinia would embrace her. It was what she deserved.

But she didn't want to die. She still clung, desperately, to hope.

"You found a way to cheat death," said Waynoka.

Lavinia inclined her head. "I could choose to live briefly . . . or sleep and hope to wake . . . in a better world." Her voice grew stronger the more she spoke. The lantern's glow turned her eyes to gleaming rocks as she focused her gaze on the darkness behind Waynoka. "Now I can be with her . . . forever."

The back of Waynoka's neck crawled at the thought of Sophronia creeping around somewhere back there. Despite this, she understood. Sophronia was the person Lavinia loved most in the world, and now that the girl would never lead a normal life—would never really grow up—Lavinia could be there for her, with her, forevermore.

Though she knew it must be only the rosy retrospection of the past, Waynoka wished she had lived, instead, in Lavinia's time. Wished she could have been her friend, like Claudia was, so that she hadn't been so alone in her quest to save her daughter.

Despite knowing the terrible things she had done—despite watching her drain the life from Mads—Waynoka felt love for Lavinia. Didn't want to let her go.

"I wanted you to survive," she said. "When I was reading your diary."

"Do you . . . want to survive?"

When she thought again about emerging from the mine and finding her way through the world, she suddenly imagined this happening sometime in the distant future, hundreds of years from now: when clouds once again found their way over the desert to patter it with rain, when the people or creatures of that time might stop destroying everything around them. When things were—maybe—better.

Until then, she could sleep. She was so tired. The numbing exhaustion that had followed her into the mine now settled ether-heavy as her adrenaline dissipated. Nothing sounded so enticing as a long nap, a respite from the weariness of this world.

Maybe she didn't have to leave Mads behind, after all.

She could be like Lavinia: fierce, independent, capable of whatever it took to survive. This flesh was only temporary, anyway—borrowed for a brief moment in time, dressed up in the costume of its day. It could be shed.

"And we can be together," said Waynoka.

<hr/>

BY THE LANTERN'S LIGHT, Lavinia led her into the darkness. Back to the burial chamber, lined with bones; back through the lower level where the dark shapes of her family slumbered.

Waynoka wondered how long Sophronia had been the only one awake while the rest hibernated, keeping herself alive on bats, a very old child alone in the dark.

Through a low doorway in the burial chamber they found another set of steps and descended, farther and farther, into the depths, the place where Earth and Hell converged.

In that dry voice with its archaic cadence, Lavinia told her she was taking her to the Old Ones. "They are not like us," she said. "We were made this way; they were born this way. They are older than time, from an earlier world. If you drink of them, you will become like them."

They entered a vast cavern. Waynoka could feel the walls widening, could sense the largeness of it even if she couldn't see its exact proportions. There was a different quality to the air here. Warm and sticky, with a vaguely fungal smell.

When Lavinia lifted her light to reveal the monstrosity that lived at the heart of the cave, Waynoka fell to her knees. She was right; Lavinia's found family had all been human once, but the growth of strange life that stretched its body of enormous and improbable shape throughout this chamber, whether one creature or a colony, had never been remotely human.

Lavinia set down the lantern, which threw contortions of light and shadow. She pulled one of her own spikes from her body and used it to pierce the flesh of the Old One, pulling on it to create a small gash that oozed a dark liquid like blood.

"*Drink,*" she said.

Waynoka put her mouth against the gash, careful of the behemoth's own protective spindles and wondered what the world had been like eons ago; what it might be like eons hence.

And then, she drank.

THE END

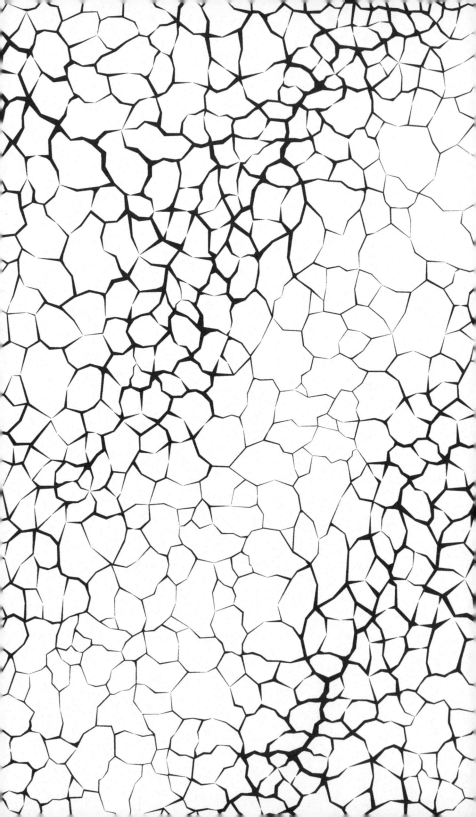

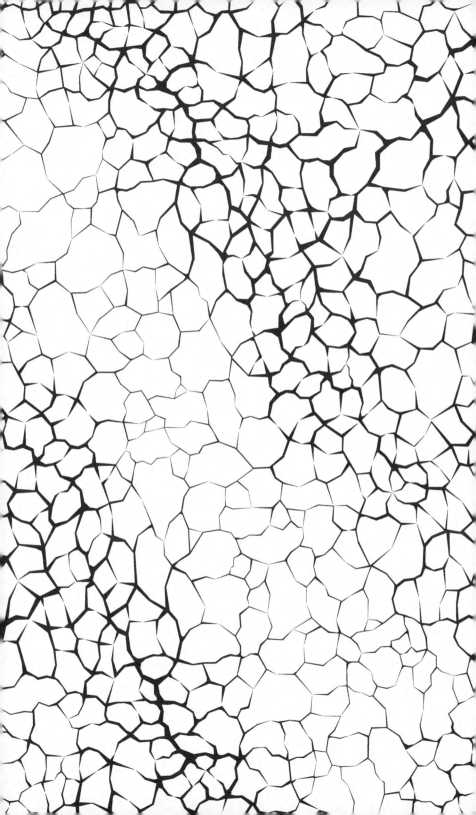

ACKNOWLEDGMENTS

MANY THANKS ARE DUE to the people who have helped me along the way. My husband, Jake Kaplan; my parents, Jeffrey and Beverly Parypinski; my sister and brother-in-law, Mallory and Marc Dahlquist, and my niece and nephew, Penny and Jackson; my dear friends, Mary Beth Sekela, Phil Sebal, and Marja and Chris Hansen; my Chapman MFA cohort including Kevin James, John Carlo Encarnacion, and Annalisa Brizuela, and the faculty there, in particular Richard Bausch; everyone in the Horror Writers Association LA chapter, in particular my cochair Kevin Wetmore, John Palisano, and Lisa Morton; all my colleagues at Glendale Community College, and the English division for welcoming me and giving me the opportunity to teach creative writing.

I wouldn't have made it this far without my amazing agent, Jill Marr; I am so grateful for everything she has done for me and my work. Everyone at CamCat Publishing has been incredible to work with on this book: my brilliant editor Helga Schier, along with Sue Arroyo and the rest of the team—Maryann Appel, Laura Wooffitt, Bill Lehto, Gabe Schier, Bridget

McFadden, Meredith Lyons, Josh Chamberlain, Elana Gibson, Abigail Miles, and Jessica Homami. I also want to thank Andrea Cavallaro, John W. Beach, Kevin Cleary, Jeffrey Chassen, Joe Derrick, Abby Ex, and Nikolaj Coster-Waldau for their work in taking *It Will Just Be Us* to screen.

Finally, there are so many wonderful writers, editors, and publishers who have supported me over the years: Daniel Braum, Scott Kenemore, Matt Cowan, S. P. Miskowski, Wendy Wagner, Andy Cox, John Joseph Adams, Jonathan Maberry, Doug Murano, Michael Bailey, Alessandro Manzetti, Chelsey Emmelhainz, Jon Padgett, Eric J. Guignard, Ellen Datlow, Kathleen Kaufman, Paulette Kennedy, Sean M. Thompson, Justin A. Burnett, Sara Tantlinger, C. M. Muller, Kenneth W. Cain, and everyone else who has picked up a story of mine or said a kind word. I couldn't do it without you.

ABOUT THE AUTHOR

ORN AND RAISED IN the suburbs of Chicago, Jo Kaplan learned early
on that she loved all things spooky. She grew up on *Goosebumps*
and *Are You Afraid of the Dark?* and began creating her own horror
stories as soon as she learned how to write. After getting her BA in English
with a creative writing emphasis at Butler University, she moved west to Los
Angeles, where she got her MFA in creative writing at Chapman University.

She now teaches English and creative writing at a local college and lives
in the foothills with her husband and two cats. When she isn't writing or
teaching, she plays cello in a community orchestra. Her short stories have
appeared in numerous publications (sometimes under the name Joanna
Parypinski), including *Fireside Quarterly, Black Static, Nightmare Magazine,
Vastarien, Haunted Nights,* edited by Ellen Datlow and Lisa Morton, and
Bram Stoker Award-nominated anthology *Miscreations: Gods, Monstrosities
and Other Horrors.* Her novel, *It Will Just Be Us,* came out in 2020 and was
optioned by Ill Kippers Productions. She is currently at work on her next
novel.

ALSO BY JO KAPLAN

It Will Just Be Us

Dark Carnival
(writing as Joanna Parypinski)

If you enjoyed

Jo Kaplan's *When the Night Bells Ring,*

you'll enjoy

David Oppegaard's *Claw Heart Mountain.*

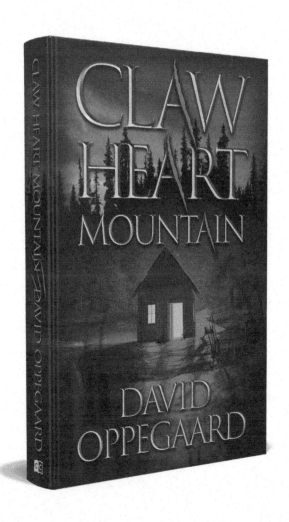

1

Windfall

C LAW HEART MOUNTAIN SAT apart from everything, like a forgotten god hunkered in thought. It looked both eternal and lonely, without a friend in sight, surrounded by rolling hills dotted in sagebrush and cheat grass, the summer sky a hazy blue above it. Nova watched the mountain through the SUV's windshield, hypnotized by its looming presence. She was driving while her friend Mackenna sat in the front passenger seat, playing a game on her phone. The three dudes—Landon, Isaac, and Wyatt—were all sprawled in the SUV's two-tiered backseat, either asleep or listening to music on their earbuds.

The SUV was quiet except for the soft roar of the air conditioning fans. Nova, who'd turned eighteen the month before, didn't like listening to music or talk radio when she drove; she preferred to focus on driving, which she took seriously. The SUV, some kind of luxury Mercedes and probably super expensive, belonged to Mackenna's wealthy family. Nova was worried she'd wreck the vehicle in a random accident, get everybody mad at her, and ruin her driving record before it had really started.

At a petite five-two, Nova felt slightly ridiculous piloting such a massive beast of a vehicle, like a toad telling a dragon what to do. Still, they'd made it this far. They'd left Greenwood Village, a suburb in south Denver, later than planned. They'd agreed Mackenna would pick them all up by ten in the morning, but she'd been late and they'd gotten a late start. Mackenna had driven for the first two hours, through the traffic of Denver and into the mountains, before claiming she was getting sleepy and asking Nova to drive. Nova protested, asking why Landon, Mackenna's boyfriend, couldn't drive, or one of the other guys, but it turned out all three of the dudes had eaten marijuana gummies before they'd even left Greenwood Village. She should have known. This was their big, end-of-summer road trip before returning to college, so why not get stoned before they even arrived at their destination?

They'd all gone to the same prep academy in the Denver suburbs and were now enrolled at Colorado College in Colorado Springs. Nova, who was a year younger than the others, was going to be a freshman, while everyone else would be a sophomore. Nova had told her parents she'd be spending the next three nights at Mackenna's cabin in Vale, with Mackenna's entire family. This was partially true—they were going to stay at *one* of the Wolcott's cabins—but it was her family's cabin on Claw Heart Mountain, across the state border in Wyoming, and nobody else in Mackenna's family would be there. The friends would be unsupervised, without a real grown-up in sight.

Nova didn't like lying to her sweet, trusting parents (and this trip was by far the largest lie Nova had ever told them) but she knew they would have otherwise said no. It was the end of a long summer for Nova—a summer that had started with getting dumped by her boyfriend—and she'd grown tired of hanging around her house and her lame suburban neighborhood, going for walks and eating her dad's overcooked barbeque while she waited for college to start. The memory of endless time on lockdown during the COVID-19 pandemic still fresh (sometimes it felt like being stuck at home, bored, had been her entire teenage life), by mid-August Nova had decided she'd finally reached the point that she might literally wither away and die if she didn't go *somewhere*.

So, basically, Nova had lied to her parents to save her own life.

Kind of.

Nova glanced at Mackenna, who was still absorbed in her phone. Mackenna was a tall, tan, volleyball-smashing Nordic beauty, with a mane of curly blond hair that cascaded down her shoulders. Nova, on the other hand, with her pale skin, brown pixie-cut hair, dark eyebrows, hazel eyes, stubby nose, and short chin, thought she resembled a woodland elf more than anything an average person would consider "sexy". Which was fine with her. She'd seen all the attention Mackenna got, both in high school and the real world, from all kinds of people, and it seemed like a huge pain in the ass. Nova would much rather float along under the sexiness radar, free to live her life without everyone drooling over her all the time.

Mackenna looked up from her phone.

"What?"

Nova looked away and focused on the road.

"Nothing."

They weren't too far across the border into Wyoming, maybe thirty miles, but Claw Heart Mountain still seemed different than the mountains in Colorado. Its outline appeared indefinite, its edges somehow blurry. Which didn't really make sense, because like every mountain in Colorado, Claw Heart must have been a part of the Rocky Mountains, which stretched all the way from New Mexico into Canada.

Mackenna leaned forward against her seatbelt and peered through the windshield. She drummed her hands on the SUV's dashboard.

"Huh. Claw Heart looks even more badass than I remember."

"How long has it been since you've been here?"

Mackenna tilted her head, thinking. "Last summer, I guess."

"You haven't been to your own cabin for an entire year?"

"We used to come here more often, but that was before we got the second cabin in Vale. Now Dad mostly uses this one for hanging out with his business buddies and entertaining clients. Claw Heart Mountain's good for hunting. Dad pays a neighbor to look after it for most of the year."

"So why aren't we just going to Vale?"

Mackenna wrinkled her nose. "It's being fumigated. Mom saw a cockroach when she was there last weekend for her book club retreat."

"Huh. Vale cabin problems, huh?"

Mackenna sat back and sighed.

"I know, right?"

Nova glanced in the rearview mirror. The dudes were all oblivious, their eyes closed as their earbuds pumped noise into their ears. Nova felt like a mom driving her kids to summer camp.

For the seventh or eighth time that day, she wondered why she was friends with Mackenna and the dudes. Or friends with Mackenna, anyway, since Nova hardly knew the dudes at all. Landon, with his good looks and blond, fake bedhead hair, was hot but sort of dumb, the kind of guy she'd normally ignore and be ignored by, the average Great White Bro. Isaac was smart but mean, a handsome Jewish kid with piercing brown eyes. Wyatt was probably the nicest of the three dudes, a genuinely sweet Black guy with a big smile who talked to everyone. He'd moved to Colorado from Minneapolis three years earlier and didn't seem worried about being popular, which, of course, made him super popular.

Nova swerved to avoid a dead critter in the road. This particular buddy had exploded all over the place and was unrecognizable. Nova felt her heart go out to the creature, whatever it had been, and straightened in the driver's seat, determined to avoid any similar roadkill. The highway sloped sharply upward as they reached the base of the mountain and climbed the first length of a switchback highway, which appeared to zigzag all the way up the mountain.

Isaac removed his earbuds and leaned forward from the backseat. Nova could smell the cologne he was wearing, a subtle musk that made her think of a dim coatroom at an adult cocktail party. Isaac pointed at the windshield.

"What the hell is that?"

Nova frowned and examined the road. It took her a moment to see what Isaac was pointing at because it was light blue, almost the same color as the sky. It was a brick-shaped armored van, lying upside down on the road, its wheels in the air. The van's small side windows had shattered and its roof was crunched.

"Holy shit," Mackenna said, lowering her phone. "Looks like an accident."

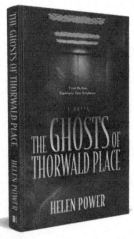
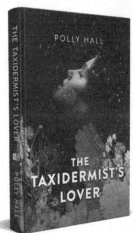

CamCat
Books

VISIT US ONLINE FOR MORE BOOKS TO LIVE IN:
CAMCATBOOKS.COM

SIGN UP FOR CAMCAT'S FICTION NEWSLETTER FOR
COVER REVEALS, EBOOK DEALS, AND MORE EXCLUSIVE CONTENT.

mCatBooks   @CamCatBooks   @CamCat_Books   @CamCatBooks